By the same author

ALEC (Alexander Trilogy, Book I)
ALEXANDER (Alexander Trilogy, Book II)
SACHA—The Way Back (Alexander Trilogy, Book III)
YESHUA—Personal Memoir of the Missing Years of Jesus
PETER AND PAUL (An intuitive sequel to Yeshûa)
ONE JUST MAN (Winston Trilogy Book I)
ELOHIM—Masters & Minions (Winston Trilogy Book II)
WINSTON'S KINGDOM (Winston Trilogy Book III)
THE AVATAR SYNDROME (Prequel to Headless World)
MARVIN CLARK—In Search of Freedom
THE GATE—Things My Mother Told Me
NOW—Being and Becoming
THE PRINCESS
GIFT OF GAMMAN
ENIGMA of the Second Coming
WALL—Love, Sex, and Immortality (Aquarius Trilogy Book I)
PLUTO EFECT (Aquarius Trilogy Book II)
OLYMPUS—Of Gods and Men (Aquarius Trilogy Book III)

Short stories

THE JEWEL & OTHER STORIES
CATS AND DOGS
Sci-Fi Series 1
Sci-Fi Series 2

Non-fiction eBooks by Stanislaw Kapuscinski

VISUALIZATION—Creating Your Own Universe
KEY TO IMMORTALITY
[Commentary on the Gospel of Thomas]
BEYOND RELIGION: Volumes I, II and III
[Collections of essays on perception of Reality]
DICTIONARY OF BIBLICAL SYMBOLISM
DELUSIONS—Pragmatic Realism

Poetry in Polish
[with illustrations by Bozena Happach]
KILKA SŁÓW I TROCHĘ GLINY
WIĘCEJ SŁÓW I WIĘCEJ GLINY

INHOUSEPRESS, MONTREAL, CANADA
http://inhousepress.ca

HEADLESS WORLD

The Vatican Incident

An Essential Sequel to

The Avatar Syndrome

Stan I.S. Law

INHOUSEPRESS, MONTREAL, CANADA

Design and layout
Bozena Happach

Library and Archives Canada Cataloguing in Publication

Law, Stan I. S.
Headless World: The Vatican Incident : an essential sequel to
The Avatar Syndrome / Stan I.S. Law.

ISBN (13) 978-0-9731872-6-7

I. Title.

PS8623.A92H42 2008   C813'.6   C2008-903535-6

This book is a work of fiction.
Names, characters, titles, places and incidents are either the products of the
author's imagination or are used fictitiously.

Published by
INHOUSEPRESS
http://www.inhousepress.ca
2008 Edition

It may be true that
you can't fool all the people all the time,
but you can fool enough of them
to rule a large country.

Will Durant
American historian, philosopher and educator
1885-1981

PROLOGUE

Washington

"Sit down, gentlemen." The Vice President's kindly eyes drifted over the group of men, embracing them all with a fatherly smile. "At ease, if you prefer," he added as an afterthought.

John Linker didn't like the atmosphere that Pentagonal comportment fostered. He thought it artificial, not conducive to creative thinking. He didn't like the pomp, the regimentation, the saluting. He liked even less the collection of metal the soldiers liked to append to their chests, as if to prove how brave they were.

"The brave ones are dead," he once told a marine colonel who looked down at officers who did not display their medals.

The brave ones were dead, and those who were brave and lived did not find it necessary to publicly display their decorations. Their heroic deeds were things of the past. "So you were brave once?" he asked another one-star, freshly baked general who got most of his boy-scout badges by sending others to do a man's job. "Just how may times have you risked *your* life, young man?" he asked, staring the officer in the eyes. The one-star freshman had not risen through the ranks. He'd risen through connections. He knew the right people.

"At ease, gentlemen," Linker repeated, seating himself at the head of the table. "We have work to do."

Actually, Vice President Linker wasn't at the head of the table. He sat at its very end. Joshua Rosengart, his Chief of Staff, already occupied the head. A good man, if a trifle too ambitious. Rosengart had the ability to talk around any subject in such a way that no one was really sure what he was talking about. He was Linker's official spokesman. The man he relied on to keep himself in the shadows.

When Linker entered, the last to arrive, all the men had stood to attention. All except Joshua. John and Joshua had been friends for a long time.

The Vice President's eyes ran over the faces. The men's bodies were now presumably relaxed, but their faces remained at attention. All eyes were turned towards him. He was the architect. He called the shots of the Plan. Not President Twigg. Only he, John Linker.

Linker smiled. He liked to smile. Just a little, a grimace almost, but it put his men at ease. At ease, but off balance.

Boys liked to play soldiers, and he needed their dedication, loyalty and expertise. He would have preferred to carry out the whole operation with the CIA, which was closer to his heart, but the plainclothes could no longer be trusted. "That would never have happened while he was in charge," he thought. It never had. One took one's orders from the President and carried them out. Now . . . now there was a smell of divided loyalty.

There had been whispers of division of power, of loyalty to the people, and such like. People? What people? Linker had never met anyone who knew precisely what he or she wanted. Not as far as the big picture was concerned. They followed the party line, or their religious leaders, or some outdated socialistic aspirations. As he had once. Then he'd read Ayn Rand. He'd never looked back. That was some forty years ago. He shrugged his shoulders, even as Atlas had.

It won't be long now, he mused, that same little smile drifting across his face.

"Brad?"

This time his voice, still gentle, carried a ring of authority. Authority which, those present knew, it would not be wise to question. There were stories circulating around Washington about mysterious disappearances. No one would presume to suggest that the VP had anything to do with them, but the stories persisted. Of course, those whispers had nothing to do with their Cause. With the Plan. After all, Linker was the Vice President, and as far as the world outside these four walls was concerned, they were here for their usual game of bridge.

It was Rosengart who had suggested calling their trysts a bridge club. One table, six men in all. Four playing, two waiting their turn. The Vice President liked the idea. He also liked the similarity to the game of bridge. It wasn't a question of which cards you were dealt but rather how well you played. A brilliant player can win at bridge even with repeatedly poor hands.

Linker made sure men reported directly to him. "The President is too busy with world problems," he'd told them. " I wouldn't bother him with details." According to Linker, all that issued from the Pentagon were details. He also made sure that all present had already read the reports presented at the meetings. This was the place for discussion, not for doing one's homework.

"Your deal," Linker said, pointing at a tall man on his right.

Brad Schwartz sat up even straighter. It was quite evident that the two-star general felt uncomfortable in the civvies. There were stars and stripes written all over his face. Now and then, Schwartz shed his uniform on purpose. He imagined that without his chest brimming with medals, he was here virtually *incognito*.

"Yes, Sir." He was hard pressed not to salute his boss repeatedly. "I put together a report as per your instruction, Sir. It lists the locations and numbers of all the silos and suspected arsenals of North Korea, Iran, Pakistan, Brazil, Syria, Egypt...." He read out another eight or ten countries before his voice hesitated.

"...and?" Linker prompted, his voice as cold as the ice cubes on the sideboard.

"And France, Sir," Schwartz finished.

"Israel?" The question came out as a whisper.

"We haven't been able to locate those, Sir," the general said, looking at a spot on the wall directly in front of him. "Not as yet, Sir," he added, his voice losing some of its confidence.

Linker didn't need to be a trained psychologist to detect a twinge of discomfort in the young general. He had only been promoted to two stars a month ago, mainly to give him greater access to classified information. One star was still controlled by the 'need to know'. Two stars decided themselves what they needed to know. A very fundamental difference.

"Brad," Linker's eyes resumed their fatherly gaze. "We must be prepared for all contingencies." And then, as the Vice President's eyes met the young general's, the blue in Linker's eyes turned to tempered steel. "If you feel uncomfortable...."

"No, Sir!" The man rose to attention. "No, Sir!" he repeated, his hand halfway up to a perfunctory salute. "You will have all the coordinates for all locations by tomorrow morning," he said, still saluting. Even if I have to work all night, he thought.

"Sit down, Brad. I know we can trust you. Sit down."

There was that grandfatherly kindness again. Linker knew he could count on the young man. He had plenty on the young man's dealings in oil during the last crisis. Brad's father had made a fortune selling oil through third-party deals to places that must remain secret. At least, for now.

Brad Schwartz had previously placed a stack of satellite photos in front of each man at the table. He went on to describe the cartographic characteristics. "We know these locations," he added, "to within inches!" He couldn't help letting pride creep into his tone. "Why, we could, right now...."

"That's enough for now, Brad," Linker cut him short, nodding knowingly. "We mustn't run ahead of ourselves."

Brad Schwartz looked nonplused. He had been looking forward to sharing his *coup de grâce* with his colleagues. Or was it friends? He glanced around the table. Does one really have friends in this business, he wondered.

There were six men sitting at the table. The average age was around forty. Only Linker was their considerable senior. At somewhere over sixty, some said seventy—nobody knew just where exactly—he commanded respect not only from the position of the Vice President of the United States of America, but by the abundant gray hair he brushed straight back from his high forehead. In contrast to all the men at the table, there was a perceptible stoop in his posture, which made the VP seem to be looking at his interlocutors from under his bushy eyebrows, as though passing judgment over his half-moon reading glasses. For a while, during the election campaign, he made do with contact lenses, but he hated them for everyday use. And, his age notwithstanding, he enjoyed excellent vision for everything but reading. He could still bring down a duck with a single shot. Not with a shotgun, but with a single bullet from a hunting rifle.

Linker himself had handpicked the other five men. "There are some things one simply cannot delegate," he told Joshua. When selecting each of them, Linker demanded absolute obedience, total commitment, and unquestioning faith. Faith in the Way. The American Way. Only from full-blooded Americans, born and bred in the American tradition, brought up in the strict confines of an established Protestant Sect, well grounded in the American ideals of freedom and democracy, could he hope to find men worthy of his Plan. The Plan he'd worked on, dreamt of and finally begun to put into practice over the last six years. A plan which would leave the world a better, safer place for all men of good faith. For men who wanted to be free. For democracy. American democracy, not some home-grown version where people who did nothing to advance the wealth of the human race demanded equal rights. "Rights are earned, not usurped at someone else's expense," he said during the last campaign, nearly two years ago. It almost cost him and President Twigg the election.

And now, here they were, advancing his Plan towards imminent fruition.

"You're next, Fred," he nodded to a man with a round face and a bushy, prematurely gray hairdo, looking more like a

professor of physics than a man involved in the most secret
mission Linker had ever undertaken. The fact that he was a
nuclear physicist by training was coincidental. Fred Finer, Ph.D.,
wore the image of an absentminded professor on purpose. No
one took him seriously or held him responsible. Except, of
course, John Linker.

The Vice President closed his eyes. He'd already read the
report. It analyzed the megatons of each country in terms of
delivery and such like. He knew the numbers by heart. He
needed the other men to know them. To be able to recite them in
their sleep. But he had to impress on those present the
importance as well as the magnitude of the task before them.

So much had happened.

Fleeting images of a boy walking along what later became
Memorial Drive... heavy trucks rolling, one after another,
carrying material to the middle of the two hundred acres of
wasteland. Over five million cubic yards of soil had been shifted.
Over forty-one thousand concrete piles had been driven into the
swamps and dumps to make up the foundations of the biggest,
the strongest, the most efficient building in the world.

The lad would sit on the curb, counting the trucks. He
remembered.

Today the swamps were lawns, leaving room for 8,770 cars
spread over sixteen parking lots. Inside, the 3,705,739 square
feet of office space housed some 23,000 military and civilian
employees. They reached their allotted desks by 19 escalators
and 131 stairways. They worked dutifully until one of the 4,200
clocks dismissed them until the following day, while the next
shift began. The building never slept.

"...an estimated 370 ICBM, each carrying five megatons,
have the capability of reaching..." the professor's voice droned.

About 200,000 telephones were dialed daily. Over
1,200,000 pieces of mail were handled every month. The army
library alone had 300,000 publications, supplemented by 1,700
periodicals in various languages.

The opening ceremony had been held on January 15th,
1943. It had been attended by John's father, John Linker Senior,

who'd made a fortune supplying the concrete. Some 434,000 cubic yards of concrete just for the building alone. A twitch lifted Linker's left eyebrow. At the time American boys were still giving up their lives in Europe, defending our allies. So many lives. So many...

A momentary flash of anger crossed his fatherly features. "Allies!" His lips formed the silent word in disgust. "Allies indeed..."

Everything connected with the Pentagon was big. It was American. It was American power.

"The logistics are complex, to say the least," Finer continued, rattling off another series of numbers. Linker was no longer listening. Even now, so many years later, he experienced a thrill when crossing Arlington Memorial Bridge on the way to his office. Oh, yes. He kept a permanent presence at the Pentagon. This was the epicenter of power. He could sleep here for a month, if need be. Here dwelt his heart. From here he controlled the future of the world.

The remaining men reported on their assignments. Two three-star generals gave their estimates on the delivery power of the latest stealth bombers and the location of the disposition of the US Navy aircraft carriers throughout the world. A discussion followed on their state of readiness. It wasn't a question of putting the Plan into action today. Or the next day. It was a question of absolute readiness the moment an opportunity presented itself.

"We have to make it easy," Linker had said more than once. As though it was meant to be, he mused.

"I shall not allow American boys to die on foreign soil," he'd said another time.

"This time we are planning ahead. Well ahead," he'd added after one of their 'bridge' meetings. Everyone knew what he meant. The last fiasco in Iraq would not be repeated. Not while he was the Vice President of the United States.

A s the other men filed out of the meeting room, Linker asked
Fred Finer to stay behind. The professor, as he was known
at the Pentagon, did not like being singled out. Too often it
proved detrimental to one's health. He smiled weakly and
remained seated. The Vice President waved him to come and sit
closer, next to him.

"How's Mary?" John asked.

Mary was Fred's second wife. His first had been murdered
on their anniversary trip to Israel. Robbed of every penny. The
VP had never talked about it, but Fred knew that it had been
John Linker who had sent the Air Force II Executive Jet to bring
him and the body back to the United States. For a while, after
that show of concern, he really liked the VP.

"Thank you, Mister Vice Pres..."

"John. At least when we are alone."

"...John. She sends her best regards."

"I asked you to stay because I have a special assignment
for you. One, I think, you will enjoy."

Linker studied the younger man's face intensely. The gray
hair added some years to his image, but his fresh complexion
belied his relative maturity.

"An assignment, Sir?" He reverted to the absentminded
professor.

The Vice President smiled. He liked the way Fred could
change his appearance from a steady, intensely intelligent gaze
into a fuddy-duddy scientist. Even his hair seemed to rise to a
discordant mop.

"Relax," John prompted. "We're friends. I wouldn't allow
anything to happen to you." He measured the scientist with a
penetrating gaze. Did I misjudge the man, he wondered. But in
the next instant Fred's eyes met his with a steady stare.

"I want you to go to Montreal," John said.

* * *

THE FIRST STEPS

...'tis in ourselves that we are thus or thus.
Our bodies are our gardens, to which our wills are gardeners.

Shakespeare, *Othello*

1

Montreal Neurological Institute

It was that blessed part of the year when the leaves have just begun turning various shades of gold, with an occasional maple showing her rubies. Yet the weather was warm enough to be able to walk around in shirtsleeves. Yesterday, as was their custom on Sundays, Peter and Anne had taken a long walk to and around Mount Royal Park. They luxuriated in the still warm, though no longer scorching, sun and reminisced about their early days, when a walk on the Mountain was their only chance to be alone.

"I'll never forget how Fluffy went after those boys who were chasing the squirrels who were chasing the peanuts the boys threw. I couldn't stop laughing," Anne confessed, a distant smile reaching back many years. Fluffy was her dog when she was a girl. He'd died more than fifteen years ago, but she always remembered him when she and Peter walked, arm in arm, along the narrow trails.

"Why should you? According to Diana you taught him to act as your judge and executioner," Peter said accusingly.

Diana was Anne's mother. She and Michael, Anne's dad, lived quietly in the Laurentians. They'd both wanted to escape the huff and bustle of city life. At the time, it had all worked out very nicely. Peter had sold the condo he and Anne had downtown, for some years, in the *Floralie de la Montagne*. The money had been used to pay cash for a lakeside cottage in St.

Marguerite. Peter with Anne, at the time pregnant with their second child, moved into Anne's parents' house, which was begging to be loved as it had been by Anne's mother and father. For a while, Gabriel, the majordomo and pretty much major of just about everything else, then in his late sixties, stayed with them in Westmount. Recently, he'd moved to the country to look after Diana and Michael. Apparently, he remained as useful as he had always been. Now and then he drove to Montreal, just to see Miss Anne. The fact that Anne's children had left home almost a year ago did not stop him from according her the youthful title. Peter and Anne both thought that Gabriel's age had its privileges. He must have been eighty if he was a day, although they both strongly suspected that Gabriel was not affected by the march of time at all. Over the years, Gabriel hadn't changed a bit.

"He'd never have hurt anyone!" Anne raised her voice in mock exasperation. "I told you a thousand times. Never," she repeated firmly. Fluffy truly was the only friend she trusted in her youth.

As a matter of fact, there had been 'stories' Peter had heard from Anne's mother. Just stories, Diana insisted, from the very distant past. Something about local animals being subjected to harsh treatment. Nothing had ever been proven. In fact, Diana wasn't even sure Fluffy had been around at the time. Peter knew with utter certainty that the Anne he held and cherished would never allow anyone to hurt anyone else in her presence. Over the years, Peter had learned that Anne's presence meant a great deal to a great many people. In a great many ways. In fact, Anne's presence affected people in ways that were nothing short of miraculous.

"Of course not, dear." He pulled her arm closer to his side. "Of course he wouldn't."

Fluffy was—and his memory must remain—sacred. A little like a Hindu cow.

Anne smiled but there was a vestige of a hurt expression on her lips. She didn't know that that gentle pout she assumed following such inconsequential spats drove him wild. Anne also didn't know that when she left him behind on her frequent trips, Peter missed her lips the most.

He wished she could give up her missions. Once and for all. Each time she left, even for a short time, he worried about her. How could he not worry? She went to places a grown man wouldn't venture alone. Especially not at night.

"But they need me," Anne would say simply, as if this justified risking her life.

L ast week, on Friday, Peter had been notified by the Administration of the Montreal Neurological Institute that yet another delegation from the Great Republic down south was coming to visit his Department. Over the years, there had been many such delegations from various American universities. Harvard, Johns Hopkins, Stanmore, UCLA, all had their representatives living in Montreal. But this was the first time that a personal emissary of John Linker, the VP himself, was heading a delegation. Peter usually steered as far away from politics as he could, but it was common knowledge, even in Canada, who held the reins in Washington. Linker—the power behind the throne. The President was the spokesman. The front man. Peter had no idea what they wanted.

Once Peter had taken over as the Head of the Neurosurgery Department, he had achieved positive results in memory control. Within a year the Department of Experimental Sonic Neurosurgery at the MNI became known throughout the world. Well, at least the neurosurgical world.

It was becoming fairly certain that particular ultrasonic vibrations affected people's memory cells. More often than not, the effect was temporary. In the early days, Peter experimented with sound to erase traumatic memories in women and some children who suffered from acute psychosis brought on by abuse. That part did not bear particularly good results, because he found that while he could bring about general temporary amnesia, he could not get at specific memories.

It was an all or nothing proposition.

The promising part and the part that had kept the funding coming was that when the memory had returned, there were certain aspects of the traumatic experience which had been relegated to the deep recesses of the mind, so much so that they no longer immediately affected the patient. It was regarded as a tremendous step forward in treatment of certain types of psychoses. A ten-minute treatment bore results similar to five to ten years on a psychiatrist's couch. No mean achievement for a research scientist still in his forties.

"Dr. Brown, I presume?"

The man facing Dr. Peter Brown, the Director of the Department of Experimental Sonic Neurosurgery, or simply DESN, did not look like any of Peter's previous visitors. Einstein, Peter thought, Albert Einstein's doppelganger. Or it could just be that other Albert? Albert Schweitzer, who in a single lifetime managed to achieve fame as a philosopher, missionary, physician, scientist, humanitarian, theologian and a skilled organist. Peter somehow doubted his visitor would prove a good missionary. He looked too... scattered. Humanitarian? Scientist? Possibly. But if the latter, then that would draw him closer to Albert Einstein. Or perhaps....

Peter nodded his head, acknowledging the complex image before him. Whoever managed to arrange each hair on his visitor's head to point in an entirely different direction had done a marvelous job. "Dr. Einst..." he bit his lip.

"My name is Finer. Doctor Fred Finer," the man said, handing Peter his card.

The little rectangle of slick cardboard looked impressive. Frederick Finer, Ph.D., Special Assistant to the Vice President of the United States of America. The address that followed was short and equally as impressive. PENTAGON, United States Department of Defense. No street number, no telephone. Not even e-mail.

"Won't you sit down, Doctor?" Peter pointed to a chair in front of his desk. He'd inherited Dr. Brent's office when he retired. John Brent had run the Institute for years from this relatively small office. The new Director of the MNI chose to oversee the considerably larger Institute from an equally larger office located in the new wing of the Montreal Neurological Institute and Hospital. The MNIH as it was known throughout the world.

"Fred. You are a doctor. I am Fred. I don't heal people," the short man replied. He was a good six inches shorter than Peter.

"I don't succeed too often either. I rather try to create conditions in which the patient cures himself. Or herself, of course." There was something contradictory about the man. His smile said one thing, his eyes another. For some reason Peter doubted that Fred Finer had great interest in healing people.

Nevertheless, Peter's statement was true. After the erasure of offensive, traumatic memories, the repair job was accomplished by the organism itself. The human brain, left to its own devices, mobilized the neurons which seemed to select and maintain only such memories as were the most beneficial to the organism as a whole. Peter still had no idea how it worked exactly.

"I've heard otherwise, Doctor. I heard your name mentioned with the highest regard."

Peter smiled. The man was either pumping him by exfoliating his ego, or he desperately wanted something. He glanced at his watch. The VP's special envoy had arrived an hour before the appointed time. There was always talk of the United States attempting to buy the best and the brightest from Canada. If not the world. The States would buy 'the brains'—a single investment—and then export their expertise to the rest of the world at great profit. Finer looked suspiciously like a man on a fishing mission.

"Perhaps we can discuss it later in the day," whatever 'it' was... Peter got up from behind his desk. "I'm afraid I have a meeting I cannot miss."

He really did have another meeting. The Washington delegation hadn't given him enough time to reschedule his agenda. Also, he did not have the slightest intention of discussing being bought by Washington, the Pentagon or even the White House. Montreal was his home. What was much more

important, it was Anne's home. And the children's, he thought.
He wondered when they would be home next.

They shook hands. Finer's was surprisingly soft yet firm. A
man of contradictions.

"What time will you find it convenient to see me, Doctor?"
Finer asked, still holding Peter's hand.

Peter had no time to explain that he had no desire to see the
emissary at all. Ever.

"Around three?" he offered.

"I shall be here, Doctor," Fred Finer said and was out of
the door without another word.

I wonder if I offended him, Peter wondered. And then, the
left, orderly, rational and logical hemisphere of his brain
whispered, 'I hope so'.

Like so many great discoveries, Peter came across the
neuro-sonic effect by accident. During the construction of the
Third Wing of the new MNI, the contractor proudly affirmed
that he could carry out certain work with a minimum disturbance
to the patients and scientists alike. By using ultrasonic tools, he
could reduce the noise that the mental patients, exposed to
previous bouts with construction, found quite unacceptable.

"You won't know we are here, Sir," the builder had told
the Director with a great smile. No one had believed him. But he
had been right.

Unbeknownst to the builder, and for that matter to
everybody else outside the MNI, within two weeks of the
employment of the new ultrasonic tools, saws, drills and suchlike,
the MNI staff had observed two side effects. One, a number of
patients had suffered temporary amnesia. And two, there was an
unusual number of stray dogs seemingly gravitating towards the
Institute grounds for reasons which no one had been, at the time,
able to understand. It had taken Peter three years to put two and
two together.

The next challenge was to discover a method of controlling
and directing the ultrasonic waves onto specific areas without
affecting other people in the immediate vicinity. By
manipulating various wavelengths, Peter began obtaining quite

unpredictable effects. He was only now beginning to feel that he'd achieved a degree of control over the ultrasonic emission.

Peter couldn't help wondering what unholy machinations had brought his work to the attention of the Department of Defense of our southern neighbors.

Peter's meeting ran into the late afternoon. He had his secretary call Dr. Finer and apologize for his inability to meet that day. Peter suggested that Dr. Finer might care for a guided tour of the MNI, which his assistant was ready to provide.

Such meetings, like the one he'd attended that day, took a large portion of his time. He'd never truly appreciated what an incredible job John Brent, his boss until some years ago, had been doing. To retain some control over the latest research and to control the administrative duties at the same time was a near-Herculean task. John Brent, the scientist-turned-physician, then neurosurgeon, had taken it in stride. True that he'd never married, and thus did not have to serve two masters, or mistresses, but even so, his duties had been much more extensive than Peter's.

On the other hand, Peter had initiated a completely new branch of neuroscience. He was venturing into the unknown. It was one thing to realize that sound affects our well-being, quite another to control and direct the ultrasonic waves at specific neural passages to obtain specific results.

The positive effects of classical music on study habits and house plants had been known for years. Likewise, the negative effects of heavy metal and certain electronic music were also well documented. The ultrasonic vibration of the contractor's tool had come in at just the right time. Within six months Peter had published his first paper. Within nine months, a department had been formed with him as its Head.

The rest, as they say, was history.

Peter loved his work. As an aspiring violinist in his youth, and then having witnessed the greatest gift nature had ever bestowed on a single musician, his own Anne, he knew, instinctively, that the medical profession had not paid sufficient attention to the influence of sound on our health. Sound surrounded us on all sides, it blared through the open windows of tall condominium buildings facing each other across narrow streets, it spewed out from cars' open windows, and it even drowned the words which actors spoke on both the big and the little screen.

"Please, Peter, please...." he'd heard so often when he and Anne attempted to enjoy some program on TV. She would raise both her arms to block her ears. He knew at once to switch off the sound of their boob tube.

Lately he and Anne seldom watched television, just to avoid having to listen to the noise. It seldom, if ever, had anything to do with the story line. Even sporting events, which were a means of relaxation for him, became impossible to watch. An army of commentators destroyed his pleasure with an insatiable running commentary as if the broadcast were on the radio and not on TV. His viewing was reduced to just that: viewing, with the sound turned completely off.

What was even worse was that the omnipresent noise, going under the misnomer of music, seldom carried any melody, any inspiring harmony or even relaxing rhythm. Percussion, and only percussion, boosted by overwhelming amps, displaced music as the food of the masses. There was not a single advert on the TV which was not accompanied by a cacophony of drums, brass plates, or simply cooking pots being struck by metal and wooden implements. At least, that was what the 'music' sounded like to him. He often imagined how Anne must have suffered when she was exposed to such gross abuse of her privacy. Anne, the once genius....

Peter needed music. After all, it was music that brought him and Anne together years ago. It was at his first dinner with the Howells. His boss, John Brent, must have had something to do with it. He probably noticed Peter's particular preoccupation with young Anne's welfare. It had been just after Anne's second PET scan followed by a series of fMRI's at the Montreal Neurological Institute. Dr. Brent had just confirmed the enlargement of the pons Virolii, the bridge between the right and the left hemisphere of her brain. As this had not been considered bad news, Peter had been invited to a celebratory dinner.

First, he had been given a personal tour of the house. An angel crowned with a massive red halo that bounced up and down with each jaunty step led him, leaving no nook unexamined. After dinner, Anne, under some pretext he couldn't recall, invited him into the garden.

It was early autumn....

There and then, with the smell of the first fallen leaves lingering in the air, their lives took an inevitable swerve towards each other. He found himself demonstrating to Anne his skill of playing the violin. One stick served as the violin, another for the bow. He must have created the right impression. Anne's words still rang in his ears.

"Mommy! Dad! Peter can play the violin!"

She was all fluttering, her eyes filled with an enchantment that illuminated her face. "He was playing the Sibelius," she announced, catching her breath, "The violin concerto. He is brilliant!"

Peter grinned at the next memory. It was the sonorous voice belonging to the Howells' majordomo.

"I thought your rendering of the andante was particularly engaging, Sir," Gabriel had said in a voice worthy of an *ex cathedra* proclamation.

Dear Gabriel. They both owed him so much.

It had been later that evening that Anne had asked if she could study the violin.

These days, on early autumn Saturdays, they would spend time together in the garden. Peter would pick up a pair of sticks and play a mock concerto. Anne would take over the cadenzas. They would stare at each other, hearing each note, precisely, as if really playing on the best Stradivarius Anne had once used around the world. Peter would see the girl in an emerald dress, long curls of fiery red cascading down her shoulders.... After the triumphant world concert tour, Anne had announced that her virtuoso days were over. She'd never played another note. Except on the sticks, with Peter, in their garden.

The long tresses were gone, too. Only the rich, reddish gold remained.

It had to be so. It would have been too dangerous for Anne to travel alone looking like a vulnerable girl. She'd cut her hair three years ago. Di, their daughter, had cried for a week.

"Mommy, how could you? How could you...." She was eighteen then.

"My head is still here, darling. And the hair can regrow," Anne assured.

Johnny, their firstborn, had taken it much better. "Makes you look half your age, Mother. Really," he assured. Being almost twenty, he deemed it a mature thing to say.

"Why, thank you, kind Sir Galahad," Anne said, bowing low before her son. "I think...." she added, not quite sure how old that made her look. Probably a little younger than her own daughter. "We could be sisters," she turned to Di.

This seemed to cheer Deirdre up. She smiled through her tears.

As for Peter? Well, Peter hadn't been asked for an opinion. He loved Anne's hair well enough, but he would take her and keep her if she were shaved naked.

Those were the good days.

The past was so beautiful. So enigmatic. Anne's incredible world tour, their first child, the first word he uttered, their daughter.... Such beauty that it almost hurt to look at her... Their life was filled with miracles. And there was Anne's work. Miracles one never saw. Miracles that came about long after Anne had left the object of her inimitable influence. Of her Presence.

Some time in her youth, Anne had had an operation to remove a minor, benign tumor in her frontal lobe. In a follow-up fMRI scan, the medical team discovered that Anne had apparently grown new neurons (an unprecedented occurrence) and enjoyed an over-developed *Pons Varolii*, the bridge between the left and right hemispheres of her brain. Of her cerebrum, to be more precise.

Years later it had been observed—details to this day remain rather murky—that when Anne walked the wards, visiting John

Brent's patients, there took place a number of inexplicable spontaneous remissions. They'd all wondered, ever since, if the additional neurons which had grown into the space liberated by the excision of her tumor, and the enlarged pons, had anything to do with these remissions and with Anne's incredible musical talent.

While the children were at home, Anne kept her trips to a minimum. She travelled alone, in men's clothing. Peter had insisted on that. He knew Anne could take care of herself, but he felt safer that way. He couldn't afford to go with her. He was as needed at the MNI as she was . . . as she was wherever she went. The slums, the favelas, the east end of New York City, the Vancouver needle district. You never knew in advance. She went for just a few days at a time. Sporadically. She often returned looking haggard, tired. She would sleep for ten or twelve hours. Then she would be her wonderful self again.

Waiting was tough on Peter. "If only you'd tell me in advance..." he tried a number of times. "Perhaps I could... Perhaps I could go with you?" he'd offered on other occasions. He had gone with her at the very beginning. Before they had children.

After, she would say, "One of us must remain here, darling."

"I know . . . but...."

She knew what was coming. She'd learned to read his mind, the way Gabriel had taught her. "I cannot go when I want to, Peter," she confessed again and again. "I must go when I have to."

He'd never understood this explanation.

"I thought we are all enjoying free will?" he suggested quietly.

"No, Peter. Not all of us. Sometimes we must do what we must do...."

The next morning Dr. Finer was waiting at Peter's door. An intern was desperately attempting to explain to him that to see Dr. Brown one needed an appointment. Fred Finer stared at the younger man as though having absolutely no idea what the intern was talking about. The absentminded professor persona was driving the intern frantic.

When Peter approached, the American detached himself from the young doctor with amazing ease. One moment he was there, the next the intern was talking to the wall.

"I thought I would drop in on the chance that you might be able to spare me a few minutes," Dr. Finer said affably.

"Please, come in." Peter had no plausible excuse.

For about thirty minutes they talked about Peter's work. Peter was quite impressed by how much Dr. Finer had learned on his tour the previous day. His questions were pointed, precise, with little room to maneuver. Gradually his visitor led him towards the heart of the matter.

"I assure you, my dear Doctor, we have no intention whatsoever of exploiting or even exploring your discovery for military uses," the pseudo-Einstein assured Peter after an hour's discussion. "Just the opposite."

Peter waited for the opposite to reveal itself. He never imagined that Fred Finer would deign to speak the truth. At the same time, he couldn't help wondering when the scientist was going to open his mouth and stick his tongue out in imitation of his famous hairy predecessor. Peter secretly had a poster of Einstein with his tongue hanging out hanging on the inside leaf of his wardrobe.

"We have great problems with post-traumatic syndrome," the physicist said, painting a duly concerned expression on his face. "Our boys return home from patriotic missions and seem to suffer from images imbedded in their subconscious, which they are unable to come to terms with...."

Translation—the young men had been sent out to kill women and children and now they suffered from prolonged nightmares. Peter felt sorry for the boys, and girls, who undertook to serve in the US Army. On the other hand, the army consisted of volunteers.

"If you bring one or two here, Doctor Finer, I would be happy to see what we can do."

There was a prolonged silence. Dr. Finer fidgeted in his chair as if suddenly finding it acutely uncomfortable.

"We were hoping, Dr. Brown, that you might consider transplanting yourself to Washington. If only for a little while?"

"A little while!?" Peter almost spat out the words.

"Say, a year or two...."

Peter had to hold on hard to the relaxation exercises Gabriel had taught him so as not to laugh outright. Either that, or simply throw the man out of his office, preferably through the window. Instead, he swallowed hard, twice, and merely looked toward the window. Apparently the world outside was still turning on its axis, as it should.

"It may have escaped your notice," Peter said very calmly, "but I am the Director of the Department right here, in Montreal?"

The gloves were off. "We would make it worth your while, Doctor."

"Are you trying to buy me?" Peter's voice was barely above a whisper.

The answer was delivered in a tone so steady that it belied the mask, which his interlocutor was offering to the world. "If necessary...."

This was no absentminded professor. This was a man who was a special emissary of the most powerful man in the world. He felt a cold draft running up his spine. He didn't like it one bit.

* * *

2

Frederick Finer, Ph.D.

Doctor Frederick Finer spent a good part of the next morning on the telephone. He enjoyed the privilege of a coded connection to the Vice President at any time of day or night. He enjoyed even more that such confidence had been placed in him. Particularly since his wife wouldn't trust him to stoke the fire correctly in their fireplace. He was allowed to take out the garbage on Mavis's day off. That was about all. The maid did all the chores, his wife all the thinking. He, well, he was the absentminded professor. He also supplied the money. For some reason his wife never let on that she had no idea how he managed to do that.

Fred Finer loved the American Way. In his mind, the Vice President embodied all the qualities that an American should have. He was kind yet strict, intelligent but not flaunting his knowledge, firm but willing to listen to reason. But most of all, he was willing to share the American Way with the whole world.

He recalled how pleased he'd been as a boy that America had already conquered the other planets. Even the very distant Krypton. After all, he reasoned, Superman was American. Didn't he fight for Truth and Justice and the American Way? Years later he'd transferred those very expectations to John Linker. To John. That was probably what he liked most. When the Vice President and he were alone, it was first names only. If only his wife knew.

"Mister Vice President?"

"Yes, Fred. How are you?"

They spoke like friends. Like equals.

Before calling the VP, Fred Finer had spent three hours checking his facts with his own team of experts. This is what his job was. He was trained as a physicist, having received his Ph.D. from MIT, with a postgraduate program in particle physics. As a hobby, almost out of his youthful homage for Superman, he had taken another postgraduate program in statics and dynamics, which put him in good standing on all subjects dealing with missiles and ballistics in general. He also loved reading. Never having read a novel (except for the Superman series), his general knowledge was staggering. He could hold his own on any subject dealing not only with physics, but with chemistry, biology, or practically any other "-ology" one could think of. At forty-eight, he was the man the VP most leaned on.

Officially, he coordinated a group of experts in diverse fields of science. John would give him a hint, and he provided the facts. Then John would use the information as he saw fit. Fred trusted his boss implicitly. In his moments of fancy, he saw John as his own outer persona, as the front for his own brain. His critical faculty was guided by facts, and facts only, never giving sway to questions of morality, which he regarded as a glorified method of keeping up with the Joneses. In a sense, he was completely amoral; yet, or perhaps because of it, he loved the strict moral code the VP adhered to. The unbending, uncompromising moral code of the righteous. For himself he preferred the mask of an absentminded professor.

"I don't think I can buy him, John. He seems to be one of those men...."

"I can't stand the virtuous ones. They are always hiding behind some illusory principles."

"I know." They could practically read each other's thoughts. "May I use the...."

"Whatever it takes. I rather think that Brown has exactly what we need. Only it might need a little more development."

"Thank you, Sir."

They hung up in perfect unison. When Fred was told to apply such pressure as was necessary, he always confirmed the authorization by addressing the Vice President as Sir. That kept the responsibility with the granter, not the grantee. He could always say that he was carrying out orders. After all, he had his wife to look after. His wife and two dogs. Ben and Ladin. They never failed to amuse him. The dogs, that is.

He now had to arrange for another meeting with Peter Brown. He didn't call him. Instead, he made an appointment with Dr. Richard Penman, the Director of the MNI. Dr. Penman was a fully accredited physician, but had given up his chosen profession to run the Institute. He never thought of himself as having given something up. He loved the respect that was showered on him whenever his balding head appeared in public.

"It's tough, but someone has to do it." He would repeat the trite truism whenever he had an opportunity. "I've given up a great deal," he would add, if the first statement fell on deaf ears.

Fred Finer was already known to the MNI Administration. He'd met with Dr. Penman on arrival, if only for a minute or two. Now, he would play the part of a Greek bearing a gift. He would offer the Institute a substantial grant in exchange for 'borrowing' Dr. Brown. He had been authorized. Finer always carried out his orders.

"Dr. Finer, please come in." A svelte secretary ushered him into the director's office.

Finer noticed again how different the office was from that occupied by Peter Brown. Or by John Linker, for that matter. Twice as large, with a magnificent seating area presumably designed for visiting dignitaries. Some said that the MNI complex had grown more in the last twenty years than any other institution in the world. It occupied the whole of the southeastern slopes of Mount Royal, swallowing the Old Royal Victoria hospital in its path. It was no Pentagon, of course. Nothing was close to the Pentagon. But for a scientific institution it had no equal.

The two men shook hands like old friends. They were both masters of the counterfeit charm better known by some as 'people skills'.

"So very nice to see you, Doctor. Please do sit down. A little refreshment, perhaps? A drink?" Dr. Penman glanced at his watch. "A soft drink?" It was ten in the morning.

"I'm just fine. Perhaps some water." Fred Finer never touched hard liquor. He did drink, however, an astounding amount of water every day. Flushes the poisons out, he claimed.

A girl appeared from nowhere, placing a tray with a jug of water, a tumbler of ice, and two glasses.

"How very kind of you, Doctor," Finer thanked the girl indirectly.

It all looked like a Chinese tea ceremony. Slow, measured, almost distinguished. At long last, with both men sitting comfortably in deep leather armchairs, each having wetted his lips in the cool water, Finer was ready to broach the subject of his visit.

"I have been asked, Doctor Penman, to make a donation towards the splendid work you are doing here. The Vice President is following your research with great interest." He took another sip. "He told me to thank you personally and to assure you that the United States of America is well aware that the whole continent, indeed the world, is grateful to you."

Penman, his lips shaped into a humble smile, was busy inspecting his nails. He wondered what was coming. Ten million? A hundred? Two hundred million dollars? Don't be greedy, he chided himself. We are working for humanity, he affirmed, glancing at his opulent office. And humanity is doing pretty well, he thought. He had come a long way since John Brent claimed that working here, at the MNI, was a privilege. Well, it still was, he supposed. Only....

"How very kind. Be sure you thank the Pres... the Vice President for his kind words. We are only doing our duty. Doing our best to justify the trust so many people, indeed so many countries, place in us." Now that sounded pretty good even to his own ears.

Fred Finer, like velvet, cast his lure. "The Vice President suggested a modest sum of One Billion Dollars. US, of course." The amount as well as the currency sounded very capitalized.

Penman took a deep breath. This was dangerous. One does not part with vast sums of money, even other people's money, without expecting something in return. He already had a list of favours he had to discharge for his previous grants.

"How can we possibly thank you, Doctor Finer? Such generosity...."

"...can be discharged rather easily," the envoy interrupted gently. The little blue irises, peering from under the high forehead half covered with the unruly hair, drilled holes into Penman's own eyes.

"Really, Doctor?" It was never that easy, he thought. Never.

"We would like to borrow one of your men."

There it was. Was that all? Dr. Penman let the air out of his lungs in a slow, controlled sigh of relief. Was that all, he repeated to himself? His smile broadened.

"And just which of my men, my dear Doctor, is worth one billion dollars to the Vice President of the United States?" His voice was as smooth as silk.

Fred Finer had underestimated Penman. He was facing a skilled negotiator. Very skilled. Penman didn't fall down and roll over at the sound of a billion US.

Finer took another sip of water. It was turning tepid.

"We never thought of it as a trade, Doctor. The two things are quite independent of each other."

"Of course." It took all Penman's skills to keep irony out of his voice.

For a while they sat stealing glances at each other. Both were used to such deals. Both knew that the only way to win was to present a win-win proposition.

"We need to borrow your Doctor Brown. Doctor Peter Brown."

"We need him, too. He is in charge of the Department of Experimental..."

"...Sonic Neurosurgery," Finer completed the title.

Penman raised one eyebrow. "Ah, yes. You've already met him."

"Yes, I have." Finer sounded non-committal.

"And what was Dr. Brown's reaction to your offer?"

"Have you spoken to him recently?" Finer didn't expect Brown to be a man who would hide behind somebody's skirt.

"You are here, aren't you, Doctor Finer?"

"Of course. He was not very well disposed towards our offer."

So Brown refused. Pity. A billion dollars would go a long way towards the new wing for Sonic Neurosurgery, not to mention recent 'improvements' to his own office. Money didn't go very far these days.

"Perhaps you would like me to have a word with him, Doctor Finer?"

"That is all we ask. That is all I ask," he repeated. John Linker didn't take kindly to failure.

"Leave it with me, Doctor Finer."

They shook hands.

"What would you say if we moved to the USA for a little while, Anne?" Peter spoke offhandedly as if he were inquiring about the weather in Madagascar.

"What, dear?" Anne usually ignored rhetorical questions. Then she realized that Peter's face was frozen into an expression of considerable concern. "I thought you were in the middle of your experiments," she said. There was something disturbing about Peter's forced indifference. His shoulders were slightly forward, his lips pressed together as if he'd just swallowed half a lemon. "What is it, darling?"

"I don't want to go," he said.

"Then we shan't," she said.

"It's not that simple." His lips were ruminating on that lemon again.

Peter had met with Dr. Penman that very afternoon. It
hadn't been an easy rendezvous. It never was with the Director.
It never had anything remotely to do with his work. It dealt with
money, staff matters, the possibility of strikes, matters of
publication copyrights and suchlike. When there were no
problems, Peter was left to his own devices.

"You're considerably over budget, Peter," Penman had
begun.

Every department was always over budget. That was what
Penman was for. To locate and acquire new grants. One cannot
cross new horizons without going over the budget. Only when
the work was advanced did it begin to bear fruit. Financial fruit.
Experimental work was pure overhead.

Penman had told Peter about Finer's visit. He was quite
open about it.

Peter loved his work. He loved Montreal. He loved crossing
new grounds. He loved his house in Westmount. He did not like
Washington. He disliked the Pentagon down to his toenails.

"It wouldn't be for long," he said in spite of himself.

"Would I have to go with you?"

He'd never thought of that. Surely, if it was just for a while,
he could go on his own, discharge his duty to the MNI finances,
and be back with Anne. His subliminal desires added: 'in no
time'. Only he didn't really think so. What if it turned out to be
a month? Or two? Or even a year? A billion dollars didn't come
cheap, he thought, quite unaware of the oxymoron. It wasn't the
biggest donation ever, but it was no hay, either. The greatest
recognition of the MNI's work still belonged to the Right
Honourable Jean Courtier, the late Federal Minister of Health of
a government long retired. The three billion dollars he'd
assigned to research were never matched, not even by our rich
cousins down south.

"I don't know," he murmured. He couldn't imagine being
away from Anne for more than a week. Since her World Tour
more than twenty years ago, they'd never been apart for more
than a week. Eight days at most. "I don't know, darling. I just
don't know."

"What is it, Peter?" Anne sensed something much deeper. Then she had it. Almost. "Where is it that they want you to go?"

For the first time he looked her straight in the eye. "The Pentagon," he said.

Somehow this single word sounded ominous. It stood for everything that Anne and Peter held in lowest regard. Contempt wouldn't be too strong a word. To them, it was practically the source of all evil. Or something close to that. It wasn't the building, of course, nor even what it stood for. Every country needs an army to protect itself from outside interference or even invasion. But in the case of the Pentagon, to Anne and Peter, indeed to their many friends, the word stood for the imposition of the will of the mighty over the little, the—at least relatively speaking—helpless. Korea, Vietnam, the installation of a puppet dictator in Iran, all in the early 1950s, through the many savage incursions into Guatemala, Chile, El Salvador, Nicaragua, Panama, and later, on an even more massive scale, into Afghanistan, Iraq . . . abuses of power too numerous to mention....

"Why?" Anne watched Peter shaking his head as though clearing it of unpleasant memories.

"It's a long story."

He told Anne the cock-and-bull story that Finer had given him at their second meeting. The stuff about the post-traumatic stress disorder. How they were hoping to alleviate suffering of their ex-combatants by applying his experimental techniques.

"Would they work?" she asked, watching him intensely.

"They might," he nodded. "How do I know? I've never treated anyone for post-traumatic stress disorder. My work is still at the experimental stage. I suppose if it doesn't work they'll just shoot me."

Even Anne didn't place the Pentagon on such a dismal level of evolution.

"They wouldn't shoot you, darling," she said with a straight face.

At this, Peter started laughing. The tension created by the meetings with Finer and Penman was released in seconds.

"Perhaps I can irradiate Finer. Make him forget why he came here!" he offered.

"Come. Let's go for a walk. It's still light enough."

This was their panacea. Their walks healed their nerves, dismissed worries over their children; even Anne's fatigue after some of her trips to obscure destinations seemed to dissipate in minutes. Mount Royal was within ten minutes of their home. The cure was there for the taking. Only this time, it didn't work.

Peter told Finer that he must think about the proposition. "You must realize that I am in the middle of a number of experiments that I cannot delegate without training someone to take over," he started defensively.

"No one is indispensable, Doctor..." Finer murmured.

"Then why do you need me?" Peter looked coldly at his tormentor. He knew that Finer had full backing of the Administration. Penman would do anything for the money. To be sure, it was his job.

"*Touché*, Doctor." For the first time, Peter saw Fred Finer smile, really smile. Not the polite, nondescript smirk that politicians used during negotiations, but a real smile of amusement. If Peter hadn't been so angry, he would have smiled himself.

"I have a wife and children," he said instead.

"We can take care of them, Doctor."

Peter wanted to shout for Finer and his Pentagonian cohorts to keep their dirty hands off his family. He swallowed hard. I must get a hold of myself. I must relax. Peter took a deep breath. Then another. He thought of Gabriel. In seconds he was himself again.

"How long would it take you to tie up the loose ends, Doctor?"

So this was it. There was no way he could get out of it. "You haven't told me how long you'll require my services, Doctor Finer."

"That depends on the results of your work, Doctor. Only you can answer this question. Once we're there, of course."

"And why is it, Doctor Finer, that you can't bring your patients to me?" Peter regarded his adversary with a fixed stare.

"It would be political suicide, Doctor. We are talking about thousands of men and women."

"Thousands!?"

"I would appreciate it if you kindly kept your voice down. Everything I tell you, Doctor, is classified information. I said thousands, counting back to about three years ago. Once you teach us to apply your techniques, we can take over. I can't be more fair than that."

"And I can't teach you the technique here?"

"As I said, Doctor, the problem itself is classified. If the media got hold of the sheer numbers of cases we're facing, it might cause...."

"...the President to resign?"

Finer didn't say anything. Once again he was busy studying his nails. His hands were very well kept.

"I don't like it, sweetheart. I just don't like it," Peter confessed that same evening. "There is a rat there, somewhere. I can smell it, but I can't see it. Not yet. Not just yet...."

Anne stroked his hair with the gentlest touch imaginable. It always relaxed him. She had hands that could perform miracles. Actually, Anne's presence alone was often enough for miracles. And I have her to myself, Peter thought. All to myself, he mused in disbelief. How lucky can a man get?

"I tell you, I smell a rat in the state of Washington. Or in the District of Columbia . . . or whatever they call it," he mumbled, his tone no longer tense.

Later that evening, Di called from Vancouver. She was in her third year of Political Science. Neither Anne nor Peter could fathom what made her select this particular discipline at the

University of British Columbia. She could have studied the same
subject at Queen's University in Kingston, closer to home, but
she wanted to experience the West Coast. The young ones didn't
live anywhere. They experienced it.

"I miss you, Mommy," she said. Johnny had long matured
to calling her mother, but Di held on to her youth. It sounded a
little incongruous from a twenty-one-year-old, but in Peter's
eyes she could do no wrong. "When are you coming to see
me?"

"I rather thought you might drop in to see *us*," Anne
admonished in a gentle voice. She, too, loved her daughter
beyond measure. She could never understand how it was that Di
was tone-deaf. Her daughter could only recognize the National
Anthem because people stood up and removed their hats.

Peter came on the other line.

"Hello, Pet," he said, "how much?"

"Daddy! How can you!" There was a momentary silence.
"I found a ticket for half-price." More silence. "Nine-hundred
and eighty return?" Flights had doubled in price since oil
stabilized at $100 a barrel. People in Alberta were laughing all
the way to the bank. The rest of the world was flying much less,
driving smaller cars, or walking to work, as Peter did.

"Love you, Pet."

"Me too, Daddy."

Anne and Di talked for another twenty minutes. When
Anne hung up, Peter looked at his wife questioningly.

"All's well," she said. "She just misses us. 'Tis all." But
her smile carried no mirth. She missed both her children
terribly. Teaching autistic children filled in her some of the void,
but not enough. Not yet. Perhaps some day. And Di was still just
a little girl. They needed each other.

Over time, Anne found that there was something in her that
could and did communicate with the autistic children at a level
apparently not accessible to other teachers. It was neither verbal
nor telepathic. Nor was it even at a strictly emotional level. Yet, it
was there. In a manner of speaking, there were moments when
she became autistic herself, or at least one with the reality from
which the children observed the world. Our world. She would

remain in this state until leaving the classroom. Then, all would be well again. The children loved her.

When Anne's Johnny and Di were little, there had been hardly four or five children per ten thousand diagnosed with Autism Spectrum Disorders. Now, the number had risen to close to a hundred. The ASD included the Asperger and the Rett's Syndromes and a number of other acronyms, such as PDD or NOS, which to Anne were just strange, meaningless words. She did not care for the name or for the disease. She cared only for the children.

Due to her irregular disappearances, Anne could not hold a permanent position at the Montreal Children's Hospital. She visited the Autism Spectrum Disorders Program whenever she could. Her talents became *sine qua non* when one-on-one therapy became the preferred vogue of treatment. Only Anne seemed to maintain one-on-one contact with a number of children simultaneously.

After the initial year or two, Anne, without any medical training to her credit, became an invaluable if unpredictable member of the psychiatric team.

Di was as different from her brother as her mother was from the rest of the world. Johnny was precociously independent. Originally they'd called him Johnny to distinguish him from John Brent, a frequent visitor in their house. It stuck.

Johnny had chosen to follow in his mother's footsteps. In a way. Or in the footsteps of both his parents. He studied composing at the Juilliard Conservatory in New York, better known simply as Juilliard. The school embraced dance, drama and music with equal passion. To finish Juilliard meant to write one's own ticket in the art world. It was that good. Johnny was a darn good pianist but, he held, the world was starved for music. New Music, with a capital M. Music that would do justice to what his mother had once offered to the world.

"We must bring the past into the present, and then step into the future," he'd once said. "Not to repeat the past, but to be inspired by it. Right now we seem to abide in a limbo. Musically speaking, in no-man's-land. It's time we came into our own."

Once, on holiday, he'd asked Gabriel what he thought of music and composers.

"Don't try to make music," the giant had told him. At the time, Gabriel was just about twice Johnny's size. "Don't make music, just listen."

That was all Gabriel had said. Soon after, Johnny won first prize for impromptu composition.

Di's call made Anne realize how much she missed both her children. As Peter was already preoccupied with his inseparable portable computer, she allowed her mind to wander to bygone days. The days of music, of a reality which today seemed hardly possible.

While Anne approved of Johnny's ambition to bring the 21st century up to the standard of the musical genius of the Past Masters of the 18th and early 19th centuries—he regarded most later composers as dismal failures—she, in that shortest of all careers, managed to find beauty in practically all she played. Perhaps, she reasoned, she played what the composers had intended, rather than what they had failed to convey on the impersonal sheets of music paper.

For that reason, she or her music had been outside the confines of time altogether. She was in the realm of spirit, where there is no time. People had sensed that, which in turn explained their insatiable hunger for her music. Even as she, when teaching children, moved to a different reality, so then, by some magic she hardly understood herself, she had transported her listeners to the realm the various composers entered, when stirred by Euterpe.

She recalled Johnny's words.

"I must make sure that when another Anne appears in the East, music will be waiting for her," he confessed when she and Johnny were last alone. "We cannot continually reach into the past for inspiration. We must live in the present and still find beauty, tonality, harmony and poetic vitality within us."

Gabriel had left his mark.

She glanced at her husband. He was still busy.

When she'd told Peter about their son's ambition, he'd wished him luck. Peter hadn't fallen for Anne just for her magic bow, but he understood how it might have left an indelible mark on his son. Even just on CDs. He loved music himself, long before he'd met Anne, but not really with the same passion that seemed to consume his only son. In a way, Peter had been instrumental in Anne's becoming a musical avatar. A messenger of the gods. To him she still was. As he was sure she remained to many, many others. Only now, in such a very different way.

Peter closed the lid of his laptop. He was tired. For a moment he closed his eyes. The next instant, Anne's image in an emerald dress, with masses of curls cascading flamboyantly down her back, shimmered behind his eyelids. The greatest violinist of all time, he thought. And now Johnny. Would he ever be that good? Would anyone?

"Will he ever be that good?" he asked out loud.

For some reason Anne knew exactly what he was asking.

"Only if he learns to lose his ego," she murmured.

"What's that?" Peter asked. He was still lost in his thoughts. Anne smiled. There had been moments lately when they shared more with silence than with words.

They were equally proud of both their children. Di was their sweetheart. Johnny was mature beyond his years. If anyone could turn the tide of what passed for music these days, he would. He was his mother's son.

* * *

3

The Needles

The dark phantoms moved of their own volition. Dim lights from infrequent lampposts cast long shadows, hardly breaking the nocturnal penumbra, which offered a degree of safety for the night creatures that roamed these environs. They slept during the day. They had to—they were stoned. Deprived of free will, their bodies squeezed into dark doorways, hiding behind low walls of half-ruined, dilapidated buildings, or stretching out under low bridges and highway overpasses. Wherever there was a chance to escape from the omnipresent, droning, monotonous Vancouver rain.

They were not easy to see.

An array of cartons discarded at the nearby shopping center served them as camouflage. They melted into the background of other debris, newspapers blown in by the wind from the Pacific or passing cars. During the night it didn't matter. The rain helped to wake them up. To allow them to move under their own volition. Like self-winding robots fueled by hunger for another fix.

Anne had seen it all before. It was the fifth time that she'd visited this particular district. The old shadows—awakened by her presence—had moved on. And new ones, multiplying as inexorably as wild mushrooms in the droning rain, had taken their place.

A vicious circle.

A Sisyphean effort?

She, too, would sleep during the day and walk around the forgotten, unkept streets at night. Not just the streets seemed forgotten. So, too, were the people who lived there. If you could call it living. Perhaps surviving? For a while. All too often a very short while. Not that time mattered. Soul, the essence of man, went on. Continued. Whatever accounts one didn't settle in this life, one would bring back in the next.

Anne smiled at her thoughts.

How wonderful it would be, she mused, if the churches were right. One would live one's life, say 'sorry' in the end, and go up to heaven. Perhaps a year or two in the halfway station of purgatory, like public baths, and up you went. Even if one forgot to apologize at the prescribed hour, there was that promise of Infinite Mercy that, surely, would never allow a creature as stupid as a human being to suffer eternal damnation. That would be like punishing your dog for not cleaning up its own poop. We, the human apes, seem to wallow in our own excrement. Day and night. Like those lost souls she would tend to tonight. Again. And again, if need be.

When she arrived in Vancouver that afternoon, she took a taxi to the hotel she'd stayed in once before on Granville Street. It was cheap but quiet and near to her nightly objective. She managed to get a room facing the backyard. No view, but quiet during the day. At the desk a young girl greeted her with a fixed smile.

"A room, Sir?"

Always the same. She was now regularly recognized as a man. Her hair cropped short, a little dishevelled, no makeup, good padding in the shoulders. She refused to wear lifts. Shoes such as short Hollywood stars wore to look taller. More macho. If she was to be a man, she would be a short man.

"Have a good day, Sir," the girl said, handing Anne the key to her room.

Somehow the greeting seemed inappropriate. She didn't care much about the day. Not today. Or tomorrow. She dreaded the night. Not because she wasn't going to sleep. She was used to that. At home she often read till first light, a throwback to her concert days. She dreaded the pain she was going to experience by drawing it out of the derelicts she would visit during the dark hours. But 'Have a nice night' would have sounded even worse. For one of those she would have to wait until she got back to Montreal. If only there were another way to help them. Perhaps Peter will invent something, she thought. Something that cleanses the sheath which we all build, unwittingly, around our Self. That sheath that thickens, building up layers of habit, of mental and emotional minutiae, until we can no longer see our way through.

All the way from the airport, her mind had been full of disjointed bits of memories, each trying hard to get out. Like the Self. Like her inner Light. So many memories....

"Each according to the capacity of the recipient," she'd murmured to herself, looking through the taxi widow, open so she could breathe some fresh air. Surely, we weren't meant to breathe the recycled gunk the airplane fed us.

Her mind had turned to Gabriel. She remembered him sitting with his left heel drawn below his perineum, the right resting on the opposite thigh. The pose of the spiritually enlightened. The *siddhasana*. He sat silent for the most part, occasionally uttering a word or two.

"Whatever is received is received according to the nature of the recipient," he'd said. Sometimes she thought his lips didn't move when he spoke. Yet she'd heard him distinctly.

According to our nature.

Nature is what we are. The Hebrews called it the *nephesh*. The animal soul. The sum total of what we have accumulated in our subconscious. Our thoughts and emotions, our likes and dislikes. Our dreams . . . both good and bad. Our nightmares. Our loves and our hates. Sometimes we had to clean out the dross, wash clean, or at least wipe the surface of the slate so that our true nature might be able to peek outside. To see the world we've created.

"Ye are gods...." King David? He'd made his share of mistakes, but he'd also cleansed himself. Why can't we do the same, she wondered?

If people only knew that we, and only we, control our nature. That's what having free will is all about.

"That'll be thirty-two dollars, Sir," the driver had said.

She'd given him a decent tip.

"Have a good day, Sir," the man said smiling. He had a nice, open smile. Not too much dross.

"You, too," she said. "You, too, driver."

There was not much left of the day. Soon her work would start. She unpacked her belongings from her shoulder bag. She didn't carry much. One change of underwear, a pair of pyjamas, an extra shirt. No tie. Men didn't wear ties any more. Too constricting. She hung her raincoat in the open wardrobe, a recess with a single bar and some hangers. That was it.

Before going out, Anne called Montreal and left a message for Peter. On all her trips, the message was always the same.

"Love you, darling." That meant that she was all right.

She always called their home number when she knew Peter was at work. She didn't want to speak to anyone. Not anyone who was coping on their own. She had to conserve her energies. Particularly, her emotional energies. Every last ounce of them.

She went downstairs.

"What's the shortest route to the ocean?" she asked. It had been four years since her last visit, and although she had no definite plans, she didn't want to get too lost.

"Take the 49th West to Marine Drive, Sir. You can't miss it," the girl said.

The late afternoon was surprisingly good, weather-wise. The sun was only partially misted by the coastal fog. Someone must have known I was coming, she thought.

She walked fast, trying to combine her walk with exercise. She was also hoping to take a nap before her night rounds. That's what she called them. John Brent had taken her on her very first rounds. At the MNI. Twenty-seven people had enjoyed remission that day. She wondered how long they remained healthy after her visit. She shrugged. It was up to them. Up to their free will.

These days, she no longer healed their bodies. Just minds. Or emotions. Or really she healed nothing. She simply empowered people to heal themselves. She had an idea how it worked, or merely a dim idea. One day she would write a paper about it. Perhaps it would help Peter in his work, though she doubted it. Peter dealt with results—she initiated the activity of the cause. Or was it Cause? But surely, she argued with herself. When Peter removes negative memories from his patient, doesn't the organism, the brain, the memories, heal itself? She and Peter weren't so far apart. She, however, didn't need complicated machines. She could do it by walking around. By making the rounds. She never knew in advance when she would have to go anywhere, but she always knew where. The moment she saw herself in her mind's eye in a certain location, she had to go. It was as if she were an instrument and, once it was tuned, she had to play it. Or... or the energy, the power or whatever it was, would dissipate. Like music to which no one listened. Like a tree falling in an empty forest. It would affect nothing and no one. She would see herself in certain surroundings, walking. Just that. Walking. The rest was up to them.

Just walking. Except for the pain. Sometimes it would last for weeks.

It did not matter. She had no say in the matter. She believed that whatever is given to the recipient must be used. It wasn't a question of choice. Not even duty. For her, it was as necessary as eating and breathing. And loving. Yes. Mostly loving. One could not survive without love. Not for long.

She wondered if the people she would visit that night still loved someone. Or something. Perhaps their drugs? They were alive, after all. They had to love someone or something. Love and life were synonymous. One couldn't experience one without the other.

She took off her shoes, rolled up her trouser legs, and waded into the Pacific. For Vancouver, it was quite warm. The summer had been hot here. There was a bunch of kids playing with a ball some distance away. The ball splashed in the water next to her.

"Mister, can you pass us the ball?" She looked down. "Pleeeease?"

She kicked it expertly. Like a man. Like Johnny had taught her in the garden.

She wondered why the children weren't in school. She'd hardly attended school at all. Mostly, she'd been tutored at home. Mother told her that she'd had problems relating to other children. Or had it been teachers? She'd cleaned herself up since. She got on well enough with just about everybody. She wondered about the Pentagon. Poor Peter....

It was time to go back. She ate a snack in a cafe on the way to the hotel. A large slice of pizza. With olives. She loved the olives. It wasn't bad. She washed it down with a cool beer. As a man would. Boy! Would men have a surprise!

Her face widened, showing her teeth in a naughty, bacchanalian grin.

An hour later she was dozing off again. Sleeping in an airplane hadn't been that relaxing. Constant noise. And lack of oxygen, of course. She hated flying. Again, no choice. Perhaps one day people would learn to fly. To just think of a place and be there. Instantly. She'd read that some yogis could do it. Wouldn't that be nice? Teleportation?

She flew.

She spread her arms wide, kicked off and she was airborne. Somehow she managed to go right through the wall. It didn't hurt at all. She soared over Vancouver. Afar she saw Stanley Park. Green. Tall trees reaching out for the sky. She could touch their crowns. It wasn't hazy any more. It was perfect. Everything was perfect. The sky, the trees.... And suddenly she was among them. Rough barks, proud enormous boles, hundreds of years old. Momentarily she wondered how her skin would look if she were that old.... Then she was up again, admiring their complex, fractal crowns. They looked different from when seen from the airplane. Now, she could see every single leaf. They differed minutely in colour. It depended how much life they held. How much vitality had been given them. She saw the veins pulsating inside the tree, working fulltime. If only we worked as hard. We would be as beautiful as trees. In Stanley Park. Or anywhere.

It was a lot cooler at night. She was glad she'd brought the mackintosh. And a hat. A fedora like the one Humphrey Bogart wore in the *Maltese Falcon*. Or was it *Casablanca*? The hat was mostly in case of rain. As she neared her destination, street lighting progressively deteriorated. All large cities have their slums. Usually large, semi-developed tracts of land, waiting for a brave developer about whom everyone could later complain. Vancouver was different. It didn't suffer from *favelas* that extended their tentacles over a large segment of the mountains in Rio, nor a whole district—as in New York, where no sane person would dare to walk alone at night. In Vancouver there were pockets of depravity where human worth was rated at par with stray dogs. Often lower. People, the so-called normal people, living comfortably around these areas, left the vagrants alone, provided they did not become too visible. What you don't see doesn't hurt, they thought.

And visible they were not.

At night the human, perhaps half-human, derelicts came out like echoes of forgotten eras, in stark contrast to the few normal people rushing home to enjoy the safety of their expensive houses. In a strange, seemingly automatic way, the forgotten ones all moved to pre-established zones, where they knew, from experience, they could hope to sate their burning desire. To stifle their pain. Their hunger.

Drugs were not hard to come by. One or two minor robberies, perhaps a handbag or two, would last for a week. Of course, you had to be careful. It would not do to stay in one place too long. Two, three nights at most. Otherwise the police would trace your footsteps and recover the stolen goods. In a strange way, the dispersal of the needle districts helped protect the customers. Small—but many. Not too far apart, but far enough for the police dogs to lose their scent.

Anne knew them all. She raised the collar of her raincoat. Somehow, when she approached her beat, she did her best to also become invisible. To melt into the shadows, to become one with the ways of the people she searched out. Usually she didn't meet any. Not face to face. Only sometimes would someone actually acknowledge her presence.

"Why are you doing this to me?" one shadow spoke in a whisper. "Leave me alone."

"You are never alone," she whispered back, not even attempting to see the face behind the cardboard box.

She was ready to walk on when the voice spoke again.

"Isn't it too late?"

"It is never too late," she replied. It sounded trite, like tired slogans delivered by a local preacher. Only she knew from her own experience that it really was true. "Not if you don't interfere."

"I never interfere." This time the voice sounded aggressive.

"If you don't interfere with yourself," she added.

She leaned against the wall, wondering if the person behind her needed her any more. The verbal exchange was an integral part of her work—her mission, as Peter called it. Often it broke the ice, established contact. Something else took place at the non-verbal level, something that, even after so many years, she was still unable to put into words. Peter was the only one who, per force, knew about what she did on her trips. Neither her mother nor her father suspected the truth. Anne, Peter had told them, is occasionally consulted on matters of autism. As a matter of fact, she did give occasional consultations, but not nearly as often as she traveled. To do what she had to. She once told Peter that if she didn't, she would burn up inside. She cited the case of a German healer, Bruno Gröning. They, the stupid people, mostly the jealous medics, stopped him from exercising his talent. He died soon after. An autopsy revealed his lungs had literally burned out. Charred. His last days must have been hell.

"This will never happen to me, darling. Not unless someone finds out what I do."

"Stay away from Salem," Peter murmured.

"What's that? I am not being solemn," she shook her head vigorously.

"You think they'll burn you at the stake?" he persisted.

"Don't be silly, darling!" Anne laughed. But Peter detected a whiff of discomfort in her laughter. He never broached the subject again.

Usually her secret ministrations took weeks, sometimes months, to bear fruit. People woke up slowly. It had taken them years to sink to their present level. They recovered much faster, but it still took time. It wasn't like miracles. Anne never said, 'Arise and walk. Thy faith has healed you.' She wasn't a healer. She was a channel that absorbed the pain that people had imposed on themselves. At least, that was how Anne had perceived it. Pain that often left her tired beyond words. Until she managed to dissipate it into the ethers. To restore the balance.

When the silence continued, Anne walked on. This wasn't like a one-on-one consultation. When words were exchanged, they always originated with the sufferer. Anne preferred to just walk and let the thought-waves, vibrations, energy, or whatever it was that passed between them, do its job. All she knew was that when she returned to the same place sometime later, things were very different. There was lightness in the air. Like the freshness you feel after an April shower. As if a great weight had been lifted. Sometimes she could even feel it on her second or third night. Some years later, new waves of nausea would almost overpower her on the same streets. It seemed that certain states of mind gravitated to similar environs. Until a developer dug deep holes, drove piles and erected skyscrapers for those who could afford them. Then the derelicts moved elsewhere. There was always an elsewhere. Always.

She stopped short of the next corner. She heard laughter. Slowly she peeked round the brick wall.

A man, perhaps in his fifties, was dancing in the middle of the street. There was no traffic, but still, she wished he'd stick to the sidewalk. He jumped up and down in a hip-hop type of dance, so popular among the youth of today. It wasn't strictly dancing, in the established sense of the word, but it consisted of uncoordinated, disjointed jerks and twists and hops which, for some reason she could not understand, were an unmistakable expression of overflowing joy.

"Ha! Ha! Ha!" he laughed outright. The man just couldn't contain himself.

Anne emerged from around the corner. The man hopped towards her, grabbed her hand and pulled her into his peculiar dance. It happened so quickly that Anne had no time to plan her defense. She spun with him in a small circle. They looked like two Dervishes ready to rise on an effusion of faith and joy.

"I am free," the man sang out. "I am free I am free I am free...."

"Me, too!" Anne called. Suddenly she understood. It was his liberation.

He let her go as he danced his way down the street. The night swallowed him together with his joy. Only pain remained. Anne leaned against the wall. She was all right in minutes. Spontaneous remissions took a great deal more out of her. She was learning to handle them, but the load the man had left behind must have taken years to accumulate.

She walked on.

She was back in her room by 5 a.m. She managed to hang out the 'Do not disturb' sign before staggering towards her bed. She collapsed fully dressed on her back. Three hours later, she got up, undressed, went to the bathroom, drew the curtains, pulled back the sheets and went to sleep.

The next evening she returned to the same area. It seemed a little easier. Fewer pangs of pain crossed her awareness. It wasn't her body that hurt. It was the rest of her. Her mind, her emotions. The sort of pain one feels when a loved one dies. Or your lover leaves you forever. The people who'd experienced release shared in their new-found joy. They began to suspect that there was a future for them. Future in life.

When she got back to the hotel, she again called Montreal and left the usual cryptic message.

"Love you, darling."

Frankly, there was nothing cryptic about it. She missed him more than she could say. And besides, he would be happy to hear her voice.

As she boarded the plane, she looked sadly through the tiny oval plastic.

"So close and yet so far," she thought. She had been so close to her daughter.

Di had digs on the other side of Granville Bridge, along 4th Avenue West. She wanted to be close to UBC, which stuck out into the Strait of Georgia. From the tip of the peninsula you could see Stanley Park, the mountains of West Vancouver, and the Sunshine Coast. With field glasses, Vancouver Island, and along the Georgia Strait all the way to Texada Island and, on a clear day, beyond. You could see all that from a single spot. From the University grounds. Now and then a yacht would move silently through the protected waters, or a majestic ferry would pull out from deep inside the Horseshoe Bay, taking people and cars all the way to Nanaimo. Water framed by mountains and forests. No wonder Di wanted to experience the Pacific Coast.

It was a beautiful spot.

"Students should be in beautiful surroundings," she had said. Was it just two years ago? It seemed like ages.

Deirdre agreed. Beauty fed the soul. It brought them, the children, the youth, closer to order and harmony in their own lives.

Anne had been so close. I could have walked there easily, in less than forty or fifty minutes, she mused. In no time at all.... In less than it takes to help a dozen people.

The roar increased as the airplane taxied towards the runway. The tarmac was so impersonal. Deserted. Soon Anne was airborne. Di remained on the ground. At least you live in Eden, Anne whispered. Yet somehow this knowledge did not ease the pain of the parting. Parting after a reunion that never happened.

* * *

4

John Linker

Within minutes of landing at Dulles International Airport, Fred Finer was whisked up by an army helicopter and deposited safely within the grounds of the Pentagon. The airport was only minutes away by road, but, here, back home, it was a question of safety. Canada had managed to avoid the recurrent dismal attacks, which discontented terrorists imposed on our southern neighbors. At any rate, Linker liked to look after his own. It would take him years to train another man like Finer. In addition, Linker had learned to trust Fred. He could count on his complete obedience. And that he needed for the Plan to work.

The Plan, though never mentioned outside the walls of the Bridge Club, was quite simple. To instill democracy in all nations. To assure fair and equitable division of the global resources to all nations. As needed. And last but not least, to rid the world of terrorism. Once and for all. It was true that since the USA began their campaign in that venue, things had gotten worse. Some said a lot worse.

No matter.

"It is always darkest just before dawn," John told his group. He liked trite, established adages. People believed them. After all, that's what established them. "Trust me," he liked to add. It was a strange predilection, as he trusted no one. No one outside his small entourage. And even then, he had other people reporting to him on their movements.

"God protects those who protect themselves," he'd once said, in a moment of weakness, to Joshua Rosengart, his Chief of Staff. He would never admit that he took his Biblical references seriously. Even if he quoted them wrong or out of context. After all, he no longer enjoyed the luxury of reading the Bible daily. Or at all. Time was too precious.

"There is a time to read and a time to work," he misquoted another proverb. Or what he deemed would have been a good addition for the Book of Proverbs.

It didn't matter. No one knew any better, with the possible exception of Fred. Fred was Jewish. At least by origin, as he put it. But Fred would never correct him. Unless asked. Fred knew an awful lot. About almost everything. Probably the Bible, too.

In spite of Linker's often verbatim quotations, Fred considered Linker's knowledge of the Bible relatively limited. Relative because, since childhood, Linker had stuck to a strictly fundamentalist interpretation. He had never gone behind the surface and read the Bible as a veritable gold mine of secret knowledge hidden under a veil of symbolism. Strange for a man who, in virtually all other fields, never took what he heard or saw at face value.

His memory was virtually photographic on subjects really close to his heart. Whatever he read or whatever data he asked his staff to provide him, was duly filed in his gray cells for instant recall, if needed. He could also recite some American poets, just to impress people.

"It's our heritage," he insisted. "It's the American Way."

Two years remained for him to carry out his Plan. For two more years he would wield power, with an iron hand, through the kid gloves of President Twigg. It wasn't that Twigg was a weakling. It was just that Linker was infinitely stronger. Stronger than most people.

"I leave the details to you, John, my boy," GW would say.

GW stood for George Wilbert. John and about a dozen other people pronounced it Geewah. GW liked to be called Mr. President or Geewah. It kept him apart from the shadow of his father, GH.

Basically, details included everything that did not include cameras. GW loved photo ops. He often spent hours looking through telecasts of himself delivering inspirational words to his people. Suitably edited, of course. Linker made sure of that. It was useful to protect the President from as much reality as possible.

It had taken Linker years to arrive at a clear image of what he really wanted. He owed a lot of his knowledge to Fred Finer. This man had a talent for extracting information from obscure sources. Like that time they discussed democracy. They were alone in Fred's garden. Mavis was supervising the preparation of dinner, chatting with John's wife. The Rosengarts hadn't arrived yet.

"What do you make of it?" Linker asked quite candidly. He had his own ideas, but he found it difficult to express himself.

"There are many versions, John," Fred told him. "Which one are you referring to?"

"Run them by me," John replied. His image was still dangling on the tail end of the Greek definition. *Demos*––the people, and *kratein*—to rule. *Demokratia*. A government by the people, direct or through elected representatives. For some reason, he found the Greek version highly unsatisfying. It lacked something. The problem was that there really were as many interpretations of what constitutes a democratic system as there were nations in the world. Even dictators claimed to head democratic regimes. The word became a status symbol, no matter how badly the principles were applied. After all, even in Attica, the extended territory of ancient Athens, of some 250,000 people fewer than 30,000 were fully paid-up citizens, and of those, only some 5,000 regularly attended more than one meeting of the popular Assembly per year. Not much, considering that, in Aristotle's day, there were forty such annually.

And worst of all, Fred wouldn't presume to tell Linker that democracy, by whatever definition, had to be earned, never given let alone imposed.

"Well, I would start with the question of democracy and the media," Fred said, stretching his legs. He loved his garden. "The Brazilian bishops supported the plan to democratize the media. They meant that the multinationals should be disbanded and control of the media put in the hands of the people. They stressed the importance of grassroots participation. This would lead, of course, to a 'new-world Information Order'." He glanced at John. His face was a mask of concentration. He was metabolizing every word.

"And..." John guessed what was coming.

"And this would mean loss of control by a system dominated by the Western industrial powers. Not good for democracy," Fred concluded. He meant the American version of democracy. The American Way.

John nodded. It certainly was not his idea of democracy. The people who ruled had to be the people who owned. And vice versa. Otherwise you had communism. Thanks to his father, Linker started his life as a millionaire. Since then, he'd multiplied the family influence, as he called it, many-fold. Financially, he controlled billions. Through third parties, of course. There was no conflict of interest. But you had to maintain the influence. To do that, you had to tell the people what democracy really was. Dictators forced their people; we had to educate them. Or, on occasion, to scare them witless....

"You need the media to educate people," he murmured.

"Precisely," Fred smiled surreptitiously. He pointedly avoided the use of the word *propaganda*. Since Goebbels, Pravda, and other demagogic regimes, the word had acquired bad connotations. What had been good enough for the Third Reich and the Kremlin wouldn't fly in Washington. Fred smiled at his own thoughts. Couldn't whitewash the White House, he smirked.

"Go on..." Linker appeared to be studying a fly walking up his sleeve, but his eyes didn't focus. "Continue," he urged.

"We seem to prefer the corporate oligopoly," Fred continued. By such he didn't necessarily mean the whole economy, of course. Just the control of specific commodities and services—in this case the media—by a relatively small group of very influential people. "The other options are those of State control, which could change at each election, or the model proposed by the Brazilian bishops, which is still relatively untested."

Fred, knowledgeable as he was, did not realize just how advanced the testing of the new system for controlling the media in South America was. It went on under many guises. It began at the grassroots, then crept along in tiny surreptitious steps, hoping to arrive at a *fait accompli* before anyone noticed. First the villages controlled the dissemination of news. Then small towns, larger towns, cities, districts, and finally.... Or at least the bishops had hoped so. Fred actually suspected all that, but he couldn't back it up with real evidence.

"Nor should it be. I'm referring to State control as being unacceptable. As for the Brazilian bishops, well, their interference is as yet untested. I got all that." John was ahead of him. "Go on."

"Well, John, we all agree that power must rest in the hands of the few who understand the problem. Ronald Reagan and George Shultz called the scourge of terrorism a plague that was spread by depraved opponents of civilization itself. But they did little about it. The USSR collapsed under its own weight. If we are to prevail, we must be in a position to impose our ideal, by...."

"...by whatever means are necessary," Linker said, expressing the view that he'd always held. He also already knew that control of the media was the key to success. "The dictators, of whatever persuasion--socialist, religious, or even intellectual—must be eradicated. You cannot serve two gods!" he concluded triumphantly, as Mavis called them to the table.

Media was the key to ownership—and ownership to power. And then, in an elaborate if twisted way, in Linker's mind, power led to democracy. Fred still failed to follow Linker's reasoning.

Almost six years had passed since Fred shared his ideas. Linker was now convinced, more than ever, that Power had to rest in the hands of those who owned the lion's share. And if government was an expression of power, then that, too, had to be controlled. The American version of democracy, the only democracy that made sense, assured that in whatever country the

American version ruled, there could be no war between them. The same interests would be shared by both countries, and you don't attack your own interests.

John Linker was going to liberate the world. Liberate it from the masses and give it to the people who deserved it. Who had earned their right to rule. Who were all determined to raise the human race to a new height. And between such men and women, democracy didn't have to be enforced. It was as natural to them as it had been to organize great conglomerates that offered employment and a decent wage to all willing to work. Yes, even to the masses.

But it was also at that dinner that Linker realized that there were parts of the world that would forever threaten the welfare of true democracy. People who took from others. People who contributed nothing to society yet would rob and diminish those who did. People who pretended to be Robin Hoods only to line their own pockets. The socialists hiding under the banner of liberalism. People like trade union leaders. Like some charitable organizations that wanted to distribute American wealth to others with impunity.

Well, no more.

"Not if I can help it," he'd told both Finer and Rosengart.

And if success required restricting the vile tentacles of some countries, even by radical surgery, then so be it. They had all been given a chance. America had shown truly divine patience. No more. The time for action had come. The day of reckoning was drawing closer. Hour by hour....

Closer to the final victory.

Democracy, Linker knew, was a secret trust. Real Democracy. The American Way. True democracy existed in its most noble form among those who controlled the wealth of the country. Another name for it was 'dog eat dog'. Or 'no holds barred', as in the wrestling he had done in college. Then they'd called it 'catch as catch can'. He always had. He was the champion of his weight class.

He leaned back, admiring the wall screen he had had installed in his office. The world at his feet. Or at least within the reach of his laser pointer.

"We are the only knights in the world. Even if we do not wear shining armour."

But a time will come, he thought. He knew. His back straightened, adding inches to his height. It was up to him.

The masses, he was convinced, swayed with the wind; like blades of grass, only to return to their point of origin. They did not advance. Did not assume new forms nor create new possibilities. Just rotated in the same space. And time. Only individuals stepped forward towards the unknown. Always the unknown. Without those pioneers there would never be any progress. The human species would still be fighting for the best cave, the best hunting ground.

He actually got up from behind his desk to embrace Fred. He owed him a lot, he felt.

"Sit down, Fred. It's good to see you."

Finer felt a little ill at ease. He'd done his job, but not completely. Linker immediately sensed his discomfort.

"Is something wrong, my friend?" Linker was quite effusive today. A rare occasion indeed.

"Yes and no, Sir," Fred answered obliquely. "He will come."

Linker raised one eyebrow. His eyes narrowed, the smile brought about by his friend's arrival dissipated into a scowl. "Out with it," he said very quietly.

"Eventually," Fred answered. He knew that his reply was highly unsatisfactory.

"When?"

Finer felt a chill along his spine. "The moment he ties up the loose ends, Sir."

"When?" Linker repeated. This time the word was hardly above a whisper.

Finer got up and started pacing the width of Linker's office. He managed five steps.

"Sit down, Fred." The ice was gone. It took patience to get the best from his lieutenants. "Tell me," he said in a normal, almost friendly voice.

Finer described his meetings with Penman and Brown. He omitted no detail which might prove pertinent to his mission. He then looked up from his hands. Finally he felt brave enough to look Linker, his friend, in the eyes.

"There is always a way," Linker said softly.

Finer knew that Linker's solution would not be a pleasant one. He waited in silence, doing his best to look relaxed. In a way he was. He'd passed the problem to his boss. Whatever solution Linker found, it would be his job to carry it out. But it would be Linker's responsibility. He, Fred Finer, would be just carrying out orders.

And then the Vice President told him.

Peter picked up Anne at Dorval. After years of squabbling about the airports at Mirabel and Dorval, Dorval won. Only now it was called the Pierre-Elliot Trudeau International Airport. Hardly room enough to fit the name on an itinerary. Nevertheless, the airport had been completely overhauled, virtually rebuilt, to match the best airports in the world. For years people had put up with the inconvenience of taking roundabout routes from their planes to the arrival lounge. Now it was all automated. As good as it comes.

Anne looked tired. She usually did after her trips. She always said that she rested on the return flight, but she invariably rushed back home the moment she felt she could. Even without seeing their daughter.

"I can't mix the personal with the universal," she'd once told him. He'd never asked her what she meant by that.

To be able to recover fully, she needed Peter . His kindness, his understanding, his love. But even more so, Peter didn't ask her for anything. She not only didn't have to give, she could actually draw on his strength. If she was a giver to others, Peter was the giver to her. He recharged her batteries.

They never discussed her trips. At least not till some days later. And even then, Anne's impressions came as disjointed fragments of events, words and actions, which were often hard to link together into a cohesive whole. He didn't mind. In a way, from his point of view, all her trips were similar. He measured their success by the degree of her tiredness. The more tired she appeared, the greater success she had scored.

Peter was the best, perhaps the only real friend she'd ever had. Except for Gabriel. But Gabriel wasn't here any more. And she was no longer a little girl.

Anne thought it strange. As a child, she had never had any close friends. She'd played with equal enjoyment, equal equanimity with any boy or girl she'd met in school or anywhere else. But there was never a special friend. She wondered why she'd never felt lonely. Later, she suffered a great many admirers, but not people with whom she would want to share any of her troubles. Quite the reverse. They invariably wanted to unload their woes on her. Only later, when she took off on her enigmatic, frankly incomprehensible trips, she always felt, on leaving, that she left behind a whole army of dear friends. People, men and women, who were willing to bare their soul to her. They never offered to share their torments with her. In a way, she had to drag their torments out of them.

Strange, she thought. After all, none of them knew that I had anything to do with their.... with their change of heart. Or mindset. Yes, mindset was closer to the truth. Yet right then and there, whether she met them face to face or not, she felt an unbreakable bond forming between them and herself. They were the distraught, and they became the hopefuls. She, it seemed, provided the link.

It was only then that she began to understand her own childhood. She had been prepared for loving all equally, favouring no one. After all, she was no more than a channel. No more than an instrument on which someone or something was playing strange melodies. She'd heard that music sometimes. Pythagoras called it the music of the spheres—an ethereal music produced by the movements of heavenly bodies. Yet she knew it was more than that. Unless Pythagoras had been talking about quite different heavenly bodies.

"Love you, darling...." She said it five or six times before they got home. She really meant 'I need to be loved'. It was practically a cry of anguish. It asked: 'Why me?' It asked: 'Will it never stop?' It asked.... There were so many unknowns.

Peter virtually carried her to the front doorstep. Whatever adrenaline kept her going when surrounded by strangers was now waning. In spite of her men's clothing, her fedora and the lack of makeup, she looked like a beautiful flower that was wilting for lack of water.

Peter took her straight to the bedroom. He helped her undress and laid her gently on the king-size bed. A meal could wait for later. She would probably awaken refreshed by the evening. They might even go for a walk. In the meantime, Peter tiptoed out of the bedroom and jogged to the MNI. He still had work to do.

His secretary caught him the moment he entered his office.

"Dr. Penman needs to see you, Sir. You can go right up at once, if you wish."

He didn't wish, but he went anyway. It didn't pay to ignore Penman's urgent messages. Research scientists, no matter how famous, subsisted on grants. Penman administered them. In some ways, Peter was at his mercy. He hoped against hope that it had nothing to do with Finer. With the Pentagon. He really had more important things to do than to protect the good public image of President Twigg. Let him get out of his mess on his own, he muttered to himself as he walked down the sterile corridor.

It was a long walk. It seemed that it got longer every year. The walls changed from pale green to beige to pale blue. Why is it always pale, he asked no one in particular. Why must even the walls look sick? As he entered the Administrative wing, the sterile aroma gave way to a pleasant air freshener. Peter hated air fresheners.

Penman wasn't in his office. That's all I need. Two hours to bring Anne home and now Penman on his sabbatical....

"He just stepped out to the washroom, Sir," the receptionist, trying hard to look efficient, told him. She wasn't hired for her efficiency. Penman's secretary sat in her own little office.

"Can't he wash at home on his own time?" Peter grumbled under his nose.

"I beg your pardon, Sir?" Peter wondered if she'd heard him.

Just then Penman walked in. He moved directly to his desk and pointed to a chair in front of it. No good morning, no hello, no how are you. It was the Pentagon, Peter knew.

"We must talk," he said. When Peter opened his mouth, Penman silenced him with a wave of his manicured hand. Apparently he had to talk, Peter had to listen.

Peter thought that Penman would be wise to get himself a smaller, or at least a lower desk. Why was it, he wondered, that people who held administrative positions invariably needed enormous desks to hide behind? Shouldn't they try to impress people with their own stature rather than with their furniture?

"I was under the impression, Dr. Brown, that we had an understanding," Penman began.

So this was going to be formal. Peter waited to see what would develop.

"You've given me to understand that you would take advantage of the Vice President's gracious offer and reciprocate his generosity."

Penman was looking sternly at his desk. Obviously he needed it for moral or immoral support. When Peter still said nothing, Penman looked up. "Well?" he said, his facial expression belying a certain lack of confidence.

"You want that billion, don't you, Richard?" Peter murmured. They'd been on first-name terms for years. Ten at least.

"This is not a laughing matter, Peter," came a dry reply.

"I'm not laughing, Richard. And I haven't refused the Pentagon," Peter spoke quietly. "They want an expertise I haven't got."

"They don't know that," Penman said, immediately regretting his words. Money came first, then thinking, then honesty. "What I mean is that you are in a position to do your best to help them."

"Aren't we all." Peter wouldn't be swayed. He knew he would probably give in, in the end, but he hated being bought. Even for a billion dollars. He remembered the story about a woman who had been greatly offended by an offer of a hundred dollars for her intimate services. When the offer was upped to a million, and the donor assured her that the money would be given to some sort of church charity, she began to waver.

"...well," she said, "for such a worthy cause..."

The man immediately handed her a ten-dollar note.

"What do you think I am?" she asked haughtily.

"That, Madam, we've already established. We are only haggling over the price."

It was an old story but, well, Peter wasn't haggling over the price. He wanted to get on with his work, no matter how small his compensation. He could make four times as much as a neurosurgeon. He had in the past.

Even as he watched, Penman seemed to be shrinking, like a doll with the air escaping through some invisible hole. He drummed his fingers on his desk, made a feeble attempt at a smile, and allowed his head to drop down to his chest. "I need your help, Peter."

Penman didn't give a damn about the Pentagon, and little more about Peter. He was a master at getting cooperation from his staff, from anyone who crossed the threshold of his office. He did not seem aware that Peter was onto most of his tricks.

"I'll do my best, Richard," Peter pretended to be mollified.

"That's all I ask...." Penman whispered, his arms spreading in a pontifical blessing. "That's all I ask," he repeated, glancing at his watch. There was another mission he had to perform this day for the good of the MNI.

Peter left his office with some misgivings. Would Penman find a way to punish his research if he refused? How far would he push him to get his way? Peter knew Penman to be misleadingly devious. Yes. Misleading and devious. He was also eminently successful, from the point of view of the Institute. Since John Brent had run the MNI, Penman had tripled the financing for research scientists.

I suppose I'll have to comply, he mused. Even if for just a while.

As Peter reached his office, a familiar face was waiting for him. He could see it through the little window. His secretary had let him in. Fred Finer got up and stretched out his hand.

"So good to see you again, Doctor Brown. May I sit down?"

Peter murmured something and nodded.

"I've spoken to the Vice President," Finer started, still standing. "We understand that your wife takes occasional trips abroad," he spoke very quietly, his tone conspiratorial. "We could provide security for her, if you wish," he said as he sat down.

Peter hadn't become the Director of the most intensely growing department at the MNI by being stupid. This was a direct, thinly veiled threat. He couldn't think of anything more dangerous for Anne than to be given the Pentagon's 'protection'.

He sat down, heavily, behind his own desk. "When?" he asked.

"I booked the flight for tomorrow morning," Finer replied, examining his nails.

"I'll be available three days from now." He needed at least that long to be there for Anne.

Finer's face opened up like sunshine cutting through clouds on a rainy day. "I shall change the reservations personally, Doctor Brown. First Class, of course."

The next moment he was gone. Only something vaguely unpleasant lingered behind. Peter recognized it as the smell of blackmail.

* * *

5

Gabriel

Gabriel evidently had access to information that was out of bounds to mere mortals. He arrived at his previous home, in Westmount, the day after Anne got back from Vancouver. As usual, he came unannounced, yet somehow he never failed to come at the right time, when his particular talents were in great demand. Gabriel had spent years at the Westmount residence as majordomo, performing the tasks of an exemplary servant, being a font of esoteric information, and acting as a friend and defender of Anne's fate in ways that no one else could match. He must have sensed, somehow, that he was needed.

At eighty-something, Gabriel looked only sixty-and-a-bit. Not that anyone attached much importance to biological age any more. Some people were pushing a century and remained active professionally, though not necessarily in their original professions. Suffice it to say that Gabriel no longer wrestled. Unless we included other people's problems as things he had to wrestle with.

He once told Peter the story from Genesis, about the man who'd wrestled an angel. To him, Holy Scrolls were a periodic table in which all the chemical elements had been arranged according to their atomic numbers. The scriptures, as the periodic table is to a scientist, were the basis, the starting point of his mental acrobatics. That is to say, when he didn't rely on his intuition alone.

Only Gabriel never took the writings literally. He treated them as stories and parables that were meant to inspire men today to recognize their true nature.

The story he'd told Peter was about Jacob, Esau's twin brother, who wrestled with his own nature. As a result of the near mortal combat, Jacob became known as Israel. You can apply the story to every man and woman living today, he'd said.

"Esau represents your material or physical nature. Jacob stands for a man who became aware of his potential. Israel is a man who is fully cognizant of his divine nature. That's a poetic, scriptural way of describing a man who rejects all limitations. On our own, it is of little importance with which point of view we regard the world. But when we deal with others, we must always address the divine within them. Otherwise we shall enter a vortex of duality from which there is no safe escape."

For some reason, Peter thought of this story the moment he saw Gabriel at the front door. He realized that he had been approaching both Penman and Finer as Jacob had approached Esau. At the lowest level possible. What if those men deserved better? What if I gave both those, ah, gentlemen a fair chance?

Peter found it really hard to apply the title 'gentleman' to either of the two . . . gentlemen. Nevertheless, the moment Gabriel stepped into his home, Peter knew that his relationship with his two tormentors would never be the same.

Gabriel's perception of reality was different from normal people's. Different from ordinary people whom we recognize, erroneously, as normal. He saw us as states of consciousness. He possessed the ability to see through any mask we donned to protect our fragile egos, and zero in on our inner turmoil.

"We all live in a state of turmoil," he'd affirmed many times. "Our job is to restore order and harmony in our lives."

On many occasions Peter had no idea what Gabriel was talking about, only to discover, some time later, that he was hitting the nail on the head.

At the front door, Gabriel waited for Peter to extend his hand, only to be embraced by Peter as though greeting a long-lost father. The huge man—Gabriel was over six-foot-six and some two hundred fifty-odd pounds—reached over Peter's extended arms and returned the bear hug.

"I wondered when you'd come, my friend," Peter said, having finally released Gabriel from the embrace. "You knew we needed you?"

"I am delighted to see you, Sir," said Gabriel. Then he smiled. "I am delighted to see you, Peter. No, you haven't offended me, although your calls have dwindled to near zero."

It was a long-standing joke between them that Gabriel only addressed Peter as Sir if the latter had offended him.

"Guilty, but insane, my friend," Peter confessed. "To tell you the truth, things have been getting hectic this last week or so."

Peter expected Gabriel to say 'I know', but if Gabriel did possess some extrasensory abilities, he'd never confirm them. "It is only a question of listening and watching, Peter. Everyone is clairvoyant if they only step out from behind the mask that obscures their vision." That was supposed to explain how Gabriel invariably knew what was about to happen or, even, what you were about to say.

"Your in-laws send their regards," Gabriel said. "I trust the four of you are equally as well?"

Peter nodded. A rhetorical question. Of course we are, now that you are here.

"Come and sit down. Anne will be back in seconds. She just stepped out and...."

"Gabriel!" a scream of joy reached them from the front door as Anne rushed in.

Anne made a running jump for Gabriel's arms. Her fatigue from her trip to Vancouver was gone. "When did you come?" she asked. "I'll never forgive myself if I missed even...."

"I am still coming in, Miss Anne."

She pulled him by the sleeve. Miss Anne remained Miss Anne even after he had agreed to be a godfather to her firstborn. In Gabriel's eyes, Miss Anne was something between a minor goddess and a major angel. Possibly, the other way round. He treated her like a Fabergé Egg wrapped in strands of golden filigree interwoven into the Shang dynasty ethereal *peau de soie*.

It was evident that his love for her was completely undemanding. Unconditional. The sort the Greeks called *agape*. He laid his heart at her feet to do with as she chose. Peter suspected that she loved him just as much. They seemed to have a bond that was invisible yet absolutely unbreakable. Gabriel once told Peter that he and Anne were individuals. When Peter looked at him questioningly, he explained.

"Individual comes from the Latin, *individuus*, meaning indivisible."

"You mean you are tied together by some invisible...." Peter felt lost. At the time he was just a little jealous at the influence that Gabriel appeared to wield over Anne.

"No, Peter. I meant that both, she and I, are indivisible from our source."

Half an hour later all three were sipping tea on the garden terrace. Anne looked radiant as if recharged by Gabriel's presence. He, in turn, regarded her with the deference one accords someone very dear yet, in a strange way, inaccessible. Peter thought that Gabriel, at some level of perception, thought of Anne as someone he always wanted to be; but as this was impossible, he seemed to draw vicarious pleasure from her spiritual powers and abilities. Anne seemed quite unaware of his quiet devotion and, for her part, poured love and dedication at his feet, always regarding him as her mentor and spiritual adviser.

He'd raised her from moments of acute depression, which had manifested as withdrawal from reality in which we all, or at least the vast majority of us, have our being. In a way, he'd restored her to life. There truly had been a bond between them, a bond that lasted to this day, when the two could communicate non-verbally, just by sharing the same space. Gabriel always referred to it as his sharpened powers of observation, but Peter hadn't believed it then, nor did he believe it now. The two employed powers which had no corresponding equivalent in the world he lived in.

Miraculous? Spiritual?

These words meant different things to different people. Peter thought that what most of us regarded as spiritual, to them, to Anne and Gabriel, was normal. Every day.

"How are mom and dad?" she asked, looking him in the eye.

She knew the answer. *They miss you.* He didn't say it but she understood him. In turn she answered his question before he'd asked it. "I'll drop in this week," she said. "If only for a while."

Gabriel nodded. He sensed that Peter needed her even more than her parents did. At least, right now. There was something Peter wasn't saying, but he took his time. Gabriel never pushed. 'If you are to know something, you will,' he'd told them both. 'It is quite unavoidable,' he would add with a big grin. To Peter it was quite evident that Gabriel believed in predestination. He, in turn, called it simply 'order and harmony'. 'If the universe managed to unfold itself over billions of years in a reasonable facsimile of order and harmony, I'm sure these attributes will trickle down on us, its conscious members, at the appropriate time.' Rather like Reagan's economics, Peter thought. Only, hopefully, a little better?

"Can you come with me?" she looked at her husband. She was thinking of the trip north to Lake Marguerite.

"I'll do my best," he assured. He didn't sound very convincing.

For a little while they sipped their tea. Anne's eyes drifted to the bed of roses. The roses Gabriel had planted over twenty years ago. They forever remained Anne's pride and glory. She watered them, gave them fertilizer, trimmed them and covered them with mulch for the winter. She treated them like a shrine to Gabriel's memory. Sometimes she just stood next to them and she could hear his voice. Or thought she did. Is there really a difference, she wondered? If you are sure you imagine something, is it not real to you? At least, at the time?

Gabriel smiled. He'd followed Anne's line of vision.

"Thank you," he said. He seemed about to say more when Peter interrupted.

"I must speak to you," he said. It wasn't clear if he meant Anne or Gabriel. "I must speak to both of you," he explained. Perhaps he, too, was learning to read their thoughts.

He described the meetings he had had with Penman and Finer. He held nothing back, including his distaste of the Pentagon, his distaste for the VP, his dislike of doing something of which he was still uncertain, of risking people's sanity. He talked for a while without interruption. Finally, he recounted Finer's offer of extending the Pentagon's protection to Anne.

"I'd rather entrust her safety to an army of devils," he concluded. "At least she would know how to deal with them."

"There isn't that much difference," Gabriel murmured.

"What's that?" Peter said, looking away from Anne.

"There isn't that much difference," Gabriel repeated. "Devils are creations of our own mind. If we act like devils, we are devils. If we act like masters, we are masters."

"Ye are gods," Anne whispered. She was alluding to the Psalm of David.

"Define gods..." Peter sighed.

"Gods are people who reject all limitations."

He expected Gabriel to come up with some sort of metaphysical nonsense. "And Satan?" he pushed, drawn into this discussion which was furthest from his mind.

"You would have to have satans, or devils. Plural. They are people who reject all limitations," Gabriel repeated with a straight face.

"Are you suggesting that the two are the same?" Though he hadn't practiced any established religion for years, he found Gabriel's statement incredulous.

"Not in the least. A knife serves to save a life or to take it."

"We are instruments, Peter. But what or whom we serve does not dictate our ethics," Anne joined the discussion.

"The Source is one. We all draw upon It. The good and the bad. We are gods," Gabriel repeated. "Or devils," he added quietly. "Often it's hard to tell..." he concluded.

There was a momentary silence. There was something hanging in the air that would not let them continue.

"But that is not what you want to talk about, is it, Peter?" Gabriel coaxed gently.

"Well, in a way it is. I am not sure if I am dealing with devils or, well, with devils."

"No one is completely bad. There is a tinge of error even in the best amongst us. This is the nature of dualistic reality," Gabriel said.

His tone was always quiet, relaxed, yet it carried undertones of deep confidence that would not be questioned. He never sounded as though he were trying to convince anyone of anything. He just stated facts and let them germinate on fertile soil. The other fields had to wait.

"So Linker isn't so bad?" Peter asked, his voice a near sneer. He was blaming the VP for Finer's messages.

"No, Peter. No one is all bad," Anne cut in again. "No one," she repeated, holding Peter's gaze.

"You are both against me, aren't you?" Peter pretended to whimper.

They laughed. If ever love was more palpable than at that moment in the garden Anne maintained with such care, Peter was not aware of it. He was physically appreciative of gentle waves of serenity, of compassion, washing over him. He felt the touch of angels.

"Help me," he said finally. "I need to understand."

"Wisdom comes with maturity, not with biological age. It is the ability to perceive purpose in the world around us," Gabriel resumed. "As Anne told us, we are all instruments. We must learn to play the most beautiful melodies we possibly can."

"When you say we, you don't actually mean, ah, you don't really mean *we*, do you?" Peter perceived a glimmer of light he couldn't quite grasp.

"When I say we, I mean the players. The instrumentalists. The virtuosi. Not the instruments."

We are the instruments and the players, Peter thought. We are both. Just then a strange idea exploded in his mind, like lightning that came out of nowhere. I and my Father are one. Who said this? There was someone who understood this... this truth, centuries ago. Millennia? The instrument and the player are one and the same. Is this what duality is all about? It is only we who separate the cause and the effect from each other? Can you separate the *Requiem* from Mozart? Neither could exist without the other.

Gabriel and Anne were regarding Peter like a wonderful child who had just passed his first exam. Peter's eyes remained wide, wondrous, still unsure of his ground, yet seemingly facing the unknown with renewed confidence.

"I shall go to Washington, darling. Will you forgive me?"

This was the last statement Anne expected from her husband at this particular moment. Somehow all her thought-reading abilities eluded her.

"Are you sure, darling?"

"I must play my tune, Pet. We all must." And then he looked up at Gabriel.

"You are a very wise young man," Gabriel said.

"Not too bad for fifty-three, eh, my friend?" He said 'eh' in a truly Canadian style. He would have to protect his Canadian soul when he walked among the Americans. We all speak the same language, but somehow we sound different.

"I wonder what it is?" he mused aloud. "Is it the instrument or the musicians?"

For once he felt his two friends weren't sure what he was talking about. He was wrong.

"Or the thespian...." Gabriel smiled at his suggestion.

We all have roles to play. We don the roles of husbands, and fathers, and scientists. Others act out their lives in a million and one different ways. We often play different roles during the same day. Indeed, we are thespians all.

"And what of the virtuosi?" he asked, a little lamely.

"That's a much higher ground. Don't climb the mountain until you are strong enough. You must first cross the river."

Anne had told him about the 'river'. Rivers, streams, any expanse of moving water symbolized change, usually drastic change, in the state of consciousness. One could not pour fresh wine into old skins, he remembered. Again, the instrument and the player. After all, like his father-in-law before him, he had gone to a Jesuit college. He'd been brainwashed with the best of them. Or had there been something there he could actually learn? He'd never thought about it. He was always too busy just living. And loving. And developing his work at the MNI. But maybe there was something to the old Biblical stories.

At first, there didn't seem to be any connection between the players and rivers and the Jesuits. In school, the Jesuits had kept the symbolic meaning of scriptures hidden under the general blanket of 'mystery'. Peter was well prepared to face the world he could perceive with his senses. For scientific research this was adequate. When he had to make pragmatic judgments in the area of 'good and evil', he was as helpless as a child. His mind rebelled against the simplistic conditioning of the fundamentalist doctrine. Slowly, under Gabriel's influence, he began to discern an invisible world of diverse shades, of all the colours of the rainbow. As a scientist he knew that all colours originate in single golden whiteness. Now he saw that only through the prism of our consciousness could we discover different shades, hues, in the makeup of our fellow men. So far he regarded people as complex cellular structures, as objects of his scientific curiosity. Now he began to see them as actors and players, each enacting his or her personal drama, tragedy or, with luck, comedy on the stage of his or her life.

He began to see that there must have been something to those biblical stories Gabriel and Anne alluded to. After all, you can't fool all the people all the time. And a great many people believed them, even if they had no idea what they meant.

As a matter of fact, he also remembered Gabriel talking about the higher ground. It always symbolized prayer, or a state of raised consciousness. It was all about consciousness, he thought.

"It's all about consciousness," he said out loud.

Anne and Gabriel smiled simultaneously. Peter knew that he'd just risen to a different level. He would never regard the universe, even mundane reality, in quite the same way. It's all about consciousness, he repeated silently. And for the first time in his life, he knew exactly what he must do.

The next day, the moment he got to his office, Peter called Finer.

"Yes?" Finer sounded shy. Perhaps he wasn't as evil as all that, Peter thought.

"When do you want me?" Peter asked.

"Yesterday?"

"I have one condition," Peter spoke very slowly. There was an audible sigh coming across the wire.

"Yes, Doctor Brown?" More negotiations? Conditions? More conditions? John wouldn't like....

"I need you to swear," Peter hesitated, "I need you to swear on the Torah, the Bible, that you will stay away from my wife. This is not negotiable," he added when silence greeted the first part of his statement.

"I shall be happy to swear on my mother's grave, if that makes you happy, Doctor Brown." Finer's voice was an ocean of relief. "At any time at all, Sir." This was the first time Finer had addressed him as Sir. Was this a good sign?

"Be here before noon," Peter said, as if commanding a subordinate.

"Yes, Sir," Finer repeated. He would address the devil himself as Sir to get his own way. Isn't that what successful negotiations were all about? He smiled at his own thoughts. Mission accomplished. His face was almost smug.

By one in the afternoon, Peter had signed a contract with Finer for a preliminary period of three months. Shorter, if Peter managed to get results sooner. At this stage Peter refused to discuss any extensions. The only surprise Peter found in the contract was his proposed remuneration. In addition to the billion-dollar grant, he was to be paid $100,000 US per month for his services. Only then did Peter realize just how much they really wanted him. Perhaps I can do some good there after all, he mused. Or are we just haggling over the price?

Peter didn't haggle.

"My work is too important here," he argued. "Anyway, if I don't succeed within three months, chances are the method you intend to apply is not doable. At least, not with our present technology."

Finer found it difficult to argue with Peter's logic.

By five o'clock Peter was discussing his impending departure with Anne and Gabriel. He tried to elicit from his wife, and from his friend, some sort of reaction to his decision. They didn't try to dissuade him, nor encourage him. Yesterday Peter had entered a new level. The club of the mentally unstable. Or the spiritually enlightened. Take your choice. He had to play his own fiddle. They said little, but the two pairs of eyes that followed his every move seemed to say, 'No one ever said it would be easy.'

It wasn't.

If the Pentagon were getting their claws into him under false pretenses, a proposition foremost on Peter's mind, he would have to deal with it there and then. There wouldn't be any of Gabriel's wisdom, nor Anne's love, to aid him. He would be alone. Like a grownup. He smiled at his thought. Here he was, a man in his early fifties, the Director of Experimental Neurosurgery, yet feeling like a schoolboy who was given a new assignment. This, he sensed, was not just a question of science. That he could handle. He had, for years.

"Something still smells in the state of Columbia," he murmured, seemingly to himself.

"You are never alone," Anne and Gabriel replied in unison.

Perhaps they could read each other's minds, after all.

* * *

6

Away from Home

Perhaps for the first time, Peter realized how Anne must have felt each time she left on one of her trips. She went on missions designed to help people, not knowing if she would. The results of her efforts might show up only years later. She did what she felt was her duty, although she never explained exactly to whom she felt such obligation. She never spoke of God, or Jesus, or any of the Great Avatars of the past. Whatever or Whomever she served seemed to dwell deep within her heart. Only she had contact with that Source which, on occasion, seemed to take over her life, virtually her free will.

Sometimes he wished he held such an allegiance. Such unquestioning faith.

Peter was faithful to Anne, to his children and to his science. He thought that if he served them well, then whatever powers supervised the comings and goings in this world would be kind to him. He would never admit it, but he'd never completely freed himself from the image of God, the benevolent Father, the Master of the Universe, who could smite him and his

loved ones with a flick of His little finger. He also held a
dwindling hope that if he behaved himself with certain decorum,
with honesty and perseverance, he would be rewarded. Not by
his work or by worldly success, but in some other place and time
by this very same benevolent Being.

"We are never punished *for* our sins," Gabriel had told him
some twenty years ago.

"You're kidding. What of the billion Christians?"

Gabriel had ignored his interruption. "We are punished *by*
our sins," he'd continued, as though Peter hadn't spoken. This
single sentence had stuck in Peter's mind. It meant that he alone
was the judge and the executioner. The only one truly
responsible. It placed a great deal more on his shoulders. From
that moment on, there was no one to blame for his fate. He was
creating his own universe. Idea by idea, thought by thought,
deed by deed, consequence by consequence.

Whatever applied to our sins must apply to our rewards.

He looked out the window. The plane had already veered
toward the south and was fast climbing to 33,000 feet. It was
about a third of the way up when it passed Westmount on its port
side. Tiny Westmount, a patch of green in an ocean of roofs and
tarmac. Only Mount Royal matched its verdant crowns.

Far, far below, there were Anne, Gabriel and, yes, and Di,
who would fly in tomorrow. He hadn't seen his daughter since
Christmas. With September only days away, he missed his
daughter badly. This summer Di had taken a hiking tour of
Vancouver Island. When she dropped in to Montreal, he was
away lecturing. And now, he would be away again. It wasn't easy
being in charge of your own life. He had no one to blame. Not
any more.

Peter wondered what Anne would do in his absence. The
three of them—Anne, Di and Gabriel—would probably drive
north to see Anne's parents. What a feast that would be. He
wondered if they would have time to miss him.

For a moment he felt sorry for himself. The old 'why me'
cry formed in his mind. Then he remembered, once again,
Anne's words, 'Ye are gods.' That was it. Gods not withstanding,

he still felt a little sorry for himself. He ordered a Scotch on the rocks. The svelte stewardess, who managed to look both smart and sexy in the US Air Force uniform, served him a twelve-year-old Johnnie Walker Black Label. Here's to you, Johnny, Peter murmured, thinking of his son. This thought made him sad again. Johnny, too, had spent a week with them at Christmas. And now, he would be flying some ten kilometers over his head and not even say hello?

"Hello, my son," he murmured, raising his glass. It was a very good Scotch. As was the next one he ordered after leaving behind the yellowish haze that hovered over New York City.

Peter was determined to do his job at the Pentagon as fast as possible and return to Westmount. He would invite both his children to fly in for a long weekend. He would be rich then. One hundred K every month would go a long way towards paying all the expenses. Not that they had ever lacked money. Anne's royalties from way back were still trickling in at an impressive rate. It seemed that for many people she never really stopped playing her violin after all.

The plane was equipped with a conference table, at which Finer remained during most of the flight. He seemed busy pressing keys on two computers while talking on a telephone mounted on his head. Only some half hour before landing did Fred Finer get up, stretch, and sit on the seat adjoining Peter's. Finer and Peter were the only passengers.

"Protecting your investment?" Peter murmured. We must be getting close to the dungeon, he thought. That was how Peter thought of the Pentagon. The dungeon. He wasn't sure he would ever get out of there alive.

"A beautiful day for flying." Finer sounded happy.

"Beautiful day for just about everything," Peter agreed noncommittally.

Finer ordered a club soda to keep Peter company. He then half-turned towards his prey, trying to catch Peter's eye. When he did, he said softly, "I want you to know, Doctor Brown, that I shall do everything in my power to help you with your experiments."

Peter nodded his appreciation. Of course he would. It was probably his job.

"I've been studying the work you do for some time now. I truly admire your perseverance. Your ability to put together seemingly independent fragments of information into a cohesive whole is truly remarkable."

Peter's face softened. Maybe the old coot wasn't as bad as he sounded.

"I also want you to know that if there has been any gray area in our relationship so far, I was merely carrying out my orders," Finer assured, his voice even more conspiratorial.

"Forget it," Peter said magnanimously. "I'm sure you did what you had to." That left him a lot of scope.

"Thank you, Peter. May I call you Peter? We shall be working together a great deal, I imagine. I shall be responsible for making sure that you have all the scientific tools you need."

"You may call me anything you want, Doctor Finer," Peter said pointedly.

"Fred," Finer corrected. "Frederick sounds so pompous," he added when Peter didn't respond to the bait.

"Fred," Peter repeated, taking another sip of Black Label. Somehow it had lost some of its relish.

By 2 p.m. the helicopter deposited the two would-be friends at the East Wing of the Pentagon fortress. Peter was reminded of the elephant's leg. There is a story about a number of Hindu men trying to discern what object they were facing in the middle of a moonless night. Each touched a different part of an elephant. Each man claimed to have faced and touched something different. Some even said they touched a tree trunk, a hairy animal, a slithering serpent or some other substance. The moral of the story was that you couldn't tell the whole by witnessing only its part. So it was with the Pentagon. Peter was pleasantly surprised how normal the building looked. He'd expected platoons of fully armed marines guarding every square inch of the place. He'd also expected roving cameras to record his every move. Well, if he was under such scrutiny, then the cameras remained conspicuously hidden. He and Finer were greeted by a smiling girl, not even in a uniform, and escorted to an elevator which took them directly to Peter's new lab. His living quarters would come later.

To put it mildly, Peter was amazed.

At first sight, he could have sworn that he was back in Montreal, in his lab at the MNI. Every detail had been reproduced with infinite care. The lab was exactly the same. The equipment might as well have been lugged from Montreal. Identical in everything to the last detail. Peter blinked repeatedly. There were even fresh flowers on his desk, in his office, such as his secretary placed there on special occasions.

"Do you find this acceptable, Peter?" A quiet voice reached him from afar.

Fred Finer was standing at the door, grinning. It was quite obvious that he was enjoying himself. It had been he who'd ordered a dozen minor officials to make a thorough study of the MNI Department of Experimental Sonic Neurosurgery. He'd given them one week to arrange an exact copy of the laboratory and Peter's personal office. All this happened without anyone's knowledge. At least Penman had not given Peter any inkling that something of this sort was going on. Perhaps he didn't know, either.

"For now, Doc... Fred. For now. This enables me to continue my work. Not necessarily to broach new ground...." Peter mused aloud, still in a state of shock. Then he turned on his heel. "I expect you have reproduced my home with equal precision?"

"No, Sir. As a matter of fact, though you may find it hard to believe, I did not authorize anyone to go anywhere near Westmount. You still think of us as uncouth barbarians, don't you, Peter?"

It was judicious not to answer that, though he was sorely tempted to say: 'Not uncouth, Doctor. I never thought uncouth...' "I'm impressed, Fred. Very impressed," he said instead.

"We use pressure in order to achieve results. Different pressures have different effects on different people. I want to apologize for one particular pressure I applied in your case."

By some means, Finer must have guessed, learned, or surmised that Peter did not hold the Pentagon in the highest regard. The financial gift he'd offered the MNI was little more than an extra jab that placed Peter in a difficult position. He never doubted that his offer to 'look after Peter's wife' was the real clinching factor. He'd used Peter's own image of his organization to achieve the desired effect. It was sneaky, unprincipled and very clever. It was a psychological twist, rather than one of underhanded blackmail.

"When do I start?"

"We have a coordination meeting at zero three hundred hours. We still have time for you to visit your living quarters and make yourself at home."

Peter followed Finer down the corridor to the elevator. There they rose to the top floor. His suite faced the inner court. Nothing in the world could induce Peter to guess that he was at the heart of the most powerful organization in the world. For a moment he felt like a fly trapped in an enormous well of honey. The feeling passed when, once again, his eyes fell on a vase of red and white carnations.

"Your national colours, I believe?"

Peter gave up. Either these people were all understudies of Machiavelli, or they were human, after all. Time would show.

"I'll pick you up at zero one hundred hours. I thought we might have a snack together."

The door closed quietly behind his host. Peter listened intensely for an extra click that would suggest that his door was locked. He waited a moment and then tiptoed to check. The door opened to a deserted corridor. "It's a funny prison," he murmured, unconvinced. He walked out into the corridor, made a little circle, and went back to his room. There was no hiss of a camera following his movement. Again, there was no extra click in the door lock.

He was reminded of a story about English boys, long before the UK joined the Common Market in 1973 that later became the EEC, who had been told to write an essay about foreigners. Most boys handed in a page or two about their continental neighbours that allowed for a certain latitude of opinion. One particular boy handed in his paper with a single line: "All foreigners are bastards."

The teacher told the lad that the French had schools and museums, the Germans had modern factories and produced their own cars, the Italians.... and so forth.

"Now go back and write another essay about foreigners," she admonished.

The boy came back with the original sentence crossed out. Below there was a new one.

"All foreigners are sneaky bastards," it said.

Peter smiled at his own thoughts. "It's a funny prison," he repeated. And then his smile faded into a strange feeling of disquiet.

A month at the Mayo Clinic, or two months at the most expensive SPA resort on the French Riviera, would not have given Anne as much rest, joy and relaxation as the single week she spent at Lake Marguerite. The villa following the contour of the hill descended towards the water that seemed to change colour every second moment. It ranged from offering a perfect reflection of the clear blue mountain sky to brooding darks verging on black, which seemed to conceal mysteries of local Nessies or even more terrifying monsters. Densely forested slopes of mature conifers surrounded the lake in an embrace of evergreens that never changed, the year round. In their midst, Anne felt protected from the unforgiving outside world.

Diana, Anne's mother, was overjoyed at seeing her daughter. Michael, her Dad, couldn't stop talking about how Diana had been preparing for her arrival by giving the house a thorough spring cleaning out of season, and Deirdre, little Di, danced around exactly as Anne used to, her long hair bouncing, sparkling, bringing sunshine into the house. Only Johnny wasn't there. He'd called that he would try to come, but... alas, he couldn't. He claimed he was conducting one of the experimental pieces he'd composed and was to present to the public. Michael suspected that he'd found a new girlfriend.

"No matter. Christmas is not far off and we shall all be together again," he asserted with conviction.

"No one mentioned Peter," Anne said, a little hurt.

"We were talking about him just before you walked in, darling. You know we all love him very much," Diana was quick to assure her daughter.

Anne missed Peter. In fact, for the first two nights she tossed and turned. On the third day she relaxed. All thanks to the indispensable Gabriel.

"If you close your eyes, you'll find him there," he told her.

She did and she found him. Whenever she needed him. But, well, it still wasn't quite the same. Nevertheless, the next five days were heaven on earth. The water was still warm enough for a daily swim, and in the afternoons Di took Anne out for a spin on their laser sailing boat. Anne's parents were both too old to handle the small craft, but they kept it in case either of their children or grandchildren dropped in. It was a sort of lure. They knew that all four loved to skim across the lake carried by the wind. The stronger the better. There was no fear in any of them.

At the week's end Anne said her good-byes and drove Di to the airport. She hated saying good-bye. Why is it, she wondered, that although we are all one, we must be so far apart? The question didn't quite make sense to her, but that was how she felt. They were one, yet they were apart. The old conflict between the universal and the parochial. There had been moments when she felt greater immediacy, greater affinity with her autistic children than with her own. Perhaps one day the human race would rise above this duality, she mused. But somehow she doubted it. She thought it more likely that, as some individuals rose to a higher plane of existence, others would rise from lower levels of the animal kingdom to join the ranks of men, and women. At the same time, she wasn't at all convinced that humanity stood at the apex of dualistic reality.

Dolphins, she thought, never killed each other. They didn't conduct wars, didn't pollute the atmosphere. But there was ample evidence that they risked their own lives when attempting to save human beings. She'd read stories that a pair of dolphins had supported a human body between them and carried the man into shallow water. There were fewer cases of man attempting to save dolphins. We preferred to exploit them and make them do silly tricks for screaming children.

The house was very empty.

First Johnny, then Di, and now Peter. Bless Gabriel. He promised to drop in weekly while Peter was away. She loved Gabriel dearly, but she couldn't cuddle up to him. Not in bed. Or anywhere. She walked the rooms like Lady Macbeth, looking for she knew not what. If only she had more hours at the school, at the Montreal Children's Hospital, to look forward to. As long as she was at the school, the children consumed all her attention. At home, she was alone again.

"Like on the world concert tour," she mused. "So many people, yet . . . so alone."

And then she had it. She switched on the computer and clicked on her bank account. She forgot her password. She found it. She waited with excitement building in her heart. 'Oh, let there be enough, let there be enough...' she prayed.

The screen displayed her account. There was over $17,000 in the credit column. She only used her account for her 'travels'. She held that if the powers that be wanted her to do their work, they had better provide the finances. So far, they always had.

The sum was more than enough. She thought of the billion dollars Peter had brought to the MNI. With Peter making so much, she would dare to propose her idea. And for once she could travel as herself. Not *incognito*. After so many years.

Peter called that same evening.

"Love you," he started, in case she wasn't there.

"Love you too, darling. Miss you. Are you all right?" She still wasn't sure how Peter would fit into the Pentagon environment. It wasn't easy to remain oneself among people who were so very different. Who had such different priorities.

"I'm just fine, darling," he assured. "But . . . I feel guilty about you sitting there, all by yourself."

She cleared her throat.

"I have an idea," she didn't sound quite sure of herself.

"What is it?"

She told him. She told him in great detail. For a number of years she dreamed about visiting some of the venues where she'd once performed. She wanted to be there without crowds, without spectators, *paparazzi* or sentries. Just to revisit the atmosphere.

"Wouldn't you rather we went together? I won't be here forever, you know?"

"No, darling. I want to do it alone. For once I want to be somewhere, alone, and walk the streets during the day. Not sneak around the whole night."

Peter thought that over. Then he sighed so deeply that she asked him if he was all right.

"Yes, darling. I'm quite all right. And I hope you have a wonderful trip."

They talked some more about the family. They avoided talking about their work. Their telephone calls were always very personal. Just for the two of them.

When Anne hung up, she felt excited. There was something about her idea that reached beyond what she'd told Peter. Only, she didn't really know what it was. But there was something very exciting. For a moment she sat down to gather her thoughts. And, as she closed her eyes, she saw an enormous machine that rotated like the world, all around her. She saw Peter and herself as cogs, without which the machine wouldn't be able to keep turning. She wondered what it was that was so important about Peter and herself. When she awoke, her head was still spinning. 'What was so important?' she mused, still in a half dream.

By the time she was to discover it, it would be too late. She could no longer back out.

For the second time that month, Anne boarded an airplane. Not just to visit the concert halls she'd once played in, but to visit them in total anonymity. She couldn't possibly visit the whole world, but Europe was closest to her heart. The next decision had been the itinerary. She had performed in London, Brussels, Berlin, Paris, Rome, Madrid, Warsaw, Moscow, Oslo, Belgrade, Copenhagen, to mention just a few from memory. She couldn't possibly visit all these capitals. Time and money would be prohibitive.

The answer had come from the travel agent. As the Pope was about to offer Plenary Indulgences, the Italian airline, ever keen to oblige the Vatican, had been offering near half-price tickets to Rome. After all, the Vatican provided more traffic, more passengers to the airlines, than any other attraction in Italy. The Vatican was good for business.

Anne had been delighted.

Where better to start her tour than from the city of the seven hills. She also made provisional bookings for Paris, Brussels, London and Oslo. That would reawaken enough of her memories to last a long time.

When she'd given up playing the violin, she seemed to have given up most, if not all, of her memories. Perhaps it would have been too painful for her to re-experience the euphoria she felt when performing.

"When I listen to my own CDs, I am listening to a total stranger," she once told Peter. "It sounds like meeting someone who was very, very dear to me, long, long ago, yet whom I haven't seen for many years. And now that person is no longer the same. Still dear, still loving, but, well, too much water has flowed under the bridge."

So much water....

For Peter her music was as fresh and as close as on the day they'd practiced together. For him, she remained the genius who allowed him, a mere mortal, to experience her gift.

"Not for me, darling," he'd said at the time.

"I know," she murmured. "In a way . . . I am jealous." There was sadness in her eyes.

In part, this was what she had to discover.

But for now, the wings of the old 848 would carry her to the Aeropuerto Roma Fiumicino. Known to most as the Leonardo da Vinci Airport, it already held memories. Yes, she remembered the places. The facts. Not the emotions, not the... the experience. She couldn't think of a better word. That was what the young ones always talked about. She wasn't travelling to see, to learn, but to experience. Perhaps Peter had been right. It was the experience she wanted to recapture.

Soon she would be walking the gardens of the Philharmonic. Then... L'Accademia Filarmonica Romana. She remembered it vaguely. All those interviews... She read about them in *Il Giornale Della Filharmonica*. They had all been laudatory. Every one of them. Such sweet people. It was all coming back. Already. But most of all the concert she'd given in the garden of the Philharmonic. There must have been thousands there. In a sudden flash she remembered their tears. She played an encore. Then another. More tears.

The flight attendant touched her shoulder.

"Are you all right, Madam?"

She hadn't been Madam, then. She had been Miss. A stripling of a girl.

"Why, yes. Is something wrong?" Anne asked. There was genuine concern on the stewardess' face.

"I'm sorry, Madam. It's just that you looked so pale. I thought...."

"I must get out more," Anne assured her. "In the sun."

Rome was full of sun. Always. At least when she was there. And the Filharmonica. Just a short stroll from Fiume Teverne.

How many years was it? Twenty? Thirty? Did it matter?

And then there was the Parco della Musica of Rome. The Sala Santa Cecilia with the ceiling undulating rhythmically like the waves in Brahms' violin concerto. Concerto in D, she remembered. She remembered the expression on Johannes' face. He approved. It was all her imagination, she knew. Just imagination. And yet.... So many years....

What time is it?

She fell asleep. She had no dreams. Her life was too vivid for her to dream. Too intense.

"We are approaching Rome. Please buckle your seat belts," the voice droned.

And then the wheels touched down. She reached out for her Stradivarius. She smiled instead. She'd given it back to Sir Ian years ago. She stepped out into the September sunshine.

* * *

CONVERGENCE

I fear that you will not reach Mecca, O Nomad!
For the road which you are following leads to Turkestan.

Sheikh Saadi, *Rose Garden*

7

The Camerlengo

He was a short man, even for one dedicated to a profession in which physical size did not matter. Almost exactly Anne's height. He smiled at her, beckoning her to come closer. In spite of her original intention to appear very feminine, Anne was dressed in her protective camouflage: a simple loose black jacket and well-pressed black trousers. At night, or in dark corners, she remained near invisible. Not that there were many dark corners in Rome. Built predominantly from local limestone and marble, Rome shimmered even at night.

For the occasion, Anne had tied a perfect Windsor knot in one of Peter's ties. Just before she left her hotel, she'd changed her mind. The day being a little cooler, she removed her shirt and put on a white polo pullover. It suited her sense of humour. From any distance at all, she looked like a Catholic priest.

'What can be more protective in Rome?' she asked herself, examining her reflection in the mirror. 'Peter would be pleased,' she thought.

She'd already called him this morning. To her amazement, he came on the line. No 'Won't you wait, Madam?' or 'I'll see if he's available?' Just: "Brown."

"Love you," she uttered her standard code. It also meant,
'Are you free to talk?'

"Love you too, sweetheart. What time is it there?"

She told him. She was six hours ahead of him. Peter was in
bed. Only then did she realize why no secretary had intervened
in the connection.

"I'm sorry, darling," she sounded contrite. "I'll call you
later. Bye now."

"Love you," Peter repeated. It was great to hear her voice.
Even at two in the morning. She'd promised him to call the
moment she got settled. He recalled how she always rambled
about the characteristics of time. She always claimed that time
was a nuisance. "It's for the birds," she'd concluded. "They
need it to get the worm."

The short priest kept gesticulating.

"I have all your CDs," he blurted out the moment she
approached him.

Anne was taken aback. "Just how did you recognize me?"
she asked him.

"I wasn't sure, but I was hoping. Sometimes one's prayers
are granted," he pointed to the sky and smiled. "I was talking
yesterday with Sir Ian. Frankly, you've been on my mind ever
since. If I may say so." He looked down at his hands as though
embarrassed at his directness.

"How very flattering," Anne jibed the young man
mercilessly.

The cleric swallowed hard. "Sir Ian told me you'd cut your
hair. And the last time he saw you, you wore black. I've just
been listening to your Sibelius. I listen to you virtually every
day. It keeps me going."

There was a disarming honesty in the priest's voice.
Perhaps living in the Vatican wasn't all peaches and cream. What
a strange simile, she caught herself in time. She was glad she
hadn't voiced it out loud.

Anne hadn't seen Sir Ian Barton in two years. He was her
first conductor. He'd put her on the world map. He . . . he must
be an ancient now, she thought. The cleric read her thoughts.

"Sir Ian doesn't get out much, these days. He lives in Rome, now. He has a villa at the top of Via Di Porta Pinciana, at the very top of the famous Via Veneto. He says he likes the view."

Anne looked at the padre questioningly. Rome has seven hills, each offering unparalleled views.

"He takes his breakfast at the Hotel Eliseo. The breakfast room is on the top floor of the building and offers a most delightful view of, as he calls it, the Eternal City."

It sounded like Sir Ian. He probably felt immortal here.

"In early spring he flies to England, just to visit his origins, he told me. But his heart is here, he said. In Rome. He thinks we, Italians, are the only people in the world who know how to enjoy life."

"He always was good at that," Anne put in.

The priest nodded. "His Holiness gave him a private audience yesterday. They've been friends for some time. They are about the same age." This last sounded like an excuse. "His Holiness loves symphonic music. Yours, too," the priest added, embarrassed. "They are both about as close to liberation," he added sadly.

"Libera..." As close to death, she realized.

So Sir Ian was about to meet his maker. The Pope had been sick for some time. The Vatican was abuzz with speculation and unofficial polling as to who would succeed him. Cardinals talked to cardinals. Quietly. The Pontiff would leave big shoes to fill. *Il Papa* was a true fisherman.

"Would you like an audience with his Holiness?"

"Me?" She was taken aback. She didn't practice her religion, Catholic or otherwise.

"Well, I have a certain pull with His Holiness. I am... sorry, I am known as the Camerlengo. *Il Papa*'s private secretary."

"Camer..."

"...lengo. Actually my name is Giovanni Pesci. Rather fitting, don't you think? Something to do with fish." Anne laughed. The Camerlengo did not lack a sense of humour. Only now did Anne notice that Giovanni spoke English with just a charming hint of a British accent.

"I would be honored to have an audience with his Holiness."

The Pope and she were, after all, in the same business. In the business of enabling people to be all that they could be. Admittedly Anne chose a rather unorthodox way to accomplish her aims, but to each his own, she mused. To each her own. "I would be honoured," she repeated with greater conviction.

"Give me your telephone number and I'll call you as soon as I can arrange something. Will you be staying long in Rome?"

"A day or two. A sort of journey of nostalgia." She gave him a little map she'd picked up at the front desk with her hotel and the telephone number.

"Then we must hurry," the Camerlengo said. He lowered his voice only for her to hear. "Papa just will not slow down. He keeps busy. I think he wants to die on his feet."

"How very wise," she managed, but Giovanni Pesci was already gone. Apparently not only *Il Papa* kept busy. She made a mental note to find out who or what a Camerlengo was. 'Just a secretary' sounded too glib. Personal or otherwise. The cleric looked as young as the Pope looked old. Somehow, too young. Perhaps Camerlengo meant an office boy. Or a messenger?

The next moment, the Camerlengo turned on his heels and jogged towards her, his cassock flaring with every step.

"I forgot to mention," he said a little breathlessly. "Sir Ian let me make a copy of the photograph you gave him two years ago. On my computer," he explained, flashing the picture in front of Anne's eyes. And he was gone again.

So that's how he recognized me. But it hardly explained why a young cleric was carrying a photograph of a middle-aged woman on his person. A lot of separate things must have happened for me to meet this man, she mused. I wonder why?

Anne had decided to leave her reminiscences for the evenings. She'd only seen her concert venues under artificial light. When she had arrived for rehearsals, she had been whisked by a limousine directly to the artists' entrance, escorted to her dressing room, the stage, and then back to her hotel. Admittedly, she'd given all her interviews during the day, but they were the last things she wanted to recall. She needed the evenings to truly recreate the images of her past.

In the meantime, she decided to visit the Vatican.

She walked the ancient corridors, the halls and chambers that still reverberated silently with the steps of hundreds of thousands if not millions of past pilgrims. The walls bore evidence of the Church's contribution to humanity. Paintings, sculptures, frescoes, mosaics and the architecture itself were a living testament that, whatever the Church's failings, the lovers of art and beauty had an enormous debt of gratitude to the Vatican. A living museum accessible to all who cared to come.

There were funny contradictions, though. Come to me, all who are tired... wasn't that America's motto? Here you could also come and rest, provided you walked through two metal detectors and were massaged by hand-held instruments, which were supposed to further confirm your integrity. Then you were allowed to stroll the halls of history while an army of cameras followed your every step. "It's a strange world we live in," Anne murmured to no one in particular. Yet she admitted to herself that she would rather submit herself to a hundred metal detectors than lose the works of art.

Incongruously, just as Anne cleared the security at the entrance, she thought of the Pentagon and, once again, her thoughts drifted to Peter. I wonder how many metal detectors he had to go through to get into the Pentagon, she wondered. And then she realized that the Pentagon was unlikely to store any priceless works of art. And people? People were very replaceable. She knew from her own experience the world over.

As she wandered the halls of the Vatican, she thought about the Camerlengo. The small priest had been like a breath of fresh air. How can one be so young in an environment that is so old? Could I do that? Could I spend any length of time here, in the Vatican, and not become a relic? And then an idea flitted across her mind. If I died, she mused, and were declared a saint, which parts of me would they worship as relics? She drew her jacket tighter around her shoulders.

Peter was still in awe of the Pentagon. Three days had passed since his arrival and he'd made little progress. What Finer wanted, what 'they' wanted, was the exact opposite of what he'd been working on at the MNI. Back home, his efforts had been concentrated on reducing the effectiveness of the ultrasound projector to the smallest area possible. He worked, with a number of assistants proficient in physics, on a directional amplifier that would emit sound waves only toward the patient, without affecting the doctor administering the treatment. Or anyone else, for that matter. Finer's bosses, who still remained in the background, wanted both—directionality and spread.

"We simply have too many, ah, patients, to treat them one by one. We have to be effective in large numbers, two or three hundred, at least. Preferably without their knowledge."

When Peter first heard this comment, he was ready to go back home. It was completely against his principles to administer even an aspirin to a patient without his or her knowledge. To affect their brain, with all the inherent risks, was unconscionable.

"Doctor Brown, trust me," Finer tried a different tack. "We are not playing with other people's free will. The patients we have in mind have suffered, often for years, from post-traumatic disorder."

"You mean battle fatigue," Peter sneered.

"If you must, Peter. From battle fatigue. What you must realize is that a great many of our ex-combatants are not really capable of making decisions. Not as complex as this one."

Peter remained silent. He still hated the idea.

"To tell you the truth, we feel, the Vice President and I, that we are responsible for the damage these men and women have suffered. Now it is our responsibility to restore them to health."

So there is someone in the Pentagon who actually wants to take responsibility for his actions. At long last. Peter still found it immoral but, in some ways, a persuasive argument.

"We would never do such a thing in Canada," he murmured, buying time to think the problem out.

"No. You wouldn't. You also wouldn't supply eighty percent of the troops in eighty percent of armed conflicts over the last fifty years."

And a great many of them against our better judgment, Peter thought. Still, the damage had been done. Perhaps he could help to restore peace to those men by erasing some of their memories. It may be justifiable under some circumstances. Maybe. He was no longer sure. He rebelled against having to make all the moral judgments. He didn't want to play with these lives. To play with their brains. He wanted to help them....

There, I've said it, he realized. He wanted to help them. The argument was not whether to help them or not, only how to administer this help.

"I can't do everything," he said half-loud.

"We will supply you all the help you ask for." Finer misunderstood Peter's statement.

Peter looked at him for a while as though he didn't know what Fred Finer was doing in his office. His inner battles, matters of moral decision, kept him off balance. He wished Anne were there. Or Gabriel. There was no one. He was on his own.

Suddenly he felt tired. He wasn't ready to rise to the higher class so quickly. 'What would Gabriel do?' he asked himself. Or Anne, for that matter.

What would they do?

The telephone woke Anne up from an afternoon nap. The flight and jet lag had taken a bit out of her and she wanted to be fresh and well rested for her evening's memory stroll. She picked up the receiver.

"The Holy Father would like to see you in his chambers for dinner, tomorrow at 6 p.m. Would that be convenient?" The Camerlengo sounded excited.

Dinner with the Holy Father? Surely, this was some sort of a joke.

"Hello?" the Camerlengo inquired after Anne remained silent.

"Is this Giovanni Pesci, the Camerlengi?"

"O. Camerlengo. Yes, it is. Are you free tomorrow evening?"

Suddenly Anne felt weak in the knees. The Holy Father... Why didn't I go to church all these years, she wondered. Not even once. Not even to pray. I could have...

"Miss Howell?" he asked, hearing only silence.

"Brown," she said.

"I beg your... ah, of course. Your married name. Can you come, Miss Brown?" The young cleric was beginning to sound desperate. Or perhaps a little exasperated. He was used to the Pope's invitations having a profound effect on people, but....

"I shall be happy to come, Father Pesci," she said. She felt a little silly calling a man younger than herself father.

"Gio, Miss Brown. I mean Mrs. Brown. Everyone calls me Gio."

Actually, very few people called him Gio. Father Giovanni Pesci wielded enormous power. It just rested lightly on his youthful shoulders.

"How do I find...."

"I'll send a limousine to pick you up. Shall we say around five thirty? We might have a Sherry before...."

"Yes. Yes. That w-w-would be just fine," Anne half stammered.

"Thank you, Mrs. Brown," the Camerlengo said politely.

"Thank you," Anne echoed, but the line was already dead.

That evening, revisiting her old venues was strangely anticlimactic. She did her rounds, but the places did not carry overtones of the past. They looked different. She was beginning to wonder if the whole idea of a trip down memory lane hadn't been a mistake. Something important, something very important was about to happen. She wasn't sure if it would happen to her, or perhaps to Peter. Or maybe even to the Pope. But whatever it was, wasn't going to happen in these old empty concert halls. Not any more for her, anyway.

She felt as if the forces that spun the earth on its axis were about to come into her life. With something unheard of.

Back at her hotel, Anne found a computer she could use. She hated those inanimate flat boxes that seemed to know more than she did. Yet this was one of those rare moments when she regretted not doing what Peter always did—carry an ibook with her. She clicked on the Internet and began researching data on *Il Papa*. There were a great many pages. She settled on one that looked most promising.

Ioannes Paulus PP. III.

John Paul the Third. She wondered what the PP stood for. No matter. The man was born in South America. People said he would do for Brazil what John-Paul II did for Poland. Liberate the people. Not from communist oppression, but from the rich, then from poverty, then from... no one was sure from what. The fact remained that Brazil was a dream that hadn't happened. Not yet. The Brazilian bishops were working with the media to liberate the people from the control of the oligarchy. The last time she'd visited the favelas in Rio, nothing much had changed.

John Paul III was eighty-two years old. A man whose charisma matched his namesake's, and completely overshadowed his immediate predecessor. A man tall for his origin, of a dark complexion, possibly a mixture of Portuguese and native blood. In his younger days he had been beautiful to look at. The photos attested to that. They said that nuns weren't allowed to come within a mile of him.

Just in case!

He was still active, although the disease of the old, osteoarthritis, played havoc with his posture and hands. He could hardly write. He wore thick gloves to conceal, at least partially, his manual deformity. Others said he was blessed with stigmata, like Father Pio. His detractors claimed that he didn't want to shake hands with the common man. In truth, each handshake brought him enormous pain, which he covered with a smile.

Anne searched for some of his encyclicals. She didn't want to make too many *faux pas*. It was a bad idea. He'd written seventeen of them. Mostly dealing with the return to our roots. By those His Holiness meant the Christian roots. Not the roots of religion, but the roots of Christianity. The more she read, the closer she found the Pope's teaching to her heart. Anne was beginning to like this man. There were masses of information. Like his namesake, he'd ruled a long time. There was too much to read for one day. She decided to wing her way. Somehow. Perhaps the pope would ask her something about her music?

Funny, that, she smiled. There was both sadness and wonderment in that smile. Funny that Peter and I never talk about music....

She searched for *Camerlengo* next.

The title of certain papal officials, she read. From Latin—*camerarius*. Camera, she knew meant chamber. But in low Latin it meant the treasure of a prince, a monastery, or even royal treasury. There were other Camerlengos. Immediately on the death of a pope, the cardinal Camerlengo assumes charge of the papal household. Was Giovanni a cardinal? He hadn't been wearing the fancy colours when she'd met him. Anyway, he must be too young. Aren't all cardinals ancient? Something to do with the wisdom of age or something.

On the pope's death, in the presence of the household, the Camerlengo strikes the forehead of the dead pope three times with a silver mallet, calling him by his baptismal name. That would be, she looked at her notes, Jose Manuel Garcia Da Rosa. Now here's a mouthful, she smiled. Long enough to wake up the dead. Sorry, she scolded herself. The Camerlengo then proceeds to remove the papal ring and break the papal seal.

How gross, she thought. It sounded like robbing the dead. She stopped reading. "The less I know, the better," she concluded. A young man sitting at the adjacent computer looked up.

"Soma silly stuffa dera," he said. She loved his accent. She loved Italians. She loved Rome. She thought Sir Ian was right. She was apprehensive about meeting the Pope. 'It's not me they want,' she consoled herself, 'it's the memory of my music.' They, too, may have wanted a trip down memory lane.

She slept badly. Peculiar dreams invaded her subconscious with such force that she tossed and turned all night. She woke up tired. It was almost like the first night on her past solo trips.

One particular dream stuck in her mind. She saw a woman, all dressed in white, waving to people from a balcony. Her face looked vaguely familiar. The woman looked a little like her daughter Deirdre. For a moment, Anne thought that she was looking at the princess of Ulster, from the Irish legend. She had no idea why she imagined that, other than the origin of her daughter's name. The woman seemed to be saying something, spreading her arms as if trying to catch the pigeons that whirled nearby. Anne's first chimerical impression was that she was looking at an angel. Then she thought that Di was trying to tell her something. Just before the dream ended, she saw the woman looking down at a crowd of people. They were all sleeping. Just sitting and sleeping. She waved her arms and they all rose. And then a pigeon landed on her face.

It was a white tulle drapery that the wind had blown, from the open window, over Anne's naked body. She woke up immediately.

What is she trying to tell me?

The princess of Ulster eloped with her lover to Scotland. She committed suicide when her guardian treacherously killed her lover. Had something happened to Di?

She picked up the telephone. This time she did glance at her watch and decided to let Di sleep another few hours. Then she realized that in Vancouver it was around 10 p.m. Six hours separated the Vatican from Montreal, then another three to the West Coast. Di must still be wide-awake. No matter. I mustn't become hysterical over a silly dream, she told herself. But she remained uneasy.

Anne felt guilty for not having told Di that she'd visited Vancouver hardly two weeks before Di had flown to see her in Montreal. True that from Montreal she'd visited Grandma and Grandpa, but . . . would it really have hurt had she stopped in just for a minute? Or even two, or three? Di would never divulge her mother's comings and goings. But if she had told her, she would have had to tell Johnny when she visited the New York slums. And then she would try to influence her destinations by the location of her children.

I did the right thing, she told herself grimly. But what did Di want from me then?

After breakfast Anne thought she would try some of her other past concert venues. Perhaps they would be more rewarding. But the first looked quite impersonal. As her taxi fought its way through the dusty, honky, screaming streets of Rome to the next concert hall, Anne began to doubt if places had anything to do with her missing memories. She could retrieve parts of them by sitting still, the way Gabriel had taught her, and see the rows of people, their faces frozen in expectation, waiting for the first stroke of her bow. After that, she had no memories. It was just music. Maybe that's all there was to find.

At least the drive was distracting. Dozens of scooters buzzed around the car in and out of traffic, and for a second she had a glimpse of long forgotten familiarity. A police escort of a dozen *carabinieri* on motorcycles; lights flashing, surrounding her darkened limousine. Then it was gone.

After lunch she called Di. She was fast asleep. It was 2 a.m. in Vancouver. Apart from that, Deirdre was just fine.

Next she called Peter.

"Di sends love," she told him.

"Tell her I love her, too. How are you, Pet?"

"Guess who invited me to dinner tonight."

"The Queen of England. Ah, sorry, forgot you're in Rome. The Pope?"

Anne was crestfallen. With his twisted sense of humour he'd taken all the wind out of her sails.

"You know already?"

"It was in all the morning papers," he laughed.

"Peter?"

"Yes?"

"I love you," she said. What more was there to say?

At 5:30 precisely, a black limousine pulled up in front of Anne's hotel. It bore the insignia of the papal office. She was already waiting downstairs, wearing her usual camouflage. She didn't want to be recognized as Anne Howell. Not any more. By anybody. The driver looked at her with suspicion. He was expecting a woman.

* * *

8

The Experiment

They were sitting behind a thick wall of glass. The expressions on the men's faces were indifferent, restrained, perhaps not sure of what they were about to witness. In the middle of the row, the Vice President, John H. Linker, moved his chair slightly forward, as though that would assure him a better view. He was flanked by Fred Finer, his personal envoy, his right hand, his jack of all that is difficult and unpleasant on one side and by Joshua Rosengart, his Chief of Staff and public image, on the other. His team from the Bridge Club occupied the remaining seats. They represented the three branches of the military. The Air Force, the Navy and the Army. The most powerful military in the world. Probably the most powerful military the world has ever known. Six men who held the fate of the world in their hands.

As for the six or seven white-coated scientists, no one seemed to care what their names were. Except for Peter Brown, of course. He was the prima donna who was about to perform.

Outside, on the roof terrace, in a rectangular space fenced off from the rest of the roof, about a dozen people were moving about. Everyone else, the maintenance staff and even the security detail, had been cleared away since early morning. The small group, mostly men and three women, stayed fairly close together, as if feeling strength in numbers. They seemed to be wandering aimlessly, not knowing what all this was about. All of them had been told that they would be awarded an Order of Merit for their service in the military. Ego has power of its own. Every invitee turned up with time to spare. For reasons of security, they had been told to report to their old bases. From there they had been flown directly to the helipad atop the Pentagon roof.

The roof garden had been Rosengart's idea. He thought it might come in useful for just such an occasion. Rosengart engineered many 'occasions' that were best enjoyed in the outdoors, yet well protected from the peering eyes of the media. Not that he didn't have most of the press under his protective, unyielding wing. A number of experimental weapons for hand-to-hand combat had been demonstrated on this roof. The Chief of Staff was very proud of his creation.

Peter was busy making final adjustments. He had done his best to explain to them that the shield was unnecessary. The ultrasonic emissions were strictly directional. The wave couldn't travel backwards. Or laterally, for that matter. That was the whole idea. There was a reason, however, why Peter had advocated the roof for the experiment. The ultrasonic waves could run through walls. Not all, but most walls.

Peter was manipulating a tube atop a tripod. The cylinder appeared to be made of plastic, with layers of transparent polymeric material surrounding it on all sides. At one end there was a small opening that looked like the lens of a camera, only without a lens, equipped with a protruding cylinder, of even smaller diameter, similar to a zoom tube on a camcorder. There were a number of buttons, little wheels and discs that turned with a clicking sound, and a single four-foot mast that looked very much like an antenna.

"I bet you could listen to Beijing on one of those," Rosengart quipped.

No one laughed. Neither the distinguished guests, nor Peter. Peter was too busy. This morning he had been told quite simply, "Show us what you've got." Up until then, they'd given him a staff of experts above and beyond the expectations of any dream team, including his staff at the MNI. And, more important, they'd left him alone to his work.

It was Finer who'd delivered the message this morning. "We shall be at your disposal at 1500 hours in the West Garden." There was no east, north or south garden, but at the Pentagon people liked to be precise. Peter had six hours to prepare a demonstration of how far along he was in his work.

"But I'm not ready," he'd pleaded belatedly. But Finer was already gone.

Peter took a deep breath and pressed a button.

There was no sound, no light, no visible effect. The group of people milling in the garden stopped momentarily, then resumed their aimless wandering. The group behind the inch-thick laminated glass would soon know if anything had happened.

A middle-aged woman was the first.

"Where are we?" she asked. Her voice, picked up by one of the concealed microphones, sounded genuinely concerned.

"Who are you?" the man next to her asked.

Finer checked his list. The two had flown in together, this morning, on the same helicopter. They'd fought in the same platoon for nine months.

The group behind the protective shield remained silent. "Does it work?" a voice asked from the side of the row of seats.

Two more men in the garden began talking. They didn't look angry, just lost.

"I was having this coffee and, hey, presto, here I am. Where are we?"

"Damned if I know. I was watching a movie. High Noon. You know? With Gary Cooper." This was an older man.

"Who the hell is Gary Cooper?" A younger man joined the conversation. He wore a Marine Corps uniform with sergeant's stripes. His chest was riddled with chunks of metal, medals of honour, all polished to perfection. As a member of the Marine Corps, he must have earned them.

"Yes, Mr. Vice President," Peter replied. "The ultra waves have affected the subjects' memory. What we don't know is to what extent, for how long, or if any collateral damage has been inflicted."

"We are not shooting at the enemy, Doctor Brown. We do not intend to have any collateral damage. Or any damage, for that matter." John Linker spoke softly, yet Peter detected an undercurrent of chill. Peter had used the military expression on purpose. He'd learned to quite like Fred Finer. This change of heart did not extend to the Vice President.

"If we could find out when High Noon was last screened, we would have some inkling of when the last thing that man remembers occurred. Except that the other man had no idea who Gary Cooper was. He either doesn't like oaters, or he is too young, or his memory fails him for a much longer period of time."

A woman in an Air Force uniform started crying.

"Easy, girl," a man patted her on her shoulders. "There now, what is it?"

"He's dead," she whimpered, tears smearing what little makeup she wore. "He's dead..."

"Easy, girl," the man repeated, putting his arm around her.

"They told me he would. I told him not to do it.... I told him, I really did..."

The others turned towards them.

"I told Charley not to touch them pills. I told him...." and more tears filled her eyes.

"If we can find out whom that lady lost, probably on an overdose in recent months, or years, we would get a handle on the time factor in memory repression."

This was a great bit of luck, Peter thought. He made a careful note of his projector's settings. Every click could mean a week or a month. Of course, different people could react in different ways. The scientist in him was drawn into the problem he had to solve.

"Just what the hell are we supposed to see here?" This was not a man in the garden. It was the Army liaison, with three stars on his over-padded shoulders. Fred Finer had sent out a memo briefing the whole group, including the Vice President, on what they were going to witness.

"Are they going to die or what?" he asked.

John Linker's face took on an unholy hue. He nodded to Rosengart.

"Get him out of here, Joshua. Now," he said. There was no animosity in his voice. He had to work with what was available. He was simply dismissing a child who hadn't done his homework. He was sending him home. For now.

In the meantime, Finer's fingers were playing *allegro con motto* on his portable computer. His whole attention was zeroed in on his work. If a bomb exploded next to the Pentagon, he might have noticed. Short of that, he was absent. Periodically he glanced at Peter, as if searching for some sort of confirmation.

"Charley, right?" he asked.

Peter nodded.

"But... but that's only three months ago." He looked at Peter in disbelief. "Just three months?" Then Finer looked again at the PC screen. "Three months and eight days."

He looked sideways at Linker.

"One hundred days," he murmured. Then he said something only Finer could hear. "It will just have to do."

Peter was observing the reactions of other men in the garden. All the data, every facial expression, every word uttered by any of them, was being duly recorded by a host of cameras, hidden microphones and surreptitious devices that could detect the heartbeat of a fly. The masses of facts would be dissected in minute detail by the staff. None of them had been told what they were looking for. Just to relate what they heard to a time frame.

One Hundred Days? God created the world in just six. One hundred days covered the issues of Twigg's nascent presidency. The second term. Not much for history books. The murders of Rwandan and Burundian presidents were followed by one hundred days of slaughter. By mid-July, 800,000 Rwandans had been killed in one hundred days. Linker looked up from his notes.

"Is that all you need for genocide? One hundred days?" he asked. He did not expect an answer.

Linker took a sip of coffee. Lately he drank a lot of coffee. It wasn't good for him, but, well, he needed the extra waking time. Finer had prepared the notes to show Linker what could be done in just one hundred days. Just for fun.

Fred Finer and the Vice President were sitting in front of an open fire. It was still warm outside, but the fireplace was probably the Vice President's only indulgence. He had the air-conditioning turned down and the fireplace set up. Just a little. It helped him to relax. He'd spent two hours with the President today. That always left him tired. He had low tolerance for stupidity.

Linker pushed the coffee away and raised his snifter. He regarded the open fire through the rich hues of Remi Martin. He didn't really drink it. He merely swirled the glass in his warm hand for it to release its bouquet. Then, with half-closed eyes, he sniffed the fragrant effulgence his caress had liberated.

"You are a good friend, Fred," his eyes remained on the glass, but there was a trace of emotion in his voice. Joshua is more fun, he thought, but Fred? Well, Fred made you think.

Finer looked down at his notes. "In one hundred days," he read, "Napoleon conducted the Waterloo Campaign. Having escaped from Elba, Napoleon arrived in Paris on March 20th. June 28th that same year marked the restoration of King Louis XVIII. One hundred days." Finer looked up. Not a good example, he thought.

Linker didn't move.

There were two more pages of notes. Linker wondered how on earth Fred had time to put together such nonsense. Just to please him? Perhaps. Finer really was a nice fellow. A buddy. A little too erudite, but he didn't lack a sense of humour.

Linker got up, stoked the fire and returned to his armchair. "We are idiots, you know," he started. "We are seeing the problem from the end, instead of the beginning."

Finer followed Linker with his eyes.

"We are not interested in erasing memory of the last hundred days." The Vice President's eyes were filled with epiphany. "We want to know for how long the amnesia will last!"

"But the trauma...."

"We don't want to erase people's memories, after the fact. We want to do it before...."

Finer was lost.

"Let Brown work on the trauma angle all he wants. What I want to know," once again Linker stood up and this time towered over Fred Finer. "What I want to know is for how long the amnesia we induced in the group on the roof terrace will last."

"Assuming it will ever come back, you mean?"

"What? Ah, yes. Assuming..." His back straightened, taking years off his posture. "Just think what we could do in one hundred days."

Linker was right. Peter's report had advised that some subjects of the experiment had lost memories reaching back four, even six years. As for the recovery time, it was much too early to tell.

P eter called Anne just before she left for the Vatican. She was already dressed. On her way towards the door, she glanced at the full-length mirror. She nodded in satisfaction. She had half a mind to let the telephone ring, but it sounded like long distance. Actually, she had a good five minutes to get downstairs. She just didn't think it was appropriate to let the Pope's limousine wait for her. That's silly, she told herself. Yet she picked up the receiver with a touch of reluctance.

"Pronto?" she said, emulating the local people.

"Love you," he said.

"Me too. I'm just going out," Anne told him.

"To see the Pope?" Peter asked. He didn't attempt to hide the humour in his voice.

"How did your experiment go?"

"I don't know if I am allowed to talk about it. It's top secret, you know?"

"Is that what they told you?"

"No, of course not. If it were top secret, they would have to give me some sort of a clearance, I suppose. No. As a matter of fact, they give me all the latitude I need to get on with my work."

"How very nice of them," Anne commented dryly.

"They are paying me a living wage, you know."

"I know. I'm sorry. I just can't get used to the idea that my husband is working for the Pentagon."

"Not so much *for* as *in*," Peter corrected. "When I finish, the knowledge will remain with me."

"That is true. As I told you, I'm also a bit nervous."

"The Pope?" Peter asked.

"Well, yes."

The silence stretched for seconds. Long seconds.

"Darling?"

"Yes, Peter?"

"You are not really going to eat with the Pope, are you?"

It was Anne's time to laugh. He who laughs last, she thought. "I did tell you...."

"I was sure you were joking."

"Would I joke about having dinner with His Holiness?"

There was another silence. Finally a weak voice answered. "Yes," he whispered. "This is exactly the sort of joke you would make."

"Well, I didn't."

More silence.

"Darling?"

"Yes, sweetheart?"

"I really must go."

"Would you give the Pope my regards?"

She hung up with a bang. Peter could be quite trying at times. He just couldn't be serious for very long. On the other hand, that was precisely why she loved him. That, and for a thousand other reasons. She missed him badly.

Peter stood staring at the receiver. This was the first time that Anne had hung up on him. First time ever. Surely I haven't offended her? Not that they'd never argued. Everyone did. They were both mature people of diverse interests. It would have been impossible not to have an intense argument now and then. But somehow, they managed, on most occasions, to adhere to the Hegelian triangle. Georg Wilhelm Friedrich Hegel was one of Peter's heroes. At least, a hero of his youth. He had convinced Anne to apply Hegel's philosophy to everyday life. Well, a small part of it. If Peter proposed a certain thesis, Anne would come up with its antithesis, and soon they would both try hard to arrive at a synthesis. Rather like that story about God being what the opposites have in common. Peter loved that definition.

This was different. Peter was sure that Anne was annoyed. And then it hit him. Anne really *was* going to have dinner with the Pope.

"What a fool I've been!" He slapped himself on the forehead a lot harder than he'd intended.

He grabbed the receiver and dialed Anne's number. He was told that Mrs. Brown had left the hotel. Of course she had. She'd said she was in a hurry.

My God! Dinner with the Pope?

He sat down at his desk, wondering what to make of it. Here I am, playing with my little ray gun (the Chief of Staff had called it that) while Anne is dining at the top of the world. Actually, many would say that I am at the top of the world, he mused absentmindedly. How strange, we are both rubbing shoulders with Ultimate Power. Temporal and Ecclesiastic. Frankly, Peter always thought that the Vatican also exercised temporal power. They were controlling people's minds. Isn't that what I am doing? Or trying to?

Yet, somehow, the two were different. The Vatican tried to persuade; the Pentagon to impose. No. That wasn't fair. The Vatican threatened with hell and damnation; the Pentagon with, well, with hell and damnation of a different sort. He wondered which the people really wanted more. Or were more scared of.

He realized that, at least at first sight, one cannot rule without intimidation. Perhaps what really mattered was what rewards one offered, not just what punishment for non-compliance. Eternity in hell, which cannot be proven, or the loss of all one had, one's loved ones, one's life. The intangible versus the palpable.

The carrot and the stick.

Dante, Goethe, Mann, Verdi, Boito, Gounod, Liszt.... they all explored the euphoria of paradise and the ultimate depravity of hell. To mystics, philosophers, artists, composers and poets, such concepts were expressions of states of consciousness. Only religion tried hard to make eternal suffering an eternal reality. How depraved, he thought. Eternal sentence with no possibility of parole. Even the Pentagon would limit such retribution to a single lifetime.

The carrot and the stick.

Was there no other way? Whatever happened to the commonality of the two opposites? Diana had told him about Rumi's beautiful vision. He searched his memory. He had it: *Beyond the doing right and the doing wrong there is a field. I'll meet you there.* It was all about the middle ground. About the thin and narrow road that led to . . . to where exactly? To that field? Wasn't Buddha's way the middle path also? And what of Tao? Gabriel could recite the whole *Tao Te Ching* to prove a point.

"I can't recite a single verse!" he said out loud.

He looked around. No one had heard him. It wouldn't do to have a lunatic who talks to himself running an experimental lab at the Pentagon.

He looked down at his papers. He realized that he and Anne couldn't be further apart. What was it that he loved so about her? Was it the sheer opposite?

"Could it be that God resides exactly in the middle, between her and myself?" This time he merely murmured.

And as quickly as he got depressed about hurting Anne, he had it. He had the answer. Between Anne and myself there is only love, he asserted with utter confidence. And in that same instant he felt that, at long last, he had a handle on God.

Whatever Spinoza claimed that God may or may not be, the name of his God was definitely Love.

And being with Anne was like abiding in heaven. Beyond the doing right and doing wrong. Just loving. Dear Anne....

A knock on the door interrupted his reveries. Peter pressed the button on his desk.

"Finer," came an electronic version of Fred Finer's voice.

Peter pressed the enter button. This precaution saved hours of work. With a touch of a finger he could switch off the intercom and complete whatever train of thought he was working on. There was no need now. I'm already in heaven, he thought, a smirk of satisfaction playing about his lips. Then he laughed. In the Pentagon?

"That was some show you gave us, Peter," Finer's face was smiles all over.

Peter had no idea whether his experiment had been deemed successful or not. He'd explained, in as simple words as he could, what he'd achieved in the relatively short time he'd worked at the Pentagon. Other than the short exchange with the Vice President, not one man had asked a single question. In the end, they all got up and filed out like chicks following a Mother Goose. He doubted that the VP would approve being compared to a goose but, well, that was what they all looked like. The big chief and the underlings. Only Fred had given him a surreptitious wink. It was better than nothing.

"The Vice President has a question for you, Peter," Finer began in a guarded voice.

In Montreal, Finer spoke to him in a normal voice. There had been variations in the intonation, as were normal in a discussion. Here, at the Big P, whenever Finer talked to him, he sounded as if he were risking his life just by opening his mouth. Or as though he were sharing with Peter the secret of the ages.

"Then let him ask," Peter replied.

Finer smiled a short, nervous smile. "He wants you to concentrate on trying to assess how long the effect of your ray gun will last."

"This is not a ray gun. It is an ultrasound wave projector. Why must you people express everything in terms of artillery?"

"Sorry. The projector. Does it erase memories forever, or just for a while?"

"How the hell am I supposed to know? This is exactly why I wanted to stay in Montreal. Rather than attempting to zap dozens of people at the same time, I was modulating the UWP for different frequencies, different duration and continuity. I was beginning to get results with emissions based on AC rather than on DC. A form of quantified waves rather than continuous stream."

Peter only half-knew what he was talking about. This particular experiment had been suggested by John Brent, his past boss and present friend, on one of his visits to the MNI. He'd helped Peter set up the electronic aspect of the UWP. The rest had been up to Peter.

"Can you try?" Finer was examining his nails—his traditional expression of patient neutrality.

"It will take time. The only way to be sure is to wait and see. Anything else would be pure speculation. It would also mean setting up MRIs, CTs and other means of studying parts of the frontal lobes of people exposed to the waves. And even then, we could only arrive at an approximation."

"How about a hundred days?" Finer would not give up.

"Hundred days what? For me to get some results?"

"Hundred days' loss of memory."

"You mean that people would lose their memory for a hundred days and then recover them, or that the last hundred days in their lives would be erased permanently?"

"Either will do." Then Finer scratched his head. "No," he corrected himself, "the former."

As loyal as he was to the VP, Fred Finer did not want to carry on his conscience any permanent erasures. He might be erasing the memories of some important events. A first love affair, a childbirth, a death of a loved one, or a budding Einstein visualizing the muscular shapes of the universe. Finer was a romantic at heart.

Peter didn't answer. Silence stretched until Finer began fidgeting. "Well?" he said at length.

"I think it's safe to assume that our friends in the garden will not recover their immediate memories within the next few weeks. The memory lapse might last for a few months. The synapses in the brain have to develop new connections between neurons, to compensate for our interference. Other than that, we are in no-man's land. No one's ever attempted to do what we did in that bloody garden."

Suddenly Peter was getting tired of the whole thing. The initial instruction they'd given him to erase the memories that might have produced the post-combat stress syndrome had got lost somewhere along the way. Frankly, he had no idea what he was doing any more.

"I need a rest," he said.

Peter had been working eighteen-hour days. He suspected that that was what was expected for $100,000 US per month. Finer would drop in, just to say hello, anytime between seven in the morning and eleven at night. He'd never given an impression that he was checking up on Peter. Yet it did show that Finer's hours were hardly in the nine-to-five category. Peter still couldn't force himself to respect what the Pentagon stood for. But he was beginning to respect the effort that the staff, senior and junior alike, put into their work. These people were believers in their cause. But what, Peter questioned, was the cause itself?

* * *

9

The Protocol

The ride was as smooth as any Anne remembered from the old days. Now as then, the darkened panes offered protection from peering eyes. Once she'd thought that only dignitaries needed such protection. But back then she'd needed it more than any dignitary she could think of. Way back when.

What strange days they'd been....

Being whisked from one destination to another, avoiding contact with anyone who wasn't on the agenda prepared by her guardians, protectors, manipulators. All for her own good, they'd said.

"We still have an hour of Tuesday. Perhaps you would like to visit..."

Not that she ever had a choice. And it had never been an offer to visit an interesting site. Or a park. Or a beach in Rio. She may have been brilliant, and her handlers had made sure the world knew about it. The 'extra hour' had always been some carefully orchestrated appointment to further her meteoric career.

Anne smiled at her own choice of words. Orchestrated. How droll.

She hardly noticed when they pulled up in front of a building. The chauffeur was opening the door for her. Another man, in a black cassock, was waiting at the door, his hands crossed at his chest. Do they use priests for everything here, Anne wondered. Of course, the man might have been a deacon or a seminarian. Give him a surplice and he could be a chorister. A few popes back, a seminary had been established at the Vatican. It was created as an example for all the other seminaries.

"Won't you follow me, Mrs. Brown."

My! They were well versed. No more Miss Howell.

She left the Borgia Courtyard behind and followed the cassock indoors. It was darkish, old, but not at all musty; the hall was—the cassock was black. At the Vatican they kept their air-conditioning up to date. Perfectly balanced—state of the art. They had to. Otherwise their priceless works of art would be long gone. Even so, they still have problems.

The lights came on as if by magic.

On the wall straight ahead was the Last Judgment. Not something Anne wanted to look at just before dinner. Up above, God was breathing life into Adam. Or giving him the finger, depending on your point of view. The Sistine Chapel was as beautiful as it was impressive. It was stunning. Overwhelming. At the same time, Anne wished she were more in the mood to enjoy it. Blocking the altar was a huge shape of a man. What, no cassock? The man turned.

"Ian!" she almost screamed. "Ian," she repeated in a more normal voice. "How wonderful...." Her eyes filled with tears. They often did so when she saw Sir Ian Barton. They shared something that no one else did. Something even beyond friendship.

Sir Ian held his arms open, a cane hanging from his elbow.

"His Holiness was kind enough..."

"Let me look at you!" Anne was beside herself. "You look wonderful!" Sir Ian's voice boomed round the empty chapel.

"I'm very much afraid that Italian pasta agrees with me," Sir Ian confessed with visible pride. Indeed, his girth matched, if not exceeded, the one he'd sported when they'd first met. Then, for a number of years, Sir Ian had lost his portentous contours. Anne wasn't aware of it, but her own meteoric rise to stardom swept Sir Ian in its wake. For a number of years, he became the most sought-after maestro in the world. Even more so than before he'd met Anne. He, the self-confessed gourmand, hardly had time for a decent meal. Now, at long last, he evidently worked hard to recover his lost contours. Judging by the rotund results, he'd worked with a vengeance.

Someone in the shadows cleared his throat. The Camerlengo was all dolled up in an impressive cassock and mozzetta, with tiny buttons running from his neck all the way down to his toes. A simple gold cross shimmered on his chest, while a broad sash bound his middle and hung down his left side. A red skullcap adorned his . . . skull. He stood in front of a side entrance, evidently enjoying what he'd just witnessed.

"It's a joy to see you both together again," he said. " I knew there had to be a special bond between you, Mrs. Brown, and you, Sir Ian. I just knew it."

Sir Ian and Anne looked at each other. "It shows, does it?"

There was laughter. Laughter in the middle of the Sistine Chapel. Was one allowed to laugh here? At the Vatican?

The next moment the Camerlengo all but disappeared in Sir Ian's embrace. The cardinal's head only just cleared the big man's paunch. Luckily, or he would have been stifled. Anne saw the headlines:

Cardinal Camerlengo dies in Sistine Chapel
Sir Ian Barton apprehended in flagrante delicto

The Camerlengo's meeting with Anne was a little more formal, but still quite effusive. Anne decided, there and then, that she and the Camerlengo, Gio, would become friends.

"I'm so glad you could come," he told her. He made it sound as though Anne were doing him a great favour. "As is the Holy Father."

This put a stop to Anne's light-headedness. The knowledge that in the next few minutes she was going to meet John Paul III put her again into a slight state of shocked panic. Somehow wandering the slums of New York or the favelas of Rio never made her nervous. Here, she reached out for Sir Ian's hand for reassurance.

"He's a very nice man," Sir Ian whispered in a voice that bounced off the Last Judgment. "He doesn't bite at all," he added. Then, as Anne didn't seem to be sufficiently at ease, he added, "It's the teeth, my dear. At our age...."

"If you'd kindly follow me," the Camerlengo interrupted.

"Right behind you, Gio," Sir Ian assured, and he pulled Anne by the hand.

Anne entered the part of the Vatican seldom if ever seen by outsiders. They weren't going to the Official Audience Hall. They were going to the Pope's private chambers overlooking St. Peter's Square, a short walk from the Sistine Chapel.

The walls alternated between frescoes and countless paintings by an array of Italian painters. They may have been the lesser-known artists, but Anne could hardly tell the difference. She was pulled, physically, into the innards of the greatest museum the world has ever known. The general public never saw these halls, not even on the news. Those museums accessible to the general public were way over on the other side of the Belvedere Courtyard.

Anne dragged her feet, her mouth half open, like a child taken for the first time to Disneyland. Only there was much more magic here.

At long last the Camerlengo left Anne and Sir Ian in a room as splendid as any number they'd passed on the way. By Vatican standards, it was a little small, but still vastly bigger than any room Anne had in her house in Westmount. The ceiling alone was high enough for a good game of badminton.

The table, in the middle of the chamber, had plates set up for four people. Just as they came in, Anne noticed a shadow disappearing through a curtain at the far end. The kitchen? She wondered. Are we going to be served by cassocked men? Or were nuns allowed to serve the Holy Father? Here, she'd read, all was protocol. Even the way you served food.

Before she drew any conclusions, a door opened and a man dressed in white entered the room. He stopped at the door, leaning against the ornate frame. He seemed out of breath. He and Sir Ian may have been the same age, but the man in white looked much older.

The moment passed.

"Permesso mi presento." First words give the measure of a man. The Pope, standing in his own palatial chambers, was asking for permission to introduce himself to Anne. He smiled serenely. *"Ioannes Paulus,"* he said with a slow nod of his gray head. "I'm so glad I could meet you before the Good Lord decided that I had already had enough fun."

As he talked he approached the odd couple waiting next to the table.

The Pontiff extended his hand to Anne, completely ignoring Sir Ian. He led her around the table to her appointed place. Then he waited until she sat down before turning to Sir Ian.

"I can tell you are not one to miss a good meal, my friend." He winked to the Camerlengo. His lips formed the word *'gracias'*.

"Giovanni gave me no choice under the penalty of excommunication," Sir Ian said with a straight face.

"As if an old pagan such as you would be moved by such a threat," the Holy Father replied in kind.

Anne was taking it all in. The room, the table with superb place settings, the incredibly high yet light as feathers wine glasses, the table cloth which must have been hand woven by some artist from the middle ages . . . it was all too much. And, yes, she was completely put off by *Il Papa*. She'd expected a reasonably severe man, looking at her as though trying to detect her sins. She half expected to be asked: 'When did you attend your last confession?' Instead she observed a mild, smiling, soft-spoken man who apparently loved people.

They talked about this and that. No one raised the subject of the violin. Sir Ian must have briefed the two priests. Only towards the end of the delicious *osso buco* entrée—a sublime rendering of braised veal shanks—the Holy Father leaned over to Anne and put his hand over hers.

"I cannot let you go, my dear, without thanking you for the hours of pleasure which this hand has given me. I shall forever be grateful to you."

She smiled. She had no idea what to say. For some reason, the Pope's hand continued to cover Anne's. His face changed in expression from profound gratitude to one of surprise. He turned his body to face Anne directly. For a timeless moment he held her gaze.

"I see," he said slowly. "*Capisco, capisco,*" he repeated, nodding his head. "I understand."

The last time Sir Ian had been privy to a similar scene was some twenty or thirty years ago, when he saw Gabriel looking into Anne's eyes. Whatever had passed between Anne and Gabriel was as incomprehensible to him then as the scene he now witnessed. The Holy Father's face remained frozen, his eyes unblinking, a look of concentration displacing his usual warm smile.

The next moment *Il Papa* smiled, let go Anne's hand and spread his arms.

"I am terribly sorry," he said to his guests. "I have some urgent duties to perform."

With that, he rose and the Camerlengo helped him to the door. At the last moment, already framed by the door, the Pontiff turned. His right hand performed the sign of the cross.

"*Benedicat vos omnipotent Deus. In nomine Patris et Filii et Spiritus Sancti,*" he said. His voice was as strong as a young man's. Then he was gone.

Sir Ian finished the last drop of the excellent Valpolicella from the Pope's favourite vineyards.

"And what do you make of that, my dear?" His tone was light, but his eyes were drilling Anne's.

For a while she was speechless. "I've been used," she whispered. "Just like in Vancouver . . . and New York, and San Francisco . . . and Rio...." she seemed to be playing for time to find the right words. "Only, oh, I don't know. It was the same yet different."

Sir Ian had only the vaguest idea what Anne did on her nocturnal escapades. Peter once tried to explain to him the principles underlying her actions, but Sir Ian was too set in his ways to understand. Or, possibly, to take Peter's words seriously. It was something about being a channel.

"How was it different, my dear?" he asked. Not that he would be able to tell the difference.

"Well, it sort of happened both ways," she said, her eyes searching Sir Ian's. "I have also been told things. Only I have no idea what they are. Does this make any sense?"

Sir Ian reserved his judgment. There were still cheeses to come. He knew that the Holy Father's pantry was the best in the world. The Pontiff seldom ate much, but he was a most amazing host.

Ioannes Paulus III, born in a small village south of Belo Horizonte, in Brazil, baptized Jose Manuel Garcia Da Rosa, died that night. Sir Ian Barton and Mrs. Anne Brown had been his very last guests. Camerlengo, Cardinal Giovanni Pesci, was at the Pontiff's side when he died.

Now, the protocol took over.

The Vatican thrived on protocol. It was the blood and guts of the City within the City. It was the life that throbbed and coursed through the corridors of power. For weeks now, some say months, factions had met with factions, offers and deals had been made by secretly appointed councils, conciliators, go-betweens, agents and scarlet advocates of their preferred candidates.

Whispers abounded everywhere. Folded notes were exchanged discreetly, surreptitiously. Smiles announced support, acquiescence. Approval. *Quid pro quo. Pro bono publico. Pro Ecclesia.* For the survival of power in the hands of the few.

The front runners remained above it all, never declaring their intentions publicly. Their hands remained clean. Like those of Pontius Pilate. Innocent. But everyone knew the few men who thought they should be the next Pope, the successor of Peter, the bishop of the Eternal City, of Rome.

Protocol ruled.

Cardinal Giovanni Pesci, the Camerlengo, did his duty. No matter how distasteful. He struck the beloved Pontiff on the forehead, three times. He broke the papal seal. Smashed it. But not before the Pope drew him to his side....

Last night, after Sir Ian and Anne had left, the Holy Father beckoned the Camerlengo into his sleeping chamber. Officially, the Camerlengo managed the Pope's secular affairs. That having been said, his duties extended much further. He was a man who had unrestricted access to the Pope. He knew the Pope's most intimate secrets, and, should he have also been his confessor, would have known the secrets that could never be divulged. And thus, the Camerlengo's influence administered not only the Pope's secular affairs, but his spiritual well-being as well.

In the Pope's bedroom, in addition to the bed and the bedside table, there were but two other pieces of furniture: a small kneeling bench, a *prie-dieu*, and a desk at which the Pope jotted down thoughts that came to him, often in the middle of the night. There were two simple, hard-backed chairs next to the desk, one for the Pope and one for the virtually ever-present Camerlengo.

These two men were not only the highest officials of the Vatican Empire, they were fast friends.

"Sit down, Gio. I must tell you things," the Pope said the moment they came in. "I must tell you things under the conditions of confession."

That meant binding silence. Forever.

Giovanni was surprised, to say the least. People never confessed in their own bedrooms unless they were on their deathbeds. However, Gio never challenged his friend's requests. When the Pope confessed, it covered a great deal more than his presumed sins. What was right for the masses, was not enough for the Pope. The concept of sin originated in the sport of archery. The Greek word *hamartia*, or *hamartano*, translated in the New Testament as sin, simply meant—missing the mark. Doing something well does not mean scoring the bull's-eye every time.

But confession meant a great deal more. It helped the penitent to discuss things with his spiritual guide in full confidence that the discussion would remain just between the two of them. Yes, forever.

Cardinal Pesci reached out for the stole hanging next to the Pope's bed and placed it around his neck. The Pope waved his hand, dismissing the usual protocol, so beloved by lesser men.

"I want to talk," he said. "Just talk."

The next half hour was the strangest thirty minutes in Giovanni Pesci's life.

"I shall tell you things that no one must know. Unless," the Pope smiled as if telling his friend a good joke, "unless you decide otherwise."

This was going to be a strange kind of confession, the Camerlengo thought. Never before had the penitent himself released a priest from the secrecy of the sacrament. For an instant he searched his mind if such an action would be permissible under the Church Law. Then he shrugged. He was listening to the man who created the Church Law. The Pontiff. The Infallible One.

"I had a vision," the Pope resumed. "I saw a woman sitting on my throne. She was small; she looked like a man. All the cardinals were lying down at her feet. They looked asleep. Yet they weren't. They were all listening to the woman talking. This went on for a long time. It was as though time had stopped and it did not matter at all. The strangest thing of all was that the woman was talking to each one of the cardinals separately, yet, apparently, not in turn. It didn't make sense."

The Pope looked up at the Camerlengo.

"That's not all. On the other side of the.... I don't know where they were, but it could have been the nave of Saint Peter's Cathedral, well, on the other side, there were also vast numbers of people who were not even priests. Yet the woman was also talking to all of them. Also individually."

The Pope stopped and poured a glass of water, standing at the side of his desk. He raised an eyebrow, asking Gio if he wanted one also. The Camerlengo declined.

"What do you make of that?" the Pope asked at length.

The Camerlengo cleared his throat. "It is evident that the Holy Mother is taking affairs into her own hands." The Camerlengo was thinking of Lourdes, and Fatima and La Salette, where the Virgin Mary had left instructions for the Church.

The Pope remained silent.

"Yes," he nodded, "that is the obvious answer." He looked pensive.

"But?"

"God acts in mysterious ways. He chooses his emissaries according to His will. As does the Holy Mother."

This time the Pope sounded as though he were talking to himself. He then asked his friend to help him to his bed. He didn't undress, just sat down and allowed Giovanni to lift his legs and let himself be stretched on the pillows. His face looked unusually pale.

"Stay with me tonight, Gio." There was a plea in his voice.

"Si, Papa, of course I will."

"Bear with me, Giovanni." This was halfway between a plea and a command.

"Yes, Papa, of course I will."

"Trust me, Gio?" the Pope asked, his voice barely above a whisper. But the Camerlengo wouldn't dream of doing otherwise.

"Yes, Papa. Of course I do," he repeated.

Ioannes Paulus was very weak. He didn't move on the bed at all. His eyes were directed at the crucifix on the wall directly in front of his bed. The Camerlengo pulled a chair next to the bed and sat gazing at the old features of his friend and mentor. Gio was just a boy when he first came to the Vatican. The Holy Father was a bishop attending a synod. Bishop Jose Da Rosa had asked the youthful Gio if he would consider being his secretary. Da Rosa took an instant liking to the young cleric. It was Gio's vitality, his complete absence of posturing, of the holier-than-thou attitude, that Da Rosa liked so much. "If we are to help people, we must be like the people. Not above them," he had said at the time. Gio had never forgotten those words. Even now, as Camerlengo and Cardinal, he would often go out into the streets of Rome dressed only in a simple cassock. They said that he was the most accessible cardinal in Rome. They also said that he would defend the Pontiff's life with his own.

"God acts in mysterious ways," John Paul repeated after a while.

He didn't explain his words. They sounded almost trite. So often overused by clergy who were unable or unwilling to explain their own actions.

"Gio," Pope's eyes didn't leave the crucifix. "Bless me, Gio...."

The Cardinal put on the stole and repeated the words the Pope had spoken on leaving the dining room.

"Benedicat te omnipotent Deus, Pater et Filius et Spiritus Sanctus."

"Graci," the Pope whispered. "Gio?" His voice was distant.

"Si, Papa?"

"Ricorda ottocento cinquanta cinque..."

Those were his last words. The Camerlengo closed the Pontiff's eyes. For a while he sat praying. Then he sighed deeply. There had been no time for the last rites. None. The Cardinal walked to the telephone on the Pope's private desk. The Pontiff's death had to be certified. The protocol demanded that he, Camerlengo, certify the death of the Pontiff. Gio demanded that a physician be present. He dialed a number.

And then, the protocol took over.

The Camerlengo racked his brains over the Pope's last words. There was a tradition in the Church that the last words carried the weight of the Last Will and Testament of the departing pope. They had always been regarded as being of utmost importance. What was difficult in this case was that John Paul had chosen to utter them under the protection of the holy sacrament of confession. And then, for some reason, the Pope had given him papal dispensation to do what he wanted with the words he had spoken.

What could possibly be of such importance for the Pope to have negated the tradition spanning hundreds of years? Canon Law 983 #1 states that the sacramental seal is inviolable. And actually, the history of the secrecy of confession could be traced only to the fifth century, when Pope Leo told the confessors not to divulge penitents' sins. The command had only been established as law in the year 1151. But it was only in 1215, at the Fourth Lateran Council, that the whole Church had become bound by the secrecy. The secrecy had been formalized by Cannon 21. There were other dates, none of them being close to 855. Assuming 855 was a date.

"Ricorda ottocento cinquanta cinque..."

Having set the wheels in motion, and having administered his own obligations under the Church Law, the Camerlengo retired to his own room. He hadn't slept last night at all. Yet even now, rather than get some well-earned rest, he switched on his computer. There was too much to do. He scanned sources where dates or numbers appeared. By 11 a.m. he collapsed on his bed. An hour later he was up again. He splashed some water on his face and looked at the gentle glow of his laptop. He'd forgotten to turn it off.

He sat down at his desk. And there it was. Glowing in the semi-darkness was the figure 855.

"Have I been working in my sleep?" he said out loud. He had no recollection of seeing such a number on the screen before. He read on.

According to an amply examined legend, John VIII, the brief successor to Leo IV in 855, was Joan, an English woman who fell in love with a Benedictine monk, fled with him to Athens, and, after his death, continued to Rome, entering the priesthood in disguise and enjoying great success as Ioannes Anglicus (John of England). The subterfuge was effective until she died in childbirth during a papal procession. Writers who declare the legend to be utterly without foundation have tended to be utterly Catholic in their outlook.

The Camerlengo leaned back in his chair. Eight hundred fifty-five. A woman. A woman who became a Pope. The Pope's vision told of a woman in white clothing, standing on the balcony, the customary place from which Popes bless the crowds in Saint Peter's square.

A woman?

He switched off the computer and walked slowly to his bed. I must get some sleep, he told himself. As was usual for him, when very tired, which was most evenings these days, or mornings for that matter, he switched on his CD player. He stretched on his bed. Soon he would have to join the world outside and take charge of the funeral and the election. As he lay down, the CD began playing the *Adagio di molto* from the Sibelius violin concerto. It was his favourite piece of all, and Anne Howell gave it heavenly quality. Yes, definitely heavenly quality.

Anne's image, now Mrs. Brown's, stood behind his closed eyelids. A simple black suit, a white polo shirt around her slim neck. How simple she looked. She could be....

He sat up with a start.

"Joan.... eight fifty-five.... a woman.... a woman Pope...."

The next moment he collapsed on his bed, exhausted beyond measure. He slept for four hours. Like a log. The music played on.

* * *

10

Opportunity

L inker had known for years that his opportunity was coming. He certainly didn't consult tarot cards like his wife, or speak to astrologers like those favoured by the First Lady. None of that nonsense for him. But he knew.

John Linker had learned patience at an early age. He had inherited a goodly sum from his father, but only after his father's death was he given a chance to quintuple the family fortune. He converted millions into billions. And he did so in such a way that few people knew about it, and those who claimed they knew were not really sure. Most of his money was dispersed throughout the whole world, wherever the GNP of a country was growing at a faster rate than its neighbours. More profit to be made.

Many said that he took enormous risks with his money, that in the process of making his fortune he'd lost millions, but he always made more than he lost. To him money was merely a hobby. Others, who knew him better, said that it was the means to an end. Fred Finer knew that both factions were right.

"The point is, my friend," the Vice President sounded particularly kind this morning, "that when the opportunity comes, you must grab it."

And the opportunity was knocking on his door. The Pope had died. Soon countless heads of state, large and small, benevolent and dictatorial, tough as nails or wishy-washy—the sort who steered his or her country so as not to offend anybody—they would all be there. And the accumulation of the Who's Who in the ecclesiastic circles would be an added bonus. Linker was thinking of the smug, self-righteous imams or mullahs; the sonorous, almost sweet-sounding preachers hiding behind symbols of their religion; or equally as self-righteous black-clad, long-bearded, uncompromising rabbis who thought that God had allotted them a special place on earth. All of them appeared to look down at everyone as though they alone held the keys to the Kingdom of Heaven.

"Heaven they want, heaven I shall give them," he thought.

As for the Catholic Church, Linker thought that it needed a little cleansing of its own. The Church's insistence on the prohibition of contraceptives put a great strain on US finances. The masses multiplied like vermin, eating, talking, complaining, demanding, never giving anything to others. That is not right, he thought. To give is human, but it feels divine, he muttered to himself. He wasn't sure this was a biblical saying, but it sounded right. At any rate, by those criteria the masses were not even human.

The problem was that the people who supplied the Vice President with statistics (misrepresented as facts) found it expedient to state only that which they assumed the VP wanted to hear. They omitted, for instance, to mention that in Swaziland, where 42.6% of the population was infected with HIV, only about 5% were Catholic. In Botswana, where the adult infection rate was 37%, only 4% were Catholic. Likewise in South Africa, over 22% of the population were infected and only 6% were Catholic.

In Uganda, however, with 43% of the population being Catholic, just 4% of the adults had been infected with HIV. These were not facts the VP would have enjoyed nor appreciated knowing.

In either case, according to Linker, the Church committed other transgressions. All too often it, or they, butted into things that were none of its business. Most ungodly, he thought. The Vatican, for instance, had denounced the US invasion of Panama, the Gulf War, the NATO war in Serbia, the campaign against

Afghanistan, the invasion of Iraq. Yes, they were definitely busybodies. They should be taught a lesson. They should stick to what is God's, and leave Caesar alone.

A month ago, one of the men on his Team, General Brad Schwartz, still behaving like a freshly baked two-star upstart, had prepared for him a list of countries which, according to John Linker's definition, needed corrective measures. The list included nations that harboured ill will towards the United States. Not militarily, of course—the USA was much too powerful for that—but countries that would not recognize the American Way.

The list also included the locations of all the major military installations in all those countries. North Korea, Nigeria, Iran, Pakistan, Sudan, Syria, Egypt, virtually all other Arab countries as well as Brazil, Venezuela, Colombia, and a number of other 'regimes' which, for purely economic reasons, had to be taught a lesson. The Vice President firmly believed the biblical admonition that if you spared the rod, you spoiled the child. He regarded the nations outside the US as his errant children. The US military might—the rod. The corrective measures, well, those would vary according to the transgression of each individual country. Or regime. John Linker firmly believed in being scrupulously fair.

"Tell the boys to get their butts to the Bridge Club," he told Finer.

Lately Fred Finer had replaced Joshua Rosengart as Linker's right-hand man. Rosengart took care of the media, of public image, and of liaison with the White House. That was important. After all, to most people, the White House was still the Seat of Power. You had to be a really good liar to do Rosengart's job. Finer was not. But he was coming up fast. Besides, Rosengart was busy buying controlling interests of selected media in Great Britain, Germany, France, Italy, Brazil, China and Russia. They would tow the line, if necessary. Usually, it was—especially after the US eagle flapped its wings. People had funny ideas about freedom of the press. They thought that you could feed people lies with impunity. Well, no more.

"We are the sentinels of the world, we have to protect people's minds," Linker had told his boys at the last bridge session. He'd meant every word.

The group of six met in the 'bridge club'. As usual, no one spoke until the Vice President sat down and began the discussion. This time, Linker remained silent for an unusually long time. Finally, for the first time ever, he rose to his feet.

"Gentlemen," he began, "the time has come."

Everybody held their breath.

"Tomorrow we start operation code-named 'The Plan'. You all know what that means. Within weeks, months at most, the American Way shall be shared with the rest of the world."

The Vice President sat down. After a momentary silence, first the Chief of Staff, then the rest of the men, began a slow clap. Next, they all rose to their feet. The uniformed men saluted, desperately confused in their attempt to salute and clap at the same time. The two men in civvies remained at attention with hands free to express their admiration. One could feel electricity in the air. A moment to cherish, to remember. Finer, first to recover, thought he might see at any moment a legionnaires' salute with a congruent shout, "Heil Führer!"

The Vice President gave quick instructions. Every man present knew exactly what he had to do. The three representatives of the Armed Forces left first. Joshua and Fred lingered longer. Only they knew the real story behind Linker's Plan. And Linker doubted that anyone could drag it out of them with wild horses. What he would do to them would be infinitely worse. The two gentlemen knew that, too. It was a tacit understanding. Yet, for some reason, both men felt that they were playing Russian roulette and placing bets with the distinct possibility of forfeiting their lives.

Linker walked to the side cabinet and returned with a bottle of Kentucky Rye. An All-American liquor. He, himself, poured good portions into three glasses. He put one each in front of the two men, keeping one for himself. He then raised his tumbler, holding it at arm's length.

"Gentlemen," he announced, his voice choked with emotion. "I give you a toast."

Rosengart and Finer got up, straightened up, and raised their glasses.

"Gentlemen," Linker repeated, "I give you the American Way!"

All three emptied their tumblers in a single gulp. It would be the last drink any of them would take until all was over.

Peter sat down feeling that the world was collapsing on his shoulders. Finer had just given him a tour of the west wing of the top floor of the Pentagon. He'd wanted to impress on Peter just how seriously they were taking his work. Peter had visited every room, peeked in every corner, examined every nook of the huge wing dedicated to his work. He had been told that there was additional storage on lower floors, and that the latest devices had been placed, under guard, in the basement. He couldn't believe his eyes.

Every single stage of all the projectors he had been instrumental in producing had been duplicated, then reproduced in triplicate, then, 'just in case', nearly mass-produced in considerable numbers. As new models appeared, the old ones had been discarded. Some parts had been reused, others....

Money was no object.

"Why do you think we are paying you a hundred grand a month, Peter?" Finer asked him. "We are not playing games, my friend."

"Why do you need so many?" Peter asked. He was in a state of shock.

"There may be ancillary applications. The Pentagon hates wasting money," Finer said as though stating the obvious.

If there had been one hundred thousand ex-combatants who were to become beneficiaries of his ultrasonic devices, then perhaps the military was right. They would need a number of his 'tubes' to do the most good in the shortest time possible. But so far ahead of schedule? And even then, hundreds?

"B-b-but . . . so many?" Peter still couldn't believe his eyes. "You could try and cure people a few at a time. Like on the roof. We still don't know how...."

"We know that people's immediate memory is disabled. That is a very valuable weapon."

"Weapon? I've been working on a weapon?"

Finer was studying Peter's face as a teacher or a parent would when suspecting, without evidence, that the child has done something wrong. A vague look of disbelief was gradually displacing Finer's expression of surprise.

"You are working at the Pentagon, Peter. Do you think we produce machines for poaching eggs?"

Peter reached out for his telephone. He tapped the button a few times. The instrument had been disabled. He swung on Finer.

"Am I being held incommunicado?" he asked, his eyes growing wider.

"We all are. But only for a few days, Peter. Come, you've done a great job. We're all very proud of you. I am sure you will find a generous bonus deposited in your bank account."

Peter sat down heavily. What a fool I have been. What a fool....

Fred Finer studied him for a while without saying a word. Peter's naiveté had got the better of him. At the same time, he really liked the scientist who believed in his own principles and much as he, or rather as John Linker believed in his.

"What would you do if you had a pile of money?" he asked after a while.

Peter was slowly recovering from his disappointment. Up to this day, he was actually getting close to changing his opinion about the Pentagon. Not diametrically, but at least he was ready to give it, or them, a fair chance.

"I have no idea," he replied, still working to control his voice. "I'm not really interested in money."

"Humour me, Peter. Say you had a few billion dollars. Your own. Money you've earned. Say you had an invention from which the whole world benefited and you had made billions from marketing it. What would you do?"

"As I said, I have no idea."

"I want you to listen very carefully. John Linker is by far the richest man I know. His billions can be counted in hundreds. He has controlling interest in production companies the world over. He assures a regular supply of 19% of the crude oil the USA needs for everyday life. He is involved, vicariously, in thousands of acres of farmland which feed about 15% of our people and there are thousands of tons of surplus comestibles made available for export. Shall I go on?"

"Why should you, he's probably already rich enough," Peter shrugged.

"Well, that's the funny part of it. John Linker eats less than half of what most of his employees eat. He hardly ever takes a drink. He doesn't smoke. Never did. He prefers to walk than to drive a car. He flies only when he absolutely has to. His house is much smaller than any house belonging to any of the CEOs of his countless companies. And I also know from personal experience that he wears the same two or three suits for years at a time. Now why do you think that is so?"

"He's saving for his old age?"

Fred Finer shook his head from side to side. "Think about it Peter. Think what you would do, for the world, if you had virtually unlimited power to do it. If you had the opportunity."

With that Fred Finer got up and left Peter's office without another word. For some reason Peter felt that Fred Finer wasn't joking. He felt that Fred really wanted to find out what he would do. What Peter would do with countless billions of dollars and virtually unlimited power.

For the first time in his life the Camerlengo felt really tired. Those who believed in both, *visibilium omnium et invisibilium*, the visible and the intangible, would say that until now he had been uplifted by Spirit. That his energy came from an inexhaustible Source. Now it seemed that catering to the dead was much tougher than catering to the living. Gio became extremely conscious of his Master's admonition: *Let the dead bury the dead.* His Master had also said: *God is not the God of the dead, but of the living*....

On the second day following his death, the late Pontiff's body would be moved to the Basilica of St. Peter for public veneration. The body would be laid out in a simple white cassock and surplice, chasuble, pallium, and sandals, such as worn by his compatriots in Bel Horizonte. The red slippers with gold brocade will have to wait for a better day. A gold-coloured miter would adorn the Pontiff's head. People would come by the thousands. Perhaps millions. For many this would be the first chance they would have to be that close to the Pope.

To the Pontiff's body, at least.

Protocol forced the Camerlengo to bury the dead. It was a long, officious, in some ways beautiful, but mostly a tiresome process steeped in tradition. For a day John Paul III would lie in state in the Clementine Hall. There the dignitaries would be given a chance to pay respects in relative privacy. Then his body would be moved to St. Peter's Basilica for four days of public viewing. The coffin would be placed just in front of the High Altar with its thirty-meter-high canopy. Swiss Guards would protect his remains. Finally, the coffin would be moved, weather permitting, outside into St. Peter's Square for the funeral Mass. There, on the raised part of the square leading into the Basilica, the body would rest in a simple pine box. Looking out from the Basilica, the clergy would sit on the right, the dignitaries on the left. Way out in the square, millions would witness, millions would pay final homage.

Overlooking the wooden altar, the clergy and the dignitaries, the *loggia*, as the roof terraces surrounding the square were known, would accommodate the media. Hundreds if not thousands of them already there, setting up their equipment. The funeral and the burial in St. Peter's crypt would follow in greater privacy. Only the select few would attend.

But the Camerlengo's duties would not end there. He must then sequester all the cardinals into the Sistine Chapel. There they would deliberate, *conclave*, under lock and key, until they chose the successor. It might take a long time. The longest it had

ever taken in the past was 1,095 days. That was in 1271. Today,
many cardinals were past eighty. They could no longer be
elected, but they would still participate in the protocol. For the
first twelve to thirteen days, unanimity is still required. Only later
is a concession made for the elderly, and a simple majority is
sufficient.

Such was the Protocol of the Holy Roman Catholic and
Apostolic Church.

The whole world was affected. The flags at the Vatican, at
the offices of papal nuncios throughout the world, were already
flown at half-mast. Cardinals changed their habitual red
garments to violet. And, what Giovanni Pesci found most
annoying, until the election of the new Pope, all cardinals would
receive the same elaborate signs of respect from the Swiss Guard
that were normally accorded only to the Pontiff. This last also
slowed the Camerlengo in the execution of his duties.

After the doctors had declared the Pope's demise, he, the
Camerlengo, issued the official statement. "The Pope is truly
dead." Only then was John Paul's pontificate officially over.
With those words they entered the interregnum.

In rare moments of freedom from his endless duties as the
chief organizer, Gio escaped to his room. He found that now,
more than ever, he needed time to pray. His prayers had seldom
anything to do with asking for anything.

"What else could I possibly want?" he'd once asked Sir
Ian. "Look around you. I live among the greatest works of art
the world has ever known. I love the people I work with. I have
wonderful friends," he added, nodding pointedly towards Sir
Ian. "And I serve God by serving the successor of Saint Peter."

Yet now this same service had become a little taxing. Try as
he might, he couldn't dismiss from his mind the late Pope's last
vision, and their last discussion. He racked his brain if any of the
Orders of Nuns who wore white vestments might resemble the
woman the Pope had seen. There were the Franciscans,
Dominicans, Benedictines, Augustines, Carmelites, each
consisting of several Orders. And then there were countless

others. Not even the official central Catholic Church data bank had arrived at a complete listing.

He gave up on the nuns.

No matter how hard he tried, there was the number eight hundred and fifty-five. There was also the image of Anne, albeit in her black suit, yet there were just too many convergences to dismiss Anne from the picture. And if the Pope did point his dying finger towards Anne, then what was he trying to tell me, he wondered.

"Pray Papa, if you can hear me, tell me."

Alas, *Il Papa* remained stubbornly silent. Let Thy will be done, Gio whispered.

The Camerlengo decided that the moment the first rush of activities diminished, he would organize the College of Cardinals in 'congregations' to coordinate the Pope's funeral and arrangements for the Conclave. He did. He issued the necessary instructions, appointed the right cardinals for the right jobs. By next morning, he breathed easier. In hindsight, he found it almost bizarre how men, many years his senior, Princes of the Church, accepted his decisions without question. He felt a little embarrassed telling some of them what, when and how to do things. Nevertheless, he was the Camerlengo.

A day later he called Anne. It was too late. Anne was gone. She'd left Rome.

Anne was gone.

He still had to organize the *novemdiales* before the funeral. The *Universi Domini Gregis* specifies that the Pope's body must be prepared for burial between the 4th and the 6th day after his death. For nine days, in a tradition that goes back for over six hundred years, Mass would be celebrated for the repose of the deceased Pontiff's soul. The nine days were known as the *novemdiales*.

"Please, Papa, help me to understand."

The Camerlengo stood alone in front of the body. The candles flickered nervously, reflecting light in the golden miter. The Pope looked relaxed. What a strange thought, Gio thought. The Pope is finally relaxed. No more duties. No more meetings. No more thousands of painful handshakes. Yes, during the last nine months of his life, the Pope had been blessed with the stigmata. Stigmata is mostly associated with Roman Catholicism, but not exclusively. And there is still conflict as to whether they are caused by psychosomatic agencies, like bleeding ulcers, or are indeed echoes of a raised state of consciousness.

And no one knew about them. It had been his wish.

A nne got nervous. She called Peter twice a day, only to hear the recorded message: "Love you, my Pet." That was all. For a moment she thought that Peter had left Washington and forgot to erase the telephone tape. On the fourth day she called the Pentagon. She pressed a hundred buttons, waited minutes that seemed like hours, while recorded messages gave her the royal run-around. From the second day onward she also called home.

Silence. At home, in Westmount, there was also silence. Anne's parents also didn't know anything.

"I'm sure everything is all right, dear. Peter is a very resourceful young man."

In her mother's eyes, all men under seventy were young men. Most of them resourceful. Anne contemplated calling Johnny or Di, but she didn't know how to ask them about their father without worrying them to death. She felt very alone.

The next day she boarded the first flight she could get for Montreal. She had overstayed her welcome in Rome. The streets were already impossible to walk. Millions were converging on the city for the Pontiff's funeral. Everyone was flying in. Flying out was easy.

If I cannot find Peter, then at least I shall be where he can find me, she reasoned. The flight was uneventful. She took off at 8:45 a.m. and two hours later was at Dorval—once she changed her watch to local time, that is. She took a cab home, half expecting to meet Peter at the door. It did not happen.

Peter had disappeared into the innards of the Pentagon.

The moment she sat down, there was a ring at the front door.

"You forgot your key!?" she half screamed, rushing to the door. She flung it open. Blocking the whole width was a huge figure silhouetted against the setting sun.

"I thought you might need me," said the shadow.

Anne collapsed into Gabriel's arms. He lifted her easily, his strength belying his age. To him she was still as light as a child. He carried her into the living room and placed her gently on the sofa. In that instant she opened her eyes.

"How did you know, Gabby?" she whispered. "How did you know?"

He only smiled. After all these years she still had to ask. "You called me," he answered simply.

I must have, she thought. I always do when I'm in trouble. I must have called him from Rome.

"Am I in trouble, Gabby?" Her voice sounded like that of the little girl Gabriel had first met a long time ago.

"No, Anne, you are never in trouble," he murmured. "Sometimes the world is in great trouble...." he added.

* * *

11

Convergence

There are people who feel that they know precisely where they've gone wrong. Strange though it seems, few of them ever knew their original destinations. We tend to cover a great deal of ground just walking in circles. And then, when we get to any particular destination, we are not quite sure why we set out on a journey to start with. Ultimately, no matter how circuitous a route we take, we all end up at the cemetery.

There are lesser destinations. Merely stops on the way to the final convergence.

Over the years, many of us have taken pilgrimages to various holy places. The Holy Apostolic Church of Rome lists many such destinations. People converge on some of them in the hopes of a miracle. So it is with the millions milling around the Black Stone of Mecca. Or at least around the great mosque, al-Haram, enclosing the Kaaba. So it is with the Hindus who seek salvation on the steps leading down to the Holy Waters of the most holy river, the Ganges. They are all places of convergence.

This time, people arriving in Rome had a much better idea of why they had come. Thousands came to pay their last respects to the late Pope, John Paul III. Ioannes Paulus. *Il Papa*. The Holy Father of us all. Not all people truly realized this, but most did. Some did and were devout followers, personally hurt by his death. They came out of love. Some claimed allegiance but ignored his teachings and admonitions. Most of them came out of guilt. Some had heard of the late Pontiff, but they neither liked nor respected him. He asked, they said, too much of them.

They all came, for whatever reasons, to witness the occasion, craning their necks out of curiosity.

The lofty walls of Sala Clementina, the Clementine Hall of the Apostolic Palace, were covered in magnificent 17th century Renaissance frescoes. An enormous chandelier, uniformly aged with a green patina, hung at the center of the rounded ceiling. It was surrounded by images of angels reaching out for the Holy Spirit symbolized by a pure white dove. The Sala had been built in honour of Pope Clement XIV, and it was used ever since for private audiences with visiting dignitaries. On that day, some of the same dignitaries came for the last time for a private audience with the Pontiff, this time prostrated before them on a raised platform. As usual, he looked in great repose.

After resting in state for a day, in the relative seclusion of the Clementine Hall, the procession carrying the Pope's coffin proceeded out through the Bronze Door, through St. Peter's Square, and into the Basilica. The great Bronze Door through which distinguished guests had been admitted to the Apostolic Palace was then locked. For now, the official residence of the Pope would remain closed. It would only be opened after the new Pope was elected.

The procession proceeded slowly. An angelic voice intoned the litany to all the saints. It sounded like a distant Gregorian chant, carried over the heads of the people gathered from the four corners of the world. After each invocation of a saint, a chorus of equally ethereal voices answered *Ora pro eo*. Let us pray for him....

"Sancte Petri.... ora pro eo....
"Sancte Paule....
"Sancte Andrea....
"Sancte Jacobe....
"Sancte Ioannes... ora pro eo... ora pro eo... ora pro eo....

Sancte Ioannes... pray for him, Saint John, whose name he had chosen....

The voice carried the coffin along as much as the shoulders of the Swiss Guards did. Raised above human heads, even as they bowed in silent homage. At the steps of the Basilica, the convoy turned momentarily to face the hushed crowds.

Santa Lucia....
Santa Agnes....
Santa Caecilia....
Santa Catharina....
Santa Anastasia....
            ora pro eo... ora pro eo... ora pro eo....
Omnes Sancti et Sanctae Dei, intercedite pro eo....

As the procession turned to face the doors of St. Peter's, two long rows of red skullcaps turned also. Beneath, short white surplices over red cassocks and long mozzettas followed the wooden box inside. The great nave swallowed them all even as the men carrying the coffin deposited it gently on a raised platform in front of the Main Altar. There the Camerlengo sprinkled the catafalque with Holy Water. The last ablution.

Prayers followed.

....may perpetual light shine upon him....

The cardinals filed past the coffin. Some bowed, others came to a momentary pause. Still others blessed themselves with the sign of the cross. They were followed by bishops, priests.... These were the final private moments. Soon this part of the rite would be over. Soon ordinary men and women would be allowed to say the ultimate goodbye to their Holy Father.

And they were many.

Thousands. Some said even millions.

On that day, and the days that followed, all roads really did lead to Rome. Strangers embraced, exchanged smiles, shed tears. Together and united by a single need. This was the time of the great convergence.

The Pope's body resting in a simple pine coffin was laid at the feet of the High Altar. And people came.

The event wasn't new for the people of Rome. Some decades back, another such convergence took place for the death of Pope John Paul II. Then another, albeit a smaller one, followed, as his successor ruled but for a short time. John Paul III had ruled the Church for more than two decades. And Brazil was a country much more populous than Poland, or even Germany.

People flew in to any airport that would receive them. Then thousands of buses, converted trucks, extra rail coaches, brought in from far and wide, wheeled them into Rome. All sports arenas were converted into hostels for the pilgrims. Thousands of great tents were erected, thousands of stands dispensing food and water were put up at every street corner. Thousands of movable washrooms filled the side streets. It was a great mess. A mess that people were more than ready to put up with. The pilgrims—with gratitude. The Romans—as their last gift to their beloved Pope.

For four days the endless crowds snaked along the streets from all directions, converging on Via Conciliazione, a street that stretched from the Tiber to St. Peter's Square. The street of the great reconciliation. The street where you left all your troubles behind and single-mindedly paid homage.

Shrines were erected *en route*. Spontaneously. A poster of *Il Papa*, a dozen candles grew into hundreds in minutes. Then came little cards, wishing the Pope Godspeed on his final journey.

"Ciao, Papa!" "Ciao... ciao, good Father," this was from a little boy.

"Sancto!" "Sancto subito!" others chanted. Make him a saint, people demanded. "Quickly!"

"It's inspiring to be here, this man is a saint!" a man with skin as black as ebony affirmed. Almond eyes at his side nodded in agreement.

"By mid-afternoon on the first day, the mass of humanity was so thick outside the Vatican's walls that people had to line up just to get into the official queue," reported one man trying to protect his head with an umbrella from the unrelenting sun. By the time the creeping mass of people reached Via

Conciliazione, the monstrous snake measured twenty-five people wide.

The great convergence.

"How I wish Mrs. Brown were here," the Camerlengo said to his secretary. "Call Sir Ian Barton. He might be able to locate her. I must speak to her."

The Cardinal's secretary was used to strange requests from his diminutive superior. The Camerlengo had to deal with so many different issues that only he was able to tie the loose ends together. The secretary dialled Sir Ian's number from the Camerlengo's electronic address book. There were over 11,000 phone numbers and addresses there.

There was no answer from the villa at the top of Via Di Porta Pinciana. It was almost impossible to reach anyone in Rome that day. The lines were busy trying to cope with the influx of people. Of the mourning millions.

"Keep trying," the Camerlengo admonished.

Cardinal Giovanni Pesci looked down from behind the thin veil that protected the now empty window from which the Pope had so often given his blessing. As far as the eye could see, there were people. They didn't seem to move at all. Now and then, a ripple of easterly wind seemed to blow them towards St. Peter's, and the ocean of heads advanced a step or two. Just that. A step or two. The Camerlengo stared, unable to move.

"So many loved him..." he said half-loud.

"They still love him, Your Eminence," a small voice said behind him.

A nun had brought him hot tea. He grimaced. "You must drink, Your Eminence. No more coffee. Doctor's orders. Your heart cannot take it," the nun said. She sounded like a nurse whose orders could not be questioned, even by a priest. Not even a cardinal.

The Camerlengo moved away from the window.

"Thank you, sister." He sat down at the small table. Even here there were papers scattered on the whole surface. Papers,

papers, papers. We are a church of the Holy Paper, he thought. One day a great Paper will come down from the sky and cover us all, he mused. He sipped the tea. It was pleasant. It took his attention away from his work. So many papers....

"And you must take a nap," the nun commanded. When the Camerlengo didn't move, she added "now."

The Cardinal smiled. What would I do without the sisters who protect me from myself? He hadn't slept more than five hours during the last two days. He didn't seem tired. Just numb. He thought that we, humans, provided we are sufficiently deprived of sleep, would make excellent robots. Like I am right now, he mused.

The robot got up and walked to the sofa.

"The bed," the sister admonished.

But it was too late. The Camerlengo was already asleep. All he needed was permission. The sister had provided one.

Anne, too, fell asleep on the sofa. She'd had problems sleeping the last three days. Her wrought-up nerves contributed to her exhaustion. On top of her inability to contact Peter, both her children seemed to be *incommunicado*. Obviously they were busy with their own lives.

"They all have their own lives," she told Gabriel. "I only have other people's."

Gabriel covered her slim body with a cashmere blanket. It was the last present he had given her just before she and Peter had moved to the house in Westmount. She kept it almost like a security blanket. When lonely or worried she would reach for it, and she felt that Gabriel was there, nearby, to help her. He usually was.

She slept for almost two hours.

In the meantime, Gabriel prepared a light meal—a sandwich with smoked ham, fresh lettuce and tomato and onion salad. It was steeped in sunflower oil with just a touch of vinegar and a squirt of lemon. Anne's favourite.

She excused herself to take a shower first. Fifteen minutes later she came back refreshed. The black suit had disappeared. She wore a light dress with a small pattern of what looked like lilacs. Each time she moved, the lilacs swayed in the wind.

The moment she sat down, the worried look returned to her face. She had an amazing capacity to cope with other people's problems, but was a total child when facing her own.

"What should I do, Gabby? Should I fly to Washington?" she asked, not touching her food.

"Do you like the tomato salad?" Gabriel asked, undeterred.

She began eating. After the first bite, her interest in food grew enormously.

"And what would you do in Washington?" he asked, after a good half of the sandwich and most of the salad had disappeared into her rapacious mouth. She hadn't eaten much lately. Somehow Gabriel had known that.

"I don't know," she said. "I really don't know," she repeated, looking into his eyes. "What should I do?"

"Relax," he said. It was his magic bullet. He always told her to relax. In Gabriel's philosophy, a state of relaxation was at the beginning of all action, not its conclusion. "Things always happen exactly the way they should." This was his second dictum.

"Do they?"

She knew he was right. He'd proven it to her a thousand times. But it was so much easier to try and do something yourself. She recalled Lao Tsu. *Wu wei.* The concept of taking no action. Doing by not doing, or something like that. Waiting was the hardest thing of all, she thought.

"You heard about the Pope?" she asked. It took her mind away from her own problems.

"Yes, Anne. He was a great man."

"I met him, you know," she said, as though talking about the weather.

"It was in all the newspapers."

For a moment there was silence. Then Anne jumped to her feet. "Really?"

"No, dear. I'm just joking. Sorry. I didn't mean to upset you."

He hadn't upset her. What he had done was call Anne's attention to the fact that the rest of the world continued to rotate on its axis, whether she approved of it or not. Somehow Anne understood what he'd tried to do. I must get some perspective, she thought. I must stop thinking of my own problems. I am not the center of the universe.

"People must be converging on Rome," she said.

"They will. For the next four days. Then . . . they will go back to their old ways."

Was the world really that prosaic?

Peter sat for a long time, thinking about Fred Finer's words. Not that he cared about John Linker and his billions. Not even what he might do with them. He was thinking that there must be some people who, for some karmic reason, were destined to rule. Even as he had been given his task to perform, not at the Pentagon but generally in the field of science, so Linker had to fulfill his destiny. Linker had to discharge his own karma.

What else could he do? Peter recalled the day Gabriel had told him about the *Bhagavad Gita*. In that epic poem imparting the wisdom of the Vedas, the hero was a soldier. There, on the Battlefield of Kuruksetra, his job was to fight and kill. Had he denied his destiny, he would have been scolded by Lord Krishna himself. Is this true of all of us, he wondered. Must we all dance to some invisible piper, to do our jobs as best we can, and limit our judgment only to the quality of our performance in terms of our destiny?

So Linker was rich. He offered livelihood to literally thousands of people, probably tens of thousands the world over. He was no longer confined to a single if great North American continent. He was the paradigm of universality. If the Indians, or the Koreans, or the Chinese did a better job at whatever they were doing, then, according to Linker, they deserved to do that

job. Of course he made money. But having made it, he
channelled it into new fields, new opportunities for a greater
number of people than any man in history.

Was he fair? Was the wage he offered fair and equitable?

Is it my job to judge him? What employment had the labour
unions ever provided for anyone, other than for their own
bosses, who grew fat on their members' dues?

Is it my job to judge them?

He looked at his desk. He was good at his job. He did what
no one else in the whole wide world could do. Was it his
responsibility to assure that his invention was used wisely? Did
Einstein bear the brunt of the responsibility for Hiroshima and
Nagasaki?

"Is it my job to judge him?" he said out loud. He was
thinking of Linker again.

In the same moment, he recalled the old adage: Judge not
lest ye be not judged. Such strange sayings seemed to come up
to the surface of his mind from his youth. Only when he needed
them. The rest of the time....

The rest of the time he ignored them. Judge not, so you
shall not be judged. So, what of Linker? Is he like Arjuna, whom
Lord Krishna, his divine charioteer, commanded that he do his
job? Unquestioningly?

All those thoughts of the *Bhagavad Gita*, of quotations
from the New Testament, combined to invoke Gabriel's image.
What would he say to all this? How would he react?

Peter realized that what really stood in his way from making
a just judgment was his anger. When emotions take the higher
road, reason is the loser. There was a difference between
discrimination and judgment. He needed one to guide his
actions. He had to avoid the other to gain control over his
emotions.

Now Peter was angry, mostly at himself.

"What a fool I have been," he told himself. "What a
bloody fool!"

For a while he had forgotten the veiled threat which Finer
had dangled in front of his face. Now he recalled Fred Finer's
exact words.

"We can take care of them, Doctor."

He remembered his fury. Peter was the gentlest of men, but he would think nothing of killing a man who tried to hurt his wife.

He took a slow, deep breath.

I must not take it out on Fred, he thought more calmly. If anyone had empowered him to say such things, it must have been Linker. He, Peter still felt sure, would stop at nothing to achieve his end. Perhaps . . . perhaps Linker feels about his mission the way I feel about protecting Anne. Somehow this idea sent chills up his spine.

He got up and started pacing his office. Ten steps to the left, ten to the right. He looked through the window. It was sunny outside. The trees seemed oblivious to anything going on in his heart. Or in the whole wide world. Inconsequentially, he recalled what a small difference there was between the genome of a human and that of an oak. We are cousins, he thought. Somehow this thought gave him comfort.

Do trees know something I don't?

Judge not and ye shall not be judged, the oaks replied. Peter found this admonition difficult. Almost impossible to incorporate into his psyche. Again he looked around. I have my job to do. My karma. My destiny.

He returned to his desk and dove headlong into his work.

On the day after John Paul III died, five men sat in silence at the corner of the southwestern face of the pentagonal structure. Fred Finer was reviewing, in his head, his last meeting with the Vice President. Joshua Rosengart was attempting to tell the men what he thought was a funny story. No one laughed. Joshua shrugged and closed his eyes. The Chief of Staff had a gift he had never admitted having to any man. Or woman. Not even his wife. It was, he thought, his secret weapon. Or, more accurately, his secret defense. He could smell danger. And this time, he smelled danger exuding from his every pore.

The door opened and the Vice President walked in. The door closed automatically behind him. The men remained seated. The VP had told them, some time ago, that all those aerobics got on his nerves. Stand if you want to, but don't keep hopping up and down, he'd told them.

John Linker took his chair. His eyes examined the faces on both sides of the table. What a useless lot, he thought. Apart from Fred's ability to think and Joshua's talent for lying, the rest wouldn't get anywhere if he hadn't placed them in positions of influence. He maintained them in those positions and controlled them with fear. He deliberately allowed the stories that circulated about his men watching the men who watched other men. The more they fear me, the harder they'll try.

"Last week I gave you instructions to put all our armed forces on standby. You were told that it was a test of our readiness. An exercise."

He glanced at the faces of the three men controlling all the military. None of them spoke, probably afraid that their particular branch may not have performed as well as they ought to have done.

"You have done well," Linker told them. The men breathed easier. As a matter of fact, he had no way of checking how well they'd done. But he certainly wasn't going to admit that.

"Today, gentlemen, I propose the second exercise in the series. All three of you are to put your branches of the military on war footing. Code Five. We cannot be too careful," he added as an afterthought.

Careful of what? The three men looked at each other. Only the President could issue such an order. Usually, with the approval of the Senate. Linker studied their faces. A trace of a smile crossed his fatherly features. The features he'd cultivated for many years.

"The President asked me to congratulate you on your excellent performance in the previous exercise. He hopes that you will prove yourselves worthy of his trust during the Code Five operation."

So it really was Code Five. All three men rose to their feet. Automatically their right hands rose to their heads in a perfunctory salute.

"Yes, Sir!" They said in perfect unison.

Joshua Rosengart visibly relaxed. It was danger indeed but, at least for now, not to himself. I wonder what the Old Man has up his sleeve, he mused. The Chief of Staff seldom shared his qualms with anyone. Certainly not with the Vice President. Never mind their friendship. For as long as he needs me... was his next fleeting thought. But his nose no longer disturbed his peace of mind.

Fred avoided looking at Linker. Contrary to Joshua, he continued to feel the chill. The Vice President was planning something that even he didn't know about. He didn't like that. He couldn't prepare for what he didn't know was coming. And now the gathering storm clouds on the horizon were approaching at great speed. Perhaps it was already too late to avert them. Assuming it had ever been possible.

I must let Peter go home, he thought. He felt responsible for Peter. Almost paternal. Peter was the only man with whom Fred could talk. Just talk. It's not really his business, Fred thought. But he had no idea how to orchestrate it. He was sure that his friendship with the Vice President would not protect him if he broke the direct order that: "Everyone working on the projector is to remain *incommunicado* until further orders."

That was the fiat. You do not break fiats given directly by John Linker. Thick clouds. Clouds abounding with tempestuous thunder.

For the forthcoming week, the weather forecast for Rome was sunny with intermittent clouds. People, armed with bottles of water, gathered on side streets in the hope of joining the main current that would carry them to the Basilica. A meter every ten or fifteen minutes. At this stage, the streets were still clean. Just as a precaution, the mayor of Rome had ordered a thorough wash-down on the day of the Pope's death. He was old enough to remember the last time three million people converged on his city, doubling its population.

The first day wasn't that bad. The Basilica remained open for twenty-two hours a day. The two hours were needed to clean up the debris that thousands inadvertently left behind on the marble floor in their shuffling. Like an army of snails, thought the mayor.

Already on the second day the hotels, the hospices, convents, monasteries, sports halls, schools, and all other places that could possibly be used to accommodate people, had reached their full capacity. People slept on makeshift portable cots, light sponges, inflatable beds and even the floor. Those arriving on the third and fourth days slept in the streets.

No one complained.

There was an air of joy mixed with sadness. Smiles and tears were interchangeable. Some elderly men and women collapsed. They were helped on the spot. People offered them water, leaving themselves short. Others were taken away on stretchers.

Some, few, asked the police to move the barriers so that they could leave.

"I am sixty-eight years old. I've been standing for the last five hours. I can't take it any more." His wife remained in the procession.

People had come a long way. From Brazil, they'd been travelling for more than ten hours. Those whose airplanes touched down outside Rome, much longer. In 2005, the Fiera di Roma exhibition center had been converted to a 5000-bed dormitory. This time it was a field hospital. By the end of the third day, it was full.

The great convergence brought people together. It also tore them apart.

* * *

12

The Funeral

O n the fourth day, in preparation for the requiem Mass, twelve men, somber in black suits, all wearing white gloves, lifted the wooden coffin containing the body of the late Pontiff and placed it outside the Basilica for the world to see. The whole world. A wooden coffin, on a wooden platform, in front of a wooden altar.

Sic transit gloria mundi.

Hundreds of television cameras were passing the humble images to countless millions, perhaps billions, who were following every step of the Pontiff's final journey.

"Unto the ends of the earth...."

Finally the prophecy would come true. Thanks to the miracle of television, the whole world would hear the Word of God. Would participate in the rites.

In Protocol.

Directly south of the coffin, to the left when facing the Basilica, a tall white candle reached out toward the cloudless sky. It symbolized the joy of resurrection. Of heaven's favourite son, Ioannes Paulus. All was ready. The dean of the College of Cardinals approached the altar. He would celebrate the requiem mass. He would face the coffin and the people with the Basilica behind him. He would be assisted by other cardinals. All for John Paul.

A few steps lower, but still close to the altar, dignitaries were already being seated in long rows of straight-backed, red velvet upholstered chairs. The colour of blood. Of martyrs. By the time all the chairs were occupied, some two hundred very important people would be packed close together. As if they were friends. They would have to spend some three hours at peace with each other.

Facing them towards the south, across the square, most of the eminencies of most world religions were already seated. The cardinals, bishops and archbishops of various Christian denominations, metropolitans of Eastern Rite churches, illustrious elders of various sects, the learned imams and mullahs who could recite the whole Koran from memory, rabbis from Israel and other important countries, His Divine Grace the long-bearded Swami of the Hindu, the Divine Dalai Lama, the clean-shaven Buddhists, and many others sat shoulder to shoulder, united in sorrow. Or so they looked. Their faces were sober, underlying the solemnity of the occasion. Some wondered, for once silently, if any of them would ever merit such overt, exorbitant if not unprecedented final respects.

They all abided in serene equanimity under the clear blue sky of the Eternal City.

On the west side of the square, directly opposite the eminencies, the President of the United States sat in the front row. Next to him were the representatives of the House of Windsor. Other presidents—European, Asian, South American and African—sat intermingled with prime ministers, ministers of foreign affairs, of all the world's major democracies. And some not-so-democratic regimes as well. All the dignitaries wore solemn expressions becoming the dignity of their office. Only sometimes a smile or a quick handshake across the backs of chairs would break the monotony. They were all important people. They all looked important. These were people who, together, forged the head of the world. The ultimate secular power. They were Caesar.

They had to be here.

They had been drawn by the power of the great convergence, like lemmings, without questioning the logic of their actions. Just like the masses stretching as far as the eye could see along the Via del Conciliazione. All the way to the river. The masses they ruled. It was their job. Their destiny. Their karma.

The dean of the College of Cardinals, His Eminence, Cardinal Archbishop Boris Ivan Gramotny, raised his arms in blessing. His somewhat controversial appointment had been political more than anything and had opened up Eastern Europe for the Roman Church.

In nomine Patris et Filii et Spiritus sancti....

The Cardinal was blessed with a rich, beautiful *basso profundo.*

Requiem aeternam dona eis Domine: et lux perpetua luceat eis....

Silence spread like an invisible film stretched over the hundreds of thousands of faces, all turned toward the altar. The faces became quite indistinguishable as they receded towards infinity.

The Mass had begun.

A woman in nun's habit read from Chapter 10 of the Acts of the Apostles, announcing the good news of the resurrection. She read the lesson in Portuguese.

Farther east, behind the world leaders, was a line of security guards, and behind them hundreds of nuns sat in a large block, side by side with lesser dignitaries. They were the children of a lesser god. Separating them from the masses were six hundred *carabinieri.* The defenders of the faith. And of the dignitaries. Their automatic weapons hanging loose from their shoulders, their fingers less loose, poised on the triggers. Others, plainclothes men, intermingled with the lesser dignitaries. And plainclothes women, their flowing habits of the Carmelite nuns concealing more automatic weapons, Mini UZIs with folded stocks, sat among the humble, unassuming nuns.

Ioannes Paulus must have felt safe in his coffin. As did the dignitaries in their places of honour.

The Lord is my shepherd... I shall fear no evil....
It was a beautiful voice. A voice that rose straight to the sky and took everyone along. The first tears of many poured freely. Not just from the nuns. Men and women, all standing their final vigil, assisting in the final journey. *"Sancto, sancto,"* some whispered. *"Sancto subito,"* others echoed, as throughout the last four days. They wanted a saint. A new saint. A saint in whose beatification they had taken part. They wanted one who had told them to love one another above all else. Hadn't someone done so before him? A commandment that we love one another? What was that....?

A nne and Gabriel sat side by side, watching the ceremony on TV. "I wonder what made me leave so suddenly?" she asked, knowing full well that it had been for Peter's sake. Her Peter. Not the splendour of the Saint she'd left behind. " I wonder how the Camerlengo is doing. What a nice man he was," she mused aloud before Gabriel could answer her first question.
He maketh me lie down in green pastures....
They both followed the activities on the screen.
"Nothing ever happens without a reason," Gabriel said softly, so as not to disturb the beautiful psalm intoned by the choir. Like most people's, it was his favourite. He'd studied mostly Asian philosophies, but he kept a book of psalms on his night table. He called it his little bible. The Psalter and the *Bhagavad Gita* lay next to each other. The latter bore a title, 'The Song Celestial'. It lacked explanatory notes, but it was translated into beautiful poetry by Sir Edwin Arnold. He, too, must have loved it. Like Gabriel, he'd learned Sanskrit just to be able to translate it.

No one knew that along the balconies, or *loggia* as they were known in Rome, embracing both sides of St. Peter's Square, sharpshooters, approved by a commission of seven nations and seven principal religions, insinuated themselves among the hundreds of press agents. They were all busy pointing their cameras, their telescoping lenses and directional microphones at the dignitaries below.

"Like sitting ducks," an English reporter remarked.

People strained their ears to catch every word.

...he restoreth my soul. He leadeth me in the paths of righteousness for His name's sake....

Sobbing could be heard from the rectangle where nuns were sitting. "He restoreth my soul...." This is what they've come for. To have their souls restored. It wasn't easy sometimes. They had all sworn obedience. Didn't God give us free will? Are we not all equal in the eyes of God? Restore my soul, oh Lord. Please, Lord. Am I not free in my soul?

Peter turned on the TV in his apartment, but he'd missed the beginning. He watched the proceedings for a brief moment and then he returned to his office. The TV in his office was bigger. Someone was reading a letter from Saint Paul to the Philippians. He wondered if Anne was watching. He wondered about Johnny and Deirdre. And Gabriel. They were bound to be watching. And listening. Di could speak four languages. She would probably understand most of the liturgy.

He glanced at his desk. He should be working. He was not being paid an enormous sum of money to watch TV. No matter how important. But he was still angry.

How long had Saint Paul stayed in prison? It would be nice to be able to walk through the wall as he had done. He and Saint John. Together. Through the iron bars.

He looked at his notes. A reading from the Book of John would be next. *"For this is the will of my father that everyone*

who sees the son and believeth in him may have eternal life."
That would put John Paul III in good stead. Where will I end up
when I die? Probably in some fantastic lab, studying the genetic
structure of angels' wings, or something.

Right now he wasn't going anywhere.

The gospel procession began forming among the cardinals.
The Princes of the Church removed their pointed miters, the
fish-heads, signs of wisdom, and showed their age. They exposed
a sea of gray heads, protected only by tiny red skullcaps.

"Lovest thou me?" the celebrant intoned. "Lovest thou
me?"

"Lord, you know that I love thee," replied a thousand
priests, nuns and deacons. The lesser dignitaries of the Catholic
Church.

The hearts of the cardinals trembled: "Lovest thou me?"
What if I were asked this same question? Would I be told to feed
His sheep? Would I answer Him even as Peter did? The Great
Peter, the Rock, in whose footsteps we walk. All his footsteps? Do
we love Him enough not to betray Him? Never? Not even once?
How sure am I that I'll be told to feed His sheep? Did I? Had I
fed His sheep throughout my life? Lord, you know that I love
you. Don't you?

The moment passed.

The celebrant began the homily. Applause. "Present here,
in St. Peter's Square, is the Spirit of Christ...." More applause.

The Camerlengo drew the curtains. Earlier that morning
he'd collapsed. He'd recovered in minutes but had been too
exhausted to attend the Mass down below. He watched the
procedures from behind the curtains. He had welcomed the
dignitaries. He'd made sure that everything would go smoothly.
Now it was their turn to do their jobs. For now, he'd done his.
Until the Conclave, when it would begin all over again. The Holy
Bedlam. The gentle heckling. Elbow twisting. Influence
peddling. Promises. He preferred to remain in the shadows.

Credo in unum Deum Patrem omnipotentem....
They sang beautifully. The declaration of faith.
...visibilium omnium et invisibilium....
The Camerlengo's chest moved in a deep sigh. So much must be taken on faith. Jesus was born, suffered under Pontius Pilate, was crucified, died and was buried. There is some evidence for that. The rest is myth. A myth we all hold so dear. Is it so important? Is loving one another not enough?

The large-screen TV took up half the length of the east wall of his office. It faced three deep armchairs that were seldom occupied. The Pope's Funeral was on but the sound was off. The Vice President was busy at his desk. Stacks of papers had to be discharged. He dictated his instructions into a number of microphones disposed about his office. It was the only way. He spoke as he sat, as he paced up and down, to and fro and back to his desk for another piece of paper. Another decision that would affect thousands, hundreds of thousands of people. He took his duties in stride.

He worked, occasionally glancing at the screen. Now and then he nodded, as though confirming his thoughts, a nod of satisfaction. People were counting on him to do his job. He had never failed them. Not once.

The funeral was proceeding just as Fred's notes had described. "It won't be long now," he mused aloud. Unwittingly, he kept his voice down. "It won't be long now," he repeated, taking a deep breath.

"Do you think he's all right?" Anne kept staring at the screen, but her thoughts kept returning to Peter. Frankly, they'd never left him. She was in Westmount, looking at the Vatican, but her heart was in Washington. In spite of Gabby.

"Yes, Anne. He is all right," Gabriel replied simply. What else could he say?

He'd come here to reassure Anne. For close to thirty years he'd known whenever Anne had been worried. There was a strange connection between them. He felt elated by her successes, worried by her sorrows. He often wondered how such a connection could have developed. Then he remembered. It hadn't. It was always like this.

"I am sure he's watching the Mass, even as we are."

Of that Gabriel was sure. He even thought that that was the way Peter kept in touch with them. With the world. Strange how the death of one man could unite the world. Isn't that what had happened in the past? Isn't that why Christ died? He had to remove himself from the equation. "Behold, the kingdom of God is within you," he'd said. "Don't look at me, look within.... How is it that ye do not understand?" he'd cried many a time. Will people ever understand? Will the priests? The bishops, the scarlet princes of the Church? They paid lip service to some of His words, but ignored the essence.

"Thank you, Gabby. I'm so glad you're here."

"It won't be long now," he assured Anne.

Somehow Gabriel just knew. He sensed that whatever kept Peter away was coming to an end, even as the Mass soon would. So many people. Millions. They said over four million. More than doubling the population of Rome. For what? Couldn't they have served the Pope while he was still alive? Couldn't they have listened to his words then? John Paul III was not like his immediate predecessor. Not even like his namesake from years ago. If Jose Manuel followed in anyone's footsteps, it would have been those of John XXIII, the fourth child from a family of fourteen, who rose to be known as 'the good Pope'. He didn't dwell on protocol. He didn't tell people to follow rules and regulations. He didn't threaten them with hell and damnation.

"Listen to your hearts," he'd admonish anyone who would listen. "Listen to your hearts...."

Some did.

Prayers were said in Latin, in Italian, then in Portuguese, and then in eleven other languages. It helped to reward the people who came from far and wide. Each prayer was followed by a short song. It was quite fitting. Even the songs were in their native tongues. It united the people. Made them feel as one. For a while....

Then came the rite of incense.

An angelic voice began singing another lonesome Gregorian chant. The choir responded in near monotone. Otherwise, the hundreds of thousands present remained transfixed by the sacred silence.

As the patriarchs, the archbishops and other elders approached the coffin, Cardinal Gramotny swung the censer in slow, rhythmic motion all around the coffin. The gentle wind spun the sweet aroma, as though trying to spread it far and wide. Then, assisted by other cardinals, the celebrant proceeded to sprinkle the coffin with Holy Water. About halfway round, he stopped. He continued waving the now empty sprinkling brush limp in his hand. He seemed unsure what to do with it. One of the cardinals took a step towards him, only to stop in consternation when he touched his elbow. By now, other cardinals looked bewildered. They continued standing, holding their skullcaps in their hands like treasured possessions. Their eyes searched each other's faces.

Cardinal Gramotny managed to return to the altar. He rested for a few seconds, then bent over the table.

"For this is my Body..."

He didn't finish. He leaned heavily over the altar, his face hidden from the people. By now no one was looking. Not those sitting nearby. The priesthood, the illustrious dignitaries, the lesser men and women sitting lower down but still close enough to be affected, sat in abject silence.

"What is going on?" whispered those farther from the altar. "What on earth is happening?"

The choir, positioned on the steps of St. Peter's Basilica, intoned the song of the Eucharist. The Transubstantiation. The mystery of the Holy Mass. Only Cardinal Gramotny never raised the Host above his head. Some said that he ate it. Swallowed it whole. Others said that it vanished into thin air.

By now people on both sides of the altar began rising. They questioned each other like strangers asking for directions. The Presidents crossed over to the bishop's side; the imams approached prime ministers—all looking for answers.

"Who are you?" asked the Prime Minister of Great Britain, addressing his French counterpart. "Who are these people?"

"*Et vous êtes qui?*" the Premier replied in kind.

"I . . . I am not sure...."

"Where are we?" an Archbishop asked one of his colleagues.

"I don't know, Your Emmi... Your Emmi... Your Emi? Can you tell me?"

One man looked a little more lost than others. The President of the United States of America walked straight up to Cardinal Gramotny.

"I demand that you tell me who I am!" he commanded. Even as he spoke, his face lost its self-assurance. The Cardinal looked at him with a mixture of surprise and suspicion.

"Please?" the President added plaintively.

"Who are you?" replied the Dean of the College of Cardinals. "Have we met?"

* * *

THE HEADLESS WORLD

Uneasy lies the head that wears the crown.

Shakespeare, *Henry IV*

13

The Beginning

For a minute or two Cardinal Giovanni Pesci didn't move. What he had just seen was too stunning for words. The Church witnessed her share of miracles. Never in the 2000-year history of the Church had something like this happened. Never.

He had to think fast.

He picked up his cellular. He hated using it. It was too easy for others to eavesdrop. This time he had no choice. Inside the Basilica, twelve men waited to pick up the coffin and take it, accompanied only by the most senior cardinals of the Church, to the crypts for burial. He hoped that at least they were all right. He'd noticed that people sitting farther away from the altar looked normal. At least they weren't wandering about like a bunch of lost sheep.

"Yes?" asked the senior pallbearer.

"This is the Camerlengo," Giovanni used his official title. He needed to be obeyed without question. "Listen carefully. Go now to the altar, avoiding contact with any of the people. Pick up the coffin and carry it to the Basilica. At the steps, turn around and face the people one final time. Then go inside St. Peter's. I'll meet you there."

That was the number one priority. The second was security. He called the commander of the Swiss Guard.

"Are your men OK?" he asked.

"Most of them. What happened?"

"I don't know. Contact the other commanders, those farthest away from the altar. I want the inner square completely sealed off. No one is to leave or enter. I don't care who they are."

"Yes, Sir. I mean Your Eminence!"

Gio could see the man from his veiled window. The man took the call standing up and then saluted as though facing his superior.

The Camerlengo glanced at his watch. As he looked up, he saw two of his assistants standing at the door to his office. They had not been allowed to sit with their colleagues in the square in case he needed them. A wise choice, he thought.

"Go downstairs and get me some physicians. As many as you can. I believe there may be some farther away from the altar who may still be in command of their wits. Bring them here." Both men turned on their heels. "Do it discreetly," he called out. Not that it mattered. There was nothing discreet about the behaviour of the cardinals or the dignitaries.

The Camerlengo got up, walked to the window overlooking the square and peered out. Twelve white-gloved men were proceeding down the steps of the Basilica with the measured steps befitting pallbearers. They would surround the coffin, lift it up, turn and return towards the steps. There, they would turn.... He had a few minutes before he would be needed downstairs.

He dialed Sir Ian Barton's number. Sir Ian hadn't replied to his earlier call. Could be out of town. Sir Ian picked up the receiver himself.

"Barton," he barked. He had been watching TV and hated to be interrupted. He just couldn't get used to not having a secretary.

"Gio Pesci," the Camerlengo introduced himself. "*Come stae....*"

"What the hell is going on, Gio? I've been watching...."

"I don't know, Ian. I'm sorry. I have a favour to ask you."

"Fire away." Sir Ian sounded anxious.

"I must get hold of Anne. Mrs. Brown. Would you know her whereabouts?"

"I don't, but I'll find out. You want her to call you?"

"I might be difficult to get hold of. Perhaps you could ask her to come to Rome, again. I assume she's already left. I really must see her."

Sir Ian was dying to ask what all this was about. It took all his self-control not to. "I'll do what I can."

"We shall pay for her flight, of course. First class," Gio added as an extra inducement.

"Leave it with me. Can I ask you something, too?"

"Of course."

"Will you let me know what happened? When you find out yourself, of course. It's just that one simply cannot trust the media any more."

"I shall, Ian. And thank you."

They hung up simultaneously.

The moment Cardinal Pesci put down the phone, he realized how strange his request must have sounded to Sir Ian. As far as his friend was concerned, he and Anne had only just met. This, the Cardinal smiled wistfully, was not quite true.

He was a young man when he'd heard Anne play at L'Accademia Filarmonica Romana. It had been during the encore that something happened to him that had marked him for life. Anne had played Bach's Sonata number 2, in A minor, for the unaccompanied violin. During the second movement, Gio had experienced what he thought of later as a moment of communion with the Infinite. He found himself stepping out of his body and spreading his awareness over countless light-years. It had been at that moment that the youthful deacon had truly anchored his faith in God. Only then, in that ephemeral moment, God was a beautiful melody. Anne was little more than a girl then, but for him her image remained irrevocably linked to a lofty seraphim, wrapped in green taffeta swept majestically with flamboyant hair.

And then, recently, when the late Pontiff had told him the date that led him to the discovery of the female pope, for an instant Anne's face had shimmered before his eyes. Not Mrs. Brown's of today, but Anne's face of yesteryear. Anne that sounded like Bach's violin sonata. He'd never told anyone about his experience at L'Accademia, yet now, today, for no

reason he could justify at an intellectual level, he felt convinced
that Anne would prove instrumental in resolving the present
dilemma.

Cardinal Pesci took a deep breath. If Anne Brown cannot
help, I don't know who will, he muttered to himself. He grabbed
his biretta and literally ran downstairs. Thank heaven I donned
the ceremonial cassock and mozzetta, he thought as he ran down
the staircase. Cardinals didn't normally run, up or down
anything. I must look like a giant bird, like a cardinal, he
thought, a chuckle in his throat. A princely bird of the Church.

He met the pallbearers just as they were turning the coffin
for the final farewell to the crowds. He stood at the head of the
tiny convoy, resplendent in his violet garment. Only his miter
was missing. Usually, the cardinals would follow the coffin inside
the Basilica for the funeral rites. It was not to be. He could not
allow anything to detract from his beloved Holy Father's rite.

No matter.

He waited for the men to turn and then faced the doors of
St. Peter's. As they walked past the choir, about half of them
began singing. Apparently, only half of them knew that
anything was wrong.

*May the angels accompany you into heaven, may the
martyrs welcome you when you arrive, and lead you to Holy
Jerusalem....*

The Camerlengo walked slowly. Once inside the Basilica, he
led the men down the steps into the grotto. There the coffin was
finally closed with red bands, sealed with both papal and Vatican
seals. The cypress coffin was then placed in a second casket of
zinc, and within a third made of walnut. This outside casket bore
the name of Ioannes Paulus III, his cross and his papal coat of
arms.

Giovanni wished he didn't feel so alone. Not one Vatican
prelate was there to give him strength. He was saying goodbye to
a man, a friend, he'd known half of his life.

Lord, grant him eternal rest, and may perpetual light shine upon him.

Somewhere behind him, among the living, someone began singing *Salve Regina*. Even as Cardinal Pesci walked up from the grotto, the crowds picked up the hymn. Soon tens of thousands of people were singing farewell to Ioannes Paulus.

The Camerlengo rushed back to his office. Four men were sitting there. One in a cassock, the other three in civilian clothing—the physicians Carlo had brought at his request.

"Well?" he asked them.

The men fidgeted uncomfortably. No one spoke. As he repeated his question, they all started talking at once. None of them said anything of value. They were as lost as he was. An act of God? A miracle? But why? Are we to reduce the protocol, to become simpler, more accessible? Are we to break barriers between the dignitaries and the believers? Weren't the dignitaries believers also?

Probably not.

The Camerlengo sat heavily. He'd never felt so alone in his life. The four doctors were blabbering without rhyme or reason. And he looked out the window, hardly hearing them.

Gabriel handed Anne the telephone. Probably her mother, he thought. They had been watching TV, uncertain, indeed at a loss, as to what was happening in Rome. It was flabbergasting. Never, never had anyone imagined that someone would want to interfere with the burial of a man beloved by so many. But who? And why? What could possibly be the point?

The behaviour of those nearest the altar, some two hundred dignitaries on the left, and an equal number of senior representatives of various religions on the right, were acting as though they were drunk. Milling around aimlessly, ignoring the rows of seats assigned to them. At least the coffin had been removed with due decorum.

"That's Gio," Anne said the moment she saw a diminutive figure leading the burial procession. "He always knows what to do." She reached out for the receiver almost absentmindedly.

"Peter!" Anne screamed. "Darling, are you all right?"

The usual trite question. Of course he was all right. He was calling her. Wasn't he?

"Love you," he replied.

"I love you too, sweetheart." Anne forgot all about the funeral. "Why didn't you call? I was so worried..." All the hurt of the last few days poured out in a flood. She wiped her eyes. Tears of relief.

"I couldn't. I've been, what we call, *incommunicado*. We all were. At least, so I've been told."

"And now?" she asked, inconsequentially.

"And now we are not. At least, I am not." There was relief mixed with humour in his voice. He was stating the obvious. "Something happened that enabled us to restore our contact with the outside world," he began carefully. He had no idea if his telephone was bugged.

"I'm so glad, darling. I'm so glad you're all right. We were so worried."

"We?"

"Gabriel is here."

"Say hello to him for me. Or better still, put him on the line," Peter asked.

The receiver nearly disappeared in Gabriel's huge palm. "Hello, Peter. It's good to hear from you."

"Gabby, listen carefully. I know what happened in Rome." Silence. Peter half expected the line to go dead. He suspected he might have only one opportunity to speak, and preferred to talk to Gabby. Anne was too emotional right now.

"Yes?"

"Someone used my invention. It erases memory for an indefinite period of time. It's a prototype but...."

"I understand. Do you expect the memory to return?" Gabriel knew of the work Peter did at the MNI. Anne had also told him of his invitation to the Pentagon. He put two and two together.

"I don't know. We only carried out a single experiment on a group. We did it about a week ago. So far, no one's recovered. Their memory, I mean. In all other respects they are OK," Peter added defensively.

"Anne wants to speak to you." Gabriel handed over the receiver.

"Are you coming home now?"

"Darling, I am not next door. I still have my work to do."

"But I thought . . . I thought that...." she was lost for words.

"Sweetheart, I don't really know what's going on. I don't think they'd let me leave, not now."

Anne had no idea what he was talking about. She looked at Gabriel.

"I'll explain," he said, guessing the tenor of their interchange.

"I'll fly home as soon as I can," Peter said. "I promise. Give my love to Di and Johnny. And your parents," he hesitated. "Can I have another word with Gabriel?"

Reluctantly, she gave Gabriel the receiver.

"Gabby? What do I do now?"

"Things will unfold exactly as they should," Gabriel assured him.

This was exactly what Peter wanted to hear. There was no one to whom he could report his knowledge at the Pentagon. Anyway, unless they were congenital morons, they already knew. Not for a moment had Peter suspected that the higher echelons of the Pentagon were not in on the caper. Not that caper was the proper word. They'd interfered with the proper running of the whole world. The headless world, he thought. What a mess. And I am responsible....

"Don't hold yourself responsible, Peter. You did what you did for the good of mankind. Don't ever forget that."

"Thanks, Gabby. Love you all."

Peter hung up. It was good to hear Gabby's assurances, not to mention Anne's voice, but it was much harder to shirk the guilt of his invention.

What a fool I am, he scolded himself. I completely forgot to ask Anne about her trip to Rome. Thank God Gabriel is there. At least he has a level head on his massive shoulders.

His thoughts were getting darker.

He remembered the question Fred Finer had asked him. It seemed like only yesterday. What would you do, Fred had asked, if you were a multibillionaire and had access to almost limitless power?

The dice had been cast. John Linker stopped pacing and sat down in front of his enormous digital TV. He split the image into six parts, watching most of them simultaneously by his peripheral vision. It had all happened exactly as he'd expected. And any moment now, the Chiefs of Staff of all the branches of the military would open their envelopes. The orders were explicit:

TOP SECRET

TO BE OPENED
ONLY IN THE EVENT THAT
THE PRESIDENT OF THE UNITED STATES
BECOMES UNABLE TO FULFILL HIS DUTIES

All aircraft carriers had been given exact destinations and were to advance towards the target areas immediately. The orders were signed by John Linker, Commander in Chief. There was no date.

Linker felt an unexpected though not unpleasant quickening in his veins. For a moment he felt young. As he'd felt when he gambled most of his fortune on one of his early deals. You don't become a multibillionaire by playing it safe. Only this time he wasn't gambling with his own money. If this gamble worked, the world would never be the same.

A buzzer sounded on his desk. Without moving his head he asked who it was.

"Finer," came the short reply.

"Enter." The word automatically unlocked the door.

Fred Finer came in and remained standing at the door. After a minute or two, Linker, still without turning his head, waved his hand.

"Sit down, Fred," he said in his usual quiet voice. "We need to talk."

No matter how private a man Linker was, he had to share his plan with someone. So far he hadn't. He carried the future of the world on his shoulders. It was beginning to weigh him down. He had to talk to someone.

Finer sat down and waited. He was good at waiting. That's what he did most of his life. He waited to carry out the orders of his superiors.

"You recall, my dear friend, when you prepared a list for me, about the hundred days?"

Finer nodded, although Linker's eyes remained on the screen.

"Well," the Vice President continued after a while, "it got me thinking."

He adjusted his hand-held control module, and two more squares covering a different part of St. Peter's Square came into view. They both saw twelve men carrying a casket on their shoulders with military precision. It seemed that they must have drilled for this somber march for days. Maybe months. Linker had great appreciation for precision. It was part of the world he lived in. Part of his reality. Without it, he would still be just a multi-millionaire.

"Well, I started working on a plan which could come to fruition in a hundred days or less."

Finer remained silent. His eyes followed the activities in various parts of the many squares. It was quite evident that the malaise had affected only the people sitting in the two quadrangles nearest the coffin. The rest seemed quite unaffected.

A moment later Finer noticed a large number of men, it could have been two or three hundred, standing up, their automatic weapons ready. They were cutting off access from the round part of the Square to its inner portion, the part nearest the Basilica. Someone must have given them orders.

"He is a good man, the Camerlengo," Linker said. "I wish he worked for me."

An unlikely story, Finer thought. Or, to put it differently, not in a million years.

"He seems to think of everything," Linker mused aloud.

"Yes, a very good man."

The third square on the left of the screen, in the second row down, zeroed in on the face of the President of the United States. The President never displayed excessive outward signs of his innate intelligence. But now, even a vestige of his perfunctory wit was missing. The eyes Finer saw were vacant. The sort of eyes Hollywood directors try so hard to display in zombies. The living dead. There was no life in them. Or at least, no intelligent life.

"It seems that you got yourself a new job, Mr. President."

A small smile played at the corners of Linker's mouth. "Nothing has changed. Not as far as you and I are concerned." And then, for the first time, John Linker, the acting President of the United States, took his eyes off the strategic display. "As of now, I shall do officially what heretofore I have been *de facto* doing for the last six years."

Finer couldn't argue with that. He always knew who the power behind the throne was.

"And by the way, I've lifted the gag. People can contact their families. Call your wife. We mustn't have them worried."

If Finer didn't know better, he would have thought that John Linker really cared about the ordinary people. On the other hand, who knew what took place in another man's head, let alone in his heart.

"It's Sir Ian," Gabriel said, rousing Anne from her rest. After hearing Peter's voice all her pent-up nerves had drained her of her resistance. She'd curled up on the settee and within seconds was fast asleep.

"Sorry, Miss Anne." Gabriel took on the more formal tone when dealing with matters in which he recognized Anne as his superior.

"Sir Ian? B-b-but he's in Rome...." she said, rubbing her eyes. Then she reached for the receiver. "Ian? How are you?"

Without any preambles, Sir Ian described the chat he'd had with the Camerlengo.

"He insists that you come back to Rome. You could stay with me. We hardly saw each other," he added hopefully.

"But I've only just come back...." She wanted to fly to Washington to see Peter.

"Gio doesn't ask favours often," Sir Ian insisted. "And he's offering you a first class ticket."

"What is it about, Ian?" She was still not fully recovered from her nap. When the telephone rang, she'd been far, far away. In fact, she hadn't heard it at all.

"Have you been watching TV?" Sir Ian was running out of patience.

"Of course, Ian. Hasn't everyone?"

"Precisely. My nose tells me that Gio thinks that you might have something to do with it. I don't mean with the problem, but with the solution."

"Me?" Anne sounded flabbergasted. This was not at all her line of work.

"When can you leave?"

"I don't know. I'll have to check with Dorval. The flights...."

"You are booked on the ten o'clock, your time, on Alitalia. You have the best seat."

"Tonight?"

"Yes, dear." His voice softened. "I'm sorry, Anne, but Gio is a good friend. I think you'll like him."

"But I do like him. Only...."

"Ten o'clock then?"

"I suppose so...."

"I'll have the Vatican limousine waiting for you at the airport. Bye now." He hung up.

Anne looked at Gabriel. "You were not much help, were you?"

Gabriel contrived to look contrite. "I'll tell your parents that you and Peter are fine. And I'll call your children. And water your plants," he added, looking around. "Get some sleep now; you might be too excited on the flight."

"Wanna bet?"

Gabriel had been right. It took Anne nearly three hours before the drone of the engines lulled her back to sleep. She dreamed she was floating over the Vatican, watching thousands of people reaching out towards her. As she moved her arms, her long, raglan sleeves swooping the air, she descended over the milling masses. They cried, their voices piercing the air with a peculiar hum. Help me, help us, they cried. Some of them shone great lights into her eyes. How can I help them if I cannot see, she wondered.

Help us . . . help us....

The cries turned into a continuous, ubiquitous drone. She flapped her wings in surprise. What would they want of a dove? Am I not free to soar above the saints like all other birds? Am I not free . . . freeeee...?

When she opened her eyes, the piercing hum of the engines filled her ears. Again. The captain's voice was announcing the descent to Rome. Her second within a single week.

* * *

14

Chaos

In Greek, the word *chaos* means void. An empty space. An abyss. We have come to understand chaos to mean without due form or order. A formless matter in the vastness of space. A mess.

Linker allowed himself to be engulfed by the deeply upholstered leather armchair. It was time for a breather. A moment or two of relaxation. I've earned it, he told himself. He was musing about the mess the world was in. He was also musing about the New World order. About the American Way.

Ah, yes, he sighed deeply. The American Way.

There is another meaning to the ancient word *chaos*. A meaning that fostered and inspired a new understanding that scientists have named Chaos theory. It is a premise that postulates that chaos exhibits a predisposition towards order and harmony. Order and harmony are not visible within chaos, but the predisposition is there.

"Rather like the quarks," Finer told him. "We recognize them only by the trails they leave behind."

Linker wondered what sort of trail he would leave behind.

This was the President's favourite time—after work well done, to sit back and muse. Often great ideas were born this way. This was probably the last time he would have the luxury of allowing his mind to wander, to reminisce, to dream. He clicked on his electronic diary, scanning main headings. One day, he thought, these notes will make me immortal.

In recent years, the so-called civilized world had been showing a marked affinity towards chaos. This questionable propensity had begun about the time when the United States of America had decided to impose democracy on a number of nations. Iraq, Iran, Afghanistan, Sudan, Liberia, Syria... a long list. A noble sentiment indeed, he thought. Only it had proven an impossible task.

"One cannot impose freedom on people dedicated to the pursuit of anarchy," he murmured, seemingly unaware that even if Finer seemed determined not to interrupt his meandering thoughts, each utterance he made was being duly recorded.

"You will be free, whether you like it or not!" Linker sneered in a half-tone, imitating the voice of his presidential predecessor.

"It is always better," he spoke, staring at the wall screen, "to offer a choice!"

For the first time he glanced at Finer, daring him to contradict his words.

He scanned some earlier pages. He'd often recorded his thoughts in the form of dialogues, mirroring Plato's exhortations. "Now, there was democracy," he mused. "One citizen in fifty controlling the fate of the nation. If I can cut it down to one in five thousand, I will have done my job!"

He scanned entries still further back.

"Impose freedom?" he read slowly, haltingly. "To impose freedom was not the American Way."

He sank deeper into his armchair.

Even without Finer's contribution, Linker was well aware of the horrendous errors of the past. He'd taken it upon himself to set the record straight. Past and future. He truly believed in giving people a chance to do their own thing—provided it did not interfere with American interests. It was a sort of 'let them eat cake' dictum. Or allowing them to sell their own oil, in their own way, at their own prices. But obviously, if they chose to do so, they would not benefit from American technology or support.

"They shouldn't expect us to provide them with our know-how, our industry, our engineering skills, our pumps, drills, tankers, refineries, back-up equipment, and even our market. Your choice.... You want to do it your way? Go right ahead. But forget about our market. About our loans. Our financing. Do it your way...."

Linker stood up and towered over Fred Finer, who was doing his best to remain invisible.

"Do you know what the world has to learn, Fred? That kindergarten is over."

For the last half hour, Finer had remained perfectly still. He sat waiting for John Linker to expound on his ruminations. Usually the wait was worthwhile. At long last, Linker appeared to be finished as he sat back down in his chair. It was evident that the President felt the need to justify, if only before his own conscience, the little red button he'd pressed just minutes ago. A little red button that might well have thrown the world into unprecedented chaos. Not just the western civilizations as in the first two World Wars, but the whole globe. The Earth.

"It is not in the stars, but in ourselves, that we are underlings," Linker murmured after considerable pause.

This was the old Linker. No longer combative but reflective, philosophical, given to deductive reasoning.

The acting President loved quoting Shakespeare—*Julius Caesar*, in particular. Next to the Bible—which he glanced at occasionally, interpreting it with a strong Southern Baptist slant—Shakespeare was his other favourite motivator. He was well capable of quoting both at will. It gave the people an impression that he was erudite, well above average. He was.

"According to Shakespeare, Julius Caesar was not fully appreciated by his contemporaries," Fred Finer spoke for the first time.

Linker smiled. He didn't care whether Caesar had been popular or not. Great leaders shouldn't be. Did Moses change his tactics to please his people?

The President glanced at his watch.

"In one hour and four minutes, the *USS Dwight D. Eisenhower* shall be underway into the Atlantic. Exactly one hour later, Admiral George W. Smith will open the second envelope. There he'll discover his exact destination. Upon arrival he will open the third envelope."

Finer sank a little deeper into his armchair. They were sitting like two friends making hay. Apparently, there was little more to do. For now. For a day or two. Finer wondered why the Admiral, being a law unto himself in the open seas, wouldn't open all the envelopes at once. Just out of curiosity. Then he glanced at Linker's face. In that instant he knew, with total confidence, that Admiral Smith would do no such thing.

Finer remembered waiting for Linker in the then Vice President's office. About a month ago. He recalled examining the walls, up and down, scanning book titles on the shelves behind Linker's desk. Finally, after making doubly sure that the door was closed and that he was really alone, he glanced at his boss's desk. There he saw Linker's evidently favorite quotation. The one he'd just given. About the stars and the underlings. Having seen it, Fred quickly returned to his chair, afraid that spy cameras might be aimed at his every move. He was wrong. Linker may have been obsessed, but no more so than Rubinstein had been with his piano, or Pavarotti with opera. He thought of himself as an artist, a musician.

Linker may have been obsessed, but he wasn't paranoid.

At the same time, Fred realized, perhaps belatedly, that the Linker he'd met years ago was, and to this day remained, an enigma.

After years of working together, Linker just didn't feel like a real person. There was something very contrived, very artificial about him. Finer's world spun around Linker's slightest whim, yet Fred still was not sure if he knew who his boss truly was. Linker wasn't, in his mind, a person with a history, a background with desires and fears.

What size are his shoes? What colour are his eyes? Does he take milk in his coffee? One lump or two?

Finer had never asked him. And his eyes? Few people dared to look Linker in the eyes long enough to determine their colour. They seemed like opaque mirrors denying access.

At least he took his Bourbon straight, Fred grinned.

Linker was so surreal, so powerful, that Fred found it hard to see his human side at the same time. How does someone with that much power and influence and with so many secrets—how does a person like that really see the world? Can a person like that just leave work at work and go home to his wife and dog? In recent days, Linker seemed like a two-dimensional personification of US imperialism, under the guise of spreading democracy. He was, Fred thought, a puppet of his own deeply ingrained concept of the American Way. He was a man possessed by an idea, to the exclusion of human traits and emotions. Though Fred found it difficult to admit even to himself, the man he was facing, the man he trusted and in many ways admired, just wasn't a believable person. He was a force of nature.

"In six days, the USS Dwight D. Eisenhower, the USS Nimitz, the Carl Vinson, the Theodore Roosevelt, the Abraham Lincoln, George Washington, John C. Stennis, Harry S. Truman, Ronald Reagan, and George H.W. Bush will all deploy at their destinations."

Linker rattled off the might of the United States, the fleet of Aircraft Carriers, like quoting his favourite poem. There was a thinly veiled sheen in his usually guarded eyes. Fred saw in them absolute commitment to the cause.

Again Fred said nothing. He wasn't quite sure what was going to happen after the aircraft carriers deployed. When he was good and ready, the President would share more of his thoughts with him.

The Nimitz Class was powered by two nuclear reactors, four shafts. They measured over 1000 feet in length. The beam extended to 134 feet, with the flight deck cantilevering over to a total width of 252 feet. Their cruising speed was over 30 knots, some 34.5 miles per hour. Each carrier supported 85 aircraft delivering the firing power of a medium-sized country. In six days, any one of the aircraft carriers could cover up to 5000 miles.

The cost? They cost over $4.5 billion each.

Fred liked the adage that yachts were referred to as millionaires' toys. This? This was in a different class of toy altogether.

The President hadn't enumerated all the carriers. There was also the Enterprise, the John F. Kennedy, and the Kitty Hawk class. These were powered by eight boilers, four shafts delivering 280,000 horsepower. Not atomic, but not to be sneezed at, either. There may have been others that Finer couldn't recall at the moment.

John Linker pressed a button on his portable control and the enormous TV screen came to life. After all these years, Finer had still never seen all the innumerable applications of the screen. He realized, once again, how very private a man Linker really was.

Visually, the map of the world dominated the whole area. The screen was twelve feet wide and eight feet high. It was impressive, to say the least. It was a veritable nerve center. A very private war room. Linker pushed another button, and the North American continent with large chunks of the Atlantic and Pacific oceans filled the entire screen.

Linker stared at it for a moment. In a few seconds, a little red dot began moving in a northeasterly direction. The first of the carriers?

"Steady as she goes," the Commander in Chief whispered. "And Godspeed."

Did this man really care?

Finer preferred not to think what the rest of the President's plan might entail. He sat perfectly still, his eyes half closed. He was all ears. 'Sufficient unto the day is the evil thereof...' Finer thought.

How incongruous... my President may well have just started a global war, and I am belatedly wondering about ethics. 'Evil thereof? What evil?' Finer felt that he, too, was escaping from reality, if only into academic dialectics. His thoughts grasped at the intangible to escape reality. 'Evil thereof...?' his mind wouldn't let go. He wondered if the same applied to the 'good'. The good thereof. 'Love thy neighbour....' Finer grimaced, averting his eyes from Linker's face. Love thy neighbour, unless you need to blow him to kingdom come.

He shook his head and, with thinly disguised distaste, turned to face his master.

"Godspeed," he echoed obediently.

The man held a hand-written sign with Anne's name on it. He stood just inside the international flights arrival gate. Anne spotted him even before she went through customs. Apparently the Camerlengo had bigger clout than met the eye.

"This way, Mrs. Brown," the man said.

Anne smiled her thanks. She was escorted through the formalities without changing her pace. Rapidly, she was losing most of her dissatisfaction at having to fly so soon after the previous visit. She'd intended to cover most of Europe on her previous tour, but she'd realized early enough that the idea wouldn't fly. You cannot recreate the past, she told herself. We all must live in the present. Always.

The chauffeur, sporting a Vatican coat of arms on his upper left blazer pocket, led Anne to a side door evidently reserved for the VVIP. Very, Very Important People. Even in First Class, some people were more equal than others. Anyway, in Rome, great many people were important. Especially those who were picked up by Vatican limousines.

"I trust you had a good flight?" the man asked politely.

"I don't know," Anne replied. When the man looked nonplused, she added, "I slept most of the way."

This wasn't quite true. She'd also enjoyed an excellent meal. The best she'd ever had on an airplane. Of course, she hadn't flown first class very often. Not since her Stradivarius days. For some reason she sighed. At home, she almost never thought about the past. But here? Rome was history, and her own was intermingled with the Eternal City.

The Camerlengo was waiting for Anne in his office. He'd moved his center of operations to the office overlooking the square. Most of the people affected by the plague, or whatever it was, had already been moved. First to the Basilica, then to the Papal Palace, the rest to the Seminarium at the back of the Vatican buildings. Originally, the latter grew out of the expanded St. Martha's hostel. Once the students had been moved out, there was just enough room, provided the illustrious personages bunked two per room. At present, they didn't seem to mind. They had no idea where they were, what they were doing and, most amazing of all, they had no idea who they were. They were, however, in perfect control of all functions that originated at the stern part of the cerebrum and the cerebellum. Their automotive reflexes were just fine. They could walk and talk and eat and react. The only parts of their brain that appeared affected were their frontal lobes. Without memories, they all seemed to find it difficult to think, to make decisions—whether out of insecurity or ignorance or fear. They were almost like children, content to entertain themselves with simple games and not worry about the world outside. At least, so said two of the neurosurgeons who had been commandeered by the Camerlengo.

The only other order Cardinal Pesci had issued was to continue holding the inner part of St. Peter's Square out of bounds. He'd extended the order to the rest of the Vatican. People were not allowed to enter or leave the City within the city. Considering the import of people affected by the plague, it was a necessary precaution.

So far, there was no evidence that the malaise was contagious.

"My dear," Giovanni Pesci rose to his feet and met Anne halfway to the door of his office. "I am most terribly sorry to have imposed on you. I know that travelling can be trying."

Anne smiled, not quite knowing what to say. The Cardinal treated her like an old friend. "Ian, Sir Ian, told me that you need me, ah, Your Emine...."

"Gio," he corrected. "Please, we must work together. We must dispense with titles. May I call you Anne, Mrs. Brown?"

"I've never addressed a Cardinal by his first name, Your Eminence."

The Camerlengo winced. "This is part of the problem we have in the Church today. People seem to have forgotten that we, all of us, the bishops, archbishops, cardinals, all of us, are just men. Like everybody else," he smiled. "Some . . . a lot worse," he added, sadly. "But we are not here to pass judgment, are we, Anne?"

Anne had absolutely no idea why they were, or at least why she was 'here'. She said as much.

"Please, sit down. I must tell you a story."

Gio related to Anne, in a few words, how the late Pope and he had met. How they worked together, how they shared their vision of the Church of the future. The Camerlengo thought it important that Anne know what sort of a bond the late Pontiff and he had shared.

He then related, in greater detail, the last conversation he'd had with the Pope already on his deathbed. He was glad the late Pope had absolved him from the vow of silence.

"The Pontiff must have known that I, his friend, might need total freedom to use my own discretion regarding our last intimate discussion. He also must have known that he was dying. Hence, the confession. Needless to say, as Padre Jose Da Rosa's eyes began clouding over, I spoke the words of absolution. Though knowing Ioannes Paulus as I did, I couldn't imagine in what way the Pontiff could have missed his mark. The crowds in the square and all the way up via Conciliazione were right. The man was a saint."

There was a great deal of restrained emotion in Gio's voice. Anne listened without interruptions.

"His very last words were why I called you here. John Paul said: *Ricorda ottocento cinquanta cinque...*"

Anne searched the Cardinal's face.

"Remember eight hundred fifty five," he translated. " I racked my brains. At long last I found the only date that corresponded to *Il Papa*'s number. It was a strange bit of

history that most members of my sacerdotal fraternity feel
should be forgotten. Or, at the very least, not taken seriously."
He handed Anne the printout from his computer.

> According to an amply examined legend, John VIII,
> the brief successor to Leo IV in 855, was Joan, an
> English woman who fell in love with a Benedictine
> monk, fled with him to Athens, and, after his death,
> continued to Rome, entering the priesthood in
> disguise and enjoying great success as Joannes
> Anglicus (John of England). The subterfuge was
> effective until she died in childbirth during a papal
> procession. Writers who declare the legend to be
> utterly without foundation have tended to be utterly
> Catholic in their outlook.

He let Anne read and reread the note. Finally she looked
up.
"May I ask, ah, Gio, what has any of this to do with me?"
Gio then told her about the Pontiff's last dream, his last
vision. He sounded embarrassed. He seemed to be grasping at
straws.
"You see, Anne, some people believe that the Holy Spirit
speaks to us with a deep, sonorous voice, commanding us to do
or not to do certain things. Well, this may be true of some
people, but it is not supported by my own experience."
Anne nodded.
"In my experience," Gio resumed, "the Spirit
communicates with us through our unconscious. It usually drops
gentle hints, and when those don't work—we ignore them—then
more forceful methods are employed on wayward sons. And
daughters," he added with a broad smile.
Anne nodded again. "I agree completely, Gio." She
mentioned how she frequently became aware of no more than an
impression, which, nevertheless, propelled her into action. She
was thinking of her trips to the forgotten souls.
"I hope you don't mind," Gio said, looking a little
embarrassed, "but Ian told me a little of what you do. He didn't

know much, but I didn't need much. A gentle whisper, a hint...."

So he knew. She'd never told anyone about her work. Except for Gabriel and Peter. But, after twenty years, both of them had had to make excuses for her absences. Something had to be said. Apparently more than she'd expected.

"Mrs. Brown. Anne. I need you to look at some of my... at some of my guests. I have about five hundred of them."

Anne sat up. "Are you referring to the person to whom I think you are referring?"

Gio began to fidget with an ornate pen on his desk. Probably a gift from one of the many dignitaries he'd met in the course of his duties.

So that was it. She was to do her thing on those dignitaries. But she felt no 'call'. No gentle whisper. No hint.

"I don't work like that, Gio. I must...."

"...get some sort of a sign. Let us agree that if you meet some of them and you do not feel any . . . any, ah, well...." he had no idea how to finish his thought.

Anne smiled. Giovanni Pesci managed to look so completely miserable, so totally lost, so absolutely over his head that she nodded.

"Of course, I will, Gio. Or course I will," she assured him. Even if it kills me.

Anne was well sensitized to human misery. She even absorbed and dispersed that which most people regarded as evil. What she had never faced was the destructive force of power. And the five hundred guests the Camerlengo had been referring to had been the most powerful men in the world. And some women....

That same evening Gio took Anne to the seminarium. The rulers of the world were accommodated, for the most part, in the Papal Palace. At the seminarium, in much humbler surroundings, resided the bishops, the cardinals and elders of different religions. They walked slowly, knocking on each door in turn, gazing inside for a brief moment, until Anne told Gio that it wasn't necessary.

"If I am to help anyone, the doors will not stand in the way, Gio," she said.

The Camerlengo nodded. "How silly of me," he apologized.

They walked for about an hour. Finally Anne asked to leave the corridors. "Let's go outside, Gio. A bit farther away."

They took a paved footpath across the Largo Santo Stefano, behind St. Peter's Basilica, all the way to the Vatican rose gardens. Had Anne been herself, she would have found it unnerving to stroll, practically hand in hand with a cardinal, on a path upon which so many successors of Peter had walked. Instead she deeply inhaled the scents, nodded at some flowers as though greeting lost friends. She kept walking, slowly, until they were a good distance away.

"That's enough," she said. "Can we sit down?" They were close to the Fountain of the Eagle. Anne pulled Gio's sleeve towards its steps.

Only then did Gio notice that Anne was struggling with her every step. He, too, was exhausted, but for very different reasons. He thought she was tired from her flight to Rome. After all, she'd only flown in this morning. By the time her limousine fought its way through the gathering crowds, it was well past noon.

"I am so sorry." He sat next to her on a stone parapet. "How very inconsiderate of me."

"It's not that," she guessed his concern.

Gio understood instantly. "You . . . you felt something?" He couldn't hide how anxious he was for his guests. How very worried.

Anne remained silent.

"Chaos," Anne whispered. She was leaning back on the bench as though trying to recover from a traumatic experience. "Just an overwhelming chaos."

* * *

15

Reunion

Peter's question was rhetorical. He was reasonably sure, but thought that it might be wiser not to antagonize the people he worked with. He told Fred Finer that he wanted to fly to Montreal. "Haven't seen my wife for longer than I care to admit," he said.

Fred Finer looked at him with a quizzical expression. "Unless I am very mistaken, young man, you've been working here for less than two weeks." The term 'young man' was supposed to help Peter relax. Finer was a few years his junior.

Peter looked up from his computer.

"Two weeks?"

"Less than two weeks," Finer assured him. "Anyway, Mrs. Brown is not at home." The moment he said it, Finer knew he'd made a mistake. He'd expressly promised to leave Anne alone.

Peter got up and walked slowly towards his employer. Instinctively, Finer took a step back. He may have been Peter's senior by position, but he was very much his junior in size.

"Please, I am sorry. Really, I am...."

Another step from Peter and he would have begun stammering. Peter continued to glare at him. "I know, we promised. And I kept my promise. We were nowhere near Mrs. Brown. Really, I swear," he said, practically blubbering.

"Then just how the hell did you know that she is not at home?" Peter's voice remained threatening.

Finer was stumped. If he told Peter, they would lose the strategic advantage of keeping eyes on both Anne's and presumably Peter's future activities. If he didn't tell him, he would probably suffer from a painful case of a broken neck. Or an extended visit to a dentist. He chose the less painful option.

"We keep tabs on Sir Ian Barton," he confessed, still looking seriously worried.

For a moment Peter was lost. That wasn't what he had been expecting.

"So you know she's in Rome again?"

"I am afraid so. But we learned it only by accident."

"And just why in the hell would you want to sneak up on Sir Ian?"

"He's in with the Camerl..." He stopped too late.

"You couldn't get your dirty hands on the Camerlengo, so you bugged Sir Ian." Peter was still fuming, but his voice was calmer. "Tell me, Freddy, just how do you shave yourself in the morning? Doesn't your face make you sick?"

For a moment Peter thought he'd gone too far. Finer's complexion assumed a reddish hue, then he swayed and sat heavily on the chair behind him. He pointed to a picture on the wall, placing his finger across his lips. Then he did the same with the lamp, the telephone, the computer and the TV. He smiled sadly.

"We were doing our job, Peter. It may have escaped your notice that we are at the Pentagon."

Peter preferred not to comment on that. If Finer's mime referred to bugging devises in his own office, they probably both should refrain from expressing their sentiments on just about any subject.

"I am flying to Rome," Peter said instead. "I would appreciate a first class seat ASAP."

Finer nodded in resignation. "I'll try to get you one."

He looked like a dog that was getting thrown out because he'd peed on the carpet. I am not made for this spy game, he thought. I can wheel and deal, but not this.

He need not have worried. The dice had been cast, and everybody was much too busy to care what he or Peter or Anne did. Now or ever.

The President was nearing the endgame.

Dinner was served in the breakfast room of the hotel that took its name from its location. Hotel Veneto. Sir Ian had decided that if Anne could fly to Rome virtually on his say-so, then the least he could do was show her the very best sight in Rome. Had Rome offered a rotating restaurant atop a hundred-story building, Sir Ian would have been defeated. But until some misguided architect aided by a gaudy developer constructed one, his famous Hotel Veneto would remain unparalleled in the tourist vista department.

Anne, as she was now becoming quite used to, had been delivered into Sir Ian's arms by a limousine, which Cardinal Pesci had placed at her disposal.

"I don't expect my guests to rent cars when visiting Rome," he'd dismissed the matter with a wave of his hand. "And anyway, those same limousines are here to serve some two hundred cardinals, archbishops, bishops and other VIPs. Right now, they are all standing idle."

For Anne, the way she had been treated since her arrival struck more echoes of her former days as a concert violinist than any of her own attempts at rediscovering links with her past. She was picked up, driven, almost carried, fed, assigned the best rooms, and generally offered the best that the Vatican and Rome could provide. Actually, the room she had been assigned at the Vatican wasn't that great, but she was well aware of the temporary shortage of accommodations.

And now Sir Ian was taking over the pampering of his adopted child.

"I had to do it," he started defensively. "Gio had never asked me a favour before, whereas he'd granted me many. It was thanks to him that I met John Paul, and he was one of the most fascinating people I've met in my life. And, as you well know, my dear Anne, I've met many."

Sir Ian was lonely. People who live alone tend to talk more. They feel the need to share their accumulated thoughts, observations and conclusions with someone. Anyone. And Anne, in addition, was a woman he loved.

"Sit down, my child," he said, drawing a chair back for Anne to face the best view in town.

Sir Ian, no longer very agile, remained a perfect gentleman. In the past, he would have acted likewise, but his principal motivation would have been an inherent need to flirt. He did so shamelessly with every beautiful woman he ever met. But not with Anne. First, when he met Anne she was a mere child. And second, one doesn't flirt with a priceless jewel. For him, Anne always was and will forever remain just that. An object of admiration, of unconditional love, a girl on whom he could bestow all his unrequited paternal instincts.

Anne, on the other hand, admired Sir Ian with almost as strong a deference. He, after all, had made her what she had become, once. A nova, a supernova, that shone with a light unsurpassed in our galaxy. She came and went like a galactic comet that shed its beauty on earth and sped on into the outer reaches, never to return again.

In a way, Anne owed Sir Ian everything. She was sure that there were countless talents that remained undiscovered throughout the world. Many years ago she'd asked Sir Ian who, in his view, was the greatest tenor alive.

"I don't know, dear, he hasn't been discovered yet." Anne recalled his beaming smile. It was so terribly open in those days. "The same is true of the best soprano, the best baritone...." he'd added.

"I get the picture," she had said.

And then Sir Ian had looked at her long and hard. His eyes were so intense she'd thought at the time that she'd done something wrong.

"But I have discovered the greatest violinist. In the whole world." There was a wondrous tear of melancholy somewhere in his voice. It seemed to say, 'I found her and I lost her....'

For a while they sat in silence as Anne absorbed the twinkling lights of the Eternal City from the Hotel Veneto. The six hills rose out of an ocean of tiny sparks glittering in the moonlight. Shimmering like giant waves frozen in immobility. Countless vehicles, insignificant fireflies, moved to and fro, trembling, disappearing around corners . . . their kin reappearing elsewhere, always busy, determined, never resting. And against this shimmering backdrop rose the glistening dome of Saint Peter's, steadfast, unmoving, reassuring.

"Thirty years?" Sir Ian asked softly.

"It's more like three hundred. It was a different age. A different era. People were all young, in those days. We all were. Even you, Ian," she added with a twinkle in her eye.

Sir Ian said nothing. He missed every second of those days. Twenty-five years ago, he and Anne enthralled the world. But even before her and after her, he had been invited everywhere to lead some, indeed most, of the best orchestras in the world. He was happy wherever he found a great orchestra or a beautiful woman. Preferably an up-and-coming diva. He always loved a challenge.

"And now I am o-o-old, f-f-fat and ug-g-gly," he whined dejectedly, but his eyes were filled with the same vitality. The next instant the room was reverberating with his thunderous laughter.

"You are beautiful to me," Anne whispered. She wasn't laughing. She truly loved this man.

Not one more word was said about the past. Anne recounted to him her last two years, since Sir Ian's last visit to Montreal. He had flown in just to say hello. It had been the first time that Sir Ian had actually stayed at her house, in Westmount.

"It is the only place in the whole wide world that I really feel at home," he'd said at the time.

They filled the rest of their time together with small talk. Anne briefly described her meeting with Cardinal Pesci, Gio, but they avoided 'business'. This was their evening. Theirs alone.

On a planet that was rapidly becoming turbulent, unpredictable, Sir Ian became a rock of stability. He was so firmly anchored in the past that nothing could disturb his present. He was exactly what Anne needed.

Dear Ian, she thought. Look who is the real healer now.

D r. Peter Brown was Dr. John Brent in reverse. John was a scientist turned neurosurgeon. Not that neurosurgery was not science. But not as pure as theoretical physics *per se*. It was an applied science. You didn't study the world to understand it; you applied your understanding to a specific end.

With Peter, the reverse happened. Already a proficient neurosurgeon, capable of complex operations, his hunger took him into the realm of pure physics. Waves. Waves, like quanta in quantum mechanics, pervaded his universe. With Peter, his new passion had begun with the visual cortex. As the airplane was bringing him closer to Anne, he leaned his seat back and closed his eyes. The clouds broke up the sunlight streaking through the oblong window into tiny fragments. It was shimmering in fractal oscillations, through his closed lids. The next moment, the same light pulsated through the branches of the maple tree as it swayed in his Westmount garden. His mind drifted to the work he did on epileptic seizures, which were often caused by such fragmented light rays. Lately he'd been working on epilepsy at the MNI.

The next moment....

Behind his eyelids he saw Anne sitting back, gazing at him with admiration. It seemed like so long ago. Ten, fifteen years? How come time loses its meaning in one's dreams? Am I really dreaming? He recalled the time when he first attempted to share with Anne his new interest. They had been sitting in the garden, enjoying the sunset. The children had just left for some extracurricular activities. He and Anne were enjoying one of those rare moments alone.

"Our eyes react to photons." He could almost hear his own voice. He sounded a little pompous. He had been very proud of the knowledge he'd gained outside his immediate specialty.

Then he saw Anne again. Her eyes had grown larger. "Larger eyes react to larger photons," he affirmed in a grave tone. Then he smiled.

"Photons are quanta of electromagnetic energy. The vast range of the electromagnetic waves includes, *inter alia*, X-rays, gamma rays, radio and television waves as well as what we know as light."

"I like the television ones," Anne put in.

"The waves range from lengths greater than the diameter of the earth to others so short that a billion strung together would barely span the width of your fingernail."

Anne took the opportunity to glance at her fingernails. She loved hearing her husband talk, even if her interests lay elsewhere.

The drone of the airplane grew monotonous. Peter continued to drift into the past.

"Sandwiched between the lengthy infrared and the extremely short ultraviolet waves is the visible spectrum, ranging from violet through blue, green, yellow and orange to red. While our bodies are affected by various waves of electromagnetic energy, our eyes recognize only this tiny amplitude."

"Why?"

"A good question indeed. There is a good reason for this."

Anne looked as proud as Punch.

"We think that the human eye operates on principles similar to a camera. That we take a mental picture and store it in memory for later use. This is true only in part. The retina is not a uniform surface. Only a tiny portion can absorb information in any detail. Only about one-hundredth of the visual field can absorb an image with any precision."

He saw his own eyes shining like stars in the evening dusk. Dreams are like that. You can see yourself. In great detail. In dreams you see with your spiritual eyes.

"This area contains special light-sensitive cells." His voice droned in his head in perfect harmony with the airplane jets complementing each other. "The rest of the retina transfers its impression of whole groups of cells, but they offer much less detail. Thus, though a single glance offers an impression, thousands of coordinated eye movements, up and down and sidewise, are needed to scan a landscape or a painting in any detail."

Dear Anne... how sweet she looked in the evening light....

"...we must transfer this information to the section of the cortex, about two inches square, at the back of the head, through the optic nerve consisting of about one million fibers of rods and cones... the impulses last a tenth of a second... then the cortex is made available to the rest of the brain for cognition...."

The droning was getting louder.

"Impulses?" Her voice sounded like music.

"Like in a movie, giving an impression of continuity. Or like an AC current...."

The drone was continuous, but surely it consisted of individual impulses of vibration.

"If there were a direct neural connection between the million visual fibers and the ten thousand million neurons of the rest of the brain, our cranium would boil..."

Peter laughed in his sleep.

"Or our head would have to be as large as a house...."

"Is everything all right, Sir?"

A stewardess leaned over Peter. He opened one eye, winked and tried to get back to sleep. It didn't work. The link with the other reality had been broken.

Now in a semi-awakened state, he thought of saints and mystics who spoke of witnessing beauty beyond the comprehension of mere mortals. Some said the same thing after experimenting with mescaline. Others, like Castaneda, wrote books about what they saw after eating mushrooms....

Peter also recalled the words of a mystic saint of present-day India. 'I sit in the light,' he'd said. 'The light is me. I am the light.'

Perhaps.

But Peter's initial passion for light had been changed by Anne. Not at her request, but by her very existence. What others did with the visual cortex, Peter had decided to do with our hearing response. Since meeting Anne, he'd spent his career learning how sound affected the working of our brain.

Cardinal Giovanni Pesci felt terribly alone. He had a dozen secretaries, five nuns and some other willing clerics ready to act at his every beckoning. But he felt lonely. He had no one with whom to share his decisions. Committees of Cardinals invariably took all the decisions at the Vatican. Strength in numbers. Or at least a modicum of safety. Only the Pope made unilateral decisions. But unlike the Pope, Cardinal Pesci didn't feel infallible. He felt very alone.

"It's not work that gets you tired," he recalled an adage he'd heard at Oxford. "It's all them decisions." Some years ago a fellow student had delivered these words of wisdom in an exaggerated Cockney accent.

Many a truth is spoken in jest, Gio mused. But it didn't help. Would Anne? Had the Holy Father seen in Anne some gift, some talent that would help him in his cross?

Gio Pesci was a man who took life in his stride. He didn't dwell on mysteries. He didn't believe that you must spend hours meditating on the Church's teaching. 'Just live', was his dictum. Restore order. Restore balance. Don't push.

Restore order?

Just days ago the world and his world of the Vatican seemed so orderly. He'd organized the funeral, assigned duties for the cardinals, made sure all was going to work smoothly. Then, listening to the joyful cries of the milling masses chanting *sancto, sancto subito,* he might have indulged in some sadness, an indulgence for which he had had no time so far. '*Sancto subito',* he repeated. Not sorrow, just emotion. *Il Papa* would have laughed.

"*Mi, sancto?*" Ah, yes, *Il Papa* would have laughed. Gio had never met a more humble man. Nor a simpler one. He simply loved people. Unconditionally.

How shall I find his successor? Will my brothers recover?
Ever?

He'd also never felt quite so helpless. Hapless? Pray, Father,
what am I to do?

There was a gentle knock on his door. He never locked it.
He even left it ajar. There was no one who could enter
unannounced. There was no one left.

"Yes, Guido?" he said, expecting it to be his principal
secretary—an elderly priest who had been too weak to sit outside
during the ceremonies. Too many steps to negotiate. Now he was
indispensable. It seemed that God worked in mysterious ways.

"There is a young man here who says that you abducted
his wife, Your Eminence."

The gray-haired priest looked embarrassed by his own
words. He also could be misleading. At his venerable age, all
men and women under eighty were young.

"Shouldn't you show him in, then? I can always plead
guilty but insane," Gio replied. He was too tired to even wonder
who it might be. No new cranks were allowed into the Vatican.
The city was sealed off. Must be one of my own, he thought
sadly.

The door opened wider and a man in his early fifties came
in. He was tall and definitely handsome. There was an
anticipatory smile widening his mouth. He bowed slightly.

"I understand, Your Eminence, that you abducted my
wife?"

"And you must be...."

"I must be? Oh, yes. Apologies. My name is Brown. Dr.
Peter Brown. Anne's husband. Is she around?"

Camerlengo got up from his desk and stretched out his
hand.

"As I told father Guido, guilty but insane. Or almost so.
Yes, I do plead guilty. Please do sit down." His polite form of
address was a remnant of his early days in England.

"So my wife really is here?"

"Under lock and key. We all are. The whole Vatican."

"It is not contagious, Father." Peter said, looking Giovanni in the eye.

"Not... you are a scientist? A physician?"

"I am a neurosurgeon specializing in the predicament which has been inflicted on your guests without my knowledge."

The Camerlengo raised his eyes towards the ceiling. Thank you, Father, he whispered. Then he looked at his guest with penetrating eyes.

"But how on earth did you get in through the carabinieri?"

Only then did Gio notice that Guido was still standing by the door, looking extremely uncomfortable. The Camerlengo directed his penetrating eyes at the old priest, who seemed to shrink inside the black cassock.

"You were asleep, Your Eminence. I stood at the door and did not allow anyone to knock on your door until you woke up. They told me it was very important. They said Dr. Brown was very important. They didn't say why . . . I just couldn't let them wake you, Your Eminence. You haven't slept..."

"You took it upon yourself to act in direct defiance of my expressed orders?"

The old priest didn't say anything.

"And you allowed a total stranger into my office?"

For some reason Gio was clearly enjoying himself. It was true. Some hours ago he had taken a nap for a few minutes. God knows, he needed it. Guido must have been approached by the head of the Vatican security, and must have made his decision risking instant dismissal from the Holy See. He was both a brave and wise man. The Camerlengo rose from behind his desk, walked up to the old priest who by now looked close to swooning, and embraced him like a long-lost brother.

"Thank you, Guido," he said simply and turned to his desk. Even as the ancient priest finally backed out of the room, Gio saw the red, yellow and blue stripes of two Swiss Guards standing at the ready just outside the door. Evidently Peter had been given an appropriate escort.

"Tell me more, Doctor," he asked as if their conversation hadn't been interrupted.

"Not until I see my wife," Peter replied. He'd had his fill of broken promises.

The Camerlengo pressed a button on his desk. The same gray head appeared in the door.

"Guido, has Mrs. Brown returned from her dinner yet?"

The priest glanced at his watch. "I expect so, Your Eminence. I can check with Carlo." Carlo had been the liaison between Gio and Anne from day one, a week ago.

"Please do so. And if she is not too tired, you might ask her to drop in and see us."

"Here, Your Eminence?" The priest glanced at his watch again. It was past eleven. The Camerlengo had a habit of working most of the night and then getting up early. The priest didn't approve of young ladies visiting the cardinal after the usual office hours.

"Yes, Guido," Gio replied. "I promise to behave myself. Anyway, I have a chaperon," he said, looking at Peter.

Peter decided that he was going to like this man, in spite of his having abducted his one and only wife. The old priest looked only slightly mollified.

For a moment or two the men sat in silence. Then Gio asked if Peter would like some refreshments. "What time did you land?"

Peter glanced at his watch. It was a new one he'd been given by Finer. It had more buttons than his computer and a radio put together. "Exactly three hours ago. What time is it here, anyway?"

Giovanni told him. "My goodness." Suddenly Peter looked worried. "I'm not getting her out of bed, I hope."

"I doubt it very much. I rather think that Anne shall be taking a little walk tonight, before she goes to sleep. She was eating outside the Vatican tonight. She insisted." Camerlengo looked apologetic.

So Anne was up to her tricks. He wondered why she chose to move outside the protection of the walled city. Later that afternoon Peter learned that, at the time, he and Anne were the only two people allowed to come and go in and out of the Vatican.

"Actually, it was Sir Ian Barton who insisted. I owed him a favour," Gio added by way of explanation.

Just then Anne ran into the office. She didn't knock, didn't say a word. She ran into Peter's open arms. Gio looked away. Those youngsters, he thought. These two will never grow up, he mused. At least I hope not, he complemented his own thought.

Guido only now reached the open door. He stood there, his arms hanging limp at his sides, his palms up in abject resignations. His eyes were saying 'those youngsters,' but his mouth just hung open.

* * *

16

Conclave

Since the beginning of the last millennium, there had been no double beds at the Vatican. Kings', Queens' nor any other size. The Holy Church had decided that intercourse made a person unclean. As a consequence, married priests had been forbidden from celebrating the Eucharist.

In 1139, the Second Lateran Council imposed mandatory celibacy on all priests. Even those currently married had to separate from their spouses. So much for the inviolable indivisibility of the sacrament of marriage. It was a question of expediency or, simply, of good business. A married priest left at least part of his earthly satchels to his wife and children. The Church wanted to lay its hands on all of them.

The priests did not give up their acquired rights easily. Realizing that celibacy and marriages were principally guided by tradition, they continued in their unclean ways. They got married 'on the quiet', when no one was looking.

Celibacy as a requirement for priests continued to be argued until the Reformation. The reformers held that requiring an oath of celibacy from a priest was contrary to biblical teaching, implied a degradation of marriage, and was one reason for the widespread sexual misconduct within the clergy. This doctrinal consensus of the reformers can best be observed in the marriages of Zwingli in 1522, Luther in 1525, and Calvin in 1539.

The final blow against clergymen who wanted to marry
came at the Council of Trent, which took place between 1545
and 1563. Councils took a while in those days. The final
prohibition of marriage had been achieved through a
technicality. The Church had declared that for a marriage to be
valid, it had to be performed by a 'valid' priest and in front of at
least two witnesses. No witnesses—no marriage. The clandestine
marriages were out.

So were double beds in the Vatican.

Peter looked sadly at the additional bed that had been
quickly installed in Anne's room. The two beds stared at each
other across the pristine chamber, undefiled by the proximity of
two objects capable of instigating a mortal sin. The beds stood,
their curvilinear oaken legs some twelve feet apart, as though
afraid to approach any closer. With a little effort on Peter's part,
they gave up their shyness and, in all but name, became a double
bed.

Only one problem remained.

When Peter and Anne returned to their quarters, Anne
kissed him passionately and said that she would be back as soon
as she could. She hated leaving him alone after being apart for
so long but, by then, the little nagging voice was telling her that
her duty lay elsewhere. Not by her husband's side. Not yet. Alas,
by the time she returned, Peter was fast asleep. The last week in
Washington, the news from the Vatican, the long flight, and
finally the affliction that had struck hundreds of men thanks to
his invention, knocked the feet from under him. He felt as guilty
as he was tired. Sleep came as a welcome relief.

A knock on the door announced that breakfast was ready.
Peter stretched, rubbed his eyes and glanced at his watch. It was
four o'clock. Are they crazy? I am not a monk rising for the
matins, he was about to tell whoever was knocking. And why is it
already light outside?

"Come in," Anne said, her voice bright and cheerful.

The delicious aroma of freshly percolated coffee preceded a middle-aged nun in a spotlessly white habit as she wheeled in a trolley with breakfast for two.

While due to the quarantine other fresh produce was being rationed, they still had two eggs each, crisp bacon, toast, and fruit picked this morning from the Vatican gardens. Fresh flowers adorned the moving table. The nun smiled at Anne, doing her best neither to see Peter nor to notice the beds brought together. By then Peter hoped that she'd succeeded. He dove under the blankets and, leaving just a gap for the light to enter, adjusted his watch by six hours. My goodness, is it ten already?

The next time he peeked from under the covers, the nun was gone.

"How time flies when you're having fun," he said, jumping out of bed.

Peter always slept naked. In Washington he may have made history for the hidden cameras. In the Vatican, he would probably be excommunicated.

"Darling," Anne looked in horror, "cover yourself up! You're not at...."

"Not until I get my morning kiss," he commanded.

"Brush your teeth, Peter. You smell like a bag of...." She was at a loss for words.

Peter rushed to the bathroom, brushed his teeth, rushed back and took Anne in his arms. She no longer resisted. She'd waited for this as long as he had.

"The breakfast can wait," he murmured, dragging her towards the bed.

The next twenty minutes would have created history even in Washington, never mind the Vatican.

An hour later, the telephone rang.

"Would it be possible for both of you to attend a meeting with His Eminence?"

There was no need to explain who the Eminence was. There was only one left. As a matter of fact, there were two other archbishops, one cardinal and three bishops who were perfectly healthy. For their age. Their average years hovered around ninety. They had not attended the funeral or any other functions for some time. One was seldom named a prince of the Church when very young. Or even middle-aged.

Anne spoke for both of them.

"Of course. At what time, Father Carlo?" By now she recognized his voice.

"As soon as you can," Carlo replied.

"A half hour?"

"I'll tell His Eminence. He will be in his office."

Suddenly Anne felt uneasy. For some reason she detected a tone of panic in Carlo's voice. What else could have gone wrong?

"I don't think it was wise to send Peter to Rome, my friend," Linker said, looking at the illuminated wall map. As the little red dots moved away from the United States Military Harbors, the map enlarged to accommodate them. Linker loved the miracles of technology.

Fred Finer was about to open his mouth in self-defense when the President waved him down. "I don't think he can do us much harm, but it sets a precedent."

Finer understood. If Peter could leave his post, scientific or otherwise, so could others.

America had been placed under Code Five. That meant war footing. It was a complex enough situation. Code Five gave the President the authority to order the Military Forces to act under his command. After all, he was the Commander in Chief. On the other hand, no war had been declared on any country. As such, the President did not have to engage the Congress or the Senate in the decision-making process. As long as he didn't order the navy to fire any weapons, John Linker stood on solid ground.

Of course, Joshua Rosengart couldn't control all the media. He controlled the majority, but by no means all of them. Questions had been asked on air, in some daily newspapers, and even among the 'ordinary' people: what exactly was going on? Was the USA expecting a major attack from the terrorists? Were people in major cities in imminent danger? Are we threatened yet again?

And what of the reputedly long defunct Al-Qaeda?

Since the demise of the USSR and the end of the fear of the Cold War, the Government of the United States had been looking for a way to control people. The ever-present threat of communism had provided ample opportunity to experiment with new weaponry, to amass a great stock of nuclear missiles, to maintain military bases around the world. Since the collapse of communism in the USSR, it had become extremely difficult to justify the tax base that spent countless billions on the military. At the same time, no President was willing to concede that the USA was no longer the top banana in the world. Military or otherwise.

"We are the defenders of the faith," the Church used to say.

"We are the defenders of democracy," the United States echoed.

"We are the defenders of the American Way," John Linker modified the last aphorism. It sounded more inspiring to the constituents.

People needed aphorisms, slogans, maxims. "That's all they really understand," Linker told Finer some time ago. "Give them a Cause with a capital C, and they'll come a-running. You don't persuade them. You inspire them."

Fred Finer was listening. He felt it dishonest to oppose the then Vice President when he had nothing better to offer. Politics was a dirty game, he knew, but what was the alternative? Love thy neighbour? That didn't get anyone very far. Nor did 'thou shalt not kill'. People loved killing, no matter how much they denied it. They would shoot at anything that moved. Especially if it proved edible. If it was the only way to eliminate their enemies, their competition, and they could get away with it, the vast majority would resort to murder.

This was where Frederick Finer admired John Linker the most. Not necessarily for his political strategies, but for his concept of fair play. The President believed that we lived in a cruel world. That Mother Nature was unforgiving, untempered by any moral or ethical considerations. But the world at large, and Mother Nature in particular, was scrupulously fair. A tornado killed the rich and the poor. The tsunami destroyed the hotels owned by the rich as well as shantytowns with equal determination. It did not play favourites. Nor did the forest fires, the earthquakes, the plagues, the extremes of temperature, or even the giant meteorites with which the scientific fraternity liked to scare people half to death.

"People love to be scared," Linker said. "Otherwise, they get bored."

As usual, Finer kept silent. Not for the first time did he have to admit to himself that he was scared, just a little, of the President. Yet, for some reason, he hadn't resigned. He could make a good living at any university in the land. But the vague outline of a Damoclean sword kept him on his toes. He felt sharper, more alive. Perhaps all people were like that, even if they were not aware of it.

The President, and the presidents before him, welcomed the concept of terrorism with open arms. At last they had an excuse to continue upholding the unparalleled might of the United States. No leader wanted to be the one under whose reign the Empire of North America, the greatest empire the world had ever known, would die. Linker believed that the time had come to introduce the American Way to the rest of the world.

Or else....

The purpose of the Conclave is to decide the future of the Church. In Latin *con* means *with*, *clavis—a key*. Within locked doors. Under lock and key. The cardinals gather together in a *conclave* to elect a new Pope. There was historical precedent why such elections had been held *con clave*. The principal of them was secrecy. No one was to interfere with the process. The stakes were too high. Bribery, violence and sex scandals sullied the history of succession.

The reigns of Popes Sergius III, John XII, Leo V, Alexander VI, Stephen VI, and a number of other pontiffs had better be left

forgotten. Their history was too bloody. Too ungodly. Too sad.
All empires had their dark moments, and the Church was no
exception.

Things changed. Slowly. Later there were rules, and more
rules, which forestalled such scars as were borne by the Church's
past.

Never again, Pope John Paul II had said while introducing
additional regulations just a few decades ago. Never again,
thought Cardinal Pesci. Only . . . what am I to do?

The Camerlengo, like his brethren throughout the whole
Catholic world, was still in mourning. He would remain so until
the *novemdiales* were over. Nine days after the Pontiff's death
the College of Cardinals was to begin its deliberations in a series
of secret meetings to elect the new Pope. Only now—there were
no cardinals. Not cardinals capable of entering the deliberations.
No cardinal bishops, no cardinal priests nor even cardinal
deacons. All their minds were shut off to the outside world. They
were held, inexorably, in a greater conclave of secrecy than the
Camerlengo could ever have imposed on them.

"In three days' time we are supposed to start the
Conclave," he announced after warmly greeting Peter and Anne.
"On Thursday we are to begin electing the new Pope."

He spread his arms wide, as though searching for answers in
the thin air.

"I need your help," the Camerlengo continued when Anne
and Peter remained silent.

There was a desperate plea in his voice. He searched Peter
and Anne's faces, then his eyes drifted, absentmindedly, around
the room. Early Renaissance portraits adorning the walls of his
office didn't shed any light on his dilemma, either. Their dark
eyes peered back at Giovanni from under the red birettas—cold,
penetrating, strangely indifferent.

For Anne, the previously joyful Gio was painful to behold.
The man, already small, appeared to have shrunk even more. He
seemed to be imploding under the weight placed on his narrow
shoulders.

For a reason she couldn't understand, she chose this moment to repeat the words Gabriel had spoken to Peter as he was about to leave for Washington.

"If you are to know something, you will," she said, her voice seemingly distant. "It is quite unavoidable."

The Camerlengo sat up in his chair. He looked at Anne as one would at a bright ray of sunshine on an overcast day. Concentration was now clearly etched on his drawn face.

"You really believe that, don't you," he said slowly. "This is exactly what John Paul told me. Word for word," he said, shaking his head as if questioning his own memory. "Word for word," he repeated.

"The question is when," Peter put in, dousing the new hope.

"When the time is right," Anne added, completing the previous statement.

"When the time is right," Gio repeated her words, ignoring Peter's comment. "When will the time be right?"

There was a momentary silence. Then Peter chuckled. The Camerlengo was slipping in his logic. You relied either on mental faculties or on faith. You could not do both simultaneously. It was like trying to be a Darwinist and a creationist at the same time. Anne knew that, and she never tried. The Cardinal, very illogically, was attempting to have his cake and eat it too. He looked at Peter with gratitude.

"What a funny world we live in when a scientist teaches a man of cloth the proper attitude towards faith," he said, his mouth widening in his old, familiar smile. "Thank you, Doctor," he added.

"Peter."

"Gio."

They both reached over the desk simultaneously and shook hands. Anne looked delighted. She knew, as only Anne was capable of knowing, that the two men would soon be friends. As usual, she was right.

"Tie the camels to the palm tree and pray to Allah that no one steals them," Gio said.

"I'm sorry. What?" Peter asked, looking sideways at Anne.

The Camerlengo laughed at himself. "It's an old proverb of sorts. A caravan driver asked a sage if he should tie the camels to a tree, or just pray that they would not wander away and be stolen. The sage said tie the camels to the palm tree and pray to Allah that no one steals them." Gio laughed again. "Religious humour, I guess," Gio said, seeing the looks of confusion on Peter's and Anne's faces.

"What can we do?" he asked no one in particular. "While we wait for the right time," he added, looking at Peter.

It was about then that Peter began to feel uncomfortable. He began avoiding Gio's eyes, pulled his hand away when Anne rested her finger on it. He began fidgeting. No matter how much I delay it, I have to tell them. Both. In detail. Only, I don't really understand it all myself, he brooded silently.

Then he cleared his throat.

"You both seemed to approach the problem as though it were some kind of an act of God," he began.

Gio and Anne said nothing. They were willing to let Peter add his knowledge to theirs.

"There are some things that are purely of man's making," Peter said darkly. He continued to avoid meeting their eyes. "And man must bear the consequences," he added, as though making a formidable announcement.

Gio smiled. "All acts are the acts of God, Peter. He acts through us. We are His instruments."

"Then He is responsible for . . . for the condition of your guests."

No one spoke. Peter rose to his feet, ostensibly ready to get out of this meeting. Then he appeared to change his mind.

"I alone am responsible for what happened," he blurted out, looking straight at the Camerlengo. "I and no one else."

"Sit down, darling," Anne whispered. "You are among friends."

"I won't be when you both hear what I have to say." He lowered his voice but couldn't hide his sense of desperation. "If only I hadn't been so stupid...."

He began pacing the length of the Camerlengo's office.

"It is true that I am responsible, although I had nothing to do with the actual execution of the dastardly deed."

"The dastardly deed?" There was a little twinkle in Gio's eye; his voice was as calm as a village pond on a summer's eve.

Peter relaxed. He sat down and proceeded to describe the nature of his work. It sounded like a confession rather than a proud report of his scientific achievement. Anne knew most of it but was surprised by how far the work he had done at the Pentagon deviated from what he had told her in Montreal.

"You see, Gio," he also glanced at Anne, "the whole idea of my work was to narrow the beam in order to affect individual groups of neurons. To affect the minimum number, to switch them off, so to speak, and then allow nature to take its course. We have an amazing facility for self-repair—if we don't interfere with the self-healing mechanism of our immune system."

"And at the Pentagon, you were asked to do the opposite?"

"Not exactly. But I was asked to attempt to affect the neurons of a group of people at the same time. The nature of the ultrasonic beam would still affect only very specialized neurons, but its effect would be completely unpredictable."

"And how long would the self-healing process take?" Gio asked.

"That's just the point. We don't know. In case of the Pentagon subjects, it did not really matter. They were trying to overcome the effects of battle fatigue. In a way, the longer it took, the better. It would enable the patients, the ex-combatants, to build up new resistance, to see the world through the eyes of the present rather than the past," Peter said.

Anne noticed that her husband's previous appearance of shame and compunction was being replaced by his scientific zeal. Peter was as committed to his work as ever. For now, his desire to find a solution to the problem had overridden his sense of guilt.

"So, in your opinion, all my . . . guests will recover?"

"Undoubtedly," he replied at once. His voice did not carry as much confidence as he tried to express with his face. "Undoubtedly," he repeated, more softly.

Gio sighed. "So we are back to square one?"

"Not quite." Peter looked at Anne. "Not quite, Gio. We have Anne." This time the full weight of guilt returned to his voice and his face. "I'm sorry, darling. I truly am." He couldn't quite look her in the eyes.

She patted his hand. This time he didn't withdraw it.

"Could one of you let me in on your secret?" Gio asked.

Peter and Anne looked at each other. "You tell the Cardinal what you know. I can never describe it adequately even to myself."

Peter took a deep breath. "Well, you know I told you that my ultrasonic beam is intended to affect certain memory cells and thus to remove latent negative sentiments encoded in the brain and allow nature to heal the organism? Well, this is almost exactly what Anne does. In her own way. She seems to take upon herself the 'negativity', for want of a better word, the dross that people accumulate over the years, and this allows the natural healing process to cope with the remainder. At least, that is what I think she does."

"Tie the camel to a tree and pray to Allah," Gio said after a while. "May God bless both of you." Gio sounded as though he really meant it.

A knock on the door interrupted them. The Camerlengo did not have the luxury normally allotted to the College of Cardinals during their deliberations. Conclave also meant no interruptions. The Camerlengo was interrupted continually. Father Guido's gray head appeared in the crack of the door.

"I have the Queen of Jordan on line one, Your Eminence. She will not put down the telephone until she speaks to you. There is also the Deputy Chairman of the People's Republic of China on line two and," Guido glanced at his notes, "Abd Al-Aziz bin Al Saud, I believe, of Saudi Arabia, on line three."

"It has begun," Gio said slowly, letting all the air out of his lungs like a man who had just taken his last breath. He stood up and turned towards the window. Usually, by this time, the Square of St. Peter was filled with people—pilgrims eager to visit the Basilica. Today the square was empty. At the far end, two rows of guards, their weapons drawn, stood shoulder to shoulder, protecting the safety of the dignitaries abiding uneasily in the Camerlengo's care.

The Cardinal's diminutive body was silhouetted against the morning sun. The light streamed in, refusing to pass through him. For an instant, Anne had a fleeting image of the young Cardinal standing at the gate of the Garden of Gethsemane.

* * *

17

A Matter of Choice

It had never been a question of needing one hundred days. Finer's exercise in historical achievements squeezed into a specific time period had been compiled for the purpose of amusement. When John Linker had said that he had managed to squeeze his Plan into ninety-eight days, he was thinking of the world returning to normal functioning, as expressed and supported by the American Way. He needed hardly more than three weeks to make his Plan operational.

Linker and Finer were once again sitting in deep leather armchairs, gazing at the twelve-by-eight wall screen. Linker was playing with his laser pointer, showing Fred various points of interest. The President's points of interest had nothing to do with the usual tourist hot spots. The tiny light from the pointer danced along the continents, indicating destinations where 'stronger' action might prove necessary.

"They will all be given a chance to comply," the President said grimly. There was an unspoken 'or else' hanging in the air.

Fred Finer wiggled his body deeper into the armchair. He was starting to feel quite uncomfortable about being the President's chief ear. By contrast, John Linker often called him to his presence three times a day. Not to lounge in front of the wall screen, but to refresh his own memory on something or other. It was evident that, under a mask of studied indifference, the President needed someone to talk to. Someone who would listen, preferably without interrupting his train of thought.

"And if they don't?" Finer asked a full minute later.

Linker waved the question away.

"Let us be pragmatic, my friend. They have everything to gain, and all to lose," he said in the same voice he would use to offer Finer another cup of tea. But Finer knew better. There was a veiled threat in his composed tone of voice. John Linker was at his most dangerous when he appeared calmest.

Finer still wasn't sure what the President had in mind. The President trusted no one. Neither his immediate entourage, nor his wife nor children. Yes, he did have children, though since Finer had met him, Linker had never spoken about them. Finer didn't ask. Enough said, the President didn't trust his own shadow.

"There are always ways of finding out what you want to know," Linker once told him when Finer asked an inopportune question. "I would not want to scramble your gray cells," he added with a twisted smile. Pentothal sodium, or sodium ethylthiobarbiturate, when injected intravenously, acted as an anesthetic but also a hypnotic. In a hypnotic state, information could be extracted from the subject without his or her conscious knowledge. There had been cases, however, when excessive amounts of the drug had caused permanent damage.

Evidently there must have been people who would go a long way to discover what was in Linker's head. The only 'head' in the world still functioning. The only 'head' wielding power.

"So they have no choice?" Finer trod carefully.

"We always have a choice. We all have God-given free will. It's just that most of us usually prefer not to suffer the consequences of our actions."

Finer wondered what would happen to Linker if his plan, whatever it ultimately proved to be, leaked out. Who was there who could, even then, oppose him? Were there really men milling around the President with orders to protect him every second of his life? There was the CIA, of course, and the FBI, and the combined Central Security Force—the Homeland

Security—created by Twigg's predecessor, but would they all prove loyal? Under all circumstances? Presidents had been assassinated before. In the US of A—quite frequently.

Fred Finer felt intermittently hot and cold. Like a woman having an attack of hot flashes and cold feet simultaneously. He kept twisting in the sensual embrace of his sumptuous armchair. He crossed and uncrossed his legs. Every few minutes, his hand reached out for a handkerchief to wipe his forehead, which remained perfectly dry. John Linker remained perfectly relaxed.

"Is there absolutely nothing you can do?" Anne gazed into Peter's eyes, searching for a ray of hope. "Isn't there an antidote to your . . . your death ray?"

"I do not have a death ray, darling. As for an antidote? Unless you know how to unscramble eggs...." Peter replied, doing his utmost to relieve the tension that the meeting with the Camerlengo had introduced between them. "I didn't participate in this subterfuge consciously, darling. You know that?"

"That's what they all said after they dropped the bomb on Hiroshima."

"I did not design a bomb. I designed a cure for a very specific neuro-pathological condition." Peter was gasping for air. He felt like a man who needed help, while drowning, and he was refused even a straw.

He could have told her that in Montreal he'd already had some positive results. The method was still experimental, but there were signs of great future applications. *Future* applications. That is the nature of research. You test and test and test, and one day, if you're lucky, you get positive results. Well, he'd been lucky already. But not in applying the projector to groups of people, let alone masses.

On the other hand, Peter had seen what toll the daily, or rather nightly, visits to the prelates and dignitaries had exacted on Anne. This was the fifth night that she had spent most of her time wandering the dark corridors. Sometimes she came to bed, once or twice, only to leave an hour or two later for another round.

She was making rounds, he thought. Even as I should be doing, right now, at the MNI. Rather than playing with instruments that evil men can exploit for their own benefit. At this he swung to face Anne. He'd been avoiding looking at her for the last twenty-four hours.

"Why do you think they did it?" he asked.

"What?"

"Someone, probably Linker, put the heads of the world to sleep. Why?"

"Didn't that make him the President?"

"There are easier ways. He must have had some sort of plan. A way to exploit the situation."

"But how?"

"I asked first," Peter said. "I think we ought to have another powwow with the Camerlengo."

"He's already swamped." Anne sounded worried. The man she'd met at dinner with the late Pontiff hardly a week ago was gone. What remained was his shadow.

"I don't think we have a choice." Peter spoke as if thinking of something else. "Tell me, Anne, if you were to concentrate on just a few of your, ah, patients, would you expect results sooner?"

"I never expect results. Sooner or later. The results are not up to me."

"Nevertheless...."

"Who would choose those who are more worthy than others of my . . . of what I am doing? Or trying to do?" Anne was never good at describing her work. She'd always said that she was a channel and that was all. She didn't judge, she didn't impose. She took upon herself their . . . their weakness, she called it. Or dross.

Peter crossed the room and gently took Anne in his arms. "I know, darling. I know. You need rest. It won't be long now...."

"What do you mean it won't be long now? I'll keep doing what I'm doing till the day I die...." And for some reason her eyes filled with tears. "I'm tired, Peter. I am so very tired."

He let her cry. "They are s-s-so w-weak, tho-o-ose m-men. So s-s-selfish."

Two hundred sacerdotal elders who claimed divine guidance and the other dignitaries who usurped and held power by the efficacy of their political skills. Selfish? Peter recalled a verse from long, long ago: 'Ye serpents, ye generation of vipers, how can ye escape the damnation of hell?' On the other hand there was Gio. Wasn't he as good a man as you could find?

"It might work," Anne said, drying her eyes.

"What, dear?"

"Your idea. About concentrating on just a few. Perhaps thirty or forty. Only don't ask me to make the selection."

Peter nodded. "We have to see Gio. He's the only one qualified to decide."

At least Peter hoped so. The Camerlengo seemed like an extremely able man. Knowledge tempered by love towards man amounted to wisdom. And they needed wisdom. An error might prove fatal to the whole world.

They couldn't see the Cardinal. "Not tonight," said Carlo. "The Camerlengo is swamped with countless telephone calls. Perhaps early tomorrow?"

"Swamped by second fiddles, demanding the release of their precious dignitaries," Peter murmured.

They went out into the garden. Anne could probably get permission to make a tour of Rome, but she wasn't in the mood. She knew what was coming that evening. That night. She wanted to sit in the garden and smell the flowers. They walked slowly, arm in arm, along the noble Renaissance wall of the Apostolic Library, along *Stradone dei Giardini*. Then west, along the Carriage Museum, then turned south along *Viale del Giardino quadrato*. Finally they sat down at the Fountain of the Eagle, where Anne had rested with Gio on the day of her arrival.

The gardens were immaculate. The footpaths had been swept, the hedges clipped, the lawns manicured to perfection.

Even the flowers looked freshly watered. But there was never any sign of a gardener. Anywhere. They witnessed only the trails he left behind. The heads of the world may have been out of commission, but the body of the world was continuing to function.

"Remember the Ayrshire roses Gabriel planted in our garden? They are just like these." She pointed to a row a few feet away. Her eyes grew misty. "Di loved them so much...."

"She still loves them, darling. So do you. We all do. This...." His arms made a wide sweep of the surroundings. "This is just a dream. A chimera."

Only it wasn't. It was terribly yet magnificently real.

They sat on the stone steps, Peter's hand drawn protectively over Anne's shoulders. They talked about their children, about Anne's parents. Both of Peter's parents were dead. Not from old age. An outbreak of Asian flu got to them. His mother had refused inoculation. She hated injections of any sort. His father kept her company. They wanted it that way. They were seldom apart. They left together also.

O n the eighth day after the funeral, BBC reported unusual movements of the US Navy. RTF, *La Radiodiffusion-Télévision Française*, confirmed the data. Next came the National Radio and TV of the People's Republic of China. The last was the South American Continent. Brazil, Argentina and Venezuela were 'surprised'. They seemed preoccupied with the situation in the Vatican.

Various warships, notably aircraft carriers, were reported in the vicinity of the territorial waters of a number of countries. Three of the said countries demanded immediate explanations from Washington.

"We consider the presence of such vessels in such proximity to our territorial waters as an aggressive act towards our sovereignty," said the Brazilian ambassador in Washington.

The US Secretary of Defense replied that the President, together with a number of other Presidents, including the

President of Brazil himself, was indisposed and under the protection of and within the jurisdiction of the Sovereign State of the Vatican. Would the Vice President of the Government of Brazil kindly direct his request to the President, c/o the US Diplomatic Mission in the Vatican, who might be in a position to contact the President and answer the Brazilian Vice President's concerns.

Other diplomatic notes delivered to the White House were more explicit. "We demand to know the intention of the United States of America, *etc., etc., etc.*"

"Let them demand," Linker murmured. "Soon, we shall place a demand or two."

The responses signed by the US Undersecretary of State at John Linker's instruction were courteous, equally as explicit and completely inane.

Not even Catholics knew that the Vatican was a sovereign country. Only under President Reagan had the US extended official diplomatic status to the Holy See. It was a little unfortunate that the status that the Vatican presently enjoyed had come into existence as a result of a Concordant and Treaty signed between the Pope and the fascist regime of Benito Mussolini, a close buddy of Adolf Hitler, not that many years ago. The treaty had given the Vatican geographical autonomy over some forty-four square kilometers on the west bank of the Tiber.

The Church went into business by itself and for itself.

Many wished it never had.

"We should cater to the needs of the soul, not of the body," the late Pontiff had declared *ex cathedra*. No one had listened.

Coincidentally, Mussolini also helped to establish the Church's own bank, under the quaint name of *Instituto per le Opere di Religione*, which translated to 'Institute for Religious Works.' The *Instituto* does not make its financial transactions public.

But the Vatican's physical size was vastly exceeded by its political influence. While it did not have a vote on the Security

Council of the United Nations, it was the only religious group in the world recognized not only as a religious but also as a political and diplomatic entity. The Pope maintained diplomatic relations with 182 countries and 58 international organizations. And the Pontiff ran all this on a budget smaller than that of the Catholic University of Notre Dame in Indiana. A truly efficient organization. The various charges of the Holy See composed the Curia. The Curia, in turn, consisted of the *Secretaria Apostolica*, the Secretariat of State, the Congregations—mostly dealing with the affairs of Doctrine of the Faith, the Tribunals, the Pontifical Councils, various Offices covering the areas of Patrimony, Economic Affairs, Pontifical Household and Liturgical Celebrations. There were also eleven Pontifical Commissions, the Swiss Guard, the Pontifical Academies, Labour Office, and a number of lesser institutions.

Normally, the Secretariat of State, headed by the Cardinal Secretary of State, would perform all the political and diplomatic functions of the Holy See. At the moment, however, this same Cardinal Secretary didn't know much. He was desperately trying to discover who he really was.

The next day the United Nations Security Council sat in session. The representative of the United States of America was notably absent. The US ambassador was nowhere to be found. The other members of the Council wanted to call the ambassador from the Vatican. They realized, in abject embarrassment, that the Vatican did not have an ambassador.

The members disbanded after two hours without drawing any conclusions.

"It will not work," Gio said. "It is not a question of whom we most need, only who are most in need of Anne's particular talent." Gio was quite adamant. For the first time Peter realized that he was not dealing with power such as Washington's. The Camerlengo was guided by quite different principles altogether.

"But, Gio..." Peter began.

"Give me an alternative," the Camerlengo interrupted. He'd made up his mind.

Peter looked at Anne.

"I cannot do more," she said, looking down at her hands resting on her lap. "I really can't," she repeated apologetically.

"No one expects you to, my dear." Gio's voice changed diametrically. His tone of command changed to that of a concerned friend. Having heard thousands of confessions, he had some idea what it meant to be exposed to other people's weaknesses. He imagined that Anne's ministrations cost her a great deal more.

"It's just that they . . . that they are more helpless than any people I've ever met," she said, looking up, searching Gio's face for an explanation.

"You, from what I've heard from Sir Ian, minister to people who've lost their way. They were vulnerable but they did not actually walk in the, ah... in the opposite direction, so to speak. These people...." He spread his arms.

"These people think, or thought, that they knew exactly what they were doing," Anne finished for the Camerlengo. "They were quite incapable of thinking in any other way."

"Which?" Peter asked. "The priests or laity?"

Anne kept silent for a long time. The silence stretched until it became uncomfortable for all three.

"You must answer, my dear. Don't mind me. I've heard many confessions," Gio assured her.

Anne's eyes grew even sadder. "Both," she whispered. "Both. The priests and the laity, as Peter calls them. There is simply no difference. Men in both groups seem obsessed, and in both groups they forgot what they were obsessed about. Does this make sense, Gio?"

The Cardinal looked at her like a man who was as lonely as he was desperate.

"This is what power does to you, my dear. Hatred is not the opposite of love. Power is...." His eyes searched the somber faces on the wall. The only cardinals who kept him company. The Princes of the Church returned his stare. There was a mixture of indifference and sardonic contempt etched on their features. It shimmered in all their eyes. The artists who had painted the portraits had reached beyond mere photographic impressions. They delved into the cardinals' souls.

Peter looked away. There was pain on Giovanni's face. He was beginning to understand what Anne was going through. In the past, she had been exposed to such dilemmas just periodically. Now, it was night after night. She was submerged in human folly.

"They say," Gio spoke slowly, sounding as though he were thinking aloud, "that power corrupts, that absolute power corrupts absolutely. More often than not, we cite this expression without analyzing its deeper meaning. Why does power corrupt? Were all our kings and princes, our presidents and ministers, yes—our popes and bishops as well as mullahs and preachers, and other men and women wielding power . . . were they all corrupt?" Always? He looked at Anne, then at Peter, a sad smile softening his face. Sadness replaced the pain that had been there before. He then sat up straight.

"If the answer is yes, then how does this corruption manifest itself?" he asked, looking from one to another.

Hearing no answer, he continued.

"What is power, anyway?" The Camerlengo got up and started pacing his office. Physically he looked really small, yet his presence dominated the large chamber. "We associate power with birthright, prerogative, privilege, right, management, ascendancy, dominance, dominion, sovereignty, influence, prestige, force, strength... we are beginning to tread on dangerous ground. Power is also synonymous with authority, command, control, domination, jurisdiction, mastery, might, strings, sway, supremacy, superiority... leading directly to corruption of one who practices such on one's neighbour." He stopped in front of Peter. "But only *leading* to corruption. After all, there are many who wish to be led, who need to be controlled or at least restrained, who wish to live under the jurisdiction of a powerful Authority. Look at our guests. We must exercise a degree of power over some four hundred of our guests," he said, spreading his arms in utter helplessness.

"Hardly your fault, Gio," Peter's voice brimmed with guilt. He wanted to say your 'choice' and it came out as 'fault'.

Gio smiled his understanding. "And one may also wish to exercise mastery over one's own weaknesses," he said gently. "Still, we are now walking on very dangerous ground...."

For a moment the Camerlengo seemed lost in thought, then his face took on a strange pallor.

"We can now hear a distinct sound of suction as we steer our boots through the quagmire, laden with self-righteousness." His own words sounded painful to him. "As I am sure Anne will tell us, the corruptive influence of power is not in how we apply it towards others, but what it does to us. To our psyche. It riles the waters of our minds, it distorts our vision, pollutes our soul. Why? Surely, we've all heard about the Power of Love?"

Gio returned to his desk. He sat down heavily.

"Well, my friends," he said, his mouth widening in a sad smile, "as we have already established, this is an oxymoron. Power is the opposite of love. Even as absolute power is the opposite of unconditional love."

Throughout this tirade, Anne had sat in silence, lost in her own thoughts. Now she looked up. Her face looked sober, tired, yet in a strange way filled with wisdom.

"Power first proposes, then imposes, finally forces us to obey. 'For our own good', of course." Her voice grew as though she were coming awake. "It takes away our freedom of choice, offers to do our thinking for us, lowers our resistance until we succumb to it. Power corrupts our minds, our ability to be individuals, to respect individuality; but mostly it corrupts the one exercising such power over others. You must be noble before you can be corrupted. Corruption is another word for compromise. Both jeopardize ethics. The greater the compromise, the greater the corruption. As you have said, Gio, power is the opposite of love. But you can always compromise on power, never on love. You can give the citizen some freedom; you cannot give them only a little love. Love is indivisible."

"And compromise is said to be the soul of politics," Peter put in.

This time they sat in silence for a long time, each lost in thought. And then, jarring the serenity that had begun to embrace the Renaissance chamber, the telephone rang.

Gio put the caller on the speaker. He was tired of secrets, of wielding power behind closed walls.

"I know that you forbade me to interrupt you, Your Eminence, but..."

"What is it, Guido? Speak up."

"Well, I don't know what it means. But Primiero Ministro Francescatti just called me. He said that there is a battleship of some sort dropping anchor just outside our territorial waters, west of Fiumicino."

The Vatican did not have any territorial waters. Fiumcino was in Italy.

"What sort of battleship?" Gio asked, sounding as though he were an expert on naval armadas.

"He didn't say, Your Eminence. But I was given to understand that the ship is from America."

"America?"

"The United States, Your Eminence. The Prime Minister wanted to know if you knew anything about it." Guido still sounded apologetic.

"Get me the Prime Minister on the line," Guido said, rolling his eyes. He switched off the intercom.

"I'm afraid, my dear friends, that we appear to be under attack by the United States Navy." And then the Camerlengo started laughing. Soon Anne and Peter joined him.

It was all too absurd to be true.

* * *

18

The Endgame

"Thomas Paine once wrote that Society in every state is a blessing, but government in its best state is but a necessary evil, in its worst state, an intolerable one," Fred said, looking up from his armchair.

President Linker was standing in front of his screen. Now and then he nodded, consulted his hand-held computer, and made one or two adjustments on the screen before turning to face his friend.

"There were people in the eighteenth century smarter than we are," he agreed.

He meant it. He despised the bureaucracy that government fostered. There had to be a better way, he thought. Democracy as such worked only when based on the American model. Any other system, including the so-called democratic or republican systems, was subject to influences beyond the control of those who supported them. Indeed, who financed them. Even then, were it possible to introduce some sort of enlightened anarchy into the matrix of the civilized world, he would vote for it. An anarchy in which freedom ruled supreme, and laws existed only to protect that freedom.

"Live and let live," he often said.

In spite of his seemingly simplistic pronouncements, John Linker, the billionaire many times over, the President of the most powerful country in the world, was a complex man. He never considered himself to be part of the government. Not really. He was doing his own thing, in his own way, in his own time. He never intended for the government to impose its will on the people.

"We, the people of the United States, in order to form a more perfect union...."

He could recite from memory vast segments of the American Constitution. He thought it was the only document the United States ever needed. All the additions imposed by Congress and the Senate were just hogwash.

"They have nothing to do, so they fill their time making up laws," was his considered opinion about both chambers. He was glad that, as President *pro tem,* he didn't have to waste any time with that bunch of fuddy-duddies.

Fred listened to all Linker's mores with patience and tolerance bred of necessity. In spite of all the stories that abounded in Washington about his boss, Finer liked him. There was a strange honesty about the man. For as long as Finer had known him, the President had never deviated from his convictions. In a way, you always knew where you stood with him. On the other hand, it did not pay to go against the President's grain.

Maybe some of the stories are true, Finer thought. One never knew for sure.

At long last President Linker sat down. Since assuming the office of the President, Linker had appointed four men to act in his name, *vis-a-vis* the 'outside' world. They spoke in his name, kept contact with the Washington power brokers, smiled at babies, embraced pregnant mothers, attended funerals and other public occasions, and saw to all sorts of things that a President normally would. His excuse for not performing those functions himself was that he did not have an experienced Vice President who would do the actual work for him.

"I am all alone," he said with a plaintive face on his one and only TV appearance.

Finer thought that at least some people believed him. Those who didn't, couldn't do much about it. Linker held all the aces.

"Do you know, Fred, what a marvelous invention GPS is?" Linker asked, still gazing at the screen. In fact, his eyes seldom left it. Finer was familiar with the intricacies of the Global Positioning System. American satellites made it possible.

Linker continued as though speaking to himself. "Never before in the history of the world could we drop anchor within inches of the territorial waters of a sovereign country and not transgress International Law." A satisfied smile played about his lips. "And our missiles can reach much farther than twelve miles. Right to any target, even far inland."

Until the twentieth century, the length of a cannon shot, or some three nautical miles, had defined territorial waters, though Norway and Spain claimed sovereignty over slightly wider distances. In more recent years, a belt of coastal waters extending twelve nautical miles from the shore into the sea was regarded as the sovereign territory of a state, although—expressly for trade purposes—foreign ships, both military and civilian, were allowed innocent passage through this belt. This was not true of the internal waters, where not even innocent passage was permitted.

Finer understood the smirk on the President's face. Modern missiles, fighter planes, or even automated drones, which replaced most of the CF-18s and 19s some years ago, could vastly exceed such puny distances. A single aircraft carrier of the USS Nimitz class could effectively cover the whole territory of a country the size of Iran, without the ship's ever encroaching on territorial waters. So much for international law, Finer thought.

But what precisely were the President's intentions?

"We've covered the Vatican," the President said over his shoulder.

Finer's face went pale. He's attacking the Vatican? He picks a fight with a billion people? The man must have gone....

"My people told me that a number of nations began demanding the release of their representatives from the Vatican's care. I don't think it would be appropriate, do you?"

So that was it. The President had placed the Vatican under his protective wing.

"You want the ah... the dignitaries to remain *incommunicado*?"

"I do not believe they have a great deal to communicate. Our roof samples are as happy as can be, pretending to be ten to fifteen years younger than they are. And they aren't even quite sure what exactly that means."

So the President was keeping tabs on the 'sample' of men and women who had been subject to the experiment of Peter's ultrasonic projector.

"That's what you used . . . during the funeral...."

"My dear fellow. I didn't use anything. There were eight men who mixed with the TV reporters atop the loggia overlooking St. Peter's Square, who had been given instructions on how to use the projectile. Very sparsely. And anyway, those eight men haven't been very talkative since." This time the President's smile got broader.

My God! So the stories are true! Men did disappear... Finer's expression must have confirmed his fears.

"You have a dirty little mind, my friend. The men did not disappear in the usual sense of the word. It would be more accurate to say that any danger or, better still, any embarrassment that they might have posed, has disappeared." Linker was having fun at Finer's expense. "He who lives by the sword, dies by the sword," the President concluded with a broad smile.

"My God! You turned the ultrasonic projectors on your own men...."

"And the men who instructed those men in the operational procedures. They are all taking a well-earned holiday. Quite happy now. Well fed, too."

Linker recalled the final phase of the incident with a degree of satisfaction. The man in charge of the operation visited him but hours ago. He was a good man. A man he could trust.

He came to give Linker a detailed report. As he talked, Linker studied the cylinder with child-like curiosity—the tiny instrument which changed the course of history. Then he slowly, with mesmeric fascination, pointed the cylinder at himself. The man leapt to protect his leader. He didn't make it. Halfway through the office, Linker pulled the trigger—only, by then, the cylinder was pointing at the man. Nothing happened to the faithful agent—at least, not to his body. But he had no recollection of the meeting with his supreme commander. Nor of the event that took place at the Vatican.

"The final link in the chain of events..." Linker thought grimly, a twisted smile playing about his lips. He didn't think it necessary to tell Fred about this incident. No need to bother his friend's conscience. At least . . . not yet.

Finer took a deep breath. He wondered if the actual memories of those last days before the amnesia would ever come back to them. He hoped not. It might only result in a desire for revenge. Vengeance might taste sweet, but it was generally considered a dangerous sport. Hopefully their memories would be modified, but the men would not be aware of any lapses.

Linker's eyes returned to the wall screen.

There were now a number of little lights twinkling in the blue expanses of water close to all the countries his colleague, General Brad Schwartz, had listed some weeks ago. It seemed like only yesterday that they were sitting in the 'bridge club', reporting on assignments. That had been the penultimate such meeting. After the next one, the President had decided to disband them.

"Mustn't risk your valuable heads," he'd told them at the time.

Finer recalled two of the men's hands had moved, instinctively, to protect their necks. Sort of Freudian reflexes. John Linker had a strange effect on people. Even those closest to him, although Fred had serious doubts if anyone was really close to the President. Now or ever. Except, perhaps, the President's dog. Some years ago Fred had been invited to the Linker residence for dinner. It was during the first term of Twigg's presidency. He'd seen Linker pet his favourite German Shepherd. For those few moments, Linker was a different man.

He seemed accessible, soft, almost malleable. The dog, Caesar was his name, appeared to love him. He licked Linker's face, and the then-Vice President allowed him to do practically anything he wanted.

And then, the moment passed. The invisible shield descended. Perfect control, a studiously guarded stare, an expressionless face... Linker had become himself again.

"I think we are ready," Linker said.

For what, Finer wondered. Ready for what?

Even as the President spoke the enigmatic words, a number of additional lights, twinkling with a much darker, more violet colour, appeared in different parts of the world.

"The submarines," the President explained. "We have a fairly large number of them. Till recently, they've been rusting in their berths. The Ballistic Missile submarines, those carrying Guided Missiles, the Attack Subs, and the special Mission Auxiliary submarines. They are useful gadgets in narrow waters."

Contrary to the aircraft carriers, Finer knew little of this class of vessels. When such things were of interest to him, Fred Finer was still a member of the 'general public'. And most of the propulsion data had not been made public. And now he just didn't have the time. He knew they had the Ohio class—seventeen ships. The guided missiles—around eight. The Virginia class—over forty. The others—he had no idea.

"Like the Red Sea?" Finer couldn't resist asking. Two hundred meters depth was plenty to accommodate most subs. Some of them could stay submerged for weeks at a time.

"The Red Sea," Linker repeated. "And one or two other places where we prefer to persuade rather than to impose."

"Impose what?" Finer again was unable to hold back his question.

"Ah, yes, the Plan," Finer said, his eyes still on the screen.

"Didn't you ever wonder what the Plan was about?"

"The American Way?" Finer asked feebly.

The President's smile was gone. His brows contracted, creating a deep furrow in the middle of his high forehead. His eyes narrowed as John Wayne's did when drawing his revolver against the ungodly.

"Yes, Fred. We are playing the game to win. We are playing to instill the American Way the world over. Those who are with us will remain with us. Those who are uncivilized and do not accept our conditions will be excluded. It will be their choice."

"Or else...?" Finer murmured.

The President heard him. Finer's qualms didn't make him angry. As a matter of fact, Finer never recalled seeing John Linker angry. He may have, on occasion, painted an expression of anger on his face, but the next instant he was as calm as ever. He used some of his facial expressions to get desired effects. They always worked. Those who were close to him didn't like to see the mask that even simulated anger. Those who were not close to him invariably saw his features perfectly composed. If Linker weren't such an ardent Baptist, he could be compared to a new incarnation of Buddha. A dark Buddha, but Buddha. A gentle smile, a quiet disposition.

Appearances can be terribly deceiving, Finer thought.

As Peter and Anne rose to leave and to allow the Camerlengo to get on with his work, the telephone rang again. This time Guido's face appeared in the door without knocking. Whatever prompted him to such an action must have been staggering. For countless years Guido was the exemplar of protocol.

"It's the President of the United States of America," he said, visibly doing his best to keep his voice under control.

"I thought the President is still...."

"The other one. The one who took over...."

The Camerlengo smiled. He picked up the receiver.

"Yes, Mr. President, what can I do for you?"

"Good morning, Cardinal Pesci. I am sorry to intrude on your busy schedule."

"Not at all, Sir. I am here to serve."

"As am I, Your Eminence. As am I." President Linker was well versed in Vatican etiquette. "I am calling to lessen your heavy load. I am sure that the imposition of hundreds of infirm people keeps you busy enough, without any interference from nervous bureaucrats and politicians. Am I right?"

"Well, Mr. President, there have been a number of calls. They all have a point. In a way, a point of protocol. They have never been officially informed of what is wrong with their elected representatives." The Camerlengo was still in the process of drafting personal letters to various lesser officials.

"They have now, Your Eminence. I took the liberty to inform them. As far as we gathered from your official announcements, they suffer from a peculiar form of amnesia. We also took the liberty to place a vessel just outside your territorial waters, in case the sub-dignitaries attempt to put pressure on you. We do not believe that it would be wise to release some and keep others *con clave*."

The Camerlengo thought he detected a trace of irony in the President's words. The Conclave should have already started. The Church was officially headless, as was the rest of the world.

"That is very kind of you, Mr. President."

"I took the liberty of advising all the possible sources of annoyance of my preventive measures. I strongly suspect you will have a little more time to sleep. Goodbye, Your Eminence. And I thank you for looking after our own President."

The line went dead.

Cardinal Pesci's face showed an expression of wonderment. Since late last night, he hadn't had a single call demanding the release of any dignitaries. God works in mysterious ways, he thought. As does the acting President of the United States.

He told Anne and Peter what the President had said. They both waited at the door, torn between curiosity and the desire to give the Camerlengo his privacy.

"At least you will be able to sleep now, Gio," Anne said sadly. More sleep than I will get, she thought.

The smile that hovered on the Cardinal's face was replaced by a look of concern.

"Is there anything that we can do?" he asked. "Anything at all?"

"Pray," Anne said.

The Camerlengo realized how little time he'd had for
prayers lately.
"I promise, my dear. I promise I will."

Finer watched John Linker's face as the President replaced the
receiver. He'd had his secretary dial the Vatican, on the
speaker, and once he was told that the Camerlengo's secretary
picked up the telephone, he lifted his receiver and waited on the
line himself. Voice sounds different on the speaker. Less
confidential. There is a slight reverberation, a sort of echo.
Apparently, Linker's power did not go to his head. Or maybe,
he just liked being polite.
"How did the Camerlengo take it?"
"He'll get some more sleep now," Linker murmured. Then
the President looked at Fred Finer with a little bit of
exasperation. "We have been monitoring his telephones for
some time now. Lately he began having a number of calls from
small fry, who were trying to score points with their own voters. I
put them on notice that the Camerlengo is too busy looking after
our officials to be bothered with their petty politics. I think
they'll listen when they notice our naval vessels."
So Washington was monitoring Vatican telephones. Was
there nothing sacred to this man? At the same time, Finer was
just beginning to realize the enormous range of John Linker's
interests. The navy, like everything else the man did, or used, was
all just means to an end. Not for the first time, Finer noticed that
Linker had a hearing aid in his left ear. That, and the ever-
present computer in Linker's left hand, had made Finer
suspicious some time ago.
As the President drew Finer more and more into his
confidence, Fred Finer grew bolder. "That's not really a hearing
aid," he said.
"Well, it is, really. It enables me to hear many different
things," Linker replied.
"And the thing attached to your left hand...."

"A sort of switchboard. Most people are very good at very few things. We live in an age of specialization. I can, at least sometimes, assign the right job to the right man," he said, as if it were a perfectly natural thing to do.

Even as he spoke, the President's right hand danced on the keyboard. Apparently John Linker was capable of thinking of more than one thing at the same time. Rather like a concert pianist whose left hand was well aware of what his right hand was doing, but it did not interfere with its function.

"So what's next?"

"Now is the easy part," the President replied. "The endgame."

A term, Finer knew, often used in the game of chess. If your middle game had been good, the end game virtually played itself out. It was the natural outcome of a good strategy. The chess masters played the last part as a matter of course, already planning their next opening moves. Finer recalled hearing chess masters declaring things like 'mate in six moves!' Or 'in ten'. Or even 'in twelve moves'. To take the endgame out of context of chess, it could be compared to a dress rehearsal for a funeral. The corpse was already there, just waiting to be buried.

Finer waited for Linker to continue. This was why he was here. He knew that the President had to release the inevitable tension that must have been building up on his nerves. Some people did it by taking a few drinks. Some kicked a football. Linker did it by talking. Talking and knowing that someone was listening. An Achilles' heel?

"And...?"

President Linker lifted his left hand for Fred to see. There was a large button that was protected by a transparent plastic dome. The countless meetings with his Chiefs of Staff, the coordination with the armed forces, the synchronization of all the actions were finally over. Seemingly in slow motion, Linker lifted the plastic dome. With a studiously expressionless face he dialed a seven-letter code and pressed the button. Then he sat down. For the first time since Fred Finer had begun coming into the President's Holy of Holies, into his Operations Room, the President appeared to have lost interest in the wall screen.

"And now we wait."

Within minutes, thousands of miles away, admirals, captains, commodores and other senior officers gathered around their commanders to read and hear the contents of the third envelope.

The right armrest of Linker's armchair was also equipped with a multitude of buttons. The President pressed one of them. The screen lost some of its sheen and then went opaque. A moment later it was concealed behind a large tapestry. Finer knew it to be a fire curtain—just in case the fireplace below and behind it misfired. A moment later this same fireplace ignited itself. Gas, Finer knew, but it certainly looked real. The next moment the door behind them opened, and a middle-aged woman brought in a tray with unsalted mixed nuts, two glasses, and a bottle of vintage Cockburn.

"That's what they drink in the navy," Linker murmured. "A Porto. I thought it might be appropriate."

The woman silently withdrew. Linker poured two glasses of the excellent Porto, pushed one towards Finer and raised his own in front of his eyes, seemingly admiring its rich colour.

"The American Way," he said.

Instinctively Finer rose to his feet. "The American Way, Mr. President."

Linker smiled. "Sit down, Fred. We are alone." Then he took a tiny sip of the ruby wine before putting the glass down. "Do you remember October 14, 1962?"

It was a rhetorical question, but Finer remembered it well. "The Cuban Missile Crisis," he answered immediately. "It lasted thirty-eight days, until November 20 that same year."

"Well," the President continued as though Fred hadn't spoken. "We went about it the wrong way. Of course, we were only facing the USSR, but deploying fifteen Jupiter IRBMs in Izmir was just so much pizzazz. Any nuclear submarine could have provided greater firepower. If you do things, do them properly."

He took another sip of Porto. He enjoyed the glints it gave by reflecting the flames dancing in the fireplace almost as much as he did its generous taste.

"Anyway, to cut the story short, the purpose was to provide an effective blockade against the deployment of any additional missiles on Cuban soil. But in essence, it was much more than that. It served as an object lesson that advised the world that the United States will not allow other nations to threaten its security."

Finer nodded. "It worked," he put in.

"Yes," Linker agreed. "In spite of many obvious shortcomings, it worked. And now?" He looked at Finer with an undisguised twinkle in his eyes. "And now we have extended the object lesson to include not only the military but also the economic, cultural, religious and all other means assaulting our interests. We, my friend, have just imposed a blockade on all nations that might threaten the American Way. In any way whatsoever."

With that statement, the President tilted his head and emptied the rest of the Porto into his throat.

* * *

THE AWAKENING

We all dance to a mysterious tune,
intoned in the distance by an invisible piper.

Albert Einstein

19

Checkmate

The man was in his nineties. His cassock hung loosely on his bony frame. The remnants of his gray hair clung to his skull in a futile attempt to adorn his head with a tonsure provided by nature herself. There had been a time, long, long ago, when Brother Andrew carefully shaved the crown of his head. His only homage to vanity.

Before the Funeral Incident, he could only move about with the aid of a wheelchair. Not motorized—just hand-propelled. "The only exercise I get," he argued. He managed well enough but needed someone to give him a hand on the ramps, where his arms were too weak to push his decrepit body up the gentle slope, or to stop it from smashing into the barrier on the way down. Now? In the middle of the night Father Andrew walked by himself to the bathroom. No one saw him. No one but Anne. She said nothing.

The Funeral Incident.

This was how everyone referred to it. No one knew what else to call it. Not many people cared. There were many who said that it was the very first miracle of the late John Paul III. That the Incident itself qualified him to be beatified. After all, to get rid of dozens of plutocrats, of dictators, of pompous politicians who fed on the exorbitant taxes they imposed on people throughout the world, had to be considered a miracle. A wonderful miracle, at that.

The fact that almost half of those affected by the Incident were cardinals, bishops, men of the cloth, who, at least overtly, never hurt anyone, was studiously ignored. As was the fact that some of the secular dignitaries had also been men of stature, men of great character, of true unblemished leadership. Even in the Vatican, some whispered, you can't make an omelette...

It was much more convenient to regard the whole affair as a miracle.

Very few hard facts were allowed to leak out to the world at large. There was danger of panic, possibly riots. Quite a few people had no idea what actually happened. Not that the experts knew much more. Perhaps they thought that all the cardinals already sat in conclave. As for others, few appeared to care. People seldom hold their own leaders in high regard. And those who do, for some reason choose not to talk about it. Not in positive terms. Abject criticism is so much more satisfying. As for the religious people, well, they like mysteries. Or, perhaps, they also saw some sort of miracle in the Incident.

Cardinal Pesci didn't think so. He never ascribed it to other than human interference in the funeral protocol.

Having had power thrust into his hands by this very same Incident, he refused to judge any man, or woman, whose destiny it was to serve by wielding power. Giovanni Pesci considered all life as a form of service. The lives only differed by whom you served, and how well. But we all served, he insisted. Often against our own convictions.

Many claimed that the world had become a better place. All too soon, however, those not quite good enough to have reached the top of the pile decided to get even with the citizenry which hadn't voted them into the top posts. Those second-stringers were many times worse than their predecessors. Uncertain of their positions, always unsure if their previous bosses would not dethrone them at any moment, they decided to pad their shoulders with pride and fill their pockets with lucre as fast as possible. Within days the public realized that, with few exceptions, the 'heads' they'd disliked so much hadn't been that bad.

The vast majority adopted the stance of wait-and-see. In effect, with the sole exception of the United States of America and some minor demagogues in emerging countries who had chosen to ignore the invitation to attend the funeral of Pope John Paul III, the majority felt that the world continued to spin on its axis. Contrary to Linker's speculations, it did not come to an effective stop. If indeed that was his intent.

Although there was no one to inspire the masses, no one to show them the way, a strange thing happened. People who heretofore needed leaders, symbols they could look up to, seemed to drift along happily as if by acquired momentum. At least for the present, they seemed to have lost their appetite for idols. Till a short while ago the faceless hordes, even as the obedient sheep, needed vanguards willing to stand on pedestals to be admired—as well as to bear the blame for their misfortunes. The Lord giveth, the Lord taketh away. The same was held true of their leaders. Only most leaders hadn't been as generous in giving.

There was no one to assure people that the world would continue to rotate on its axis out of habit. Yet it did. In vast, meaningless circles. It fulfilled the first law of motion. That was all. But it was a Headless World.

The next day the nonagenarian asked a nun catering to his needs if he could be of any help.

"I don't know why I'm lying here, doing nothing, Sister," he confessed. "Surely, I must be good for something?"

"And you are...?" The nun faked ignorance.

"Why, Sister Cecilia, you've known me for years. I am Brother Andrew. Until recently, I used to look after the garden...." Recently, in Brother Andrew's memory, spanned the last few years.

The nun rushed to the supervising priest, who rushed to his senior, who contacted Father Guido, who knocked on the Camerlengo's door. He couldn't contain himself.

"Your Eminence... Your Eminence..." His arms were unaccustomedly swinging. "It's Brother Andrew..."

"Yes, what is it?" the Camerlengo asked, expecting the worse.

"It's Brother Andrew. The Nonagenarian. He's recovered...." Father Guido evidently thought the news to be on a par with the Annunciation of the angel Gabriel.

Cardinal Pesci put down his pen and sat back.

"Are you sure?"

"Sister Cecilia spoke to him. He asked if he could help. He knew his own name. He..." He wanted to share the good news that Brother Andrew could walk, but was interrupted. The Camerlengo was a very busy man.

"I get the picture. Anyone else?" When Father Guido looked lost, the Camerlengo repeated, "Has anyone else recovered their memory, Guido?"

Father Guido's animus evaporated into thin air. "Why no, Your Eminence. Not to my knowledge..."

"Let me know if they do," the Camerlengo said, returning to his work with simulated unconcern. He needed all his willpower to maintain his calm.

When the doors closed behind Father Guido, Cardinal Pesci again leaned back in his chair. Strange, he thought, yet it makes sense. Brother Andrew was a humble man, expecting little for himself, sharing all he had. He wasn't an intellectual giant, but his heart made up for it many times over. Perhaps he was the least among the men, but he must have also been the least affected by the Incident. He only sat with the sacerdotal dignitaries because of his age. He was the oldest who could still attend. It was the sort of gift Brother Andrew alone would really appreciate. He sat in the back row of the clerical congregation, in his wheelchair, yet among the Princes of the Church. He was a prince himself, if of a different Kingdom.

And he was the first to recover. How very fitting.

The wall screen was shimmering in half-light, as some computers do when they are sent to sleep. The sound was off. It would switch on automatically if awakened by Linker's voice. Linker was at his desk, deep in thought. There should have been some reaction by now, he thought. It stands to reason....

At 0300 hours a squadron of unidentified warplanes dropped depth charges in close proximity of the Ohio Class FBM submarine cruising eight knots along the deepest part of the Red Sea. The military assault aircraft was observed on the radar approaching the submarine from WSW. Permission to respond.

The message came over the device that never left the President's left ear. He even slept with it switched on. Linker dialed a code on his left arm keyboard, then set his jaw and pressed a red button below the plastic cap. It had begun, he thought grimly.

At 0305 hours, three ballistic missiles were deployed towards the target areas. At 0335 hours a drone plane deployed from USS John F. Kennedy that was cruising, at the time, at six knots in International Waters off the coast of North Africa reported complete destruction of the airfield and two other strategic military bases.

The target areas had been predetermined. Schwartz had seen to that weeks ago. There was no room for error. Justice was swift and convincing. Like the American Way. Like our generosity, Linker grinned without mirth.

These were the first reports that came in. They had already been edited and decoded from military jargon into colloquial English. President Linker read the messages again and erased them. Linker didn't need them. His own memory served him just fine. And he certainly didn't need any record for posterity. He wasn't doing this for fame.

It had to happen, he thought. Some people just didn't know what was good for them. He then lowered his body deeper into his armchair and instantly fell asleep. He was already asleep when a footstool automatically emerged from below to support his feet. The President liked sleeping in the Operations Room. It made him feel young.

A nne looked at Brother Andrew with the same satisfaction she had looked, so many times in the past, at men and women in the more seedy parts of towns and cities in various parts of the world. Never in her wildest dreams had she imagined that, one day, she would be conducting such work in the heart of the civilized world. In the Vatican.

She was a little jealous.

People to whom she had given a new lease on life, in a manner of speaking a clean slate, were so much better off than she was. She had to continue to struggle with all of her own past. Even her early days occasionally rose to the surface. If she was lucky, only in her dreams. Yet sometimes they also surfaced in her waking state, usually when she felt alone, deserted by her own children, by Peter, who periodically, even as she herself did, flew to various scientific conferences around the world.

Her most profound nightmares, or quasi-nightmares, invariably involved the autistic children she worked with in Montreal. She was well aware that by her being here, in the Vatican, the little ones who needed her most, at least emotionally, were left alone. She did her best to visit them in her dreams, but seldom succeeded. When she did join minds with some of them, those were the few moments of joy she experienced while working with the dormant cardinals and dignitaries. When she did not—she woke up with a sense of guilt and frustration.

Not that she'd ever complained to anyone. She was as fully aware of her blessings as she was of her mission. For such it was. One is never given a gift, no matter what kind, for the sole purpose of titillating one's ego. A painter must paint. A musician must use his talent to bring music to others less gifted. A surgeon must spend endless hours standing, bending over patients, straining his eyes, just so that he or she might restore order and harmony in someone's body. And even then, there was never a certainty. Not that result is expected from us. Our job is to do our best and not to worry about the consequences.

That was what Peter had done.

Anne had difficulties in convincing Peter that the results were not his responsibility. Or at least, not his alone. The world had become result-oriented. If a greedy developer ruined a beautiful design an architect had prepared, cut corners to augment his profits—the architect was blamed. If people invested money into someone else's business, they wanted results—profits. The business thrived on quarterly returns, regardless of how they were obtained. People amassed fortunes investing in the tobacco industry, or in the production of hard liquor. The trip no longer mattered; the destination was all that counted. The last few days, Peter had become moody, disoriented, expecting something great to happen to set his mind at ease. He'd begun to expect results.

"Surely, they must wake up sometime?" he asked no one in particular.

Since the conversation Gio had had with the acting President of the United States, there had been a marked reduction in inquiries about the interned dignitaries. Twice each day, the Curia, consisting of Cardinal Giovanni Pesci and his six assistants, issued a bulletin advising all the countries and organizations of the guests' physical, mental and psychological condition.

The bulletins didn't change much.

There was a slight improvement in all men, but that improvement seemed related to the dignitaries' coming to terms with their present condition, without being in the least bit aware of what that condition was or the return of any significant memories. They could best be compared to very large members of a kindergarten. Or inexplicably juvenile adults.

On the day Brother Andrew regained the command of his senses, not to mention the use of his legs, a number of other Vatican charges began recalling their late childhoods. In the course of a single day, many regained more memories of their schooldays than they remembered before the Incident.

In general, this second group's reaction was completely different from the Pentagon group, whose initial disorientation had given way to attacks of acute depression, occasional violent behaviour and, generally, a refusal to discuss their problems with anyone. Possibly, the duration of their exposure to the ultrasound had been longer, while the concentration of the waves had been less intense.

The many experiments, albeit on quite a different scale at the Montreal Neurological Institute, had suggested that both groups would eventually recover most if not all of their reasoning faculties. Though no one, not even Peter, was willing to speculate how long it would take them.

"I really think you should go back to Washington," Anne told him, practically holding back tears.

It had been three days, and Peter didn't know what to do with his time. Gio was too busy, and Anne needed rest and had neither time nor strength to cater to Peter's self-induced problems. He could have gone to see Sir Ian but preferred to stay at Anne's side. After all, that was what he'd come for. To be with her. Anne knew she would miss him, but Peter was quite unable to remain inactive for any length of time. Even on their infrequent holidays, he invariably took a number of textbooks and his trusty computer with him. While Anne would frolic with Di and Johnny in the warm waters, he would sit under a large umbrella, endeavouring to fathom the abysmal depth of the human brain.

"Go back to those crooks?" Peter sounded aghast.

"You agreed to help them with a specific problem. To my knowledge you have not fulfilled your end of the bargain," Anne insisted.

"But they abused...."

"I am afraid I must agree with Anne," Gio put in. "We cannot take the sins of others upon ourselves. That's already been done," he added, his face as serious as his tone.

"You want me to work with those . . . those..."

"Men and women whom you promised to help," Anne finished for her husband.

To his own surprise, Peter began breathing a lot easier. The Camerlengo made sure that Peter was looking at Anne before he gave her what can only be described as a lascivious wink. In a very short time, Anne and Gio had reached a depth of understanding. Sometimes a single look, a raised eyebrow or a sigh would convey more between them than a long argument. Gio fully understood that what was at stake was Peter's well-being. He recalled a statement once made by Joseph Campbell, a man who dedicated his life to the study of myths. 'A woman must be,' he'd said; 'a man must act.' Peter was very much a man.

The following evening EST, Dr. Peter Brown landed at Dulles International Airport. Dr. Frederick Finer picked him up. This time there was no helicopter, but a bullet-proof limousine was waiting at the VIP entrance.

"Just how did you know I was flying back?" Peter asked, not really expecting to hear the truth.

"We have a complete list of all passengers coming and going from the Rome International Airport, as well as landing at and leaving from Dulles International," Finer replied as though stating the obvious. Then he smiled and added, "You don't imagine that we are following your every step, do you?"

I wouldn't be surprised, Peter thought, but he said nothing. After a moment he muttered, "Why, am I not important enough?"

Finer shook his head in resignation. "Why do you find it so hard to believe that we really want to find a way to alleviate the battle fatigue syndrome in our armed forces? Is it really so hard to accept?"

"It would be a lot easier, my dear Frederick, if you didn't use my inventions for other purposes," Peter said dryly.

Finer said nothing. Even though he'd come out to meet Peter at the airport purely out of friendship, right now silence was the best strategy.

At 0600 hours, John Linker sat up in his retractable bed, drank a glass of water, went to the bathroom, brushed his teeth and sat on his Exercycle. He peddled at a reasonable speed, with reasonable resistance, for exactly 30 minutes. He then took a shower, shaved and got dressed. The bed he'd slept on had already slid quietly into the wall, only to reemerge on the other side where the sheets were changed daily.

"If it's good enough for a hotel, it's good enough for me," Linker said after one of his trips during which he'd slept in a different bed for twenty-two days running. Besides, he liked sleeping on clean sheets.

"They're crisp," he claimed.

The President stretched a little on the way to his desk.

He clicked on his computer. Among all the usual junk that could wait, that didn't require his direct intervention, were a few notices of more minor skirmishes of little or no consequence. And only one attracted his attention. It had been decoded and deciphered, like all the messages from the military. This one originated from *USS Harry S. Truman*, which was cruising just off the coast of Bushehr. The carrier had sustained minor damage. At 0412 hours the carrier repelled an attack of eleven missiles, two squadrons of fighter jets, and one old-fashioned submarine.

> *The USS Harry S. Truman had come under attack while deployed in international waters, off the western coast in the Persian Gulf.*
> *USS Truman losses—one FX-19.*
> *Casualties—none. Commander J. G. Jones recovered from the sea unharmed.*
> *The USS Truman responded to the attack by downing all but one (1) enemy aircraft, sinking the attack submarine, incapacitating eleven (11) warships, deploying twenty-two (22) missiles to cut off land links between the aggressor and its neighboring countries.*

The message was signed John Patrick Gravitz, Rear Admiral, who, like all the naval commanders, was under strict orders not to mention which countries initiated hostile action. Linker didn't want the media to know the extent of the operation. There were one hundred ninety-eight member states of the United Nations. The USA had only thirty-seven vessels capable of enforcing the blockade. There were another fifty-seven available and deployed mostly for moral support rather than for effective military action on land. Linker had to rely on the assumptions that the various non-cooperating countries would draw. Fear, Linker knew, was by far the greatest weapon. Greater than any battleship.

The enemy had lost the personnel engaged in the attack on the *USS Harry S. Truman*, but that didn't really matter.

Amazing, thought Linker, that there are still people around, who think they can surprise the US military. A few years ago a number of terrorist attacks had achieved undesirable effects, but only two of them had been aimed at the military. Since, the terrorists invariably directed their efforts against the civilians.

Much easier targets.

The Presidential Order made it quite clear that under no circumstances was the USS Navy to initiate any hostile action against any sovereign country. They were to broadcast the President's message in the language of the country at which it was directed and leave it at that. Originally, the President had considered making his announcement in the United Nations. He'd discarded the idea as soon as he'd thought about it. Had he done so, they'd all still be there, discussing the political repercussions and international law.

The President's message invited all sovereign nations to join the American Coalition for the Preservation of Democracy. The message continued that any country was free to opt out of the offer. Should they do so, however, they would no longer be invited to participate in any international trade in which the United States of America was engaged.

For the majority of the sovereign nations that were already deeply engaged in free trade, it all sounded worse than it was. There were, however, a good few that participated, but did not respect the rules of the game. For those, this was an ultimatum with no recourse to diplomatic procrastination. The American Way was the same for everyone. Any transgressor would be henceforth automatically expelled. These days, isolation meant a lingering political and economic death. No one could survive on their own. The world had become far too intrinsically interdependent for that. And this time, the US Navy assured that offenders could not easily engage in subterfuge.

At 0950 hours, the President finished his meeting with the Chiefs of Staff. As usual, the meeting was held in his office. The admirals and generals were ready to leave when a red buzzer sounded on the President's desk. It meant danger and required the President's intervention. President Linker pressed the red button.

The USS George H.W. Bush was sunk by a tsunami wave off the coast of Choson-man at 2147 hours. A mushroom cloud was observed from SSBN Nordic. Awaiting orders.

No muscle moved on the President's face. He didn't blink, he didn't grimace. The time differential placed the sinking at three minutes ago. Linker pressed another button, and the message appeared on the wall screen. It looked more deadly when spelled out in two-inch-high letters. When there are a dozen men present in any enclosed space, there is always an undercurrent of noise. A throat being cleared, a cough, a chair creaking or even the sound of deep breathing. Not then. Total silence enveloped the room like an all-permeating fog. The eerie feeling started at their feet, moved up the men's spines and finally constricted their throats. The generals, admirals and the rest of the staff held their breath.

Very slowly the President rose to his feet.

"Apparently we have no choice," he said, his voice so normal it sounded out of place. No emotion, no anger. No threat. Just a vague, undefined sorrow. "No choice," he repeated.

He pressed another button on his hand-held computer. He pressed it three times, then dialed six digits. Then three more letters and two more digits. No ship had been authorized to employ nuclear weapons without Presidential permission. For a moment it seemed that Linker was about to say something. Then he walked to the window, his feet making no sound on the thick carpet. He turned his back on the room.

"I played the game fair and square," he said, looking at the inner courtyard of the Pentagon. "The American Way. They gave us no choice. For them the game is over. It's checkmate."

By 1030 hours EST, the petty dictator, his private army, his stockpiles of nuclear missiles, his lavish palaces and toys he'd accumulated at the expense of a starving country, ceased to exist. The process of extermination was fast and thorough. The facilities to be destroyed had been known for over three months. There were no errors, no regrets.

The Chiefs of Staff filed out in total silence. Fred Finer stayed behind. He thought the President might be in need of company.

"Why?" John Linker asked him. "What have I done wrong?"

One death is a tragedy, Finer could have said. A thousand deaths is a statistic. He could have said that, but he said nothing. Somehow, in moments like these, some deaths seemed more painful than others.

President Linker would never admit it even when he was alone with Finer, but he'd more or less expected what just took place. When you remove the head of a country, the second fiddles would try to impress their subordinates, if not the whole nation, with their quick decisions, their military skills, or with their mastery over the situation. No president or prime minister would ever initiate an attack against tremendous odds. Against the might of the United States Navy. Only fools would do such a thing. Only those who would never have been elected to the top job.

Linker also thought of the men and women who died in the US counter-attack. Hopefully, they died quickly. As for the rest of the nation, they were free. For the first time in long decades of absolute rule, the people were free to determine their own future.

* * *

20

The Syndrome

The rounds Anne did every night were beginning to have results. Some of Peter's comments had given her a handle on the mass of symptoms she'd observed in her patients. That's what she called them. Patients. There were only eleven women, all over sixty. Most were men well over fifty, some pushing eighty. Only cardinals less then eighty years old were allowed to take part in the Conclave. And so they had been the only ones who had traveled to the Vatican for the funeral, intending to stay for the Conclave. The even older gentlemen had remained at home, in their countries of origin. There had been no point troubling them just for the funeral.

The symptoms were many. Anne was sure that, one day, some neurosurgeon or neurologist would refer to them as the Brown Syndrome. Or the Vatican Syndrome. It might be hard to prove that Peter had been in any way connected with the Incident. After all, it wasn't the sort of thing one would brag about. Not even to one's colleagues.

After Peter left, Anne organized her time over a twenty-four-hour cycle. Apparently, it mattered little if she visited the prelates or the dignitaries during the day or night. The state of their 'wakedness', the quality of being wide awake, differed little between the day or night. Originally she'd only made her rounds at night, because she was used to doing her work only during the dark hours. Here it did not matter. These were not the slums, and people to whom she ministered were at her disposal at any time. The problem, she soon discovered, was the intensity of her work.

In the past, as she sauntered along the deserted streets, only one in perhaps a hundred men or women would respond to her presence. There would be some sort of contact established only between her and those in dire need of help. The consciousness of others had been inaccessible to her. Even as Peter's or Gio's or her children's was. But these were no ordinary people, not in the sense of being in command of the instrument through which their consciousness manifested. Their defenses were down. Four hundred people all open, confused and as vulnerable as children connected to her.

"I wonder to what degree their soul is affected by all this," Anne mused aloud.

"Whatever is received is received according to the nature of the recipient," Gio replied. "With the consciousness that resides in and manifests through us."

She knew the expression. It belonged to Thomas Aquinas. Many years ago, Gabriel had referred to it on a number of occasions. In those days they had been discussing the talent she had manifested in playing the violin as a possible by-product of her slightly larger frontal lobe and a broader Pons Virolii, the connector between the right and the left hemispheres of her brain.

"Peter might know," she smiled sadly. "If only he would accept the concept of..."

"...soul?" Gio smiled. "People can't accept what they cannot embrace with their mind. That is why we need symbols. What we usually refer to as soul is little more than our subconscious, *nephesh* in Hebrew, or animal soul. I'm sure your husband accepts the concept of the subconscious, which surely is very much affected."

"Whereas Soul, the omnipresence..."

"...of God, is above human scheming, foibles, human desire for power and control. In a way, It is eternally unaffected."

"Indestructible. Immortal..."

Gio didn't say anything. They understood each other beyond the need for further words. They both knew that there was little point to having a mind that couldn't accept its own highest potential. And this Potential, this Individualized Presence, needed all fragments It had created to manifest Itself in this dualistic reality. It was the *nephesh* Anne was worried about—the seat of our subconscious. There resided the sum-total of what makes us human, or at least the human animal. We could not study the subconscious of the 'four hundred' without access to their brain. There was also no question of conducting PET scans or fMRI on over four hundred patients. But the principle was the same.

'You cannot squeeze blood out of a stone,' Peter had once said, 'nor force certain neurons to act outside their particular specialization.' Nor receive above and beyond the nature of the recipient, as Saint Thomas Aquinas would probably say.

At the MNI they had already discovered the equivalent of neural stem cells. Under certain circumstances, the necessary neurons could be rebuilt. But this was not the MNI. Not even a hospital. And these people were not really sick. Anne had to act in lieu of what stem cells could accomplish. What affected our brain, affected our subconscious, affected our ability to display still higher aspirations. It was all up to Anne. In a way, she had to succeed for Peter.

By the beginning of the second week after the Incident, two more elderly gentlemen, both cardinals, began to show signs of recovery. They became aware of who they were, but still had no recollection whatever of the funeral. The first Cardinal to partially recover was well aware of the country he had come from, of his rank and diocese, but he had no idea what he was doing in the Vatican.

"Until they know that a conclave must follow the funeral of a Pontiff, they are of no use to me," Gio confessed. "I need some sort of a quorum, preferably ten or twenty of my colleagues to elect a new pope. Otherwise..." He spread his arms. "Otherwise the continuity might be questioned."

The continuity from St. Peter himself. This was not entirely accurate. Peter had never been elected Pope. The early Christians had named him one only after his death.

But there was still time.

The matter, as such, wasn't tragic. In 1271, it had taken 1,095 days to elect Pope Gregory X. More recently, the popes had been elected in less than four days; but as recently as 1831, the conclave had lasted fifty-four days for the Cardinals to decide on Pope Gregory XVI. By Church standards, this was like yesterday; but what was more important, the precedent had been set. Although there was no way to initiate the conclave, theoretically the Camerlengo still had a few weeks to assure continuity, even without calling on the historical record of Gregory X.

At the same time, Gio wasn't overly optimistic.

"Since I cannot appoint myself," he told Anne with a rare-of-late attempt at humour, "I might as well name you the next Pope. Being a woman disqualifies you, but, as we are so keen on the precedent, there was always John VIII, Joan of England, back in 855." Gio's eyes were smiling, but his voice was quite serious.

Anne invariably dressed in a black suit—not white. Nevertheless, she was halfway there. But what really scared Anne was that the Camerlengo might just do it. She recalled Einstein's assertion: 'I want to know the thoughts of God; the rest are details.' The Camerlengo quoted the late Pontiff, John Paul III, who'd put a new spin on the expression: 'Love one another; the rest are details.' He'd said it many a time.

"Not to about one billion Catholics," Anne countered. "People are unable to live in the present. They cling to traditions. They live with one foot in the past."

Then Anne looked at Gio and still couldn't be sure if the Camerlengo was serious or not. Her suspicions kept churning in her tired head. In many ways, Gio was a bit of a rebel. "I would immediately name you my successor, Gio," she replied in kind.

"I'm afraid that would be illegal. You would have to slay me first," he mused aloud. "Popes are not allowed to name their successors. On the other hand, there is ample precedent of foul play in the naming of one's successor. Including murder."

"How can you talk like that?" Anne exclaimed. "You are a cardinal, a prince of the Church!" She pretended to be shocked. "And anyway, I only slay dragons," she added confidentially.

"I knew you would hold it against me." He did his best to look crestfallen. Anne assumed Gio was apologizing for not being a dragon. "Oh, well, give me a dozen cardinals, and I'll let you go free. That's the best offer I can make."

By now Anne was completely lost.

If it hadn't been for those lighter moments that skimmed the edges of sanity, both Anne and Gio would be in serious danger of joining the four hundred delinquents distributed throughout the Vatican. Anne preferred them in smaller groups. It put a lesser strain on her resources.

"I'll do my best, Gio," she promised, though she knew that it was never up to her what might actually happen. She planted the seed, but the soil had to be ripe, the water had to come down from heaven, the sun had to be warm.... It was never up to her.

After Anne left his office, the Cardinal sat for a while in silence. He remembered the dream he'd had the night the Pontiff died. It was extremely real. Even now he could recall it in great detail. The woman Pope. Was it as absurd as all that, he wondered.

Later, Anne lay down to get some rest, too. Even as she closed her eyes, she heard a silent plea.

Help me . . . help me . . . please....

During that second week, Anne also discovered that the memory lapses were very selective. A cardinal or an archbishop might remember the name of his diocese, but not the name of his secretary. He would remember the names of his parents, but not the bishop who worked with him. Partially, this could be explained by the time-line. Events and all names connected with them in the most recent past had been completely erased. The further they went back, the greater the recall. There were twenty-six doctors constantly interviewing the 'patients' and keeping strict records of their findings. There were already stacks of paper, even though only deviations from the normal were reported to the Camerlengo. Otherwise he would be suffocated under the mountain of reports titled *The Vatican Incident Syndrome.*

In his Pentagon office, Peter found a like pile of paper awaiting his review. He was lucky. He dealt with only twelve people. Anne had four hundred. Yet even then, Peter could not delegate the review of the reports. At the same time, he dove headlong into his lab work. It was as Anne had said: He'd made a commitment; he would do his best to honour it.

From day one, he found that Fred Finer liked to insinuate himself into his office under some pretext or another.

"Are you keeping an eye on me?" Peter asked point-blank.

"Do you want the truth?" Finer looked depressed.

"Shoot!"

"Well, knowing your attitude, it's not easy to explain it to you. In a nutshell, you are the only non-American, non-Pentagonian, if you will, with whom I can talk. Every other person seems to keep one eye over his shoulder just to talk about the weather with me. There is tension in the air, in the whole building."

"So?"

"Well, you are sane. You're getting on with your work without looking over your shoulder. You behave the way we're supposed to behave...."

"Sit down, Fred." Peter dropped the paper he was reading on the desk. Until now, Finer had been standing at the door, waiting to be invited. "What's really eating you?"

"It's classified." Finer looked guilty. "Really, I'm not making this up."

"I believe you. But how on earth do you imagine I can help you if you don't tell me the truth?"

"All I can say is that I am the President's, the acting President's, ear. He chose me, for some reason, to spill his guts to. I can't take it any more."

"Did you tell him that?" Peter was beginning to feel sorry for the little man before him. His head was only just protruding over the top of the stack of papers on Peter's desk.

"Don't be ridiculous, Peter. You don't tell the President of the United States of...."

"Acting President," Peter corrected.

"Whatever. Anyway, I feel he needs me."

"And now you need me?"

Finer began examining his fingernails. This, Peter had learned, was Finer's way of saying 'yes, but can't say it out loud.'

"You are welcome to drop in here at any time. But I must get on with my work."

"That reminds me." Finer reached inside his breast pocket. He took out an envelope and handed it to Peter. Inside, Peter found a facsimile of a cheque for one million dollars US. He sat back in consternation.

"It's already in your bank account," Finer said, a vague smile playing on his lips.

"I will not be here long enough to earn this much," Peter said, still staring at the cheque.

"Think of it as a bonus." For the first time in weeks, Finer was enjoying himself. He had been instrumental in procuring this cheque for Peter. He now loved watching his face. "I was hoping that you would find it useful," he said almost shyly.

Peter thought of Anne flying first class, of a better apartment for Di, of a new car for himself and for Gabriel, of installing new windows in their Westmount residence. Also, it could serve to buy one of those electronic contraptions that Johnny spoke about to help him compose. Yes, he would find it useful. Yet for some reason he felt guilty.

In truth, it was Fred Finer who was attempting to whitewash his own sense of guilt by rewarding Peter with unearned money. If they can spend billions on a single battleship, he reasoned, how much more deserving is Peter, who can save countless lives? Besides, it made him feel good to see Peter being embarrassed for a change. It was his turn.

Peter's control group, the men and women from the roof terrace, were doing very well. Of course, Peter knew exactly how much exposure they'd each suffered. There was no question here of any permanent damage, unless one considered ridding the culprit of memories that resulted in neurotic if not pathological behaviour as damage.

After only a single day in Washington, Peter had returned to being completely immersed in his work. He forgot about the bonus money, about the misuse of his invention in the Vatican. His sole concern was to help the people who were counting on him. Or rather, the people who didn't even know that he was doing his very best to help them.

And then he began to compare notes of his research in Washington with the observation he got by e-mail from the Vatican. Since his return, he and Anne kept in touch. Anne regularly sent him summaries of the Vatican reports. Apparently no one interfered; no one had put any gag orders on his freedom of communication outside the Pentagon.

Peter was beginning to relax.

All went well until, late in the evening of the third day, Peter returned to his apartment and switched on the TV. The headline consisted of a single word: WAR. He was tired of hearing about some African or Central-American top bananas shooting at their opposition. He changed the channel.

???WORLD WAR???

This time the title was splashed across the whole thirty-six-inch screen with three question marks framing it on each side. Against this background, the speaker was reciting a list of 'ballistic exchanges', 'armed conflicts', 'atomic explosions' and a dozen other headlines in quick succession. There had been military conflicts in the Middle East, Central America, South America, Africa and the Far East. Europe seemed to have escaped unscathed. Peter picked up the phone and dialed Finer's number.

"Finer."

Peter heard the usual gruff acknowledgment. Once again Fred wasn't a happy camper.

"What's going on?" Peter asked.

"Ah . . . you're watching the evening news?"

"I am. What's going on?"

There was the sound of some papers being shuffled. "Can I come over and see you in, ah, in, say, half an hour?" Finer had a *pied-à-terre* in a different side of the Pentagon.

"See you," Peter said and hung up.

"What the bloody hell's going on?" he wondered aloud.

For the first time since he got to Washington, Peter went to the fully equipped bar and poured himself a shot of Scotch. It tasted expensive. Whatever one might think of the Pentagonians, they knew how to look after their guests. They seemed generous to a fault. Printing your own money must be nice, he thought. Actually, *their* own money. Well, almost.

A few minutes later Fred Finer knocked on the door.

"Sit down," Peter said. "We've got to talk."

Finer looked towards the wall bar. "Help yourself," Peter nodded. He did not feel compelled to return the pleasantries offered by his host. In a way, Finer was his host. He more or less acted as one.

Fred gave himself a soda with a twist and sat down. He waited for Peter to have his say.

"Did Linker start a war?" Peter asked. "A global war?"

Finer stirred uncomfortably. "He didn't break a single International Law."

"Answer my question, Fred. I installed an ultrasonic device in this room. Whatever listening devices your henchmen hid around are useless. You can speak freely."

Finer's mouth opened as if to say "You what???" But it closed without uttering a word. Finer believed him. After all,

Peter was an expert on sound. Then a little smile appeared on his thin lips. He leaned back in his armchair. For the first time since Peter arrived in Washington, including his first trip, Fred Finer looked fully relaxed.

"The President does not make me privy to all his plans, Peter...." When Peter glared at him, Finer continued. "The President is determined to make the world a fairer, safer and more democratic place. And he's doing it the only way he knows how."

"By destroying the opposition?"

"He's never fired the first shot."

Peter sat in the chair opposite Finer's. For a while he remained quite silent. He realized that if he was to learn the truth, he must at least pretend to be interested in Linker's reasons, not just in how to condemn them.

"It's all to do with the American Way," Finer said after a while. "You see, there are people who believe that all people are born equal. They claim that even the Bible teaches that. Surely, you will agree that this is absolute nonsense. No two people are equal. And in a number of political systems around the world, they will never become equal, either."

"If I hear you correctly, you believe that all people have equal potential but it cannot be met due to...."

"...many factors. But the political system is the most obvious one."

Peter believed Finer's theories. Up to a point. He remembered their earlier discussion about the nature of democracy. He also remembered Gabriel talking about karma and the baggage we bring into this world from our previous life. Or lives. Still, there was something missing.

When Peter remained silent, Finer continued. "In Brazil, some twenty-five thousand people are said to be working as slave labourers, most of them clearing Amazonian forests. In Europe, tens of thousands of women and girls are cheated, abducted and forced into prostitution. In Thailand, thousands of girls work as sex slaves for tourists. In Sudan...."

"And in the USA?"

Finer's face lost some of its confidence. He looked at the standard places where listening devices were usually installed, then his eyes returned to Peter. Apparently, he was reassured.

"An estimated twenty thousand people are trafficked into the US annually, many of whom are forced into prostitution."

A smirk twisted Peter's handsome face. It was neither joyful nor triumphant. It was the sort of smile that scientists allow themselves when they cross a new boundary in their work. They still have a long way to go, but at least they know that they are on the right track. Furthermore, Peter had discovered that whatever the official policy of the USA, Finer was both fair and knowledgeable.

Peter got up and walked to his desk. There were three computer screens positioned around his swivel chair. If it weren't for the stacks of paper, he would have looked like a spaceship commander, about to embark on a trip across the galaxy. He very nearly was.

His fingers began dancing on all three keyboards. For a while they both kept silent. Then Peter sat back, an expression of satisfaction on his face.

"Correct me if I am wrong," he began, waving Finer to come and stand behind him.

Finer downed his soda and took a position behind the 'captain's chair'. Peter pressed a few more keys and once again leaned back. The screens were full of numbers, some accompanied by terse comments. Then Peter took a deep breath.

"Lincoln's Emancipation Proclamation that officially ended slavery in America was published in 1863. Abraham Lincoln was the sixteenth president of the US. Sixteenth since George Washington. Eighty-seven years have elapsed since the Continental Congress adopted the Declaration of Independence. Seventy-four years since the original Constitution was signed."

He glanced at Finer. His face was inscrutable, though he did wipe his forehead.

"We, the people..." Peter resumed. "Who were those people? Certainly not the slaves picking cotton."

Again he glanced at Finer. If Finer guessed what Peter was driving at, his face didn't show it.

"It wasn't until the 20th amendment to the Constitution that American women were given the right to vote. You know when that was?"

"Nineteen-twenty," Fred said quietly. He knew his stuff. No wonder Linker used him as a mobile encyclopaedia.

"Nineteen-twenty," Peter repeated. "Some fifty-seven years after Lincoln's Proclamation. Women remained political and social slaves till some ninety years ago. And you criticize the Arabs?" That last question carried a note of incredulity.

"The Pequot Indians had been exterminated by the Colonists in Connecticut by about 1637. This included women and children who tried to escape. But already in 1493, when Columbus returned with a force of seventeen ships, he initiated mass extermination of the Taino population. After his departure, the Wounded Knee Massacre, the 'Indian removal' and other initiatives of the newly formed United States, such as 'clearing', 'military slaughter of tribal villages', 'bounties on native scalps' and biological warfare, continued with considerable success. We could say that genocide in America was practiced diligently for some three hundred and seventy years immediately prior to Lincoln's Proclamation."

As Peter recited this last list, he pointed to the screen on his right where those and many other massacres were enumerated in greater detail. Finer walked round Peter's desk and poured himself another soda. Then he changed his mind and gulped down a goodly shot of Scotch. Thus fortified with Dutch courage, he turned as if ready to defend the honour of his country. Peter's hand stopped him.

"It took you three-hundred-seventy years to stop the practice of genocide, seventy-four years to stop slavery, and another fifty-seven years to give women, your women, your own wives and daughters, the right to vote. What is it exactly that Linker is trying to teach the world? That democracy takes time?"

Finer was ready to counter at least some of Peter's argument with the long-established mumbo-jumbo, so popular among the politicians. He knew he couldn't negate the facts, but at least he was willing to save some face for his beloved country.

But when he opened his mouth, he found he'd lost his appetite to fight.

"Is he mad?" Peter asked in all seriousness.

"Who?" Fred was grateful for a change of subject.

"Linker. Your President. Is he mad?"

Peter walked to the wall cabinet and poured two more tumblers of Black Label. He wasn't going to do much work after that. He didn't care. He didn't feel much like working any more.

* * *

21

The Wind

The enigma of memory loss was beginning to weaken around the edges. Anne and her army of physicians, the Camerlengo's wisdom, and constant contact with Peter finally began to bear results. So far they had all been groping in the dark. Now, there was a light on the horizon. And the horizon was getting much closer.

The amnesia was not related to any chronological schedule. What controlled its influence was not the time when any particular event happened, only the influence it had on the present. The degree to which it motivated the person's present behaviour. Whatever was congruent to the original psyche, or the constituents of the original self, seemed to come to the fore. Those essential elements manifested themselves. The later layers that people's egos and life had imposed on the structure of their subconscious seemed to have vanished.

"We all live in the present," Gio smiled when hearing of the scientists' conclusions.

"Evidently what preys on our mind is, by definition, at the forefront of our mind. And it so happens, the part of our brain that handles this particular preoccupation is also at the forefront of our brain."

"Very apt," Gio commented dryly, not knowing how this piece of information could advance their search for a solution.

"What it means, Your Eminence," Dr. Provost continued undeterred, "is that we can now isolate the part of the brain that has been affected by the amnesia."

"Peter knew that some time ago," Anne put in. "I'm sorry, but he thought that this was, ah, well . . . obvious," she concluded, slightly embarrassed.

"To a neurosurgeon, Mrs. Brown, not to a lowly physician. Perhaps you could persuade your husband to share some of his thoughts on the subject with us."

"I am sure, Doctor, that Doctor Brown will be happy to discuss anything you want. We'll get you his email address and phone number at the Pentagon. Now, I really must get on...." Gio assured him.

The doctor, with a slightly injured ego, and Anne both got to their feet. When they reached the door, the Camerlengo called Anne back.

"Could you spare me a moment, Anne?"

The doctor now stormed through the open door. He took his sole, individual dismissal as a demeaning insult.

"Aah, if only those people wouldn't take themselves quite so seriously," Gio smiled indulgently. "He really is a very good man, you know, it's just that, that...."

"That he is human?" Anne said, returning to her chair.

"I want to know from you what the primary difference between the recovery of Peter's dozen and our four hundred guests is."

"Three hundred and eighty-eight," Anne laughed. Gio looked confused, then smiled. "I'm sorry," she added contritely; "since Peter left I've been having those stupid dreams, and I suppose I feel a bit inane."

"Are you overtaxing yourself?" There was real concern on Gio's face. He looked deeply into her eyes. "Do you want to tell me about them?"

Anne had a peculiar influence on people. Most people quite automatically cared about her well-being. When she walked into a room on an overcast day, people were under the impression that there was a ray of sunshine that somehow had gotten lost and graced them with its presence. And this before she'd even spoken, before she'd taken more than a few steps. It was no longer her beauty, even though now, in her forties, she was still a very attractive woman. Some would still say beautiful, if she only made the slightest effort to highlight her natural charm. As for that first impression, some people called it an aura, others charisma. Or just plain old-fashioned charm. This was why, after some twenty-five years of marriage, Peter hated to be away from her. He needed to see her, to touch her, to make love to her. Intimate contact with his wife reconstituted him as a man, and as a human being.

Anne held Gio's eyes. For a while neither of them spoke. Then Anne sat back, raising her arms and then dropping them in resignation.

"We cannot serve two masters..." she sighed.

She was thinking of her autistic children and the demands of her present commitment, but she didn't enlighten Gio any further. And anyway, the biblical meaning of the phrase was quite different from what she had in mind. Also, she didn't want to burden Gio with her own problems. She could hardly tell him that she resented all the attention that was lavished on her narrow shoulders. She wanted to go back to Montreal, to hide, to visit her children when no one was looking.

"I am just me..." she started, her voice trailing off into a protracted sigh.

Gio nodded without interrupting. At last Anne sat up and cleared her throat. "When I was playing the violin, life was simple. There was no question of doing my absolute best at any particular time. I found that the only way I could succeed, consistently, was to give up any idea I may have had of what was right or wrong. All I had to do was to reach back to the heart of the composer, his very soul, and let my intuition direct my interpretation. What I am trying to say is that I found it worked best if I ignored my ego, even my will, and let myself be swept by the music itself. It was as though the composers had been messengers of gods, and I could do little more than to act as an instrument of their message. Does this make any sense, Gio?"

The Camerlengo shifted uncomfortably. He'd never had the luxury of free time to analyze his own modes of behaviour in such depth. Especially now. As for other people, the people he served in the confessional—their problems seemed fairly simplistic when compared to those raised by Anne.

"Whatever you did, Anne, bore results unparalleled in the history of the violin. You must have done something right..." he smiled at the inadequacy of his own words.

Anne did not seem to have heard him. "And now . . . and now I am expected to make decisions. I feel farther from, not closer to, the source that inspired me originally. Now I have to do consciously what before was just a negation of any interference on my part..."

Gio reached over the desk and took Anne's hands in his own. "This, Anne, is the price of growing up. Most people never reach this level. They simply react to their subconscious that is anchored in their past and controls all their automotive functions. Physical and mental. The unconscious, on the other hand, is our unlimited potential. It inspires us, it guides us when we are children. But it is the conscious mind that we must develop. The conscious and the unconscious must become one. Then we shall be as gods..."

His voice trailed off into pensive silence. Anne looked at Gio in abject embarrassment. *This man has the world on his shoulders, and he takes time to help me.*

"I'm all right, Gio, thank you. Or as well as I shall ever be with those calls...."

"...calls?"

"I hear them calling me. Asking for help. It used to be only at night. Now, well, now it's virtually all the time."

Giovanni Pesci, the Cardinal, the Camerlengo, remained silent. They were discussing matters of the soul, of the inner being, and yet he felt completely inadequate. Inadequate and helpless. A lesser man would tell her some clever, impressive words of comfort. Gio was too honest. To him, matters of soul were beyond words.

"I hear you calling right now, Gio...."

The Camerlengo shook his head. "Does it show that much?" he asked softly.

"It's hardly your fault, Gio. We all need help at one time or another. It is just that right now I must be oversensitive. Or over-sensitized—emotionally, I mean. It will pass." She sat up straighter in her elaborate Renaissance chair. "As for your question, Gio, it is hard to tell, right now. The difference isn't that they can or cannot remember. It will show itself in what sort of men they choose to be when they come out of their present condition."

"Are you sure that we have so much to say in what's in store for us?" he mused aloud.

"No, I'm not. Not at all. I think we all have a very important, an indispensable role to play in the unfolding of the universe. I also think that few of us are smart or lucky enough to realize what our role is."

"Self-realization?" The Cardinal's voice was getting softer. It often did when he was approaching what he felt was a holy subject. He'd once told Anne that God abides in absolute silence, but He manifests Himself best through music. 'Order and harmony,' he had said. Exactly what Peter always believed. As did her father.

Anne nodded, listening to Gio thinking out loud.

"Some wise people in the East call this Self-Realization. That you come truly alive only when you discover your true destiny. Until that moment you are only half alive."

"Do you think that's what they mean by being born again?" Anne was drawn into Gio's line of thought.

"No, I don't think that's what is normally understood by that phrase. But I strongly suspect that you may be right. You are not so much born in Spirit, as you become a conscious part of It. You become that which you really are."

"And always have been without realizing it?"

"I believe so. I can't be sure...." he admitted contritely.

"I can," she said. But she spoke so quietly that the Camerlengo couldn't hear her. She knew because she'd already been born anew twice. First, to offer her being to music. To have become what was universally regarded as the greatest violinist ever. And the second time? The second time she had to give up the remainder of her ego, her personality and—just be. For Anne, it had been the moment when she had handed the priceless Stradivarius back to Sir Ian. The instant when exquisite pain was released into an ocean of freedom. An instant of perfect balance. Only then could Spirit do Its work through her. The slightest resistance, the slightest attempt to have her own way, even a strong desire to help someone, to make things better, and she no longer felt alive. Not in the true sense.

"Peter once quoted Einstein to me. Apparently the man who gave us the most famous scientific theories also thought that we all dance to a mysterious tune, intoned in the distance by an invisible piper. I think he may have been right."

Gio looked at Anne with genuine admiration. "You have a very clever husband, my dear. A very wise man, too," he asserted.

"I know. I'm very lucky, Gio," she smiled her gratitude. "And now, if you'll excuse me, the piper is calling. I must go and dance...."

Gio's eyes followed her to the door. *The wind bloweth where it listeth...* he quoted from memory. There was genuine love and sadness in his eyes, in equal measure. *And so is every one that is born of the Spirit,* he said out loud to the empty room.

Out of the one hundred sixty-eight members of the United Nations, thirty-four withdrew their ambassadors and consuls and all the rest of their senior diplomatic staff from American soil. They didn't break official relations. They were brought home for 'consultations'. A euphemism for 'I don't like what you are doing.' No one ventured a guess as to how long the consultations would last. They allowed a very tenuous link to remain, however, through their representatives at the United Nations.

On the day after the Choson-Man fiasco, or the military action that had been so described by the European Press when

Linker had avenged the sinking of the *USS George H.W. Bush*
by an induced tsunami wave, one hundred forty-seven nations
voted to sanction the United States of America. The sanctions
weren't defined—at the United Nations few things seldom
are—but things had changed over the years. Since President
Twigg came to power, or became elected because power always
rested with Linker, the GNP of the People's Republic of China
had grown by over 54%. That translated into a middle class
society 50% more numerous than the whole population of the
United States of America.

Also, since Twigg's election, Europe had considerably
consolidated as a Trading Block. The population of Europe
exceeded that of the United States. Even Great Britain no longer
held onto the coattails of their American cousins but had thrown
their fortunes into the European cauldron.

The most enigmatic change had taken place in South
America. The greater the expression of capitalism in China and
India, the greater the swing to the left in South America. Yet
there was no question of any return to communism, though it
did seem that, in a global context, the balance of power between
left and right had to be maintained. It was the sort of democracy
of which the Brazilian bishops had spoken in the days of the
Liberation Philosophy.

Fred Finer had tried to explain the principles of this version
of democracy to President Linker. At the time, his boss wasn't
impressed. Indeed, he was rather distraught.

It had begun with a statement by the Brazilian bishops in
support of a plan to democratize media. At the time, Brazilian
TV rested in the hands of five big networks, while only eight
huge multinational corporations accounted for the vast majority
of all advertising. The bishops understood the political power of
the media a long time before Linker came to the same
conclusion. After all, he who pays for advertising must have
some control over the advertisement. Or, in other words,
propaganda is a necessary evil. Or good. Depending on one's
point of view.

Local villages and towns elected representatives to district
councils, who elected representatives to greater groups, who

elected representatives to districts, who . . . became the representatives in the Federal Government in Brasilia. They made mistakes, but it worked. And having at least partial control over the media, they let people know what worked and what didn't, and why.

Linker hated the idea. Those who own should rule, not the other way around.

There was a lot of appeal in Linker's concept. If you are the owner of an apartment building, you don't want the lodgers telling you what to do and when. Everyone is free to move out at the expiration of their lease. What can be more fair than that?

The Brazilians thought that many things could be fairer than that. For a while the idea was knocked about in intellectual circles, bandied about as an interesting but impractical concept. The Brazilian Conference of Catholic Bishops repeatedly stressed the importance of grassroots participation in all aspects of communication. Twenty years later, faced with Linker's blockade, it became an idea whose time had come.

When the Argentinians agreed with them, they were followed by Peru and Venezuela. Actually, Venezuela had to take a step towards the right to meet its left-of-the-center neighbours.

North America was out.

There was one country that benefited enormously from this state of affairs. That country was Canada. The US poured countless billions of dollars to buy Canadian oil, Canadian natural gas, and Canadian timber. Anything Canadian became necessary, fashionable and desirable. After years of protectionism, the Americans even stopped talking about Mad Cow disease. The Canadians always maintained their traditional neutrality in all things military. It worked for them just fine. As it had done, once, for Switzerland.

During the next twenty-four hours, there were four more 'armed conflicts' generated by Linker's attempt to share the American Way with the rest of the world. The Arab countries, east of the Mediterranean, did not appreciate being told with whom and how they could conduct trade. Soon they'd resorted to old-fashioned, proven guerrilla methods, referred to in previous decades as terrorism. The difference between the reaction of some larger countries and the smaller sovereign nations was that it was hard for the military might of the United States to respond with all its overwhelming power against a single diver carrying the very latest plastic explosives and attaching them, strategically, under the water level of the mighty aircraft carriers.

If the men waited for ruffled and riled waters, usually a day or two after a steady blow of ten to twelve knots, and were prepared to risk their lives in order to benefit from the services of a few dozen virgins in the hereafter, should their attempt to escape with their lives fail, they were more or less bound to succeed. The big boy on the block, the bully, felt as though he'd been attacked by an army of fleas, lice, or even microbes. *Nec Hercules contra plures* was the motto the Arabs evidently borrowed from the Romans, or really the Greeks. And it worked.

Three aircraft carriers had to withdraw from their positions to 'friendly', meaning neutral, harbours, to effect repairs. Not big repairs. Just a dozen small holes below the water line that, cumulatively, threatened the safety of the multibillion-dollar vessel.

For years the American Way had stipulated that bigger is better. On the other hand, the Age of Aquarius empowered the individual. The elephant is helpless against a wasp injecting its venom inside his ear. He cannot even reach to protect himself. The enormous aircraft carriers were stung by a swarm of wasps.

USS Theodore Roosevelt, 0500 hours.
Three small explosions were registered at 0340, 0342 and 0345 hours on the port side bow, approx. six feet below the water line.
Four explosions were registered at 0345, 0347, 0349 and 0352 hours on the starboard bow also below the water line.
Request permission to withdraw to effect the necessary repairs.

Similar requests came from the vicinity of Bight of Benin, where *USS Dwight D. Eisenhower* was keeping vigil. They needed repairs to three of their screws that did not respond to commands from the bridge. Their commanders recommended immediate withdrawal to assess the damage. There, Admiral Johnston could not be sure if the damage was inflicted by outside interference or by lack of proper maintenance.

Recommend immediate withdrawal to Cape Town, which has the facilities to assist.
Message authorized by Rear Admiral J.K.L Stenson USN.

"This is what happens when your navy spends all its life in dry dock," Linker said darkly. The military present at the briefing preferred not to argue. The *USS Dwight D. Eisenhower* hadn't been in dry dock for over three years.

Linker's face was growing darker by the day.

"It could be mines floating since the last intervention in those waters, Sir," said a younger general, attempting to cheer up the President.

"So our minc-sweeping equipment is useless?" Linker asked very quietly.

The general chose not to answer.

Fred Finer always attended the military briefings, though he never opened his mouth. As often in the past, he wasn't really listening. It wasn't his job to offer military advice. He wouldn't come at all if the President hadn't told him to be wherever he was.

"Where I go, you go. I want you to be my shadow. My alter ego."

Finer had no idea why the President wanted him as a shadow, but he was certainly going to humour him. In a way, watching Hercules struggling against prevailing odds was fascinating. Finer wouldn't place any bets on which side would emerge victorious. Linker always placed all his faith in the resilience of an individual. Never on the masses. Yet here, he was no longer dealing with the masses. Every ant raising its head against his dictates seemed to have a mind of its own. They were not stupid natives, nor lazy, uneducated rabble that responded only to men, or women, superior to themselves. They took initiative into their own hands. An aircraft carrier could defend itself against a host of battleships, against enemy aircraft. It could even shoot down heat-seeking missiles aimed at its engines in the middle of a cold sea. Even a small torpedo could easily be blown out of the water. But a dolphin could bump against the hull without anyone even knowing about it.

And now, Finer thought, we've made a full circle. We are headed back to square one. Unless Linker succeeded, America would come to a standstill. It would spiral down like an old-fashioned clock that someone forgot to wind. No matter how wonderful the machinery, without foreign energy supplies it was just so much metal. Metal and human ingenuity.

What a waste, he mused. What a fantastic waste....

Even as the meeting adjourned, Finer was still lost in his thoughts and stayed silent. He knew that a tiger was at his most dangerous when wounded. He preferred not to think about what Linker might do to get his own way.

Anne thought that perhaps there was such a thing as a lucky-thirteen. Since Peter had found a five-leaf shamrock on the day Di was born, and a black cat chose to cross her path on the day Johnny had been accepted to the Juilliard School, then there also might be something to the number thirteen. On the thirteenth day after her second arrival at the Vatican, the first miracle happened.

Her conclusions were twofold. First, two cardinals recognized each other, embraced, and told the supervising nun that they would appreciate it if they could see the Camerlengo. The second miracle was that they did not issue orders to that effect but politely asked the nun if she would be so good as to find out, *etc., etc.* In the past, the cardinals would have told the nun, albeit politely, to take them to the Camerlengo. They didn't. They asked. Something had changed.

The Camerlengo welcomed the two cardinals like two prodigal sons.

"You have wasted thirteen days, my brothers, what say you?"

They both bowed before the Camerlengo, although Gio was the only one present whose head did not display a crown of silvery hair.

"Indeed, we have, Giovanni. We came to make amends. Is there any function you can assign us to make up for our omissions?"

Cardinal Fresci regarded Giovanni with interest, as though seeing him for the first time. The other, Cardinal Martel, also gave the impression of not really knowing the Camerlengo that well.

"Why are you studying me with such interest?" Gio asked. "I never considered myself worthy of such scrutiny," he added with a smile, but his tone was quite serious.

"It is not that you have changed, Giovanni, it is that we are seeing you with new eyes." Cardinal Fresci glanced at his freshly resurrected colleague, who nodded vigorously.

"Do I pass?"

"Oh, we are sorry," they both said at once. Then Cardinal Martel continued. "It is not that we are judging you in any way. It is more... that we have been so blind for so long...."

Evidently Cardinal Martel spoke for both of them.

"Care to explain?"

"I can't speak for the both of us, but I think dear Jean will agree." Fresci used his colleague's first name as though they were long friends. "We were raised to our position some ten years ago. In that length of time, we have both learned to discern power in the people we have had to deal with. We had to. In a way, it was our job. And now . . . here . . . as I look at you, dear Giovanni, I detect no power. Yet, at the same time, I feel that, should the need arise, you could move mountains...."

Both Cardinals continued to study the Camerlengo like a rare exhibit that one can admire but not touch. Giovanni also found a strangeness about the two men that he couldn't define. It was neither good nor bad—that he could normally sense about people he met. Yet it seemed to inspire a realm of great possibilities. A certain willingness. For what? He had no idea.

The three princes were so involved with studying each other that none heard the door open to admit Anne. Lately, Guido no longer announced her. She was part of the *familia*. She came in quietly and stood behind the two cardinals. Gio was the first to notice her. He saw her, walked past the two colleagues and took Anne's hand. His face shone as though he'd received an exhilarating epiphany.

"Only now I understand what you mean, dear Anne. Only now I see...."

That same evening, the first Prime Minister opened his eyes after an afternoon snooze and asked what the hell he was doing there. After he looked around, at the frescoes on the ceiling, the rows of saints adorning the walls, and a number of nuns in their flowing robes floating silently about, he decided to rephrase his question.

"Where in heaven's name am I?" he asked.

* * *

22

Stalemate

C hina was first. Then came India, propped up by Pakistan, with whom they had just signed a mutual non-aggression pact. Indonesia, and the Small Tigers of the Far East, held onto China's coattails. Within a single week of Linker's non-invasive military surgery, they had all signed a single economic pact removing all trade barriers between them.

The day after the signing, Australia applied to join the Sino-Indian trading bloc.

A second bloc formed with equal dexterity in South America. Brazil, Argentina, Venezuela and The Republic of Peru, all had governments considerably left of center. The South American bloc recognized the benefits of free trade, of private enterprise, but all four agreed that there were limits to the power that an individual should have over the people. Be it an individual politician or specific international conglomerate. Or their Chairperson. Or their CEO. Or the President. Man or woman. Within three more days, the rest of South America had signed on the dotted line.

The Asian bloc united some 2.7 billion people into a single trading bloc. The second—a little over 500 million. Smaller but still more than the population of the United States. Both blocs excluded the United States from participating in the benefits of their agreement. And Europe? Europe had been dealing as a single entity for some twenty years. They were friendly but looked after their own business.

They did things their way.

The media went wild. Some headlines called for Linker's resignation; others for immediate attacks on China, South America, and whoever else dared to make money without the express permission of the United States of America.

After all, those countries' prosperity had been built on American money-making know-how. How dare they do it on their own?

There were more and more 'them', fewer and fewer 'us'.

Europe remained steadfastly neutral.

Whoever plays the game of chess knows that a stalemate is a conclusion to a game that gives satisfaction to neither player. There is a feeling, on both sides, that had they tried a little harder, surely victory would have been theirs.

This is exactly how Linker felt. He certainly did not feel defeated. He merely felt that his Plan had failed to materialize exactly as he had envisioned it. But all was not lost. There were Europe, a good part of Africa and, strangely enough, Russia, which remained non-aligned. There was still room to grow, to leave the imprint of the American Way.

He decided to let things be, for a while, and see what developed.

"Get me Doctor Brown," he said into the armrest microphone, as he leaned back in his seat.

Ten minutes later Peter was admitted to the presence. The President got straight to the point.

"How long do I have?" he asked.

Peter didn't take long to put two and two together. The man was shameless. Still, it was no good crying over spilled milk.

"Our control group has not budged substantially from their original condition," he answered. There was no way he would volunteer to tell the President that Anne might have achieved results that no one else could.

"And there?"

"At the Vatican?" A rhetorical question. "I have no way of knowing. I wasn't consulted on the exposure of the cardinals to the ultrasound." Peter had no desire to risk his neck, but he was determined to play the game close to his chest.

"Don't you keep in touch with your wife?"

So he knew. Of course he knew. Peter was desperately trying to recall what he'd written and received in e-mails during the last day or two.

"We exchange observations of symptoms. That's about all," he said.

He prayed that that had been all. Before he'd left the Vatican, Peter, Anne and the supporting medical staff agreed that they would not report to each other on total recoveries. Those, for now, were none of anyone's business. Especially Linker's. Also, Peter wanted to have an ace up his sleeve. If there were signs of remission, the e-mail would start with 'Love you, darling.' Their old code.

Peter felt a bead of perspiration detach itself from his forehead and slowly make its way down his nose.

He momentarily forgot he was in the presence of the world's most powerful man. A self-defense mechanism he'd developed when working on seemingly impossible problems back home, in Montreal. As he blinked slowly, Anne's image flashed before his eyes. It always brought him comfort. He needed her now, as never before.

"You never tell me you love me, darling," he heard her voice as if she were present.

They often joked about it, because Anne had once complained that Peter didn't tell her often enough that he loved her. From that moment on, the phrase had become a code, even though it meant different things at different times.

The moment passed. It couldn't have lasted more than three or four seconds. Peter wiped his forehead.

"Your best guess?" Linker didn't look at Peter. He seemed lost in thought, emerging only to throw an occasional question from behind a mask of simulated indifference. Peter had rubbed shoulders often enough with psychiatrists at the MNI to know false calm when he saw it.

"I have nothing to add, Mr. President. Your guess would be as good as mine. I certainly wouldn't want to mislead you. I can only tell you that there is some movement in the awareness of reality among the control group we tested on the roof. They are becoming reconciled to their present fate, but there are still no signs of any access to the memories of the, ah... of the syndrome."

"Syndrome?"

"They used to call it the Vietnam Syndrome, then the Iraq Syndrome, now we are dealing with the...."

"Yes, I know. There is sometimes a penalty for doing what's right," the President said, seemingly drifting again into his private reality.

Peter stood at the door. He hadn't been asked to sit down, and frankly, he hoped to be dismissed as soon as possible. He had serious reservations about the President's sanity.

The silence stretched. Peter wished Finer were there. During the last few weeks he'd gotten to know Fred rather well. They didn't agree on a number of subjects, but Finer was a man who, within his own terms of reference, could be trusted. At least, Peter thought so. He even suspected that Finer needed someone to talk to, even as he, himself, did right now. Other than the President. Someone a bit closer to reality. Objective reality. But there was no one else. Apparently, Fred never went home to see his wife. 'Does he have a wife?' Peter asked himself. 'Strange that I've gotten to know Fred well enough to know how his mind works, but still know virtually nothing about his private life. He must have one," he mused.

"A month?" The question came out of nowhere.

"A month? A month for all twelve to return to a functioning..."

"Do I have a month before the subjects recover their memories?" For the first time the President sounded a little annoyed.

"The idea was for the subjects to lose a segment of their memories. Not to recover them."

For the first time Linker looked up. He studied Peter for a moment or two, then got up and offered his hand.

"I thank you very much, Doctor Brown. You have been a great help." And if Peter ignored the stony, cold expression in the President's eyes, the handshake was almost warm.

Peter took this as a dismissal. As he walked towards the door, the great wall screen was just beginning to emerge from behind its protective sheath. A moment later Linker was lost in the vastness of the oceans. Now and then he touched a button or two on his left hand, and then he sank into the deep armchair.

"Stalemate," he murmured to himself. "I hate stalemates."

By then Peter was well on the way to his office.

Once Peter got there, he switched on two of his computers. The first one served as data storage for all his observations to date, the second as a calculating machine for his ultrasonic research. The third was mostly for research and e-mail. He opened his inbox.

Love you, darling. I miss you terribly. I love you, I love you, I love you. a

The little 'a' stood for Anne.

Good God, four of them? Could it be that her ministrations had made such an incredible difference? Peter desperately wanted to know more details, but there was no way to ask. I suppose I'll just have to resign, he told himself with a deep sigh. I wonder if Finer would let me go and let me keep the million. The moment the thought crossed his mind he felt deeply ashamed. It is much easier to earn a million dollars than to lose it. On the other hand, he didn't really know. Until he got to Washington, he'd never thought about money. Not even once. He was just too busy with his work. Power corrupts, he thought, and money is power.

"I am beginning to hate this country," he mumbled to himself, his face contorted in disgust. "The next thing I'll do is buy a gun and start shooting people."

Per capita, there had been more murders committed with firearms in the United States than in any other country in the world.

Anne was ecstatic. Since she'd e-mailed Peter, there had been seven more partial recoveries among the prelates. For some reason, the dignitaries still remained lost in their internal struggle. She was aware of their repeated cries for help. But there was only so much she could do.

As for the 'partial' aspect of the cardinals' recovery, it had to do with the nature rather than the depth of it. Two of the prelates began reciting the Bible. At least, she thought it was one of the evangelists until Gio put her right. What the two prelates—one reciting in Modern Greek and the other in English—seemed to be remembering was the original version of the New Testament, from which the gospels of Matthew, Luke and Mark apparently evolved.

A sort of synergic gospel.

Another cardinal took it upon himself to recite the whole of St. John's Gospel, but with a twist. In his version, parts of it sounded like fragments from the Nag Hammadi manuscripts, with particular reference to the Gospel of Thomas. In the cardinal's rendition, Gio said, the damage that bishop Irenaeus had done was removed.

Anne looked up, her eyes posing a question.

Gio sighed disarmingly. "I shouldn't be telling you all this, but, I suppose, you're a heretic already." He smiled broadly. "Well, at the beginning of the third century, Irenaeus, bishop of Lyon, expounded in his tractate, 'Against the Heresies', condemning the Gnostics. He was so successful that they made him a saint." Gio looked a little embarrassed.

"Why the reservations?" Anne asked.

"There are scholars who hold that Jesus Christ was a Gnostic," Gio confessed.

"I see," Anne nodded. "Does it really matter?"

"Well, *gnosis* in Greek means knowledge, but also recognition. The object is to recognize your own true nature. We base our religion on faith; Gnostics—on knowledge. Or really on a knowingness that only comes from within."

"So it does really matter...."

"Not as long as we love one another," Gio said sadly. "But for some people the messenger is more important than the message."

"You mean they cry Jeeeeezus a lot, but ignore His teaching?" She pictured the plump and cuddly, rosy-cheeked preachers peddling their Jeeeezus wares on TV.

Gio didn't answer. He didn't have to.

But Anne wasn't ready to let go. "And what exactly do Gnostics have to do with Nag Hammadi?"

"Well, Nag Hammadi is a small town at the Jabal al Tarif in Upper Egypt. The town, a village in those days, lies in the shadows of a mountain honeycombed with more than a hundred fifty caves. Over some four thousand three hundred years, or since the sixth dynasty, many of the caves were enlarged and painted to serve as gravesites. As time went on, stories abounded about vengeful ghosts protecting the ancient remains. They, the stories or, ah . . . the ghosts, kept the grave robbers away."

Anne loved stories of ancient times, and ghost stories always held a particular fascination for her. "And the Gnostics?" she prompted.

"When Bishop Irenaeus mobilized his men to destroy the Gnostic manuscripts, some monks in a nearby monastery, where they'd settled in an attempt to escape the Roman Orthodoxy, decided to hide them. What better place than a mountain protected by ghosts?"

Gio took a sip of water.

"Hence, the manuscripts," he concluded. "All of them lovingly translated from the original Greek into Coptic some fifteen hundred years ago."

"But how did they find the manuscripts?" Anne sounded incredulous.

"In December 1945, two local peasants stumbled on an earthenware jar, which they promptly smashed with their mallets in the hope of finding gold."

"And..."

"And finding thirteen papyrus books, bound in leather, they were determined to use them as kindling. Some of them, they did.... There isn't much wood in Upper Egypt."

Anne, quite scandalized, decided it was time for her afternoon nap. She had another heavy night ahead of her. Her efforts were beginning to bear results.

Indeed, there had been other awakenings.

A rabbi, as ancient in appearance as in fact, began singing the Torah. For an old man, his voice carried a beauty that was enchanting.

The regular Vatican Radio was not known for stepping outside strict orthodoxy. Since The Incident, its programs had been limited to statements approved by Gio himself. Much like the reports he sent out to the diplomats and ambassadors, there wasn't much new information in them.

When the clerics started their recitations, their reinterpretations of the ancient texts were the result of deep inspiration. Every single incantation, recitation or statement by the newly recovered sacerdotal prophets, or inspired seers, was to be not only recorded but also broadcast on the Vatican Radio Urbi et Orbi, without any commentary or authorship assigned to any of them.

Gio was well aware of the enormous gravity of the information he was disseminating to the world. The revisions had not been preached. They were to be put on the air without being scanned for conformity to the Orthodox Doctrine. This fact alone was revolutionary.

"My dear," Gio confessed to Anne when they were alone in his study, "I am counting on these broadcasts to accomplish, at least in part, what you have already accomplished with some of my colleagues."

"I'm beginning to feel responsible for things over which I have very little control," Anne said. She looked nervous.

"Do not worry," Gio replied, "The world will make up its own mind in due course. It is high time we stop telling people how to think."

Anne was speechless. She thought of Bishop Irenaeus. From everything she'd ever heard, the Catholic Church specialized in fighting heresies. Her face continued to show her discomfort.

"Do you know what the word heretic means?" Gio asked. "Like so many other things we borrowed, it also comes to us from the ancient Greeks. From the word *haireticos*. It simply means 'able to choose'. In my judgment, God granted free will to all of us, not just my colleagues in the Vatican."

Anne thought that Gio was lucky his colleagues were still mostly benumbed. Otherwise they would have burned him on a pyre of heretical scriptures.

There was an unexpected, almost ludicrous, fringe benefit to Gio's broadcasting policy.

Even as the Vatican radio was broadcasting on seven wavelengths, the Pentagon was diligently recording every single word of the actual text. The Vatican and the Pentagon were fast becoming the principal world authorities on spiritual knowledge.

Strange times indeed.

Peter wondered if Finer would let him go. He called him, and Fred came at once. He looked haggard. Peter asked him point-blank to be released from his obligations.

"There is little I can do until our group joins the real world. If it works, you won't need me to administer my method to other ex-combatants. If not, then the system is all wrong, anyway."

Finer weighed Peter's words.

"You have been listening to the radio, haven't you?"

It was no good lying. The excitement of what was going on in Rome was painted all over Peter's face.

"Will you let me go?"

Finer smiled. "Of course, Peter. Only promise me that if we need you again, you will come willingly." Presumably he meant without special inducements.

"Do you want the million back?" Peter was more than willing to return all the money.

"I can't. The money has been spent."

"What?!"

"Oh, not by you, my friend. By the Pentagon. When we make a requisition to the Treasury, we don't return the money. It might set a precedent."

The next morning Peter took the first flight to Rome. This time, a limousine with a Vatican crest was waiting for him. It was nice to be pampered.

Next came the *Bhagavad Gita*, the ancient Runes, then the *Upanishads* and other Vedic texts. The last to see the light of day, or the freedom of the airwaves, was Lao Tsu's *Tao Te Ching* and a dozen other obscure scriptures, the interpretation of which had been disputed over centuries. It seemed that gods were really busy talking to mankind, only we had not been very good at listening. A number of elderly men walked slowly with microphones attached to their lapels, some to their turbans; others just stood motionless in front of a mike and spoke like automatons. But not all. One particular rabbi was crying. He'd just finished singing the psalms. He confessed that he'd never realized just how beautiful they were. He also recorded most of the major prophets and was about to embark on the minor ones. One leading psychiatrist insisted that the manifestation of ancient knowledge vindicated Carl Jung's theories about archetypes.

"The knowledge has been anchored deep within our psyche, and now, under propitious conditions, it emerges in full force." The venerable psychoanalyst failed to define what exactly the propitious conditions might be.

No matter. Nobody really cared.

Anne had a flash recall, a *déjà vu* of a film she'd seen as a girl. It was called *Fahrenheit 451*, the temperature at which paper catches fire. The regime of the day was determined to burn all books. As a countermeasure, there was a group of people who decided to learn the important literary jewels by heart, and thus preserve them for posterity. They forewent their own names and assumed the names of the books they'd committed to memory.

They became the books.

New faces continued to shuffle through Gio's office. They may have been elderly, and certainly shuffling, but there was fire in their eyes. By the time Peter arrived, there were fourteen cardinals 'fully operational'. The Camerlengo thought that delaying the Conclave was no longer necessary.

"If the Holy Spirit can speak through a hundred or two, it can do so through fourteen. And these gentlemen at least know how to listen!" He winked in Anne's direction. She nodded with great satisfaction.

Peter went from the limousine directly to Anne's room. The double bed was still there. No one had dared to push the two halves back against the opposite walls. Peter stripped, took a shower and lay naked on the bed. He closed his eyes. At long last he felt clean and free. Cleansed from within.

This was how Anne found him. She tiptoed to his bed and gently insinuated herself next to him. Two seconds later, she was speechless. She had to be. Peter's lips were firmly planted on her own. What followed made up, at least in part, for the time they'd been apart. It should have. Two hours passed by the time they both got out of bed.

According to Anne, there were two other reasons for Peter's stellar performance. First, he fancied that, although not for the first time, he was still the first man in over a thousand years to have salacious sex in the Vatican. Or if one wished to be nasty, to have illicit sex. And the second reason was the door. Anne's room being in what, until two week ago, had been a seminary, the doors had no locks. Peter became perceptibly excited by the idea that at any moment a nun or some other cleric, perhaps a cardinal in an impressive miter, might walk in on them and catch him *in flagrante* or, to use a more common expression, with his pants down. The fact that his pants were neatly folded on the chair did in no way diminish his long-suffering and unreleased animus.

"My God!" Anne despaired. "I'll miss my rounds."

Peter was going to say 'My Goddess', but it was too late. "You don't need them any more. Or more precisely, they don't need you," Peter said with conviction. "You've done your job."

"Perhaps, but I can still hear them...."

"Their pleas? Some people will never stop. Remember how you act on your usual trips. You spend two or three nights in any district and move on."

"Yes . . . but...."

"Let's go and see Gio. I'll explain it to him. Then he will explain it to you."

Gio invited both of them to dinner. Not as Epicurean as Anne's first dinner with Gio and the late Pontiff, but very good. Things being what they were, with just a few cardinals and other elders around, the Vatican kitchen had few people to please. The culinary experts, chefs of some repute, were all glad to serve the Camerlengo. They'd never heard a harsh word from him. Not once.

The Camerlengo embraced Peter as he would an old friend.

"You are my next best person at the Vatican," he declared. "Right next to Anne. She is our star above all stars. Have you heard what she's accomplished?"

Peter did have some idea, but he wanted to hear it from the Camerlengo.

"In just a few days, she accomplished what every fourth or fifth Pontiff has tried to do and failed. She renewed us. She renewed the Church. She is a gift we truly do not deserve...." Gio would have gone on had Peter not interrupted.

"Don't forget John Linker, Gio."

The Camerlengo stared at him with round eyes. "You are jesting with me, my good Sir?"

"Not at all. If it hadn't been for Linker, Anne could have done little or nothing. At least not here, not at the Vatican," Peter's eyes were smiling, but his tone was dead serious.

"God works in mysterious ways," Gio said, sticking out his chest in a vain attempt to sound pontifical.

"You sounded just like our old friend!" Anne said.

"By Jove, you're right," Gio admitted, now also sticking out his stomach and lowering his voice. "I really miss the old scoundrel."

They all knew that Anne was probably the only beautiful woman Sir Ian had ever met and didn't try to seduce. They all enjoyed the memory of Sir Ian.

"I must see him before I go," Peter said. "I owe him so much. We both do," he said, looking at Anne.

A gentle knock on the door admitted Guido. He seemed to have shed ten years. In fact, everybody around there seemed younger, happier, unable to hide their good spirits. This was particularly strange considering the circumstances.

He approached Gio, bowed, and handed him a piece of paper with scribbles covering the whole surface. At least, that was what it looked like from where Peter was sitting.

"It was the gentleman from Saudi Arabia, Your Eminence. He seemed quite pleased with it." There was a smirk of tolerance on Guido's lined face.

"What do you make of this, Peter?" Gio passed the paper to Peter.

Even as Peter studied the handwritten sheet, his face began turning a different shade. He seemed surprised, amazed, astonished, flabbergasted, and then totally stunned.

"Well, what is it?" Anne and Gio asked together.

"Unless I am very wrong, this is a formula, or an equation explaining a formula, for removing salt from saline water."

"Don't we have that already?" Guido put in from the door.

"Not like this." Peter kept nodding his head as though the import of the equation were still expanding in his head. "If this is right, then the process produces excess energy, get me? The process of converting saline into potable water does not cost energy but produces excess in vast quantities. Why... this could mean free electricity for thousands, millions of people. Anne, think, clean water . . . in Africa, Indonesia, Bangladesh...." Peter stopped talking, but his mouth still hung open.

"A *perpetuum mobile*?" Gio asked.

"Not really, Gio. Once we run out of oceans, we shall be back to square one." While Peter began laughing, it was Gio's and Anne's turn to fathom the boon that humanity was about to receive.

There was a knock on the door. Guido put his head through the crack.

"Could you ask the gentleman to come in?" Gio said.

Gio was not one for wasting time. Soon the Cambridge-educated Emir of the Saudi Royal family, who'd 'awakened' only that morning, and Peter were in deep discussion. They scribbled signs, numbers and letters that no one else could understand. The word 'water' was heard between whispered oohs and aahs. Finally, Peter leaned back.

"You may be right, Your Royal Highness. You may well be right. The only problem is that no one thinks in those terms. They don't fit into our math...."

"They will," the Prince said. "It will take time, but they will."

Gio and Anne exchanged glances. Neither had any idea what the two scientists had been talking about. Nevertheless, for the first time in over a week, they felt that God was truly on their side.

* * *

23

Habemus Papem

fter a morning of roaming through the streets of Rome, crowned by a delicious lunch with Sir Ian, Peter and Anne decided to spend the rest of the afternoon lazing around in the Vatican gardens. Whatever else may have changed in the Vatican, the gardens had lost nothing of their former glory. They looked as though dozens of invisible gardeners spent all their time working on enhancing their natural beauty. The attraction was further increased by the fact that Peter and Anne were the only people among the pristine lawns, meandering on secondary footpaths between the major lanes of *viale del Governatorato, viale del Osservatorio,* up *via Posta* and *via Pio X,* all the way to the heliport.

The Vatican gardens dated back to medieval times, when vineyards and orchards extended to the north of the Apostolic Palace. In 1297 Pope Nicholas II enclosed the gardens with walls. By the beginning of the 16th century, many new buildings began to encroach on the green area. Exigencies of State.

Anne, already familiar with most of the terrain, led Peter to the Italian Garden. They stretched out on the gentle slopes overlooking the intricate box hedges, reminiscent of later French labyrinths. It was an oasis of calm in a world that, of late, was

both turbulent and angry. They wanted to talk—to discuss the
events of the last few weeks of their lives spent apart.

Stretched out on the grass, Peter let his thoughts drift back
to their morning's host.

"Sir Ian," Peter murmured so as not to disturb the
tranquility, "hasn't changed. If anything, his appearance seems
to have reverted to if not exceeded its former glory," he joked
good-naturedly.

In fact, Sir Ian's girth had became so imposing that, during
lunch, Anne had expressed her concern for his health.

"Never been sick a day in my life," he'd countered with a
roar that could have awakened the dead. He patted his stomach
lovingly. "Don't swing the baton anymore," he'd added,
presumably as an excuse for his contours.

Anne had concluded that Sir Ian's stomach functioned on
the push-through-or-I'll-give-you-more principle.

"Ian," she'd explained, "ingests food as punishment. To
make sure that his entrails do not absorb too much, he rams it
through with additional loading."

All three had laughed, though Peter did not approve of Sir
Ian's apparent folly. It was very evident that Rome and Sir Ian
agreed with each other.

Then, even as they reminisced, the Italian Gardens drew
them into their serene enchantment. They didn't talk much
anymore. There was such stillness in the air that they just sat, side
by side, gazing at the richness of greens, interspersed by narrow,
vertical columns of dark, elegantly slim cypresses that pierced
the Roman sky, creating regular segments of purest blue. They
grew silent, as though visiting a holy place.

Later they walked again, slowly, relaxed, in full knowledge
that things were looking up in the world. Or so it seemed.

By the time they finally decided to stretch out their weary
bones on something softer than the lawn, Anne found a note
from the Camerlengo waiting for them in their bedroom. It
asked Anne to drop into Gio's office at any time at all. At six
that evening she knocked on the Cardinal's door. As usual, he
got up to greet her.

For a while the Cardinal seemed to be hedging, as if unable to get to the point. Finally he took a deep breath and leaned over his desk. His eyes were filled with a strange fire that Anne could not interpret.

"I understand..." he said at long last. "I understand John Paul's message."

Anne held her breath. She had no idea what Gio was talking about. Somehow, his words created a tension in the air unlike any she'd experienced in his presence before.

"The Camerlengo holds great power," Gio resumed. "In fact, there are three Camerlengos. I am the Camerlengo of the College of Cardinals. As such, tomorrow my place will be with the Cardinals deliberating over the choice of the next Pontiff."

"You will be . . . *incommunicado?*"

"Under the penalty of excommunication." Gio's face was as serious as she'd ever seen it.

"For how long?"

"It depends. We take the first ballot on the afternoon of the first day. Then, we vote twice in the morning and twice in the afternoon. Every day. After seven days, if there is no agreement, we rest for a day. Actually we don't rest at all. We engage in, hopefully, fruitful discussions. And we remain *con clave.*"

Anne nodded her understanding.

"There is also a Camerlengo of the Roman Clergy," Gio resumed his story. "Even if he joins us by tomorrow, from his, ah, detachment, it wouldn't help because he, too, would have to be sequestered." The Camerlengo still wasn't sure how exactly to describe the state of induced amnesia. It certainly wasn't anything that he'd ever experienced in anyone before.

"So what exactly is the problem?" Anne found this interesting enough, but it hardly accounted for Gio's gravity.

"Usually it wouldn't matter. Much. But now, in the next weeks, or months, there will be a large number of cardinals, elders of other churches, and hopefully a number of dignitaries who will be coming out of their mental withdrawal. I need someone to look after them."

"I will be happy to do so, Gio. You know that."

"Yes, I know that. But I must be sure that those emerging from withdrawal also know it. I must empower you to act in the name of the Church."

"Is that really necessary?"

"I am afraid so. I have already called an assembly of all able-bodied cardinals, two bishops and about forty priests to witness your appointment."

"Appointment to what?"

"To the office of the Camerlengo of the Holy Roman Church, the man who would normally take care of things while we're in the Conclave. Officially, you will have the power to administer all the Church's domains. *In esse*, you will decide what to do with the people who...."

"...who emerge from the withdrawal." Even as Anne completed Gio's words, her face grew pale. She wasn't even a practicing Catholic. She didn't go to confession, didn't attend Mass, she.... On the other hand, what is a practicing Catholic, really? Practicing going to Mass, once a week? Going to confession, once a year? Loving one's neighbour, once in a lifetime?

"I can't do it," she said. "I just cannot!"

Gio walked around the desk and knelt on one knee beside her. "You know that people such as you and I do not have a choice in such matters. We dance to an invisible piper," he said softly.

Anne wasn't sure if she wasn't about to wake up and this whole meeting would dissolve into thin air. She felt like thin air herself. She didn't feel real.

"And you need it for what?"

"When the dignitaries awaken, you must have the authority of the Church to decide what to do with them. You alone are capable of making such a decision. Even now, I assign tasks to them, but you advise me on their capability."

Anne sat quietly, studying her shaking hands.

"And this wouldn't be for long?" There was a quiver in her voice, like an excessive vibrato on a violin.

"It could be for a day or two, or . . . for a month or two. The Church needs continuity. And of the seventeen cardinals who are already back with us, seven are so-called favourites, or principal contenders for the papacy. This was obvious even before the funeral. With such a limited choice, the Conclave cannot possibly last long...." This time Gio avoided her eyes. He knew that God acted in mysterious ways.

By the time Anne returned to her room from Gio's office, Peter was gone. There was no message. What Anne found instead was a white cassock spread out on the double bed. White as in a nun or as a quasi-pope, she wondered? She remembered the dream Gio had told her about. She realized she could wear white because the official mourning period for the last Pontiff was over.

"As if that really mattered," she said, stifling a nervous giggle.

For a while she stood motionless, looking at the white cassock. A dress, really, she told herself. I could buy one just like it in Montreal. Strange that, she mused, how come I'd never had a white dress? Not even when I got married. It had been ivory—it looked better with my long red hair. Her hand moved to her head. The long, fiery chestnut cascades were long gone.

So many years had passed....

Frederick Finer hated letting Peter go. He hadn't seen him that often, but to him Peter Brown represented contact with the outside world. The real world, he often thought, a world where people got on with their lives, without attempting to run other people's lives for them. Wasn't that the definition of freedom? Is this not what American Democracy really meant?

The American Way began to mean different things to different people.

He leaned back in Peter's chair, pretending that Peter was still in the room. It was a place that had the right 'vibes'. A place where the range of emotions, until recently, had been directed towards the betterment of the human condition. Not by force, though. He was sure that if Peter had his way, not a single man or woman would be exposed to his projector without their expressed knowledge and permission. Alas, this was no longer the American Way. Not any more. Or at least not the Pentagon Way.

The Pentagon's way was different.

For some time now, Finer had carried in his pocket notes he'd found while cleaning up his desk at home. He went home, for a few hours, after he drove Peter to the airport. Somehow he needed to be away from the Pentagon just a little longer. Some years ago he'd attempted to make some notes on recent American military history. Now, alone in Peter's office, he pulled out his notebook. He read slowly, trying to find errors in his notes, to find things he could deny or even dismiss.

1953 U.S. (with the British) overthrows Premier Dr. Mohammed Mossadegh of Iran. U.S. installs Shah Mohammad Reza Pahlavi as dictator.

1954 U.S. overthrows democratically elected President Jacobo Arbenz of Guatemala. An estimated 200,000 civilians die in the process.

1963 U.S. backs assassination of South Vietnamese President Ngo Dinh Diem.

1963-1975 The U.S. military kills 4 million people in Southeast Asia.

1973 U.S. stages a military coup in Chile. Democratically elected President Salvador Allende is assassinated. Dictator Augusto Pinochet is installed. 5000 Chileans are murdered.

1977 U.S. backs military rulers of El Salvador. 70,000 Salvadorans are killed. Later, Jesuits are murdered by the Atlacati Battalion, an elite unit created, trained and equipped by the U.S.

1980 In this decade the U.S. trains Osama bin Laden and fellow terrorists to kill Soviets in Afghanistan. CIA gives bin Laden $3 billion.

1981 President Reagan's Administration trains and funds 'contras'. 30,000 Nicaraguans die.

1982 U.S. provides billions in aid to Saddam Hussein for weapons to kill Iranians.

1983 White House secretly finances weapons to kill Iraqis.

1989 CIA agent Manuel Noriega disobeys orders from Washington. Noriega is also performing the function of Panamanian President. He is removed following U.S. invasion. The invasion results in 3000 Panamanian civilian casualties.

1990 Iraq invades Kuwait with weapons supplied by the U.S.

1991 U.S. invades Iraq. President Bush reinstates the dictator of Kuwait.

1991 U.S. initiates a weekly bombardment of Iraq. The U.N. estimates 500,000 Iraqi children died as a direct result of bombing and sanctions.

1998 U.S. under President Clinton bombs a 'weapons factory' in Sudan. The factory turns out to be manufacturing aspirin.

1999 On April 20, the U.S. enacts the largest one-day bombing in the Kosovo War. Twenty-two NATO missiles fall on a single village. President Clinton said at the time that they were striking hard at the Soviet machinery of oppression. Most missiles fell on the residential area, a hospital and a primary school. *

2000-2001 U.S. gives Taliban who rule Afghanistan $245,000,000 in 'aid'. On September 11, 2001, Osama bin Laden uses his expert CIA training to murder 3,000 people in New York.

Finer looked at the asterisk accompanying the 1999 note. He read his scribbled writing in the margin. It did not deal with U.S. ventures into other countries. It was a domestic problem.

*On April 20, 1999, one hour after the bombing of Kosovo had been initiated, there was a shooting at the Columbine High School. 12 students and one teacher died. Over 900 rounds of ammunition had been fired. This was Americans killing Americans.

There were another two pages with some twenty more entries. Finer tore them all out of his notebook, crumpled them viciously, and flung them away. His face, usually registering little or no expression, was contracted in a sneer of disgust. He lost all appetite for recent American history. He felt sick to his stomach. Was this really the American Way?

Needing something to do, some distraction, Finer clicked on one of Peter's computers. He scanned the home page, wondering what it might all mean. Not just Peter's work, but the world at large. Something caught his eye. It was a short statement that stipulated that the ultrasonic projector could be as effective through most solid materials. Apparently the ultrasonic waves hardly respected physical barriers. Perhaps that is why dogs could hear them at a distance, around a corner or on the other side of a building.

For some reason the idea fascinated him. On the other hand, the same was true of all radio waves. No big deal....

The crucial doctrine was that the state must adopt a defensive stance. In 1954 the Eisenhower administration upheld this strategy of deterring aggression by threatening the use of nuclear weapons in Indochina.

How noble! Indochina must have threatened the United States security gravely....

There was also the saturation bombing of densely populated areas in North Vietnam. There was the sponsoring of the killing of thousand of Nicaraguans in order to restore democracy. Quite true. The killing was quite democratic. Anyone could die. How dare they defend their own country against American aggression? Don't they want the American Way? Then there was Guatemala, El Salvador and Honduras. The slaves may live in relative freedom, provided they kill off those who are free first. A strange philosophy? Essential to a man who could induce fear in his own people. Such a man qualified to be called 'one of us'. Or so it seemed.

Not for the first time, Finer felt that he no longer belonged at the Pentagon. There was a certain rabid fascination with being so close to the Seat of Power. There was also a growing sense of distaste.

Guido came to pick Anne up in her room and escort her to the Basilica. He bowed deeply as he came in. For Guido, protocol was very important. After so many years, he couldn't function without it. It wasn't his to question the commands of his superiors. A woman Camerlengo? A woman? All the way to Anne's room, and then to the Basilica, he pretended that Anne was a man. After all, that was what she looked like, most of the time, didn't she?

Well? Didn't she?

The ceremony was short and very official. It took place at the main altar. No 'outsiders' were invited or allowed. Gio was at her elbow to help her.

She said the right words, some of them in Latin. Guido made sure of that. He may have hated protocol, but he was enmeshed in its tentacles. For now.

An hour later Anne emerged from St. Peter's Basilica as the first woman Camerlengo of the Holy Roman Church. Once the cardinals, led by Giovanni Pesci, retired to the Sistine Chapel, she would become the most powerful person in the Catholic Church. As she led the procession away from the Basilica with Cardinal Giovanni Pesci in close pursuit, she experienced chimerical flashes of a white dove soaring over St. Peter's Square.

That's funny, she thought. I didn't know I could fly....

The next moment, Cardinal Pesci saw Anne falter. Instantly he was by her side. They walked the rest of the way arm in arm. By the time Anne saw Peter, she was fully herself. She managed to persuade the Camerlengo of the Sacred College of Cardinals to let go the elbow of the Camerlengo of the Holy Roman Church. Gio appeared to do so reluctantly. Peter took over and stayed by Anne's side, just in case, all the way to their room.

At 6 a.m. the next day, Anne was in her new office, Gio's office actually, from which she would rule the Church with an iron hand—well, at least a smile and an ounce of persuasion. She decided not to make any additional 'rounds of the wards', since, as Peter had already observed, they were either on the mend or, translated into Anne's own words, weren't meant to be. All of them had been given exactly the same chance.

Indeed, she was right. During the night another nine cardinals had emerged and arrived shortly after eight o'clock, humbly asking for an audience. They wanted to know if they were allowed to join in the proceedings. In the Conclave.

"Permesso mi presento..." each began, bowing to Anne.

Anne felt strange, embarrassed and humbled by the sincerity of the new arrivals. These were not the pompous Princes of the Church she saw on occasion in the press. None of the usual paraphernalia adorned their stature. They all wore simple black cassocks and mozzettas. Neither birettas nor great impressive fishheads--presumably symbols of wisdom—adorned their crowns. Not even the impressive red sashes. A few wore small skullcaps. Probably a force of habit dating back to way back when....

As each face rose from the bow, it was lit by a contented smile. Whatever pleased them could not have been the sight of a beautiful woman. Dressed as she was, her hair cropped to within an inch of her skull, she might well have been a man. A very handsome man with very gentle features.

"It is a joy to behold you, Signora Camerlengo," one said, a particularly broad smile on his face.

These were not ordinary men. Whatever had transpired while they were in the state of amnesia had left a mark that was as invisible as it was obvious. Something had taken place deep within their being.

At 4:30 p.m., Rome time, Cardinal Giovanni Pesci led a humble procession of twenty-seven Cardinals to the Pauline Chapel to seek guidance through prayer. The procession was televised. People had a right to know. The world had a right to know.

The Cardinals stood side-by-side; two or three knelt. They held their vigil with their Maker in silence. In the meantime, the Sistine Chapel was being thoroughly searched for listening devices. Gio, after a chat with Peter, would not take any chances. Peter had been asked to help the normal team of sweepers.

After the prayers, they followed Gio into the Sistine Chapel. The Camerlengo supervised them all to assure that each took an oath to follow Jean-Paul II's rules requiring written ballots and secret deliberation.

Gio hated the oath part. He recalled his Master's admonition, 'Swear not at all: neither by heaven, for it is God's throne. Nor by the earth, for it is his footstool, neither by Jerusalem, for it is the city of the great King.' Still, the Church was a living Church and protocol was protocol. The Church had drifted a long way from its roots. 'Let your communication be Yea, yea; Nay nay; for whosoever is more than these cometh of evil....'

Gio sighed deeply. Could he tell them that? Could he turn their own protocol against them? Was he not appointed to his position of Camerlengo of the Sacred College of Cardinals to protect the Church's Way?

Gio didn't like protocol of any sort. He liked yea, yea and nay, nay.

Once again the Camerlengo counted the cardinals and exchanged brief instructions about the electoral rules. For now, his job was done. Yet each time he arrived at a number of cardinals, the doors opened a tad and another gray head appeared. By the time they were ready to write the first ballot, there were thirty-two Princes of the Church ready to vote.

The line formed before the altar.

Each cardinal wrote a name on a ballot, folded the paper and awaited his turn before the altar. There he swore, once again, that he was voting for the man he wanted to be the next pope. Then each man put the ballot on a round plate and tipped it into the chalice awaiting his decision. Except for the murmured oaths and the occasional clink of metal on metal, it all took place in utter silence. The cardinals moved almost mechanically, each knowing his function, each well aware of the gravity of his decision. Yet the only expression on each and every face was a gentle knowledgeable smile. It looked as though the decision rested lightly on their shoulders, as though it had already been made.

The first to cast their votes became the official counters. They checked the total number of ballots and the name written on each ballot. As they unfolded the pieces of paper, they read the name aloud.

"Cardinal Giovanni Pesci."
"Cardinal Giovanni Pesci."
"Cardinal Giovanni Pesci."
"Cardinal Giovanni Pesci."
"Cardinal Giovanni Pesci."

And on and on. One name again and again until two-thirds of the votes had been counted. Theoretically the voting was over. But the official counters continued:

"Cardinal Giovanni Pesci."
"Cardinal Giovanni Pesci."
"Cardinal Giovanni Pesci."

The cardinals read the name clearly, enunciating every syllable to assure no error could be construed in their announcement.

"Cardinal Giovanni Pesci."
"Cardinal Giovanni Pesci."
"Cardinal Jean-Paul Arizme."

The old man, whose goodness was legendary among those who knew him, smiled, turning towards Gio. He nodded his thanks. Obviously Cardinal Pesci could not vote for himself.

"Cardinal Giovanni Pesci."
"Cardinal Giovanni Pesci."
"Cardinal Giovanni Pesci."

Thirty-one times the name appeared on the ballot. With the exception of Cardinal Pesci, absolute unanimity. Thirty-one times his name had been read aloud before the cardinals present, a knowing smile playing about their lips. How could they know, Gio wondered. Some of them only awoke last night from their slumber.

There was one more stage to the protocol. The chosen cardinal had to be asked if he accepted the nomination. There had been no previous discussions, no *consistoris* or conferences to discuss the pros and cons of the candidates. Not since the funeral. Gio had imagined that the cardinals taking part in the voting had recovered their memories, and thus they would have voted for their favourites.

"Why me....?" he whispered. "Why me...."

The cardinals surrounded him, forming a protective wall.

"Because we love you," one said.

The others nodded. "We all love you...."

A simple statement expressing a simple enough emotion. What more could he ask of them? Is this not what he preached on every occasion?

"I accept," he whispered. But there was little joy in his voice. He knew that the road would not be an easy one. Not if he were to do what lay in his heart. "Love one another," he heard his own voice advocating the only thing that really mattered. "Love one another...."

Someone made sure that white smoke emerged from the chimney.

There were no usual crowds in St. Peter's Square. The inner part was cordoned off altogether. But farther down there still were some silent pilgrims who came to pray for the plague to be lifted. For their spiritual leaders to be freed from its power. Others came late, running, having seen the TV broadcast of the procession of the cardinals to the Pauline Chapel.

"They are choosing the Pope," they whispered.

"They are choosing *Il Papa*," the voices grew louder.

"*Il Papa?*"

"*Si, si, Il Papa!*"

Moments later they saw the white smoke.

By the time Gio donned the papal vestments, thousands had emerged from nowhere. All the way, up to the massive barriers, people advanced, their faces raised in anticipation.

"*Il Papa?*" Their voices were incredulous.

Anne was still in her office. As Guido brought her the news, she could no longer contain herself. She ran to the window overlooking St. Peter's Square, flung it wide open, stood on her toes and shouted into the microphones at the top of her voice.

"Habemus Papem!"

She wanted to scream that it's Gio, her Gio, her friend, the man who was the only priest with whom she'd shared so much, for so long. Yes. For three weeks. For a lifetime. Gio was Pope.

And then Gio came into his office.

He still looked in shock.

In fact, Gio looked like a teacher surrounded by a bunch of schoolboys. Only he was the younger, and many of the 'boys' were a head taller than he. But what really united them was an air of sublime happiness. They seemed to enjoy each other's company in as boisterous and youthful a way as any group of real schoolboys would on the day the school year was over. There was ebullience in the air. A palpable sense of joy.

Gio and Anne wore identical cassocks, identical mozzettas. They were both decked in pure white. They were also about the same height and about the same size in all respects. Even Gio's hair was clipped in a fashion similar to Anne's. If the Pontiff ever needed a double, he wouldn't have far to look.

"Habemus Papem," some of the cardinals were still repeating, as though wanting to hear it from their own lips. *"Habemus Papem."*

Gio walked up to Anne and took her in his arms. He held her for a long moment.

"How shall I ever thank you?" he asked.

Anne had been a Camerlengo for close to nineteen hours. Eight of which, she'd slept.

"Any time, Your Holiness," she replied. She was darn close to giggling. It was nothing, she thought. Really, nothing at all. She felt light-headed as if Christmas had come early that year. And then she did it. She giggled.

"Now don't you start," the Pope scolded her at arm's length. "I have to put up with this from them. Not from personal friends. Do I really look that funny?"

"Thank you, Gio," Anne whispered.

"That's better," the Pontiff said. "In case anybody asks you, I chose the name Ioannes Anna the First. Do you like it?"

This brought more tears to Anne's eyes than she was counting on. Once more the Pontiff, Ioannes Anna I, took her in his arms. When he let go, there was a large wet patch on his left shoulder.

"Now," he said, "let's get to work."

With a confident step, he walked towards the window overlooking St. Peter's Square.

* * *

A Matter of Timing

At 0600 hours President John Linker was alone in his Pentagon office. He couldn't sleep. He got up, went through his morning routine, and waited for his secretary to bring him breakfast. For as long as he could remember, he'd worked alone; but lately he also felt alone. Detached from the rest of the world. He suspected that people, his own people, his right-hand group of generals and advisers, his own staff, did not really understand him. He doubted even more that any of them really understood the American Way.

For a long time he stood perfectly still in front of his wall screen. Not a muscle moved to indicate a sign of life.

Then his eyes scanned the oceans, from east to west, then up and down, searching for some hint, some reason, to make his will known to the world. Should a red dot waver, God forbid disappear, that would do it. He could respond in kind. He would show them, the upstarts, what American Might really meant. He thought he'd already done that, but you never know. With the heads of state still sequestered in the Vatican, all things were possible.

He was counting on that.

He was counting on the uncertainty principle.

The little red dots, all but one, still shimmered on the blue expanse, but steadfastly refused to blink out of existence. The missing one had already been justly avenged. His ships were his power. The British Empire had been built on the power of the Royal Navy. Hardly surprising, he thought, considering four-fifths of the world is covered with water. And now they, the other ships, the merchant navy, were indispensable to global trade. For the same reason. They linked the world into a single entity. A single trading bloc. A single conglomeration.

The American Way.

Since that day at the 'bridge club', the coordinates of all the strategic locations of ballistic stockpiles of all nations, locations of all the delivery systems, reduced uranium plants, even individual silos, had been interpreted and assigned to various ships he had deployed in various parts of the world. The ships, fully armed, were already there. The coordinates of the sites he still carried on his arm. For almost a month, Linker had had in his palm, or at least in the computer on his left wrist, all the coordinates that General Bradley Schwartz had procured for him. After working all night, Linker recalled with a grim smile. The President carried those coordinates with him. He slept with them. He'd ordered all other copies to be destroyed. He alone had the power to decide the future of the world. He was the sole master of life and death.

Only on three occasions had he released the information on the need-to-know basis. His orders had been carried out to the letter. It was self-defense. Every nation under the United Nations Charter had the right to self-defense. The three sovereign states that had indulged in unprovoked attacks on his ships had been set back some fifty years in the development and deployment of nuclear missiles. Or any missiles. Or bombs. Or anything military at all that might threaten the global security of the United States of America. It was never a question of protecting the American borders. It was a question of protecting American interests. The American Way.

Linker played for keeps.

He pressed a button on his armrest. The screen shimmered and broke up into six sections. Each square, a four-foot-by-four-foot screen, covered a different part of the world. The smaller squares could be broken down further, then enlarged to four times their size.

His eyes drifted to the section in the bottom left corner. The crowds were growing even as he looked. Soon they would break through the barriers. He'd never found it easy to deal with the crowds. He'd never been part of one. Even when he helped open a new session of the Senate, he felt apart from the One Hundred faces pretending to listen to his words. He didn't like being Vice President. Nor did he enjoy being the President. He hadn't spent an hour in the Oval Office. It was a front. An image to uphold men who were so weak as to have to rely on images. The Oval Office was a symbol of power. But the true power rested in the man who could walk in and out of the office. For the first time a smile played about his lips. He needed no such props, he knew.

Holding the office, even the highest office, was a necessary evil. Like any government. But only until the enlightened anarchy could take over. Not yet, though. People were not ready. They needed guidance. Leadership. They needed to look up or they would continue to stare at their own feet. At their limitations.

" The fault, dear Fred, is not in our stars, but in ourselves, that we are underlings," he murmured.

He still liked to quote Shakespeare, embellished with his own overtones. The old bard knew that Julius Caesar had not been appreciated by his own people. That was, at least in part, why Linker always shunned people. He shunned advisers. He never told them more than was absolutely necessary. They weren't ready, either.

He pressed a button. "Finer," he said. His secretary would deliver the message.

Fred Finer was a good sort, Linker thought, but he was weak. They were all weak. What Finer did for him was to create an illusion of not being completely alone. Alone in the whole grossly overpopulated world. His wife, lately, did not even speak to him. To give her her due, he never left the Pentagon. The stakes were too high. He needed to be at the Center of Operations twenty-four hours a day. Or else he would have to delegate, and that, he knew, he could not do.

The door opened, allowing Fred Finer to enter.

"What do you make of that?" Linker asked, singling out the bottom left corner screen with his laser pointer.

"It looks like they've elected a new pope, Sir." Finer always addressed the President formally until he'd learned what sort of mood his boss was in.

"With no cardinals?"

"There is a protocol of secrecy at the Vatican, Sir. They must have had a few coming alive."

"Is there a minimum necessary to elect a pope?"

"I don't know. Would you want me to find out?"

"Doesn't matter. The fact is that some came to. The others can't be far behind."

"The other cardinals?"

"The others," Linker repeated, without elucidating further.

So the game was up. Once the heads of the world came to, there would be hell to pay. Unless it was a *fait accompli.* Everybody loves a winner. Had Hitler won the Second World War, there would be statues of Herr Führer adorning every village square in America.

Linker kept staring at the bottom left corner. The crowd in St. Peter's Square was growing by the minute. His lips formed a downward curve, somewhere between commitment and derision.

"La comedia e finita," he said darkly. "The party is over, my friend." He turned to Finer. "They will be either with me or against me." He waved his arm towards the door. This was a polite way to tell Finer that he was dismissed.

Finer left the President's office at 0820 hours, EST. He went straight to Peter's now-vacant lab. There were things he had to do.

The curtains parted and a figure of a man dressed all in white appeared in the opening. Other than Anne's outburst, this was the first time in weeks that any clergyman had made direct contact with the people from this venue. The man adjusted the microphones to his diminutive height. So many things had happened these last three weeks that the papal office was still in profound disarray.

"Remove the barriers," were the first words John Anne uttered to his people. "Let my children come to me."

There was a momentary hesitation, and then an ocean of heads surged forward in a single broad swell. No barriers could have stopped them. No army, either. The wave moved in a single motion until they filled the inner court of St. Peter's Square to overflowing. Only then did John Anne spread his arms wide in a papal embrace.

"I welcome you all back to your Basilica. Let no man ever stop people from entering what is yours. *"Benedicat vos omnipotens Deus, Pater et Filius et Spiritus Sanctus."*

With these words the Pontiff blessed the city and the world, *urbi et orbi.* People lowered themselves to their knees. They cried. They laughed. This time there was no time for the world to come to St. Peter's Square. These were only Romans.

"Papa! Papa!" they yelled. "Viva *Il Papa!*"

This was their city and their Pope. The bishop of Rome. The highest office of all.

At 0830 hours, Washington time, President John Linker entered the code on his wrist computer. Moments later, various red lights scattered over the blue surface of the screen began vibrating in rhythm, indicating that his messages had arrived. He timed them so that action would start at precisely 0900 hours, the world over, simultaneously. The little dots of red light looked as though they were nervous.

The order was ATTACK AND DESTROY as per—there followed a reference to the last briefing in the last envelope opened by the commanders of the navy. There was no doubt, no room for interpretation. They were precise orders to destroy all the known targets supplied in the message. Each message was compacted into a compressed electronic impulse that only an onboard computer could decipher. If it weren't for the satellite network, none of this would have been possible.

The wonders of technology. American technology.

Linker was perfectly calm. He did what he had to do. He had no choice. Should the heads of the world awaken, they would all revert to the wishy-washy, insipid, lackadaisical existence they enjoyed so much before the Vatican Incident. Linker liked that name, the Vatican Incident. It was just that. An incident. A single link in a long chain of events that he and he alone had planned for over six years. He was the one who linked them together.

"Enough of this *bourgeoisie*," he said out loud. "We are playing for keeps."

He sat down and cut his wall screen into two parts. He knew that, soon enough, he would start getting input from the rest of the world, a reaction to his orders. He was ready. Whether the world liked his decision or not, it was already too late. His Plan was playing itself out.

Checkmate. At last.

At long last.

Linker retained the right half of the screen as the world map and split the left side into four equal squares. He glanced at the bottom left corner. He smiled benevolently. The new Pope was delivering his *urbi et orbi* blessing. He split the Vatican screen into four more parts. And then....

Men, experts and technicians, were running around as they might before a premiere of a major Broadway production. Wires and cables were spread about everywhere. Hanging from walls, overhead—just clearing people's heads, and slithering all over the floor like a pit of snakes. No one seemed to mind. In spite of evident pressure, the men waiting to deliver and witness the broadcast smiled. They looked perfectly relaxed. Then one man stepped forward. He faced the microphone held on a long boom as well as a battery of other standard media mikes.

He looked well over sixty, a slight stoop adding years to his appearance. His gray hair was elegantly combed straight back, in a vain attempt to heighten his forehead. His face did not exhibit any particularly distinguishing features, except for his eyes, which seemed to combine a burning desire with quite inexplicable calm. His eyes were a contradiction that dominated his face.

Linker froze.

He was staring at the President of the United States, George Wilbert Twigg. He turned on the sound.

Twigg's voice was deep with authority.

THIS IS THE PRESIDENT OF THE UNITED STATES OF AMERICA. I, GEORGE WILBERT TWIGG, HEREBY ISSUE A PRESIDENTIAL ORDER TO ALL UNITED STATES NAVY VESSELS DEPLOYED ANYWHERE IN THE OCEANS OF THE WORLD. YOU ARE TO STAND DOWN CODE 001. REPEAT. STAND DOWN CODE ZERO ZERO ONE. YOU ARE TO ABORT AND DESIST AND RETURN TO YOUR PORT OF ORIGIN.

I SAY AGAIN,

THIS IS THE PRESIDENT OF THE UNITED STATES OF AMERICA. I, GEORGE WILBERT TWIGG, HEREBY ISSUE A PRESIDENTIAL ORDER TO ALL UNITED STATES NAVY VESSELS DEPLOYED ANYWHERE....

Linker's legs could no longer support him. He staggered backwards and only just made it to the armchair. He collapsed like an inflatable doll deprived of its life-giving air.

Finer went straight to Peter's lab computer and typed out the code for the map of the Pentagon. He studied it for some minutes, then he gave equal time to an axonometric projection of the building. Satisfied, he turned to the projector resting on a tripod and made some adjustments. He then turned it on its axis, adjusted the vertical angle, and set the timer.

Moments later he walked out of the Pentagon. He inhaled briefly. He'd long forgotten that air had a taste of its own. It smelled of trees and bushes and flowers and grass. It smelled the way the world should smell. Not like the canned stuff that had poisoned his lungs for the last few years.

Fred Finer looked and felt like a new man.

Stand-down Order Code 001 had been the special idiom since the early days of the Cold War in the last century. It had to be short and sweet. Sometimes only seconds stood between it and a world holocaust. On three occasions, past presidents had used it to avert global war with the USSR. Now President Twigg used it for the very same purpose. He had no idea how far Linker had advanced his military campaign, but he didn't really want to find out. The man must have been mad.

In order to reach not only the men and women deployed on American ships throughout the world, but for the whole world to see and hear for themselves, the presidential order was broadcast on open networks. The order was issued at 14:40 Vatican time, or 8:40 in the morning, that is to say 0840 hours Washington time. Ten minutes after Linker had issued his order to ATTACK AND DESTROY.

The presidential order was broadcast continually from 1440 hours, Vatican time, on all international airways. No instructions were given as to when to stop.

"You will know when they get the message," President Twigg said with a confident smile.

In fact, never before had President Twigg displayed such confidence. Certainly not in public or on public airways. He'd been known to be wishy-washy, invariably searching for words, which seemed in short demand in his personal vocabulary. Something had changed. Also, in a peculiar if unpredictable way, he seemed to be enjoying himself.

The President stood before an array of microphones framed by President Nicoli Brotoff of Russia, Prime Minister Paul Henry Prescot of Great Britain, President of France Jean-Paul Martal, and Zung Tse Ming, the Chairman of the People's Republic of China. The five gentlemen had spent the last four hours studying news reports from around the world on TVs provided by Camerlengo Anne Brown. It had been her last order as the Camerlengo of the Holy Church of Rome.

Minutes after the first broadcast, Anne performed a public striptease in the middle of the papal office. Beneath the flowing white vestments, she was fully dressed in her normal black suit. Pope John Anne I, accompanied by a group of cardinals, gave her a big hand for a job well done. As Camerlengo, not the striptease. He was no expert on the latter.

It had been a long day. Pope John Anne I, Dr. and Mrs. Peter Brown, and Sir Ian Barton were sitting at the same table at which, some weeks ago, John Paul III had shared a dinner with the very same guests.

"I always knew you would make it, Your Holiness," Sir Ian said, downing the second glass of excellent Valpolicella from the Vatican's very private cellar.

"I wasn't aware I was suppose to make anything," Gio replied. "Surely you will not hold it against me that three dozen gray-haired men preferred to lumber me with the job rather than take it on themselves, will you?"

"No, Your Holiness," Sir Ian said and then, when John Anne gave him a dirty look, he added, "No, Gio. But I always knew you had it in you."

Peter and Anne sat back, enjoying this impromptu banter. Guido told them that, in some ways, they always acted like a couple of kids having fun. This is what the old priest found so endearing. They were serious one moment and up to some juvenile pranks the next. Peter and Anne had no idea what they were talking about. Then Anne remembered the 'double bed'. Could Gio have known about that? Were there hidden cameras scrutinizing the behaviour of young seminarians? For a woman in her forties, Anne managed to display a perfectly formed intense blush.

All but eleven of the cardinals had fully recovered. Those few unfortunates who hadn't might never recover; only God knew for sure, and, in spite of their illustrious location, He (She or It, according to Peter) wasn't talking. All the other clerics and elders had awoken and were back to normal. Better, in fact. Rejuvenated in a way no one, not even Peter, could begin to explain.

It didn't go quite so well with the laic dignitaries. About a quarter of them refused to go back to politics. Whatever they'd experienced in their detachment from the reality of recent years had made it impossible for them to wield power. They hadn't become holier than thou, or mental vegetables. They simply felt that life was too short to fight for things which others would not even appreciate. Only a fool would want to be a president, and only a saint would agree to be one.

"I am neither," a man dressed in an immaculate Saville Row suit said to Peter.

Peter understood him well enough. He felt the same way.

"Don't you find it strange, Gio," Peter asked sometime during this memorable dinner, "that there are only two locations in the whole world where all the scriptures are revealed in their totality by our new prophets?"

His Holiness looked up from his plate.

"One is the Vatican, and the other—the Pentagon. Only these two organizations are sure to have recorded every single word we broadcast over the last week or so."

"I told you that God moves in mysterious ways," His Holiness replied, his eyes sparkling in undeniable contentment.

"Not only that, but even the purely scientific inventions that came out of the Incident are also recorded in those two locations. There is no copyright on those recordings. There is no one to claim royalties, to grant permission, to exploit the ideas for personal gain. They literally belong to humanity." Peter drove his point home.

"And Linker was at the root of freeing mankind from the Linker theories. He was the piper who danced to a tune he did not even begin to understand himself," Anne put in.

News from around the world was coming so fast that even Gio kept a TV set on in his office, just to keep up with world developments. President Twigg's order had come too late for two ships, which had remained faithful to acting President Linker. They had carried out their orders and then, presumably suspecting the consequence of such actions, had directed the last missile at themselves. Peter still thought this most un-American, until he learned that the naval artillery officers on both vessels had turned Moslem months before leaving harbour. Both must have suffered

from acute dichotomy during the last weeks of their life. Since
Mohammad Ali, the conversions had become more frequent but
were seldom announced. Islam was not a popular religion in the
USA.

The other ships pulled up in time to jettison their missiles into
the oceans. Many of the nuclear warheads were already airborne.
The best that these commanders could do was to re-program their
destinations by radio to fall into the ocean, away from any
inhabited islands. The same was true of the fighter jets. They
couldn't land back on the carrier with the missile or bomb load.
They, too, were jettisoned into the brine. It is doubtful that it made
the fish very happy; nevertheless, in a single day Linker had
accomplished more to disarm the world than all the presidents since
the Second World War. What remained, of course, were the
countless land-based missiles. Still, it was a step towards sanity.

"Here's to the New World!" Sir Ian raised his glass for the
umpteenth time.

"Here, here," His Holiness agreed. "Whatever that might be."

The next moment the *scallopini* arrived and soon disappeared
in the abyss of Sir Ian's stomach.

* * *

EPILOGUE

Montreal — Westmount

Peter looked at his notes. Six months had passed since he and Anne returned from the Vatican. Not for the first time was he trying to put together some sort of coherent record of that special month of his life. There was not much to add.

Finer, he'd learned, had directed his ultrasonic projectors at the Pentagon itself, zeroing in, as best he could, on John Linker's office. No one ever discovered what had really happened to the acting President. For the first month or two he hardly spoke at all. Perhaps, Fred thought, he no longer had anything to say. Finer kept most of his speculations to himself. The official report was that Linker had had a heart attack.

"It could have been a stroke," Finer said to the White House aides who clamoured for information. "A massive one at that. They should have re-taken another encephalogram." Neither the aides nor the press were impressed.

Fred Finer had flown to Montreal just to thank Peter for all he'd done. "If it weren't for you, my friend, I would have never found myself again. I would have become a permanent fixture at the Pentagon."

Fred Finer, Ph.D., was now teaching physics at George Washington University. It was only four blocks away from the White House, where Dr. Finer still acted as special consultant to the President. "Anything other than the Pentagon," he insisted. Finer was the only link the President could rely on for events before and after the Vatican Incident. As for teaching, Fred loved it. "All those fresh, unspoiled minds..." he commented dreamily.

"Not from what I hear about some of the changes that President Twigg is introducing in Washington," Peter countered to his previous comment. "I understand he's a breath of fresh air, too?"

"I meant to ask you about that." Finer held Peter's eyes. "Something happened to him at the Vatican. He's a completely different man. Something both intangible yet obvious to anyone who knew him before. Why, you can even discuss things with him. Things requiring mental acumen. The man is positively smart."

Until the Vatican Incident, no one in the whole world would ever have accused President G.W. Twigg of being smart.

"I'm telling you," Fred insisted, "it's really true."

"I believe you," Peter replied. He glanced at Anne sitting quietly, listening to the two men talking. "Strange things happen to people at the Vatican."

This time, Anne couldn't hold back her laughter.

Within a few months, Fred Finer was also running a home for stray dogs. He was known in the vicinity as the happiest man alive. Three months later, John Linker joined him. Finer felt responsible for his old boss, even if he, too, had become a very different man. Something was missing. Perhaps, Finer thought, it was his ambition.

Fred and John spent evenings together, musing over recent world events. Linker didn't lose much memory, just the last few months of obsession, but his whole outlook had changed. The conclusions he drew were different. Of course, his old philosophy of the rich ruling didn't make much sense now. Now there was talk of an abundance of food and energy—the world over. It would still take a few years to implement the program, but hope was in the air.

There was one other thing that Linker refused to talk about, even a few months after things got back to normal, or as normal as they would ever be. In a moment of unaccustomed weakness, he confessed to Fred that, for reasons that he couldn't understand, he was living under a gnawing, inexplicable sense of guilt.

"I wake up with it," he rasped with a dry throat. "I lie in bed at night with it chewing at my innards..."

Finer took pity. "Did you see a doctor?"

"You know what I think of psychiatrists, Fred. But I did go to see Dr. Schreiber. He's supposed to be the best. The Jungian school."

"And?"

"He said it was something deeply ingrained in my psyche. I gave him $200 and made myself scarce."

Fred had no heart to tell Linker how deeply it was ingrained. Perhaps beyond redemption.

A few months after moving in with Finer, Linker officially resigned from his various business interests, gave countless millions to various charities, and still remained a very rich man. A year later he founded the Washington Institute for Sonic Research. Peter became a regular visiting professor. Over time, at Fred's prodding, Peter actually learned to like Linker.

Well, almost. Emotional memories have a very long shelf life.

The scientific community continued to be challenged by the strange equations that had come out of the Vatican. President Twigg opened the Pentagon files for international research. Some of the results were quite stunning, if seldom understood. But that would come with time.

Peter's projector became so finely tuned that, within weeks, the recipients of the treatment became useful citizens of whatever country they belonged to.

Over time, jails grew empty.

Years passed.

Anne continued to rejoice in 'her' children or, as she called them, her autistic wonders. From the day after she and Peter got back from the Vatican, she dedicated many hours to commune with them.

"I don't really have to be there, in the hospital," she admitted to Peter. "But the pleasure of seeing them, of touching them, of seeing their eyes melting in mine.... well, I think I need them as much as they seem to need me. There is something I can share with them that seems impossible to share with others—the so-called normal people. With them.... with them we seem to become one...."

To this day Peter could not get anything more specific out of her. She and her children shared a world of their own. As for the little ones, many of them were eventually discharged from the hospital as cured. Yet not one of them broke the contact he or she had developed with Anne over the years. Perhaps in some way she remained their link to our reality.

Yet Anne's heart still longed for those rare days, when both her children would come to see her together. Deirdre was a frequent visitor, often with her husband, when she was not gracing the halls of power in Ottawa. Johnny, on the other hand, since the unprecedented success of his opera *Exodus*, dedicated his life exclusively to his muse. He was busy traveling the concert halls of Europe, South America and even Asia. He truly kept his promise to bring the beauty of 18th and 19th century music to the concert halls of today, yet in a manner marked by singular originality. His peers regarded him as one blessed with the touch of genius. Peter, though he would never admit it, regarded his son with something close to adoration. "Like mother—like son," he thought. "Like mother, like son."

The Vatican remained, or rather became, a source of inspiration. Not just for the faithful of what used to be Roman Catholicism, but to people of all faiths. For the first time in history, it became a truly Universal Church which, strangely enough, was what the word 'Catholic' really meant. Buddhists, Hindus, Jews, all manner of Christians and members of every other imaginable religion went there, to this single hill of Rome, to compare their findings, to rejoice in the serenity that the Vatican now offered.

Slowly, carefully, almost shyly, His Holiness, Ioannes Anna I, eliminated all dogmas. "Only our Father knows for sure," he commented when asked for reasons.

The biggest change took place in the religious expression of the Moslems. Those faithful to the Koran adopted the new version recited by one of their own imams, who had been involved in the Incident and who recorded it in modern Arabic to everyone's understanding. The sage's version was closer to those propagated by the old Sufi mystics.

It was a very new beginning.

There were some laggards, but they were mostly ignored. And for those who asked, help was given. But no one was forced. People knew that they all had a tune to dance to. Each a different tune, though played by the same piper.

Cathedrals, basilicas, churches, mosques, temples and synagogues opened their doors to the homeless. Within months there were no homeless. With energy in free fall, more men were already offering their time to agriculture. Hunger would soon be a thing of the past.

In fact, Peter had to watch his waist. He had no intention of competing with Sir Ian. Until Sir Ian died, at ninety-two, once a year Peter and Anne flew to Rome. Nowadays they could well afford it. They always had a dinner at the Vatican. They were treated like the most distinguished guests. But even more so as dear friends.

Yet after counting all the blessings—all the social, political and economical benefits derived as a direct result of the Vatican Incident--one particular benison remained practically unnoticed.

Someone once said that divinity is like water—that it always finds its lowest level. That it remains unnoticed. So did this, the most insignificant yet surely the greatest of all the benefits conferred upon the human race.

For some twenty-five years, Anne had visited, sporadically, diverse places to help those who were in greatest need of her unique talents. She didn't heal their physical needs, but she managed to restore their innate potential to rise above their own particular, self-imposed limitations.

Some years after the Vatican Incident, Anne discovered that she was no longer alone. Several dozen deacons, priests, bishops and archbishops, preachers of diverse religions, imams and rabbis, teachers, as well as nuns and sisters of various denominations—indeed, ecclesiastical members of the world's leading religions—stopped preaching.

Literally, they stopped talking.

Instead, they began aiding Anne in her work. They became that which so many of them had once intended to become—channels for the creative Spirit. Channels for that within us or, as Thomas in his Nag Hammadi gospel had said, for that which is within us and without us. They freed people of their dross, of the miasma accumulated over years of brainwashing, of false concepts, of misguided ideas—and gave them the autonomy to just be. To become that which they truly were, that which they truly intended to be. To become themselves. Some of them eventually understood, for the first time, the ancient admonition, 'Ye are gods!'

Had it all been worth it? After all, the vast majority of people hadn't changed. The good remained reasonably good, and the bad continued to be—pretty bad. A great many remained called, and few indeed decided to be the chosen ones.

Yes, it remained their decision. As it always had been.

There are contrasts in the world we live in. It seems that there always will be. We perceive our reality only by studying opposites. Our perceptions are conditioned to respond to duality. Until we decide to opt out—to be in this world but not of this world. To be free.

The last time the four of them had been together, just the four of them, was over coffee after the farewell dinner at the Vatican.

They were sitting in Pope John-Anne's private sitting room. They talked little, mostly just enjoying looking at each other. What joined them together went way beyond words.

But, after all was said and done, neither Anne, nor Peter, nor Gio, nor even Sir Ian would have missed that single month for all the tea in China, though Sir Ian was the first to return to his routine. He loved his pasta beyond all else.

Events had altered their individual lives—changed the very structure of the world. They would never again think of politicians or the so-called ruling classes, nor even of cardinals and bishops, in quite the same way. Each of them had become acutely aware of the potential that lay within each of us, the potential that was also so very precarious.

"They were all men, women, such as you or I," Peter murmured, "but they had demands placed on them that few could carry out. And most didn't, until first Linker and then Anne performed their magic."

Ioannes Anna looked at each one of his guests with genuine affection. "Nothing is wholly good, nor completely evil," he said, a wistful smile seemingly wishing it were otherwise. "This is the price we pay for the demanding yet often euphoric condition we know as becoming . . . as reaching for higher aims, higher truths, higher aspirations."

Peter nodded. "Aah... and our perceived limitations. The fault is not in our stars, but in ourselves, that we are underlings," he cited from *Julius Caesar*, quite unaware that he was citing John Linker's favourite quotation.

"Ye are gods." Anne preferred the biblical version of man's potential.

Gio embraced them both with his disarming smile.

"Indeed, but ye shall die like men, and fall like one of the princes," he completed Anne's quotation.

Peter put his notes aside, leaned back from his desk in his home office in Westmount, and thought of Linker. And then of Fred Finer. Perhaps, he mused, perhaps in a very down-to-earth way, Fred had saved the world. Who can tell, he wondered. Who can tell?

On his way out, he looked out through the window. Gabriel, his back to the house, was sitting on a small stool, yet still towered over Di and Johnny, squatting on deckchairs on either side of him. Evidently, Gabriel was talking. Peter's son's and daughter's faces were frozen in rapt attention, their eyes shining with something akin to inexplicable joy.

"There we go, again," thought Peter. "Their time has come."

* * * * *

Acknowledgments

I would be remiss were I not to thank Madeleine Witthoeft, Bryn Symonds and Adam Goldman for their diligent editing, each in his and her inimitable way. Also my particular thanks to Kate Jones for her punctilious and very indispensable final proofreading. Most especially, my gratitude to my wife, Bozena Happach, who put up with being a grass widow for weeks on end and then allowed me to benefit from her insights. Finally, my thanks to my many friends who read the galley proofs and helped to make this book a success,

Sincerely,

Stan J.S. Law

The Avatar Syndrome

A novel by Stan I.S. Law

By the author of One Just Man, Yeshúa and the Sacha Trilogy

INHOUSEPRESS presents Prequel to HEADLESS WORLD:
The Avatar Syndrome
To order, please contact: info@inhousepress.ca
101108

www.ingramcontent.com/pod-product-compliance
Lightning Source LLC
Chambersburg PA
CBHW020331180626
46812CB00001B/157